A Sense of Touch

A SENSE OF TOUCH

A NOVEL

CHRISTOPHER OSBORN

JOHN MURRAY

First published in 1989
by John Murray (Publishers) Ltd
50 Albemarle Street, London W1X 4BD

Printed in Great Britain

ISBN 0-7195-4717-2

British Library Cataloguing-in-Publication Data
is available

NIGHT

A *COUGH* breaks the silence. Male or female? he wonders, and smiles – a small, tight smile. Could you tell? Already the vibrations, rushing around according to their own laws, have explored the corners and crevices of the large empty space above him, filled it with human presence, and now fade, drown, before he can decide anything. But in his mind the cough remains a little longer. There are other coughs, of course, that is only to be expected, but this one had a story to tell . . . definitely a painful, personal cough, at first repressed and then bursting all the more angrily through pursed lips, and perhaps a handkerchief. The parable of the angry cough . . . forget it, this is not the right moment. A sharp pain shoots down his right arm; he tries to free it at the wrist. A deeply moral cough. But angry. Concentrate. You had to admit it was interesting . . . could a cough really give away anything about the cougher, about the personality, for example, or the *sex*? Unreliable, the conclusions to be drawn from a cough, a cough alone. After all, just a tickle on the vocal chords . . . you felt a tickle, and then you coughed, to relieve it; a way of scratching the vocal chords. Curious that the vocal chords should be ticklish. Perhaps every part of the body is ticklish. He knows that he is ticklish. But that is on the outside of his body; is he ticklish on the inside too? The vocal chords, after all, are on the inside. What about the tongue, a sort of half-way house: is the tongue ticklish? What if you got a tickle on one of the inner organs? Stop. Concentrate. The liver. What could you do if you got a tickle on the liver? You might die from the agony, the agony of not being able to scratch . . . or would it make you laugh hysterically? Perhaps having the liver tickled would be the greatest fun of all. Why be shy of the inner organs? If they were on view they'd be no stranger than an ear, than this hand, these fingers which he watches as they try to impose themselves against the keys. Perhaps we would go into ecstasies over a pair of well-proportioned kidneys, the curve of a particular heart, the spongy resilience of a beloved pancreas. Would we not long to touch, to caress, to feel the life throbbing darkly through them, and to press our own against them? A dim memory swims to the surface, of something seen, somewhere, sometime: a plaster cast of a male torso into which a hand has been thrust; entering just below the navel, forcing its way up, under the flesh, and exiting, fingers extended, between erect nipples. A bust in a smoke-filled room: yes, a club. Does the torso have a head? It sits on a shelf behind the bar, a backdrop to the swift movements of the barmen. It goes unnoticed, for the most part, by the clientele, who parade, chatter and flirt, and yet its presence, writhing in an extremity of pain or pleasure, insidiously influences them, heightens the atmosphere in the little room, and injects it with danger.

He reaches awkwardly for the low G; it is smudged, gone for ever, lost. These keys I am at this moment pressing down, he thinks, feeling his forehead grow wet, no – stop! This symmetrical arrangement of anonymous teeth, mechanical innards exposed to view (springs, hammers and a forest of metal wires), a hard black body like a giant kidney, three brass feet – this is the beast I am trying to coax into life, to fill with the strength and weakness of flesh and blood, mine and Robert Schumann's; both of us Robert; does that help?

A few minutes ago I sat, quite alone, in the dressing-room. It was the interval. Around me, on the walls, famous musical figures stared out from signed photographs. I examined them all, not for the first time. They are very interesting. Mostly they are dead, but here, in the 'artists' room', they are still in command. I stared at them, smiling, as if to ingratiate myself. Kathleen Ferrier was there, serenely beaming, as if lit up from within. A woman with an illegible signature stood in a long evening dress, looking hilariously out towards me; in her mighty arms, bare to the shoulder, relaxed a large Pekinese, whose face, close to hers, was profoundly mournful. I tried to penetrate the photographs, to get behind them, until there was nothing more I could extract. Then, as I sat sipping a glass of water, I heard a door swing open, and a clatter of high heels. My parents had come to visit me. My mother, wearing a green dress and a small piece of fur round her neck, was in a state of excitement. She gave me a loud wet kiss, too close to my mouth, and said: 'Never, *mon chéri*, never have I heard you play so well! You were so relaxed, so in *command*! We were talking to Mrs Schwarzenberg, you know, and she says it is years, *years*, since she heard the Schubert Sonata played like that . . . and there are so many old friends here! Just one small thing, darling, do you know how *loud* the piano is? Nothing to do with your playing, which was really *impressionant* – no, it's this dear old hall, *tu sais ce que je veux dire*, it's a bit over-resonant! Only a tiny detail to bear in mind; whatever happens – don't *hold back*!'

My father took my hand warmly and said: 'Well played, Rob. I particularly enjoyed the Debussy. The audience seems good, not too many coughers. There are definitely one or two critics here, I think. There's a man in front of us taking notes.'

'It might be William Kenny, from the *Telegraph*,' put in my mother.

'Oh good,' I said. 'To hell with the bloody critics.'

There was an audible silence. Frankly I was surprised they should be put out by one of my routine remarks about the critics. I looked at them: they were my parents, and yet they stood quite dumbfounded, fidgeting. I must admit I felt a little rush of pleasure. It was my concert, after all. But I had, of course, once again exposed my insecurity. 'You know what I mean. At this moment the last thing I want to think about is critics.'

My mother, immediately: 'Of course, darling.'

'I thought you'd be pleased,' said my father. 'It shows you're being taken seriously. And you do deserve to be taken seriously, you know,' he added, with special emphasis and a piercing stare.

'Look at this,' I said, pointing at the picture of the woman with the Pekinese. 'Isn't it funny?'

'Just like Monsieur Pischik!' she cried.

My father put on his glasses. 'And she's just like you,' he said to his wife.

'Oh, no – how awful! Isn't she ridiculous! Poor Monsieur Pischik. Darling –' she turned to me, her movements as usual swift and nervous as a bird, '– darling, I'm so looking forward to the Fantasy. You can be completely confident. You've got us all in the palm of your hand!'

'Literally speaking,' said my father, showing a little silver filling in the corner of his mouth.

The attendant appeared and announced that the interval would be over in five minutes. My parents prepared to leave.

'Wait a moment,' I said.

'We don't want to miss the concert,' joked my father.

'*Merde, chéri,*' she said, standing on the very tips of her toes as she kissed me on both cheeks. '*Merde! Merde! Merde!*' and she shook her little clenched fists in the air, looking right into my eyes.

'Oh well,' I said.

'Good luck, Rob. It's going splendidly,' said my father.

Then they went. My mother turned at the door to blow me a last kiss, and my father placed his surgeon's hand under her elbow. He winked and smiled. I heard their footsteps echo in the high corridor; the squeak of the swing door which let in, briefly, the hum of distant voices; then the door squeaked shut, and I was alone again.

I thought of my mother's brave little fists, and wondered why it was necessary to do things one didn't want to do. I was pacing up and down the room, but soon I would have to change course and tell my legs to set off in a different direction, to leave the room; and I remembered a film by Buñuel in which people are unable to leave a room; why should that not happen to me? Objectively, of course, I was in control of my legs; I could tell them, if I wanted, to walk straight out of the hall by the back exit and disappear into the warm spring evening. It would even be possible to hide in a shadowy doorway and watch the shocked and confused audience tiptoe away, conversing in hushed voices. But, catching sight of the lugubrious peke on the wall, held tight by those rapturous feminine arms, I had a kind of revelation. I was a circus dog, quite unable to act against my instructions. My whole existence, without exception, was controlled by others, for reasons which I couldn't possibly understand. I was a complete circus dog. 'This is absurd,' I said to myself aloud. But the conversation with my parents began to take on a completely different meaning. Their encouraging words were full of badly concealed threats. Or rather, not so much their words as their kisses, winks and stares. My mother's clenched fists were what I would be beaten with if I failed to go satisfactorily through my hoops. The fur around her neck was a reminder of the power she wielded over animals. My father's terrible words 'and you do deserve to be taken seriously, you know' were enough to make you shudder; and what of the metal filling he loved to show in the corner of his mouth?

The attendant came again and said: 'About one minute, sir.' The 'sir' made me smile. I sat down and opened the music of the Schumann Fantasy. The black dots and lines were really a foreign language. What was the worst, the very worst that could happen? And what was the best? I thought again of my mother's delicate fists, valiantly raised, and I was overwhelmed with love. In fact she was trying to pass me her own strength. Her words 'Darling, I'm so looking forward to the Fantasy!' came back to me, and I said 'Yes, I'll play.' She had confidence in me; why should I not trust her judgment? Scales fell from my eyes. I was not a circus dog, not at all. This was my concert, my very own concert. And the critics were there, said my father. Now that was a stupid thing to say. I had a quick glimpse of his hand shoving itself under my mother's elbow. He was always doing that, and what should be an act of tenderness was, I realised, merely a way of asserting his superiority: her elbow was no more than a collection of bone and gristle which he, as a surgeon, could dissect and reassemble without the slightest difficulty. And in fact behind all my father said or did, and nothing more than his friendliness, his *bonhomie*, there lurked an ulterior motive . . . but what was it exactly? 'Through all the sounds that sound,' I read on the first page of the Schumann Fantasy, 'in Earth's many-hued dream, there sounds a secret note, for him who listens secretly.' I was losing my train of thought, but perhaps if I could just see for a second behind the mask which I suddenly realised my father was always wearing, perhaps then . . . Out of the corner of my eye I could see the attendant waiting, a little apprehensively, by the door. A wave of fear came over me. In less than one minute, I realised, I will get up from this chair and go out on stage, bow to the public and play the Fantasy of Schumann: but how? Can I take it for granted that when the attendant comes and says 'Time now, please' (as if announcing the moment of my death) my legs will respond, uncross themselves, support me, do what is expected of them? I can rely on nothing; not even on the unconscious mechanism that links my brain to my muscles, the intricate spinal cord which carries messages I am not even aware of sending (my father has explained it to me). I can rely on nothing happening as it should; I must take a conscious part in everything, I must *tell* my legs to uncross, my body to unwrap, my lips to smile, my fingers to play; I must oversee the sending of messages from my brain outwards: but how can you oversee an unconscious process?

The attendant comes; 'Time now, sir,' she says. She is thin, wiry, middle-aged, a little desperate. I look at her, smiling, and say: 'Yes, all right.' But I feel the dilemma stronger than ever: I really will not be able to stand up. I will have to remain, cataleptic, in this chair. Is there anything to be gained from such a dilemma, anything at all? I can see my father standing in front of me smiling sympathetically and pityingly; and saying to my mother 'Poor old Rob, he grew too fast, always getting himself into tangles!' There he stands, impenetrable as a rock, a man of action who knows when not to ask questions, who cuts up the brains of others but never doubts his own, whose life is a huge success; he stands there, in my path, facing me without expression, dense, obscure . . . but for all that, *is* he a good doctor? Or a good husband? Is he perhaps neither?

The attendant comes again: 'Whenever you're ready, sir. They're all in now.' I nod. 'Yes,' I say, and adjust my tie. My hands are white and cold; a network of sickly black hairs creeps over them. The poor attendant, in her crinkly brown dress, looks worried. There is something both touching and comic about her. Out here, backstage, there are only the two of us left. She is my ally, the last person I will see before returning to the place of judgment, and the look she is giving me now, the last human look, will come with me out there. I stand up, stretch my legs and move forwards. I will rush out onto the platform, bow with a splendid smile, and for the next half hour I will spew my guts all over the piano. She is so small now, the attendant, as she looks up at me full of hope. Out there the wild beasts are growing hungry. Now is the moment: I am filled with courage; yes, I will dare to slip away, trip down the concrete carpetless stairs (no one will stop me), out into freedom, my car is waiting, for I must decide, what am I doing, what do I want, do I really want this, am I capable, do I dare . . . but already, muttering 'thank you' to the smiling attendant (my eyes discover a mole which nestles against her nose), I pass through the door she holds open for me, my legs transport me, amid the roar of the ravening creatures, into the bright lights, towards the glistening leather stool.

'It's childish, and does him harm,' says his father to his mother, in row J.

She is powdering her cheeks. 'He's probably right,' she says.

'All the same, he should be more professional. He's playing well. Why be so on edge? He only does himself harm.'

She purses her lips. It was hard to explain. 'You don't understand what it's like,' she says.

'Of course I understand, Yvonne. I just want to be helpful. I feel it's time he began to – ' but his voice is drowned by clapping. Rob is on stage again. He bows and smiles charmingly. 'What I mean is,' whispers his father, 'he should have more respect for himself. It's a matter of confidence. He's already played quite a lot. Why doesn't he have more confidence?'

There is no answer. He looks at his wife's foot. She was fidgeting. He can see the toes, inside the green shoe, moving obsessively. He touches her arm kindly. It was, naturally, a nerve-wracking experience. Yvonne was so sensitive. The French tend to be more hysterical than the English. Yvonne, poor darling, was French. He watches his hand rubbing the green silk sleeve in a small circular movement. It was a comforting hand with strong square fingers. He squeezes the arm – just hard enough to give her a little jolt without hurting. His knuckles rise harmoniously and whiten. He nudges her, tries to catch her attention; he feels playful. But Yvonne's eyes are glued to the stage. In front of him the critic has taken out his pen. The music, he realises, has started. He sighs, and resigns himself.

The resistant surface suddenly gives way as his son's trembling little finger bites into the first low G. His left hand seethes in an oceanic swell which is like the very material of Schumann's soul, the essence which colours all his perceptions; and Robert knows, despite a whole company of inhibitions which revolve inside him – underneath all these, he knows that his heart beats with a vibrant rhythm which is not unlike that of Schumann. Pressing deep into the piano keys he wants the hard wooden strips to yield and reveal the world that lies beneath them: the music behind the sound. For these notes, now flashing by like shooting stars, always speak to him in the clearest terms of a living human soul, with which he could immediately identify – and so, surely, if only he played well enough, could everyone else. For a few moments the connection between his desire, his brain and his fingertips is complete; he, the piano, the music are one. Then, with a sense of humour all their own, the words 'spinal cord' float through him, and with them they bring a faint whiff of the surgeon's paw as it grasped his mother's elbow; stifling and antiseptic it ridicules the notion of souls. The first phrase of the Fantasy, rising at full strength from the elements, is a great affirmation; but almost immediately it turns into a question; to be answered softly, from another region – with a softness, however, which in itself is just as intense. A real challenge, for the octaves in his right hand, now thin and soft, must be as highly charged as their predecessors. And this is just where his father's paw interposes itself, solid and repressive; the first of the gentle octaves is too weak; it has suffocated. He knows only that for a second his mind went blank and the thread was lost. It would be good to do it again, but the music never waits; it rushes on, rises again, questions again; to be answered differently, with a new inner voice, a trill to be played with thumb and forefinger, the melody above – and here there was nothing to be done but grit his teeth and close his eyes. Something prevented his thumb from working freely, and for the trill to take its natural place, a third voice, a soft, enigmatic vibration between melody and bass – oh, for this to happen how free the thumb and forefinger must be! It's no good, there are no miracles, only work, the right sort of work can help . . . the music rushes on. There is no peace for the performer. If he cannot lead, he must follow. There must be no regrets and no thought of the future. He is condemned to live in the present.

This is his role. He is a visitor to a rich and beautiful garden. The composer shows him the way and, chameleon-like, he follows. He looks, and sees many flowers; some he recognises immediately, others are strange. They set up echoes inside him, for he too has a garden of his own. Countless sympathetic strings begin to hum; his own inner world resounds and overflows. From notes and symbols drily recorded in printed books he fashions a living, breathing creature; half the composer's, half his own.

But the piano, with a flashing smile, comes to meet him like an out-of-control juggernaut. With clumsy sweating hands he engages in battle; much as he wishes for peace the juggernaut will have none of it. The low G is badly smudged, the trill is a battle of wills, and he seems cut off from the sound of his own playing by earfuls of cotton wool; while the public . . . the public does not like to be disappointed. The public wants to forget the banality of its life. The public has paid good money to be diverted. The public is a hungry monster; only my playing, these sound waves I am continually producing – and must go on producing – can keep it at bay. Otherwise the monster will clamber onto the stage, catch hold of me with its furry arms, drag me into a corner, nuzzle me and strip me naked; for a while we will stare at each other, but my eyes, full of human weakness, will find no mirror in the eyes of the mute beast (it can only utter squeaks); without more ado it will set on me . . . Meanwhile his hands, magically, have already carried him two or three pages further (had it not been too bad, after all?) – and there he is in a new zone, where for the first time the great tide begins to recede, the storm has passed on, leaving behind it fragments, isolated pools in a weathered landscape; gradually the melodic line breaks up, disperses, as if all its ardour were called into question; there are interruptions, hesitations, new rhythms, new thoughts; and behind the ebb and flow, which seemed unstoppable, is a small soft voice; a question from deep in Schumann's heart; it vanishes into silence. Robert sees his hands, still for the first time, as they wait for the sound of that curious little question to disappear; and he sees his cuff, the cuff of his black tailcoat, under which peeps the cuff of his white shirt sleeve, both scrupulously clean; he lifts them, and they hang above the keys, waiting; he releases the pedal, and the moment of silence begins, no stir even in the audience . . . and then, all of a sudden, he is walking somewhere, in a city, in tight jeans and a leather jacket with quite different cuffs.

To be precise: he was walking, in London, at five o'clock

on a spring afternoon, wearing tight jeans (tight even on his thin legs) and a new leather jacket. The jacket was extremely stylish. Its wide, easy shoulders and ballooning sleeves (grey, with maroon vents) gave him an undeniable feeling of confidence. He increased the length of his stride – after all, was he not six foot two inches tall? – and his back expanded, quite naturally, to include the magnificent shoulders. He seemed, for once, to be the right shape. He danced along the pavement, and if he passed a face that interested him he gave it a frank unashamed glance. A group of trendy youths stopped talking as he went by; all stared at the jacket. He fixed his eyes on a distant point above their heads. It could, in fact, be an advantage to be tall! Progressing in this way, royal and unhurried, he had the extremely pleasant feeling that the pavement belonged to him, at least as much as to anybody else. He reached a café, where he would sit by the window with a cup of black coffee and a dark-tobaccoed cigarette. He stopped and looked through the plate-glass window. The café was full of young people, boys and girls, all chattering, laughing, smoking, with earrings and freakish hairstyles, skirts, scarves and jackets of every shape and colour. He scanned the place for an empty seat. He would like to join up with these happy people. At one table two young men were talking with bright eyes and smiles. In the midst of the smoky hum these two were in a world of their own. He could sense the current that passed from one to the other, like a glittering wave; and he too was filled with delight. Then, looking closer, he recognised them: Peter and Daniel. He stepped back sharply, out of view. On his shoulders the magnificent jacket withered.

In the concert hall the moment of silence is over. The wall of his stomach tightens, and he takes a low, syncopated D at full strength. The notes which follow are also syncopated. But tension cannot be contained for ever; it becomes unbearable. In the same way, alone at night, Robert would feel the tension inside him grow, and his home would become a prison, which he would have to break out of; at a time when sensible people are just falling asleep, he would find it impossible to stay indoors. Not knowing yet where to go, he would stand outside and look at the darkened windows of other houses. Darkness was a relief, a consolation. And this feeling Schumann too must have known.

He would climb into his car without, at first, the idea of a particular direction. Sometimes he drove to Primrose Hill and walked to the top. How peaceful everything looks from the top of Primrose Hill. How peaceful the city looks from here, its lights spread out so prettily, its trees and parks providing gentle sombre contrast, how sensible, how orderly a city looks from a distance. He smoked a filterless Camel; he could feel the pleasant roughness of the tobacco against his tongue. Inside his pocket he practised a trill with his thumb and second finger. He gazed across the night-filled park, and the lamps, with their little oases of quiet light, offered comfort. Above, in the vast, still sky, stars and aeroplanes combined. Inside his pocket the fingers trilled insistently. He realised he was smiling. From up here the world, spread out before him like a map, was harmonious. It was calm and inviting. And everything had its place. Life was calling to him, rustling like the leaves of a spring forest. Shall I dive in? he said to himself. He too was alive! His fingers, tapping against his thigh, were strong and full of hope. He would go to bed now, and in the morning something new would begin, nothing less than a transformation. In one and a half cigarettes' time he was already unlocking the door of his car, his bright blue Beetle. It was two o'clock. But somebody was speaking to him.

'Oh, please, excuse me! You look so kind.' In front of him stood a strange-looking man with a slightly foreign accent. 'It has been impossible, quite, completely, impossible to find a taxi. And you are not, you do not happen, just *happen*, to be going vaguely in the direction of Golders Green?'

'Well no . . . I'm going to Finsbury Park. That's not really the right way for you.'

'Oh Finsbury Park! What a beautiful name – *Finsbury Park!*' He burst into noisy laughter, opening an unusually wide mouth from which one of the front teeth was missing. 'We'll pay you a pound,' he said.

'A pound . . .'

'Yes, look – a new one! A dear little round pound, a brand new little pound! The sort one doesn't want to part with, but for you . . . ' again he showed the gap in his teeth, into which one could just about fit a cigarette.

'All right,' said Robert. 'Jump in. But keep your little round pound.'

'You are a darling . . . no, not a darling, an angel. My name is Daniel, and this is Peter.' He held out a hand with long, thin fingers, and his companion, a small dark youth, smiled.

'Pleased to meet you,' said Robert. 'In you get. There's not much room in the back, I'm afraid.'

'Oh we don't need much room, do we? I'm always amazed how little room a human being takes up, if you know what I mean. All those brains take up so little space!' And he helped Peter into the back, guiding him firmly from behind.

'But the body is more cumbersome,' Robert joked.

'Oh *cumbersome*! But I never take the body seriously. Anyway the body likes being compressed. Oh it loves to be squeezed into tight places. I mean, look at Peter, look at his jeans!' He gave a roar of infectious laughter. 'But the brains are something else altogether. They hate tight places. If the brains aren't free, they go berserk, very quickly! I can tell you, from my own experience. Never lock up your brains.'

'I'll try and remember.'

'Other people do it to you. They lock up your brains, tell them what to eat, what to drink, what to think, when to go to bed, *where* to go to bed – and the worst of it is, the brains go along with it. Silly, oh so silly, these brains of ours!' And he clapped his head with both hands, at the same time uttering a long drawn-out moan.

There was a ripple of laughter from the back of the car.

'And even worse,' he continued, 'we do it to ourselves!'

'Does he always talk like this?' Robert asked over his shoulder.

'Mainly when he's pissed,' came the answer, so light and melodious that he had to look round.

'Pissed! Pissed yourself. Not that you'll ever be able to again. Did you see his jeans? It's not at all good for it, you know. Is it?' He nudged Robert. 'It'll shrink. Maybe disappear altogether. I can tell you from my own experience.'

'You've had a lot of experience. Locked-up brains shrunken –'

'And that's not all, I can assure you. Most of my organs have been through dramatic experiences, the heart especially, of course. But what were you saying? Shrunken what?' He had completely lost his foreign accent.

'No – you said it.'

'Did I really? Oh for a hot summer, a barn with a creaking door, a night without stars!'

'Why without stars?'

But Daniel, shaking his head mournfully, only said: 'It'll disappear. And good riddance.'

They glided through Hampstead, climbed to Whitestone Pond, slid down towards Golders Green. It was so silent in the car, as if they were flying. He was aware of Daniel in the seat beside him, dark and still as a shadow.

'Could you take the first left?' came Peter's voice. 'Or leave us at the corner. It's very kind of you.' He had a slight impediment. Was there something not quite perfect about his r's?

'Oh no, our dear friend must, *must*, come in . . . for a little drop of something or other. One for the road. Or two . . .' He laid an almost imperceptible hand on Robert's arm.

'All right.'

A short winding path and a few steps led to the porch of a redbrick house. Robert followed. On Peter's leather-clad back sparkled an elephant with its trunk raised, imprinted in metal studs. Daniel opened the door and switched on the light. He turned towards Robert and grinned. 'This is my house,' he said. 'It's rather empty, but that's how I like it.' His face was completely unsymmetrical. One ear flopped forward, while the other clung to the side of his head. He had full, heavy lips; when he smiled they pulled his whole face apart. He led into a large room with a wooden floor and windows at both ends. 'The drawing-room,' he said. From the ceiling hung a ponderous chandelier with glass pendants and brassy struts. There was an easel, and canvasses propped against a wall. Peter went to fetch three glasses and a bottle of whisky.

'Glenmorangie,' said Daniel. 'I find Glenfiddich a little sharp. How do you like the chandelier?'

'Well, it's beautiful.'

'Beautiful. Is it beautiful, Peter?'

Peter laughed. 'You know what I think of it.'

'Peter doesn't like it. Do you like it?'

'Well, I said it was beautiful . . .'

'Ah . . . now you're trying to get out of it!'

'You don't believe me?'

'You're such a gentleman, so polite. How can I tell if you're telling the truth?'

'All right . . . I think it's a bit pompous.'

'So why did you say it was beautiful?'

'I'm sorry, I just . . .' Robert shrugged and laughed.

'Of course it's revolting, quite revolting. That is, perhaps, why I like it. But you, a man with good taste, pretended it was beautiful. Why?'

'I really didn't think it was very important.'

'What is important? Isn't it important to be sincere?'

'No, I don't think so. Not always . . .'

'Ah, that is the trouble with the English,' he said, nodding seriously. 'The famous English hypocrisy.'

'Well, I agree the English are often hypocritical, but I don't think it's fair to blame me for . . .'

Daniel burst into laughter. 'I am extremely sorry,' he said. 'Oh Peter, I have been so rude!'

'Yes, you were really unpleasant,' said Peter. 'Even by your standards.'

'Let me kiss your feet,' said Daniel. Robert tried to stop him, but Peter gestured above Daniel's head. Daniel kissed his sneakers and sat up beaming. 'Thank you for letting me,' he said. 'May I be forgiven now?'

Robert shrugged. 'Of course.'

Peter was watching, taking in everything.

'What do you do?' asked Daniel.

'When?' Robert smiled, trying to be light-hearted. He must find a good moment and leave as soon as possible.

'In the daytime.'

'I lie in bed a lot.'

'And?'

'Daydream.'

'And?'

'I play the piano.'

'In bed?'

'No . . .'

'Are you a pianist? A professional, *classical* pianist?'

'Yes.'

'I like music. You see . . .' With his pirate's smile he indicated two shelves bursting with tapes and records. Robert had not noticed. The empty room took on a new aspect, as if Daniel, with a sweep of his arm, had created the laden shelves and a gleaming stereo, so bright he couldn't imagine how he'd missed it.

'And when you play,' said Daniel, 'do you put your whole life into it?'

'Well,' he laughed, 'that's asking a lot.'

'I mean – when you play, is your whole life present?'

He shrugged, smiling.

'In fact, when you play, a piece that means a lot to you, which you love, you are sending out coded messages, you see what I mean? The way you touch each note, the variations in speed, in loudness, softness, in phrasing, the pauses you make, the way you first lay your hands on the keyboard, and how you take them off – all these are messages, from which, if only we knew how to interpret them properly, we could draw a whole map of your brain!'

'I'd have to be expressing myself perfectly.'

'Yes – and then you would give everything away, simply by how you touched each note, and finished each phrase! If you didn't play well, that would teach us something about you too, wouldn't it?'

'No, you're going too far now.'

'He's mad,' said Peter.

'Isn't it strange to think you have another life, a life you lead with the piano, which is parallel, completely parallel, to your real life? Your love, your longing, your happiness, your sorrows, your fears too, and all the other hidden, half-glimpsed sensations – perhaps even this meeting tonight, and especially, perhaps, meeting Peter, will mean something special to you and so will influence your playing. It will pass through the transformer and a new element will creep into your playing, something more serious, or something more frivolous, something sadder, or something joyful . . . you won't be aware of the connection, of course, but it will be there! Just imagine, if you play a piece, a great piece, with a great range, now, if I were a genius, from the way you play that piece I could guess your whole life story . . . and even, perhaps, your future. For what you show us more than anything else – is your potential! You see, it's all there in your playing, everything that you really *are*, however grey and disappointing your real life is!' As he spoke his hands circled around his head, with extravagant gestures.

'Yes, perhaps you're right.'

'Do you think so?' He smiled, and his face split in two.

'Maybe you could understand quite a lot about me, get to know me in a way, but you couldn't actually deduce any *events*. Or how I behave with other people, for instance.'

Peter was watching him. 'Are you gay?' he said.

'When is your next concert?' Daniel asked.

'One question at a time, please . . .'

'Now,' said Daniel, 'this is my diary, and I want to know when your next concert is, and where.'

Robert told him. He looked at Peter's jacket, thrown down on the floor. The metal studs glinted. 'That's a beautiful elephant.'

Peter smiled. 'Oh yes. It's my elephant.'

'Peter has a personal relationship with the jungle,' explained Daniel.

Peter began to laugh, and laughed so much that he almost turned a somersault. With his legs curled up, and his cheek against the wooden floorboards, he said: 'I used to live in Zimbabwe. I was manager of a farm there. In the south, near Bulawayo.'

'Manager? At your age?' asked Robert stupidly.

'You're right. I was too young.'

'He's rich,' said Daniel.

'Are you? Very, very rich?' Robert teased.

'You should see his parents,' said Daniel.

'Oh, I'm happy just seeing him.'

Peter gave him a lovely smile.

'You like him?'

'Don't you? Yes, of course,' he said quickly. 'Did your parents own the farm?' And to Daniel, joking: 'Of course I like him!' And then to Peter: 'I'm sure you were a good manager . . .'

'I had to make hard decisions. Once I threw a man off the farm. He was stirring up trouble. Like you, he thought I was too young.'

'I didn't say that!'

Peter took a gulp of whisky and lay flat on his back. 'But he got his revenge. One night he broke into my house and attacked me. With a knife. Look.' He lifted his shirt and there was a scar running almost from side to side of his stomach.

'That's terrible! What did you do?'

'I threw him out,' said Peter.

'Oh, oh, oh! Did you ever see such an exhibitionist?' cried Daniel. 'Do you know why he told that story? A – so he could tell you how he threw out a great big black man who wanted to murder him! And B – to show you his belly.'

'No,' said Robert. 'He wanted to show that he was a bit young to run the farm.'

'Exactly!'

'Liar!'

'This is my friend,' said Peter, and touched him on the knee. 'He understands me.'

'How could you throw him out?' said Robert. 'You must have been bleeding.'

'I was.'

'And yet you managed . . .'

'He's strong,' said Daniel. 'Aren't you, sweetheart? Go on, show him how strong you are.'

'Shall I?'

'Yes please,' said Robert. 'Show me.'

'Stand up,' said Peter.

They stood, facing each other. The top of Peter's head barely reached Robert's chin. He looked up into Robert's face with black eyes. In the centre of his upper lip a perfectly formed channel spanned the distance from mouth to nose. He was clean-shaven. Dark little bristles, just visible, did not form an unbroken path around his cheeks and across his chin. There were patches where his beard did not grow. Its presence seemed like an achievement. Each little hair should be prized on account of its delicate persistence. Manhood should not be taken for granted. Robert's eyes travelled over Peter's chin, down his throat, where the sallow skin responded in the most natural way to a perfect Adam's apple. He thought: we are breathing the same air. The air which has been in my own lungs is flowing over his face. He takes it into the depth of his body and releases it. I absorb it again.

Peter's face creases and his teeth glisten wildly before Robert hears that he is laughing. He gives a little push and Robert falls onto the sofa. For Peter is small and yet perfectly co-ordinated. His body is slim and yet it fills his clothes. He has been created according to the mysterious laws of proportion. He gave Robert a push and the sofa obediently received him. He laughed, and Robert saw between his teeth into a watery cave where a tongue played in perfect harmony.

'You see,' said Daniel. 'Peter is strong.'

'But I wasn't trying,' he protested.

'Let us change the subject,' said Daniel pleasantly. 'Now

that the athletics are over, for the time being. What is the difference between the material and the spiritual? Take the smile, for example. On what does the beauty of a smile rest? On the physical drawing open of the lips? Or on the glimpse inside a delicious personality, which, for some reason, the smile represents? We say someone has a beautiful smile. But why should the opening of the mouth and the crinkling of the cheeks be beautiful?'

Peter had touched him. By applying force, however small, he had acknowledged the presence of an obstacle: Robert's body. Peter had acknowledged that Robert had a body; what was more, he had not shrunk from touching it.

'What did you say?' Robert asked.

'I asked about the smile,' said Daniel.

Peter smiled, without opening his lips. 'Whose?' he said.

'Well, yours, for instance,' Robert said to Daniel.

'Mine?' Obediently he disclosed the gap in his front teeth.

This smile was an excellent example. The roguish gap in itself was charming; it seemed to apply directly to his personality. 'Well?' he asked, his mouth frozen.

'You are a pirate,' said Peter. 'A gentle pirate. But still a pirate.'

'Yes!' Daniel cried. 'And now, to prove it, I will murder you.' He stood over Peter, who lay on the floor in an attitude of submission. 'I will start with the legs. Look,' he said to Robert. 'Look at this thigh. Would it surprise you to know that sometimes, when I am not with him, Peter wears torn jeans. Jeans, that is, which have purposeful tears in them. And what do these tears disclose? A man,' he continued after a dramatic pause, 'a man may fall in love with the tear in a pair of jeans. It is, naturally, more exciting than the thigh itself. For months, for years, a man may be in love with the glimpse of thigh disclosed by a tear. And now,' he took a knife from the table, 'I am going to create just such a tear in Peter's leg.' He paused, the knife hovering above the denim. 'A man who has seduced another by the tear in his trouser leg must remember just one thing – if he wants to keep him: never take down the trousers. And Peter never does.'

'I do,' said Peter.

'But of course. For whom?'

'For you,' he said.

'Peter is practising for sainthood. He believes in free sex, love, that sort of thing. And why? So that, one day, when he has experienced everything, he can give it all up. This is how he will become superior to other human beings.'

Peter took the knife and put it back on the table. 'Now come on, Jock,' he said. 'You're getting carried away.'

'Did you hear that? He calls me Jock!'

'Jocky darling,' said Peter, and put his arm round him.

'Jock was his *dog*!' spat out Daniel, only half angry.

'But I loved him.' He led Daniel to the back window, and as they passed under the chandelier Daniel's hair, close cropped, was quite grey.

Robert knew it was time to go. He remembered his glass of whisky and swallowed it in a gulp. 'Lovely whisky,' he said. But it was not easy to leave. He had become an essential part of the proceedings, like the audience at a play. His eyes wandered around the room, trying to find something to look at. The canvasses were all turned to the wall. He went over to the shelf of records and tapes. 'Oh that's interesting,' he said. 'You've got Pollini playing the Chopin Studies . . . and Gieseking playing Debussy. Marta Argerich in Beethoven's first two concertos – I'd like to hear that. And look at this – an old recording of Furtwängler doing Brahms First!' He wandered back to the sofa, hands in pockets. The chandelier twinkled merrily. He sat down. He started to hum – a Chopin Study. The slow one, in E major. He played the notes on his leg, with both hands, as if it were a piano. If the keyboard were as soft as a human body, it would be much easier to play expressively. He realised he was afraid of the hardness of the piano keys.

He saw Daniel and Peter sitting together on the floor. Peter was leaning against the wall below the window; his black hair just reached the level of the sill. His legs were stretched out across the floor. With one arm he held Daniel's head against his chest. For a while no one moved. Robert reached the end of his melody and fell silent. We could be statues, he thought, no more alive than the easel over there, the knife on the table, the chandelier. And yet, though I am completely still, I notice that my eyelids blink, and my heart is pounding. And Peter is holding Daniel's head; his eyes, though lowered, are open. And Daniel, whose eyes are closed, feels Peter's warmth and hears his heartbeat. We throb with life, and continually try to batter down the walls that separate us.

Then he saw Daniel's hand move. It moved slowly up, across Peter's leg; stopped and returned. A moment later it started again. There was a tiny reaction from the denim, the flexing of a small, invisible muscle. The hand was moving; almost inaudibly it rustled the trouser leg. With a slow, ever widening movement, it explored; across, and up, it covered the fullest part of the thigh; stopped; and reached the crutch. Then it was still; there was silence again. Robert watched as the long, slightly crooked fingers adjusted to the new shape. Daniel's head had not moved. His eyes, shrouded by thick eyebrows, were closed. He lay against Peter, his head bowed like a supplicant. He began to stroke. Robert watched, feeling the sweat run on his own body. Peter, though flesh and blood, was impassive. His stillness, his silence, was of another order; he was not part of the dreadful intensity that guided Daniel's fingers. With every second the gulf between them widened. He frowned, and removed Daniel's hand. Now Daniel began to rub his head across Peter's chest. He twined his hand around Peter's fingers and squeezed them. He slid his arm round Peter's shoulders and grasped them. His eyes were still closed. Peter became restless. He drew up his legs and tried to free his shoulders. But Daniel only clasped them tighter. He tried to stand up but Daniel would not let him. Instead he pushed him down onto his side, and lay on top of him. Again there was silence. Daniel was pinning Peter down. Both had their eyes open. Peter was staring out across the room, his eyes darker than ever. Suddenly Daniel was smiling. He was on top of

Peter, straddling him. He took hold of Peter's arm and twisted it behind his back. He looked at Robert and winked at him. Peter made no attempt at resistance. Daniel twisted his arm further. 'You're hurting me,' said Peter. 'Then get up,' said Daniel playfully. 'Please, Daniel,' said Peter; and even now his voice was high and melodious. 'You'll have to fight me off.' 'I don't want to.' 'Pretend I'm a big black man.' 'Please, Daniel.' 'I'm a pirate, remember,' he said gaily. 'It's not easy to love a pirate. You should have thought of that.' Again he winked at Robert. 'We pirates are wild creatures. We roam the universe in search of adventure. We are explorers. We are faithful.' 'Let go.' 'I don't want to.' 'You're doing yourself harm, you know it.' 'I don't agree.' 'Please, Daniel. There's no point.' Silence again. Then Daniel said: 'This is hardly the way to entertain a guest.' 'Oh don't worry about me,' Robert put in, laughing. 'Anyway, I'm feeling a bit drunk.' 'So you won't fight.' 'No.' A long silence. 'I'm not surprised. At heart you're a coward.' Then he took hold of Peter's shoulders and shook him violently. Robert saw Peter screw up his eyes and tense his body. There was a crack as his head hit the wall.

Daniel released him and stood up. He said: 'I am sorry. An evil angel has passed'; turned, and left the room.

The music gives nothing away. Again and again he takes the low C with all his strength (once he misses and plays B instead) and the sound that pours out of the piano is like a straining knot of sinews, a forest that shuts out light. And now the trill which, before, was no more than an obscure vibration, becomes pre-eminent, the two obsessively alternating notes will not yield, they grow until all other sounds drown, obstinate, alone, they swell until, uncontainable, they shatter and lurch onto a higher, single note, like a climber who loses balance and grabs an overhanging rock; then step by step, note by note, the turbulence gradually disperses, there is a slow scale downwards, a precarious ever-quietening descent, which in turn becomes preparation, the clearing of a space; like a staircase he treads a long C minor scale, reaches the low G, and waits there until nothing else remains. The stage is empty. Then Schumann writes: *Im Legendenton* – in the tone of a legend. The time-scale shifts. Out of the sound and fury a legend emerges. He bows his head and tries to build the tale as if each note, each chord were a block of granite. He feels the sweat that links his fingertips to the shiny keys as he creeps, spiderlike, from one to the next, and, as he presses, he is aware for a moment of the whitening of his flesh under the nails.

Oh no, she thinks, in row J, oh no I mustn't . . . she is afraid to let her mind wander, even for a second. The consequences of her mind wandering might be catastrophic. Nevertheless it happens, for the mind is a perverse creature. She becomes aware of her husband's hand. She sees it out of the corner of her eye. There it lies, lifeless, on Henry's left thigh, close, very close to the edge of her own shimmering dress. She immediately concentrates all her attention on the small black-clad figure up on stage. She sees him pause, relax for a moment, and launch into another section. Wonderful, passionate Schumann! She closes her eyes and her neck sways in time to the music. Her son was indeed a romantic at heart. That much was clear, and everyone would realise. This section was different, slower, and yet it was connected to what had gone before. What exactly was the connection? No doubt there was a simple theoretical explanation. But that was not, she believes, what mattered. What mattered was the spirit. She was convinced of this, and she had passed her conviction to her son. She opens her eyes and looks straight ahead; all was well.

On the very edge of her vision she sees her husband's little finger make a small lizard-like movement. She quickly closes her eyes, and even screws them up a little, for the music is so unbearably beautiful; but they pop open again and make a brief dart for that colourless blob, again lifeless, located so close to her own dress. Immediately she again stares forward; sighs, smiles; lays herself open to the mass of sound sweeping the hall. But her ears, she realises, are increasingly aware of the heavy breathing to her right. She looks to her left. There is a spare seat; but she could hardly move into it. Or could she pretend that the visibility was poor? There were no hats or large heads of hair in front. '*Merde*, I can't breathe. Rob, Rob,' she mutters, pronouncing the 'r' in the French way. 'What is wrong with me? *C'est la claustrophobie – ridicule* . . .' She changes position, rearranges her dress, uncrosses her legs, smoothes her brow; it is only Henry! And Rob is playing. But again she is compelled, as if by an alien power, on to the hand, as it lies, like a toad, on Henry's trouser leg. And at that very moment the hand comes to life (though Henry himself, staring ahead, seems quite unaware); the knuckles rise, the fingers curl and uncurl, the tendons contract; if this were a dream, she says to herself, watching in fascinated horror, I would scream now. But in fact Henry is scratching himself. She watches, amused and horrified, as the hand scrapes, extends and returns to immobility. She wonders, in a way quite uncharacteristic, but of course picked up from him, what the hand was made of; what were the precise percentages of flesh, bone, cartilage and fat? And how had these changed over the years? Much of what had once been flesh, she reflects, had now turned to fat. The skin had lost its elasticity and wrinkled pouches now enveloped the joints. Here and there, in clumps, sprouted coarse greyish hairs. She frowns: these were new, surely? She gazes at them. This was the hand, this blotched hand, that had grabbed hold of her, commanded her, explored her with expert precision. It had wielded the knife over innumerable bodies, and come home to her. In sleep she had watched as it lay beside her, half curled, defenceless as a child. Awake it had kneaded her thighs, pumped her breasts, thrust itself into her secret places. This hand, this scientific hand, had desired her – and she . . . what of me? she thinks, staring blindly at the stage. What if the hand now raised itself and – as in the old days, in a dark theatre, or even at a dinner party, under the table – laid its solid mass on her thigh and squeezed . . . was she afraid of that? She smiles. Oh no. She would act firmly and with discretion. For this was the Wigmore Hall, a place of refuge. Here the surgeon's hand, incorrigible carpenter, took second place. Had Henry, after all, ever cared much for what she considered most precious – the imagination? She smiles again. (From row G Mrs Schwarzenberg, head half turned, watches her smile; narrowing her eyes she mutters grimly: *ja*, she is happy. This is her boy. And he is good.) No! Henry was suspicious of the imagination.

Long ago, especially before Rob was born, she would talk to Henry about the books she read, about music, about her childhood and the little garden in Normandy where she spent many hours stretched on the grass, gazing up at the sky through the branches of the apple trees . . . and Henry would listen seriously, and say nothing, he would try to take her hand, but often she would withdraw it and cry: let's go to Sicily and visit the Greek temples! He would nod, and say yes, we will, whenever you like, but before long his arm was around her again, strong as an iron bar, while she chattered on, gazing into the distance; then (Henry was impatient!) his face close to hers, he would insist: 'Enough words, Yvonne!' and she would feel her own lips, even as they still tried to form words, remoulded, reshaped by the alien, prickly presence of his, the words literally squeezed out of them; and then with a fluttering protest (and the exquisite knowledge that she was essentially, and for ever, mysterious to him) she submitted. What if she had known another sort of man, a man more like her? Would there then have been no iron grasp, no forceful silencing, no giggling withdrawal into her own world while her body trembled? Now she looks at that poor old square hand and suddenly wishes it would come to life, take her in the old rough way; she moves her right hand and places it carefully on the edge of the seat. Now, she calls silently, now . . . if only he too would have the inspiration, this plump boneless little hand, so elusive, would turn to flesh and blood; and his own thick fingers would suddenly be entwined by purposeful, well-manicured, sinewy tendrils! Her lips part; she feels the lipstick crack.

But Henry remains, like a dinosaur, motionless in his seat. He is concentrating, apparently, on the performance. Oh well, she thinks gaily, you've missed your chance. And then she too remembers what is going on. Like the zoom lens of a camera, or the eye of an insect that suddenly shoots out on a stalk, she focuses with all her might, and all in a rush, on the stage. She has a moment of utter panic, the terrible fear that her lack of attention may have had disastrous consequences. But no, *Dieu merci*, it was all still going on. And she feels immense relief, the relief of a woman who has been unfaithful and hurries home full of anxiety only to find everything as usual, her husband glued to the TV, her children asleep upstairs. Now what was Rob playing? What was this gentle, simple melody? Could it be that this was already the last movement, that her reverie had been so powerful as to obliterate the entire second movement? She panics again. With telescopic vision she sees that his forehead is wet; a bead of sweat runs down his cheek and falls, like a tear, onto the keyboard.

'These little cars', he said, 'are usually very reliable. It was already old when I got it! But every now and then things start going wrong. One thing after another! You know what it's like with cars. The other day I had to get a new exhaust pipe. And then a new starter! And now there's something going wrong with the gears. I hope it's just the clutch. Not a new gear box! Are you a good mechanic?'

Everything reproached him: the squeaking seats, the uncomfortable gear change, his long legs trapped under the steering wheel; London itself, waking to a new radiant day.

'I used to drive a tractor in Bulawayo,' said Peter. 'It was hard to get spare parts.'

'I can imagine!'

Night was almost over, Peter would soon be home, and everything was returning to normal.

'Did he hurt you?'

Peter smiled a little, and shook his head.

'Well, I know he said you were strong, but still . . . I heard a crack.'

Peter tapped his head. 'It's hard,' he said.

He could feel the road beneath them, consumed by the wheels, yard by yard, inch by inch. He searched for ways of escape. But the tyrannical road grew ever shorter. He could invite Peter back to his own flat. Or perhaps Peter would like to go for a walk in the country . . . they could turn off, here, down Hendon Way, and in ten minutes be out of London.

'Would you like to go for a walk?' he suggested. 'In the country?'

Oh what an absurd idea! He laughed. 'I just thought you might not want to go home straight away . . .'

'In the country?' Peter said, smiling a little. He turned towards him. His eyes looked moist. 'No, I'd better go home.'

Robert stretched out his hand and put it on Peter's knee. 'Don't worry,' he said. His body melted. He was filled with happiness. 'Don't worry, Peter. I saw what happened. It wasn't your fault.'

'Then whose was it?'

'Nobody's.'

Now the day, dawning, was enigmatic; it almost held out hope. He felt that solid knee, square beneath the jeans, and it was clear to him that nothing could conquer such a knee, it was a rock on which an empire could be founded; and deep within it flowed the river of life, which seeped through the denim and warmed his hand. 'You must try and have a good sleep,' he said. The engine was labouring, he would have to change gear, remove his hand . . . 'I hope you don't have to get up early.'

'Well, I'm supposed to go and see someone. But perhaps that can wait till the afternoon.'

'Are you a student?'

'No. Yes, in a way. I'm going to be a priest.'

'Oh, really? A priest!'

Peter gave him precise directions. They turned into Randolph Avenue.

'Just here,' he said. 'Thank you very much.'

'Wait a moment . . . It'd be nice to see you again – will you give me your phone number?'

'Yes, all right. Here. Goodbye. And thanks again. I'm sorry, by the way.' He was getting out of the car.

'Oh no, don't be sorry. It was a wonderful evening.'

'Really? You enjoyed it?' He paused, the door ajar.

'I was happy to meet you.'

'Oh, I see.' He pushed open the door.

'Will you come and have dinner?'

'Yes, of course. Give me a ring. Anytime.'

'How about Thursday?'

Peter took a key from his pocket. 'No, next week would be better.'

'Oh all right. Tuesday next week?'

'Yes, that's fine.'

'About eight o'clock? You've got my address.'

'Yes.'

'You have to ring the top bell.'

'OK. Top bell! Bye.'

'See you on Tuesday!'

Peter slipped off the seat, straightened his knees, and swivelled with a graceful thud onto the pavement. On his back the happy elephant glittered. He inserted the key in the lock; turned and waved. The elephant's glitter suddenly filled his face. Robert tried to smile back, but his own face cracked into a thousand fragments and he could not reassemble them. Go in now, he implored. It was impossible to meet such brilliance. His own crooked smile just would not hold still. It wobbled unhappily from cheek to cheek.

The door closed and he drove off immediately, taking with him, still, something of the precious cargo; the ceiling, which grazed his head, the speedometer misted with vapour, the peeling cloth of the seats, the door handles, were alive with Peter's fragrance; he breathed in the miraculous air, in which a priest's collar, a hero's knees, an elephant's trunk, and a name, were all combined. He soared through the streets, and his car was like a bright capsule, still earth-warm, which flies in the blackness of space.

He reached his flat, and it had changed. The door into the sitting-room was purposefully ajar. On the sofa cushions, poised like frozen waves, were about to break. He stroked the stalks of purple tulips in a vase, and they threw back their heads. He peeped into the bedroom, as if afraid to wake someone. The bedclothes lay about, intoxicated. The dent in the pillow was a smile. He laughed, and tiptoed from bedroom to sitting-room and back, and back again, like a visitor to a dawn-filled garden where dew lies on the grass so perfect that to disturb it would be a crime. He leant against the piano, wondering if that too had come alive. The open lid stretched out like the wing of a shadowy bird. But the black and white keys, immobile as crocodile teeth, glinted malevolently. He touched them; depressed them slightly, so that a faint sound, the ghost of a chord, disturbed the silence. He opened a thick book of Beethoven Sonatas and sat, cross-legged, on the floor. The black dots and lines, double and triple lines, curved lines, dense agglomerations, hieroglyphic rests, leaped in jagged patterns across the page. He read the music, and it seemed more vibrant than ever before. The melody rose like the birth of a breath, hung above thick repeating chords, fell, broke off, began again, broke off. The sforzando accent there was pure pain, like the scrape of a knife in a wound; that rest, that silence, was the suspense of the soul.

He turned the page, and there was a photograph of Johnny.

He took the picture to the window and scrutinised it. Johnny's profile scorched him. His gaze was fixed on a distant point; although the slight contraction of the eyebrows suggested that, as usual, Johnny was preoccupied with himself. Robert examined the face as if he were seeing it for the first time. The high ridge of the nose; the skin drawn so tightly across the cheekbones that it gave him the look of an underfed child; the striking contrast of the strong jaw and full wide lips, faintly smiling; the forehead, slightly furrowed, on which he had often tried to lay a soothing hand, but Johnny was so restless that he would not stand it for long, except sometimes at night when he would ask for it, saying it helped him to sleep. Above the brow hair spurted densely into short thick curls, like heather gripping a Scottish moor; hair the same light brown as his skin. He never needed to fear the sun, he boasted, this resistant olive skin had been bequeathed him by his beautiful Italian grandmother. How proud he was of her! He would tell stories of her bravery during the war; once she hid three young men in her barn, burying them in the grain and bringing them food and drink. One of them, a Resistance hero, became her lover. Perhaps this was why barns held such romance for Johnny, and when once he saw one in the country he became excited, dared Robert to take off his clothes, persuaded him to spend the whole night there, pushed him into the straw, fought him, beat him, tickled him, kissed him, pretended to rape him. And was Johnny happy then? Robert called him aloud, by the Italian name he especially liked (and which for that reason Robert used sparingly): Giovannino. He held the picture tenderly, as if it were Johnny himself. He brought it to his face, kissed the nose, the corner of the mouth, his own eyes closed; oh if the profile would turn, and look at him, and give some tiny sign of life, the flicker of an eyelid . . . let me see you, he whispered. He slid the tip of his tongue across Johnny's lips, and licked the celluloid. The miracle occurred: for a second he had a glimpse of Johnny's wide open eyes, surprisingly blue in such a brown face, looking straight at him with that impossible expression. As usual they demanded a love which, seconds later, they would refuse. They demanded a love which they could not believe in. All forms of tenderness, kisses, words, caresses, were absorbed with an insatiable appetite, but Johnny remained unconvinced. Then he would invent ploys and tricks of all kinds, he showed extraordinary versatility in finding new ways of testing Robert, he laid traps for him, he was sulky, glum, he missed appointments, he pretended to be ill; he was impossible. But the glow which now poured across the picture gave Johnny back all his innocence. That face, once again, was a summons. Where was Johnny now?

He replaced the photograph and stood up. His knees cracked, and he remembered Peter. He felt a little thrill: the thrill of infidelity. He went into the bedroom and lay down, without undressing. He was surrounded by lovers.

She sees the sweat fall, a single drop, and panics. What if this were already the last movement? Curious thoughts dart through her mind. To think that poor Monsieur Pischik, her dog, was ill that very morning! He vomited, several times, it was like a kind of yellow foam. And what about dinner? She is almost sure she has forgotten the radishes. But no, she must be brave and listen. She sighs and tries to hold still. And she is rewarded. Something tells her that . . . yes, was this not . . . yes, this was the quotation, the musical quotation at the end of the first movement – had Rob not told her? – or what at least was thought to be a quotation from 'An die Ferne Geliebte' by Beethoven! She mouths the German words in her exquisite French accent, and then, thrillingly, in English: 'To the Distant Beloved'. What a world of feeling, of hope, of despair, was contained in these words! And how excited she suddenly feels as she sits, looking and listening, while Rob played, in public, an Ode to the Distant Beloved! For was not, in fact, all that was most exciting, most *real*, contained, paradoxically, in the elusive idea of the Distant Beloved! Actually the thought has never crossed her mind before. But now, as the sound waves cleanse her, the repeated mouthing of the words (in three languages; she adds 'A la bien-aimée lointaine') fills her with inexpressible delight.

She feels gloriously free; and in fact she *is* free! She could allow her thoughts, her feelings (even her actions?) to roam like a panther; she need have no fear, no shame, with Henry on one side, a doctor – and Rob, an artist, on the other. Like a panther, clad in shining green, she could glide, she could prowl, she could tease, she could spring. Could she hunt too? She could extend her wardrobe – why was she so modest in choosing clothes? She glances at her dress; yes, it was shabby. She glares at Henry. Had she ever been demanding? No, and Henry had taken advantage of her well-bred reserve. She was still a good-looking woman; was it not her right to have beautiful clothes (after all Henry earned plenty of money)? The little orchard in Normandy, where she spent so many happy hours, comes back to her. There, lying on the grass within the garden wall and staring at the incredible sky, life had been so simple; she was a princess, the world was hers, and there was no darkness, only light.

Coughing and fidgeting have started, and with the words 'To the Distant Beloved' still on her lips, she realises the movement has come to an end. She looks at Rob with enormous tenderness as he relaxes for a moment, straightens his shoulders and takes out a handkerchief. She knows Henry has turned to her and is smiling, but she decides to ignore him. For once she is not interested in other people's opinions. In the end, she tells herself, it is what you are, not what you do, that matters. She looks at Rob, her thin, overgrown offspring, covered in hair (as she remembers, with a slight shock, from a recent trip to the beach) but with such lovely, unforgettable eyes. And who, she wonders suddenly (but probably there was no one); who was benefiting from the depths hidden in those eyes? She, who was so discreet, who wanted Rob to have a private life of his own, who never enquired, who knew without being told (of course she would never mention it to Henry) that he was not *quite* an *homme à femme* (but one would never know) . . . and so, who was it? She tries, but not too hard, to imagine his furry body rubbing and sweating against another furry body, and for a second she has a picture of two tarantulas (but that was, she laughs to herself, because Henry sometimes teasingly called him 'Spider'); but no, she must be content to know nothing. Perhaps there *was* nothing, but Rob was, after all, a romantic; nevertheless perhaps there was nothing. And if there was something, that is to say another man . . . of course there had been Johnny, yes, Johnny, she had almost forgotten! But Johnny had a chip on his shoulder, he was most awkward, she remembers, he had a habit of laughing ferociously at the wrong moments; in other words he was not suitable. Rob needed someone more stable, someone to help him discover himself, to give him confidence, to do the cooking (but were homosexuals ever stable?); who would allow him his freedom, the odd little prank on the side, why not, a reliable man; preferably less hairy and a little more solid in the body.

He was late, as usual, in a terrible hurry, trying to peel potatoes, cut up onions, and wash a lettuce all at once. Hanging by the door was an apron marked 'COLMAN'S MUSTARD', a present, curiously enough, from his father, but he had no time to put it on. He rushed from the sink to the chopping board, cut his finger and swore. The oven was hot, but the casserole was not ready. It was amazing how long it took to prepare a casserole – lamb chops, potatoes, onions, carrots – especially if your knife was not very sharp, if you were not very experienced and didn't allow time for things like peeling potatoes.

He was approximately twenty minutes behind schedule. He tore open a packet of 'herbes de Provence' and sprinkled them freely. They came out in a rush, and he had to scrape some off. A few drops of blood from his finger fell in as well. He screwed down the lid tightly and pushed it into the oven. It should be ready, he calculated, by eight-thirty. For a moment he relaxed, but there was really no time. He went into the bathroom, turned on the bath, and hurried back to the kitchen. He washed the lettuce and made a dressing. He opened a box of candles, bought earlier, and took one out, pristine. But now where on earth was the candle holder, the old silver candle holder? His finger was still bleeding, he had to look for a plaster. A plaster was unaesthetic. The floor should be hoovered, but his hoover was defective. It was better at spewing out than sucking in. 'Spew out spew out spew out' he muttered crazily, and it seemed he was on stage, performing a hectic farce, but without an audience. He fetched the dustpan and brush. There was dust everywhere. He sat down on the floor and looked at it. Dust was a strange phenomenon. What were they, these tiny uniform particles that settled like mist and dulled the surface of things? There was no time for speculation. On his hands and knees he set to work. Crumbs, ash, and whirls of cloud-like fluff resisted the brush, which was too soft. The music of the filling bath was going up in pitch, swelling like a balloon about to burst; he must turn off the taps. In the bathroom he was not sure at first, but it seemed that another, more aggressive sound was trying to attract his attention. Once the taps were silenced there was no doubt. He came back into the sitting-room and eyed the small grey object, like a scorpion with a shiny coiled tail, as it yelled its mechanical head off. He toyed with the idea of not answering. The rhythm of the grating notes was simplistic: two monotonous beats followed by three of silence. And yet it was not quite accurate, it was an inept attempt at five in the bar, the attempt of a beginner. He watched his hand, his pianist's fingers, as they cautiously explored the receiver. He lifted the little plastic thing and put it to his ear, aware of the hush.

'Hello.'

'Is that Robert?' The voice was high; oh, it was a woman.

'Yes.'

'This is Peter.' A strange mistake to have made. 'Listen, I've got a terrible headache. I've had it all day. I'm really sorry to leave it so late. I hope you haven't started cooking.'

'No.'

'Oh good. I'd better not come.'

'Oh – do you think so?'

'Yes.'

Long pause.

'Of course your headache might get better. It might –'

'No, it won't. I've had it all day, you know. It's a migraine.'

'Oh.' (Cheerfully, full of interest) 'You get migraines?'

'Yes.'

'I see.'

'Luckily you haven't started cooking!'

'No.' (Awkward laughter) 'Well, I mean . . . I've done the shopping and I was just, you know, cutting up a few things. But of course if you can't . . . is it really that bad?'

'Yes.'

'Well then . . . wait a moment, shall I come round to you?'

'No, I think I'd really better go to bed!'

'Oh well then. How about another night?'

Short pause.

'Yes, another night. I'm going to bed now!'

'All right.'

'Good-night!'

'Good-night.'

'Take care!'

'Goodbye.'

He reeled; and the immobility of the room, the abandoned white candle, the grief-stricken dustpan and brush, claimed him with open arms. He lit a cigarette. For a time he smoked obsessively. He clung to the cigarettes, one after the other, holding them constantly between his lips. They were the only thing he possessed, his only support. They helped a little to dull the churning in his stomach. The smoke crept towards the ceiling in a frozen plume. He gazed at the clock (in the shape of a piano) and followed the second hand, revolving eternally. It became an effort to hold the cigarette to his mouth. He noticed the hairs, bursting pointlessly from his shirt sleeves. And the mole on his right hand, near the wrist, had begun to sprout hair too. Three or four coarse, brand new hairs, sticking straight up, were claiming a right to existence. It was clear that his life force was manifest only in the hairs that rioted from one end of his body to the other. Well, he thought, let them. Let them consume me. I will give in. He lay down on the floor and closed his eyes.

He thought perhaps he was going to be sick. His cheek pressed against the carpet, and he covered his head with both arms. After a while he tried to kick off his shoes. One of them resisted. Reaching down he wrenched it violently off his foot. He curled into the foetal position and held the shoe against his chest. In the lace was a tight little knot. He could feel it between his fingers. His cheek was growing hot against the carpet; he was sweating. He took hold of the shoe-lace at both ends and pulled savagely. The knot remained, smaller than ever, like a louse. He tried with his teeth. He could feel the loop of the lace quite clearly with the tip of his tongue, but it was not easy to get his teeth under it. The leather of the shoe rubbed against his chin and scraped the ubiquitous bristles like a percussion instrument. His beard was a wild animal, quite alien. Even after death the beard was supposed to grow. It was not a sign of life. He began to suck at the shoe lace, and it calmed him a little. It had a sweet taste; what did it remind him of? Yes . . . it was marmite, marmite with brown sugar stirred in. The texture was both soft and resistant, rather like rubber; there was something unbearable about this texture, and the softer and damper it became the more unbearable it was. He began chewing rather than sucking, and it was an obsession; he had to go on and on, nothing must come between him and the lace. It was like the sort of nightmare you could have, before waking up with a fever, a nightmare which lasts for ever but is over in a matter of seconds; desperately biting through rubber with exhausted, aching jaws, while your limbs flail in an ocean of cotton wool . . . snap. Oh, so soon! He removed the ragged remains from his mouth and examined the broken lace: it had separated into warm, soggy strands.

He tried to reason with himself. What had happened? Peter had rejected him. Peter, whom he had met only once. Could Peter be the cause of such despair? In the room the shadow was increasing. The sofa, the piano, the table, and he himself, were darker islands in the growing tide. Angles melted. The tulip flowers, and their large cups, flattened; their purple seemed to spread, infiltrating the stalks, the pointed leaves, confusing the patterns on the vase; flowed down into the table, the unlit candle, the lampshades, the floor, anaesthetising everything. He must do something. Anything. He is afraid of this deadening.

He tries out the length of his arm, stretches it right down; then up, across his thigh to the solar plexus. He slips his hand, which gleams for a second, beneath the band of his trousers, nestles in the warm tight space there, in the curly hair which is like twigs and dried grass. He tries to play a little game. What could it be, what mystery is heralded by this resplendent growth? His fingers probe and detach a small cylinder, cool and pliable; he lets out a little gasp of amazement. He loosens the trouser button, and the floppy creature lies exposed, basking in the twilight. As if this were not enough, he discovers a wrinkled pouch lurking in the background, like a wizened counsellor.

He plays with it all, eyes closed, his mind nowhere. But the game is hollow. The spongy thing is his own, after all. He is ashamed of it.

After a long while he became aware of a faint sound, a series of clicks, from the telephone. He crawled towards it: the receiver was off. He lifted it and listened. The clicking stopped; instead there was an angry, drawn-out hiss, and from time to time a distant scraping sound, as if someone, far off, were shovelling gravel. Was the connection to Peter's house still open? With sudden violence he roared into the mouthpiece, and crashed the receiver down. Then he regretted it; perhaps he could have played a more subtle game. But something else was filtering into the room, a smell; the casserole, following the blind laws of the kitchen, was still cooking. He would immediately go and switch off this shameful remnant, which should have evaporated with the telephone call, and throw it into the dustbin. He wrenched up his trousers, snapped the button into place; and stopped.

He had an idea, a small idea. He opened the French window and went out on to his little balcony. It was cool, but the weather was fine. It was still light. The drone of the traffic was like a thickly woven chord, distant and vaguely intriguing. In the yard below was his own car. He came in, leaving the door open, and walked to the bathroom. He took a leisurely bath, washed his hair, shaved, and stared into the mirror at his soft dark eyes. The idea grew, became a plan. He tried to harden his eyes and make them glint like a blade. He put on a red silk dressing-gown.

He uncorked the bottle and lit the candle. His timing was good. He sat at the table and surveyed the meal, steaming by candle-light; then plunged into the great enamel pot with knife and fork and swallowed the wine (Brouilly 1985) in huge gulps. His appetite was savage. He devoured almost the entire casserole and emptied the bottle; lapped up the salad, stuffing it into his mouth with his fingers; a perfect Camembert, two peaches, a pot of coffee, a glass of brandy; and the plan was nourished, and hummed like an electric wire.

He laid out the beautiful grey jacket, with ballooning sleeves, on the sofa. At the mirror he groomed his thick black hair, and shaved off a few remaining bristles. The chin and cheeks were completely smooth; his beard was no more than a ghost, a promise. He smiled at himself, and ran his finger over the enigmatic furrows, framing his lips, that came and went. The plan filled him, changed him. The room was no more than a decor now; the chairs, cushions, the tulips existed for him to use, they had no power of their own. He felt the air inflating his lungs, expanding his chest, the nipples tightening against his shirt. His body was an instrument.

The telephone rang; his heart leaped.

It was Flavia.

'Are you alone?' she asked.

'Yes.'

'What are you doing?'

'I'm drinking a bottle of brandy and waiting for death, like St Augustine.'

Flavia roared with laughter. She thought Robert was the funniest person she knew.

'I shouldn't be laughing,' she said.

'Why not?'

'Because I'm terribly unhappy.'

'Have you been travelling again?'

'Well, I can't sit by the phone waiting for him to call me!'

'So you went to Manchester.'

'Yes.'

'To the theatre.'

'Yes.'

'And he had a cup of tea with you, and said how nice of you to come, but unfortunately he's got a rehearsal now, and so what was the point of you coming all the way when he couldn't really see you anyway, and you knew it very well, so why don't you just wait for him to get in touch, he's very sorry but he doesn't see any other way, that's how it is, he likes you very much and now he's got a rehearsal.'

After a pause she said: 'You sound pleased about it.'

'I'm not pleased, but I think it's time you got the message: don't get mixed up with married men. You're always doing it, aren't you?'

'But I love him.'

'There are lots of handsome, interesting, devastating, unmarried men around.'

'Introduce me to them.'

'All right, I will.'

'Why are you in such a good mood?'

'Because I've just been let down by my lover. I was expecting someone to dinner, and he didn't turn up. So I had a huge meal all by myself, got drunk, and now I'm having a great time.'

He could feel her curiosity.

'Who was it? Aren't you upset?'

'No.'

'Why not?'

'Because I've just realised he's not the only person in the world.'

Was this true? Had he got over Peter already?

'Robert.'

'What?'

'I love you.'

'Me too.'

'Really?'

'Of course.'

Then Flavia, who was a singer, sang down the phone from a Schubert song: *'In Grün will ich mich kleiden, in grüne Tränen weiden . . .'*

He closed his eyes. There was something so beautiful, much too beautiful, in that music, in Flavia's voice.

'Not a bad reception, I must say, for a telephone.'

He heard her laugh at that, a silent breathy laugh with odd little squeaks.

'Why don't you come round?' she said. 'The neighbours are out, and I feel like singing. With you.'

He hesitated. 'It's late.'

'Not really.'

He felt a surge of warmth; but the plan was slipping.

'You could even sleep here,' she added.

'No,' he said. 'I'll come tomorrow. You can sing then, and I'll play.'

She sighed. 'You're a bore,' she said.

'I know . . . I'm sorry.'

She clicked her tongue. 'I need you tonight!'

The jacket, on the sofa, was waiting for him. 'I'm sorry, tonight's no good. Tomorrow, please?'

'All right.'

'Thank you. Good-night, *chérie*.'

He puts the receiver down, carefully this time, and he is happy to have resisted Flavia's appeal. But he is afraid too, afraid of her vengeance. How can he be afraid of one who loves him so much? For a second he sees this clearly. But only for a second. Because the outside world bays at his heels like a pack of hounds. Even the solitary candle, still burning, wants something from him. The wax is almost consumed, it will soon be all gone, a candle no more . . . spluttering incoherently it reproaches him for his brutality. Dissolving into tears it drips down over the candle holder, into a small shapeless pool. He blows it out. He laughs. He will not be tormented by candles. He remembers. The plan takes possession of him again, and it is a kind of return to selfhood; and yet there is something so exciting, so inspiring about it that he is not quite himself either; it is like the idea that a composer might have for a great symphony, an idea that seems to come from elsewhere, a vision of a thing not yet existent, and he is transformed as it takes root inside him. He shoulders the beautiful jacket, turns up the collar, goes down to his car, and drives away. He is free, and also possessed. He thrusts Peter behind him. He has severed his links, and light as air he is setting out on his own adventure, totally his own. The people he is going to meet now will be almost, but not quite, the creatures of his own mind, like those we meet in dreams.

And so he joins the anonymous network of cars, lights blazing, which thread the city, and takes his own place in that ever-changing pattern. 'Oh Peter,' he mutters. The gears grind, and he prays they will not give out, not yet. The upturned collar brushes his cheek as he looks to right or left. His hands on the steering wheel, he is half aware, are damp.

Observatory Gardens

THE pianist wipes his brow and replaces the handkerchief inside the rim of the piano: a woman's habit, thinks his mother with a slight frown. Women don't have pockets and it would look absurd to bring a handbag on stage. But with those capacious pockets of his! She must remember to mention it. She knows it is the sort of thing he doesn't like to be bothered with, and in fact he was bound to jump down her throat . . . of course she would make a joke of it. She knows, even if he refused to, that details of this sort were important. One day he would be grateful. But now the second movement has started, and she realises, with a little thrill right through her body, how exciting his playing can be. Henry glances at her, smiling. Yes, this type of music, virile and energetic, was something Henry could understand. Their eyes meet, and somewhere, in both their faces, is the memory of a time before life became routine. To her surprise she almost feels like blushing. And he sees, with complete clarity, the protesting girl, full of daydreams, who in the event proved to be surprisingly passionate. Looking at her he has an unexpected insight into the passing of time: it is irrelevant. He tries to grasp this thought. How can time be irrelevant? Irrelevant to what? Here, sitting beside him, is the girl he knew so long ago, and nothing has changed. And these wild, march-like rhythms, filling all their ears, are Schumann himself, the essence of Schumann, quite intact after a hundred and fifty years. Could you then say that the essence of me, of you, of Yvonne, or Schumann does not fade: once born it exists for ever, even after death? What a lovely thought. If only he could have thoughts like this more often, how infinitely less boring his life would be! But already he can feel his scientific mind, like a scalpel, hacking away, reducing: such thoughts are products of the escapist imagination, necessary to allay fear, fear of extinction, there was no objective truth in them; people are addicted to every form of self-delusion, anything to avoid the horror of passing time and certain death.

And yet there was undoubted magic in notions of soul, or immortality. Is the scalpel really capable of doing away with them? And if minds are capable of inventing such notions, is that not magic in itself? He must try to remain as long as possible in this state, this rare state, so titillating, a state of suspense, as if everything could really have another interpretation . . . Looking at Yvonne he suddenly wants to kiss her. She understands, he is convinced, she knows of the indestructible essence of things and people that lies just below the surface. He smiles at her, and it seems that this is a smile he has hardly ever smiled before: the cheeks lift, the eyes sparkle, the skin at his temples folds into a thousand creases, all quite effortlessly – as if the weight of the years, the wrinkles and pouches, the lacrimal sacs, have been disposed of, classed as irrelevant by a single idea. Now this is something to tell Rob about afterwards. What a tribute this will be to his playing, and Rob will realise that he too, his old materialistic father, has an imagination . . .

But Yvonne has turned away; once again she is concentrating on the music. Henry too fixes his eyes forward. He is shocked by what he sees. Rob is throwing himself around, bouncing up and down on the piano stool. The music, it is true, was energetic, but Rob seemed more intent on conveying this by the movements of his body than through his fingers. Even worse, Henry distinctly hears a series of croaks and grunts coming from his mouth. He closes his eyes and tries his best to recapture his serene thoughts of a moment ago. He thinks of Schumann and Yvonne when she was little, and all the other departed souls . . . But if the dead all still existed somewhere how many of them there would be! And what does a dismembered soul look like, for that matter? He couldn't help smiling. Try as he might he was stuck with the sight of his lanky, uncoordinated son flinging himself to and fro in deadly earnest, uttering strangled groans; and now the vast array of the dead and their 'essences' appears to him as a tattered collection of jerking, overgrown creatures, a multitude of clattering bones, a terrible case of St Vitus's dance . . . He opens his eyes. Thank God, Rob was quieter. He glances quickly around, to see if anybody has a nasty smirk on their face.

He walks nonchalantly, hands in pockets, collar turned up, along the sandy paths that lead to the centre of the Gardens. It is dark. He draws himself up, tries to assume responsibility for his height. His left foot has the bad habit of turning out; he straightens it. Here and there, in the hollows formed by bushes, in the shadows of low-branched trees, are human shapes. They are still, like sentries. He notes them. He feels the pupils of his eyes expand as their frame of reference changes. The ground is dry; leaves and twigs crackle as he steps on them. He walks on ridges of hardened mud. He reaches the spot where the path opens out. On one side is a thick wooded area, and on the other the ground rises steeply, treeless, covered in summer with high rustling grass. In winter it is a low, close hill, without contours. He stops and lights a cigarette: a Benson, not his usual Camel. Bensons are more useful here. As his eyes adjust the woods come alive. People stray in all directions. Some pass him on the path, and give him a wide berth. Others come close and look into his face. Staring is not bad manners here. It is expected. A small middle-aged man, bald, with a track suit and white scarf, fixes him with narrowed eyes and slowly wets his lips. Robert stands above him, majestic, gazing into the distance. Men appear from the depths of the trees, negotiate fallen branches, sinewy roots. At the path they hesitate, uncertain which way to turn; thrust their hands into pockets, take up a position, light cigarettes, and wait with keen eyes. There are new arrivals. Some come with a bright step, free at last from the shackles of the outside. Others more cautiously, as if something of the outside still sticks to them. There are old men and young, of all races, shaven heads, bald heads, motorbike helmets, ties and suits, long flowing locks, carefully mutilated jeans, chains, jogging shorts, high boots, shining black shoes, army surplus boots, sneakers, leather brogues: the diversity of a city.

Robert sees a young man leaning against a tree trunk, legs crossed in loose trousers, with short fair hair. He is not very handsome. He has a snub nose and close-set eyes. But there is something appealing about him. His sleeves are rolled up even though the spring air is cool. He has strong shoulders, and his head rises from his body fiercely, like the thrust of a fountain. A tall, bent old man, with a peaked cap and trousers too short, passes, pauses, peers at him with short-sighted eyes; the youth pretends he isn't there. The other moves on. He hardly expected anything else. Another man approaches, short, probably in his thirties, with dark hair and full cheeks. He looks like a bank clerk; his baggy suit and plumpish body are out of place here, at night, in a wood. You can be sure the fair-haired young man will pretend he doesn't exist. But no. Their eyes meet and hold. They don't budge. Then the fair one languidly uncrosses his legs. He turns, and with the slightest of glances over his shoulder heads into the trees. The dark one follows, his heart beating violently. He stumbles over roots, but the branches sway and the leaves rustle, gently encouraging. In front of him, proud, luminous, strides the fair young man. He bends under a low branch, disappears. The other hurries after him, under the same branch; the ground dips and he almost falls. The fair one is waiting. Again their eyes meet, and hold; but now is no time for hesitation. The fair one reaches out; he touches the anxious chest, draws it towards him. He slips his hand under the shirt, plays with the hair around the nipples, and slides down, across the soft city skin. He feels the other's hand on his waist, reaching for the clasp to his belt. He sees the dark eyes, abject almost, perhaps amazed, the lips parted; then he touches the flabby stomach, bulging despite all efforts to hold it in; and he stops. He restrains the hand trying to undo his belt, and mutters something. The other knows without being told. He averts his eyes. He stands, his shirt open, his belly protruding, his office suit absurd, silently calling. He needs a disguise, but has none.

The fair one smiles. 'Take care,' he says, and moves away. He regrets breaking it off, but he had no choice. The fellow was not, after all, what he'd taken him for. He wanders into a clearing, checks his belt, his zip, runs a hand through his hair (cut that day) and goes on smiling. He is aware of his strength, his success, of his thighs moving powerfully. He walks on, and the wide trousers fall about his legs like drapes. His shoes with their thick ribbing never slip. He feels like a wild animal, senses straining. On his left he hears something. He stops, dead still.

Is it the rustling of branches in the breeze? He moves closer with stealthy steps; the soles of his feet graze the ground. Twigs are crackling behind a clump of bushes. And the faint metallic clink of a loosened belt sends a shiver through him. He approaches silently, slips between leaves, and listens. He hears breathing. This is only the third time he has come here; each time he is braver. Each time, at first, he is shocked; as if, in the space of five minutes, he has stepped outside civilisation, outside politeness and prevarication, into a savage world. Now he makes out two or three silhouettes, close together among the leaves. He takes a step forward, hesitates; is he wanted? He sees arms reaching out for each other, hands diving among shirts and trousers. He feels a warmth in his groin and thinks: it is the outside world which is a sham; this is where real life takes place.

He pushes through the branches, and looks. In the centre is a tall young man, with fair hair like his own. His eyes are closed and his head thrown back, while two others lovingly unbutton him, discover his chest, his lips, his buttocks, his navel, his genitals. One of them, on his knees, buries his head between his thighs, while the other kisses his nipples and rubs his hand up and down the channel in his long back; over the buttocks, and under, between the top of the legs, where his fingers meet the face of the other. The young man moans with delight (is he pretending? Can it really be *so* wonderful?), his trousers round his calves, his shirt flapping, and guides the movements of his ravishers with his own hands. The other watches, unable to move, and now a hand reaches out and grasps him too; whose is it, he wonders, but all he can see is a close cropped head, and an arm reaching like a tentacle for the bulge in his new trousers. Is this paradise, he asks silently, and abandons himself to the fingers which explore his bursting crutch; he closes his eyes, feels and hears his zip being lowered, his trousers and then his pants eased over his hips; feels the cool air on him as his prick leaps out into the night. He opens his eyes, faces the tall young man, and longs for him to see; and that proud head turns towards him, wondering perhaps who is this newcomer that has diverted the attention which was his alone; the eyes glint, absorb him. Yes, of course, this is what he has always wanted! Two or three pairs of hands grasp hold of him and his whole body is imprisoned, caught, like a swimmer in a wave. These young bodies, and mine, interlocking and loving each other, for ever. A tongue grazes his cheek, and he glimpses the face it belongs to: a lined face, with loose lips and receding grey hair. The image is shattered: there, in the thick of this youthful adventure, is an old man! Go away, he does not like old men! And yet the hands belonging to this face caress him with all the intensity he could dream of. What should he do? The hands insist. He is aware of gentleness spreading over him; of a knot dissolving. He feels his flesh become soft, malleable as putty. He almost wants to laugh. How can he stop now? He reaches out and touches the chest of the tall young man. The purity of that body is like a searing coal. He catches sight of stars twinkling through the leaves (incredibly bright! he thinks) and suddenly, unexpectedly, reaches a climax.

He is aware of the stillness all around, as he dresses. He thinks of his work mates, with whom he was drinking earlier.

They chatted about a movie, *Fatal Attraction*, and their girlfriends. They'd be surprised to see him now! The idea tickles him; his life, his double life, is wicked . . . He does up his belt and turns to go. 'See you, mate,' he says in a whisper. The others look up. One squeezes his hand, and the tall youth gives him a smile and a wink. 'We're like twins,' he thinks, and the smile and the wink seem more meaningful than anything. He pushes his way through the leaves and low branches and comes out onto the path. It is bright here, like daylight. He passes Robert. He notices this tall young fellow, who stops and stands a few paces away. 'Skinny,' he mutters, and shakes his head. He turns left along the path, and illuminates his watch. One o'clock already. Time flies in this godforsaken place. Behind him he hears footsteps. That skinny bastard is following him. Now all he concentrates on is getting away as fast as possible. 'Fuck you,' he thinks, but without malice. In a jiffy he reaches the Observatory building (what is that? he wonders), runs down the sandy track and disappears, out among the cars and yellow street lamps. Real life begins again, he knows very well, with the roar of his alarm clock, in six and a half hours' time.

But the little group he has just left behind is still engaged. In the dark space, amongst leaves of prickly holly, the grey-haired man kneels, and explores the young lad's crutch with his tongue. What a world of its own, moist, like a tropical landscape. What a special taste it has, this part of the body. Its own senses too, its own logic, its own decisions. It has a personality, a life of its own. It has a face. Not like the face above, the daily face, with its weathered skin and crafty eyes. The face below has no eyes, like the face of some fishes which live in the deepest oceans. It has a mop of wayward hair, a little sack of wisdom, and a wild protuberance. What a face! As he works, he remembers that in the law courts the prick is sometimes known as 'the person': he smiles at the accuracy of it. Now, under his expert touch, he feels the wave swelling: the brave young man can bear it no longer; his seed suddenly floods out, and shoots like tiny luminous arrows across the dark. Tenderly he monitors the powerless, involuntary spasms, and looks at the face above, its eyes closed, sunk in carnal dream. He is part of an irreversible and primeval event; he has journeyed into the heart of the life of the flesh, to that sub-atomic zone where spirit and matter combine. And the joy of it is that, like it or not, this young man, full of such promise, has been all the way with him.

The lad is in a hurry. He pulls up his pants, takes out a tissue and cleans himself up. He is all too aware, now, of his situation. He looks at the face of his lover. What possessed him? He looks at this old man and can't understand what drove him to it. And yet a few moments ago the sight of this wrinkled face and cropped grey hair thrilled him. But now . . . he is dying to go. He hears a well-spoken voice. 'It was a pleasure meeting you.' He understands that the man is trying to detain him. He refuses a cigarette. 'What's your name?' He must answer. 'Frank,' he says – a lie, this is his brother's name. Why did he say Frank? But the man seems satisfied. 'Good-night, Frank,' he says. 'Night,' the young man replies, and parting the leaves, gives him a friendly tap on the shoulder. This tap helps to restore his self-esteem. The old man smiles. He would like to take him in his arms. He loves his haste, his confusion, his shame. He watches the boy, who is in such a hurry, at such pains to forget. But he will not be able to forget. He will never forget. That thought is very touching.

He is left alone. He stands, his eyes quite used to darkness, in the little room whose walls are made mostly of holly. His trousers are round his ankles; above his fifty-year-old erection, gradually deflating in the crisp air, hang two or three rolls of flab. He lights a cigarette and considers his position. What if he came across himself, or one like him, a half-naked satyr with all the signs of decay about him, hiding from the light, and yet exhibiting himself? He would not find the sight beautiful. But everything is relative. So much would depend on the satyr's attitude. A satyr who was ashamed of himself, who in his heart of hearts considered himself obscene: yes, that would be a sorry sight. He would turn quickly away from this creature with the horror of one who sees his own worst fears confirmed. This middle-aged decay, thrust shamefully forward, would seem the embodiment of an entire life, an entire personality. The craving for youthful flesh would be nothing but despair, nothing but a desperate, famished mouth which had long since swallowed up the rest of him. On the other hand a fifty-year-old who was proud, who stood there sporting his maturity with confidence, who hid nothing, who openly enjoyed the caress of the night breeze; who profoundly understood that life is not just a matter of youth and vigour . . . was he himself not one of these? To which of the two categories did he himself belong? He pauses, inhaling the cigarette smoke deeply, then understands, once again: he belongs to both.

It is after one o'clock. In less than eight hours time the first of the day's patients will arrive. The thought gives him pleasure. The pleasure of a boy who has once again played truant without anybody finding out. He wants to lean comfortably against a tree trunk, to enjoy his triumph. He pulls up his trousers.

Outside the little room, Robert walks past; and stops, aware of a presence. He knows that older or less attractive men usually lurk in the darkest places, and yet he looks for an opening in the leaves. The thought of Peter is not far off; it must be kept at bay. He finds a gap and creeps through, bending double. He sees a man with short grey hair and a bulbous nose; immediately he turns back. The man says: 'Don't go.' Robert knows this is a trap, he must forget about good manners and pretend he has heard nothing. 'Please don't go.' He is suddenly thrown into confusion; and in fact the man too is shocked to hear himself say 'please', he has no idea why he should have wanted to hold back this gangly youth, not particularly attractive – and, what's more, by making himself pathetic, by saying the one thing that was sure to drive him away – damn it, from what self-destructive remnant of his psyche did that 'please' slip out? But Robert is taken off his guard; there is something devastating about 'please', here in this holly bush. 'That sounds terrible,' says the man quickly. 'I really didn't mean it like that.' 'Like what?' 'I didn't mean to beg; to try and stop you going.' 'You mean you wish you hadn't said please?' It is amazing, thinks Robert, how rude, how direct I am being. They are both silent; and then Robert laughs. 'Yes,' says the man, and laughs too. I can laugh, he thinks to himself, because I do not desire him, because I don't mind if he rejects me . . .'

They leave the holly room and walk together along the path. 'What a beautiful night,' says Robert; and they laugh again, because it is clear that the beauty of the night has nothing to do with it, nothing to do with their reasons for being here. And they are relieved. They see that, in fact, the night is beautiful, other forms of beauty exist too, not only bodies, and they walk together on an island, an island of enlightenment, while the others, in the grip of their demons, prowl back and forth. In this way, without really meaning to, they reach the end of the path, where the Observatory building stands, with its round tower and blank windowless wall.

'I'd like to look at the stars through a telescope,' says Robert.

And the man thinks: he is still open to new experiences, life for him is not yet an obvious repetition of patterns, not yet bounded by a clear circle within which we play for ever with the same few building blocks, he believes that something is to be gained from a new type of adventure.

'Do you think', says Robert, 'that one would be surprised by what one saw?'

'Perhaps. It would depend on you.' He is aware, as Robert looks at him, of the very deep cast of his eyes, and he thinks: he is beautiful, after all. 'I think *you* would,' he says. And he realises suddenly the depth of his own despair. 'Life is full of surprises,' he says.

'Do you really believe that?' says Robert.

'Yes,' he answers, and searches the young man's eyes. Is it only the darkness that gives these eyes such depth? He had forgotten the existence of such eyes. He stares into them, searching for an answer. What is this sudden despair? Quickly, urgently, he must identify it, pin it down . . . he sees himself sitting in his chair, his comfortable chair, with the patient, any patient, lying or sitting in front of him – and he thinks: do I really try to help them?

'I must go now,' he says.

'Just as we were having an interesting talk.'

'Yes – but I have to work in the morning.' He wants Robert to ask him what he does. He longs to break his rule of anonymity.

But Robert says nothing.

'I'm a psychoanalyst, you see.'

And he is sure, suddenly, that he does not try to help his patients, he uses them, he moulds them to his own ideas, it is power he is after, and all to cover up his own emptiness, his own despair. 'Yes, I'm a psychoanalyst.' And despite himself he is doing the same to Robert, he is trying to impress him, by repeating this, to get control of him. And still he searches the young man's eyes. He wants to say: 'I try to help other people. But really I'm just as confused as they are.'

Instead he says: 'These gardens are the playground of the unconscious.'

Robert laughs. 'That's a good way of putting it.'

'I hope you get the chance to look through a real telescope one day.'

'Oh, I daresay I will.' He can hardly expect the man to know that he is not, has never been, particularly interested in telescopes, that he mentioned them simply as a means of conversation.

'Take care. Remember, safe sex only!'

'Oh yes, of course.'

'I really must go. Otherwise I won't be in a fit state to listen to anyone tomorrow!'

He thinks: it would be easy to ask for his phone number. He feels a rush of nervousness. He hesitates, the question on his lips. He cannot bear indecision. So he smiles at Robert, fatherly, omniscient. He turns, and heads off towards the city, with a friendly wave.

He hums a tune as he goes, perhaps something from an

opera by Verdi. And his step is strong and sprightly – not bad for a fifty-year-old! But he does not get very far. The thought of his well-furnished flat, full of interesting mementoes of travels, and the bare consulting room, is not appealing. He circles the Observatory, and returns to the same spot. He looks back along the path. He thinks he sees the young man in the distance – yes, it must be him, that narrow, slow-moving body; and then he disappears into darkness. The path is empty. He does not dare go after him. A powerful sensation takes hold of him, as if he were about to vomit. He can hardly stand upright, and grips the pointed wooden stakes, the fence that surrounds the Observatory. He bends right down, and the sharp spikes bite agonisingly into his hands. He waits. He is not going to vomit; it is only fear that is rising in his throat. The old, obscure fear. He shudders, and screws up his eyes; feels the skin pulling, cracking, as if it were about to explode, his mouth set in a rictus that could tear his face apart. He waits for it to pass. He tries to regain possession of his mind. Inside his head he talks to himself, tries to grab hold of the scraps of reason that must be there, somewhere, tiny bricks of thought with which he must, as many times before, must build a dam. There is no rejection here, none, nothing. He has had a good time, has got what he wanted, he did not want that gawky youth, he did not even try, no he did not try, he did not want to try, he has a good life, a full life, friends, success, respect, boys when he needs them, he is not alone. Gradually he raises his head. The nightmare recedes. Like a thunderbolt it passes.

He lights a cigarette and leans against the fence, his legs shaky. It seems much cooler. The ground has begun to smell, as if a dew has fallen. He runs a hand through his hair, and down, over his black leather jacket and the metal of the zip. I have failed, he thinks. I have failed to find a mate, to love, to look after and be looked after by. Instead I have devised an arrangement. I have deep, uncommitted relationships with my patients and I come here, anonymous, to masturbate boys and share with them for a moment dark, wordless sensations. In both situations I retain control. I risk nothing. And even now I want to go back, find more boys, and drown myself in them. It is the only way I will be able to forget the look in your eyes, to put a barrier between it and me, to carry on with my life. For I could love you; and you will not want me. Against your eyes, the presence in them, nothing in my life can stand. Now I feel myself smile, partly because of the beauty of your eyes; also because I know it is not true, the mystery in your eyes is a trick, a coincidence; they have, perhaps, your mother's shape, the colour and set of your father's, and in this light they seem unfathomable; but what does this have to do with you? I could take you into an operating theatre, strip you, and shine lights onto you, your funny, underdeveloped body, and into your eyes, so that I would see them for what they are, shallow, frightened lenses, a mechanical instrument for seeing, common to all creatures, nothing more.

But perhaps I would love you all the more. Perhaps I would love the fear in your eyes. I might desire you, more than I do now; and then I would be afraid to let you go free. I would chain you, like Prometheus, to a rock and feed off you. For such is my sense of loss that, although I am not cruel, the possibility of finding could turn me into a sadist. But if you did not love me would I have found anything?

He looks at his hands. The sharp wooden stakes have thrust deep into his palms, and they ache. He thinks of the process by which the body heals itself. Within a few days this tender flesh will be robust again. Does the mind have similar ways of healing itself? What about this sense of loss that he feels as he stands here, a middle-aged figure alone at night on a stretch of grass? A few yards away a lad passes, without seeing him. He notices the way he walks; there is something carefree, a touch of boldness about him. Automatically he steps out in pursuit; but the chill air reaches right into his lungs, with a sobering effect. He stops. He observes the boy walking past with complete clarity. He feels the magnetic appeal of that living, breathing creature, and yet he remains separate, aware of his own identity. He stretches out his fingers one by one, and the breeze darts playfully through them. He brings his hands together, the fingers relax and interlock. For a moment he seems to hold the conundrum of human existence, cupping it like a magic lantern between his palms. The boy disappears out of sight, but the grass he has trodden still glitters with his presence.

The man thinks: yes, the one unchanging absolute in human life is lack. The Garden of Eden is always with us. All our life, in so many different ways, vaguely or desperately, we search for that mythical environment in which we still believe. All our life we long for it. It is our sense of lack which has created religions, cathedrals, music, love; and still we are thirsty. Lack is what makes life worth living. It is our sense of lack that gives life all its vividness, that makes the world a place of tremulous possibilities. It is lack that makes love and beauty possible. Not only possible, but necessary. We are all addicts. There is nothing to be ashamed of. And yet it is a shattering state of affairs. Where does it come from, this sense of lack? Oh yes, he knows, he is a psychoanalyst, it is not too hard to analyse himself, to trace the delicate chain of cause and effect that has led him from a small father-lacking boy to the delights and sorrows of this park; and so his own personal story has trickled like a stream to swell the great tide of human lack. But what of the great tide itself, the metaphysical longing, which is, in fact, no other than the longing for God? And perhaps the only indication of his possible existence?

Easy to say, with the banality of some psychologists, that this great dissatisfaction is the result of a simple separation; the parting of the baby from its mother, the gradual end of symbiosis. But how can this be? If our destiny is to be free, thinking creatures, why should we be left with such unending nostalgia for a time when we knew so little, understood nothing, when our human adventure has scarcely begun? The painful separation of baby from mother is surely only a symbol, a single aspect of what Nietzsche called 'the eternal wound of being'. This wound is the sense, varying but ever returning, of lack, of something missing. Lack is a key, a curse and a blessing; we must learn to use it . . .

He shivers. How clear it all was! This sky, and its small bright moon, the trees with tight patient buds, darkly looming above clusters of holly, and the men threading through them, full of hope.

Daniel sits near the back of the hall, an empty seat on either side. He does not want to be seen. How can he forgive himself for his terrible behaviour that evening? He cannot decide whether to go round and see Robert at the end of the concert. He had made a public display of his jealousy, and worse, his impotence. His exhibitionism knew no bounds. He had stormed out of the house and gone straight to a little cobbled alley close by. There was hardly ever anybody here, even in the daytime. The houses were small and dark, quite unlike the usual Golders Green monstrosities. It was a separate quarter, a troglodyte quarter. At the end of the street was a huge bridge, a railway bridge. It was built of old London brick and towered above the troglodyte dwellings. No wonder the inhabitants never ventured out. The rumbling of the trains must be horrifying. But now there were no trains, no sound at all except the regular dripping of water. Underneath this bridge water was always dripping, even in fine weather. It had stained the pavement shiny black. If he were a real painter he would paint this place. But he knew that he would never be a real painter. All he was was a stockbroker, an absurdly brilliant stockbroker. He went and stood on the black pavement. To think that he had become a stockbroker by accident, as a sort of bad joke, he had applied for a job, any job, to keep himself, while labouring with the demands of his art, his great vocation. Instead of becoming a great painter he had become a great stockbroker. He had a large house now, an excellent investment in itself. Standing under the bridge he rubs his hands up and down the wet grimy wall, also stained black. There was something pleasantly familiar about this spot, he had been here many times before; it was a sort of second home. It was here that he came to humiliate himself. He had an exquisite sense of belonging here.

A small clump of orange fungus grew out of the angle between wall and pavement. He gave it a violent kick. 'Thank you,' he said, 'thank you, my darlings. Thank you so much for reminding me. Thank you, God,' he called up into the echoing arch, 'yes, I am waiting, down here, my back is waiting, lash me!' He bends over, the dripping water and mangled fungus close to his splayed-out ears, and thinks of the mushrooms he was picking one day in the Observatory Gardens, more than two years ago, when he was young. Not the hallucinogenic sort, just ordinary wild mushrooms, boletus in particular. He was a good cook then, and passionate about wild mushrooms. And he was furious because although it was October, and wet mushroom weather, there was not a single one to be found. His eyes were sharp as razors. Someone must have been there before him, and yet the English know nothing about wild mushrooms. To them they are all poisonous toadstools. An excellent reason, in fact, for living in England. Perhaps the only one. And so there he was, in a long grey overcoat, fuming, when along came a rather short young man accompanied by a large black man, talking non-stop, in whose hands was a basket containing seven or eight perfect boletus. 'Excuse me,' he spluttered, 'I don't believe it. This is England! Never before has this happened . . .' and broke off because he was being ridiculous. He really wanted to give the basket a kick and send all the mushrooms flying. The young man started laughing. 'You can't possibly have found all those!' Daniel exploded. 'And do you mind not laughing? I have people coming to dinner!' The young man delved into the basket and picked out the largest and best boletus. 'Here you are,' he said in a high sing-song voice that was not unpleasant, with a ravishing smile. This sprite turned out to be Peter.

Under the dripping bridge he stamps and squashes the orange fungus into the ground. He is forty years old. Horrible signs of age are insidiously appearing. Hair has begun to grow inside his ears. Naturally he trims it! And his legs have become smooth and waxen. He has ruined everything with his fits of childish rage. And yet Peter always comes back to him. There, under the stinking bridge, he sees everything clearly. Quite simply, Peter *likes* his fits of rage. And this is enough to drive him into a rage. Peter is turning him into a buffoon! How much longer is he going to waste his time?

He will go to Paris, which is the only place for him; marry, have two children, and write a book. He has already been married, and divorced, so why not again? With a single stroke he will cut through the bonds that tie him to London, to Peter, to the erratic life he has been leading for so many years. Daniel the buffoon will be banished. So will Daniel the Angry, Daniel the Confused, Daniel the Idiot who can't make up his own mind. And when did it all start? When he became a homosexual. The idea of being a homosexual is quite absurd. Only an idiot would be a homosexual. Look at Robert, for instance, flailing at the piano, skinny legs and arms, spotty skin, ugly pink nipples, flopping cock, big feet, anus, and hair everywhere.

Of course he will do nothing of all this. He will remain in Golders Green, for ever, a homosexual Jewish stockbroker. So why all this confusion, this impetuosity? He looks round the hall; it is like a tomb. The rows of motionless little heads peeping above the seats strike him as funny. They are all asleep, he thinks. And I am awake, too awake. I am a Jew. Yes, a Jew, he mutters under his breath. A Jew, a Jew. He swallows the wrong way, and feels he is going to cough. Yes, he is going to draw attention to himself again. He takes out a handkerchief, and tries to recall the spittle from the back of his throat. At least he must try and wait for a good moment. He swallows hard. Typical! The music is soft for the first time in this movement. He tries hard to concentrate on the music. There is something interesting about the rhythm. It is syncopated, he thinks. And there is something syncopated too about Robert's body. It seems uncomfortable on the piano stool, as if not really sitting there, only pretending to sit, on half a buttock. And his back is askew, leaning awkwardly one way and then the other. It is really quite comic, jerky like the movements of a puppet on strings. And all for an audience of corpses. Imagine how funny it would be without the sound, in an old silent film. But then the music suddenly reaches him, and he understands: it is the tension of this music, the hope, the tentative hope in the notes, the odd, uncomfortable rhythm of this hope, which is in that angular back, that buttock which will not quite rest on the stool. This young man is completely at one with his music. It lives inside him, Schumann's spirit, his sorrows and hopes, as vividly as anything in his own life. Suddenly the cough explodes, and he only just has time to get the handkerchief up to his mouth.

Robert sets off again along the sandy path and watches the man as he waves and disappears past the Observatory. He is pleased to see him go. It does not seem quite right to find a middle-aged psychologist here. He feels that this man is a sort of spy from the outside world, who comes to check up, to gather information. He has an ulterior motive. One should be granted a pass, he thinks; only naïve and innocent people admitted. No doctors, no scientists. He has a pleasantly hygienic feeling, as if he has eliminated an element of pollution. The place is pure again, and it is his doing. And so he can concentrate again on more pressing matters. He draws himself up, rearranges his collar, and narrows his eyes. He allows a subtle smile to infiltrate his lips. He treads carefully, as if testing the ground. He wants his careful, controlled steps to give the impression of great muscular power. He reaches the smooth hill which slopes up to the right. On summer nights people sometimes make love here, hidden from view by tall grasses. But now, apparently, there is no one around. He feels like a circus ringmaster. He wants to crack a whip and have people appear. This landscape is so bleak, so lacking, it cannot be taken at face value. It is up to him to create the right environment, to draw elves and spirits from the woods. What of all those creatures that were here before, only half an hour ago? His conversation with the psychologist has driven them away, talk of telescopes and the unconscious has shattered the magic rites, there is not a soul here, except him. And yet the psychologist himself had been one of them; before he spoke, before he revealed his identity. He climbs up the slope a little, to get a better view, and to exhibit himself. He towers above the path, monumental, fascinating. Now surely they will all see him and emerge from their hiding places. They are taking their time, like badgers before venturing from their setts. At last a human shape appears from the left, tiny and sprightly, and hurries along, intent on going somewhere. The superiority of Robert's position is unbearable. The little figure will be dwarfed and terrified. Robert steps down to the path. He is a knight in the shining armour of his high collar and perfect, seamless jeans. The homunculus approaches; Robert recognises him. It is the same small, bald, middle-aged, tracksuited being that leered at him before. For a moment he allows himself to be desired, staring into the black distance. The man stops, poised on chubby legs, and licks his chops.

Robert moves away. He does not want to torment the poor creature, and so he tries to introduce a flaw into his appearance. He droops his head apologetically, and walks with clumsy, unappetising steps. He turns left along a narrow path, and rubs his hand along the bark of trees. It is surprising that these tree trunks should be so solid. One would expect them to be flimsy, illusion-bound, movable, like props on a stage. He knows the little man is following, and it is annoying that people cannot take no for an answer. He tramps on, without meeting a single soul. Has there been a police raid while he was talking to the shrink? He stops, and the steps behind him stop too. He hears twigs cracking sharply, and a little quiver of excitement runs through him. He turns to look. No, it is just his bald admirer trying to draw attention to himself. The little man is delighted, encouraged by Robert's glance, and with amazing speed undoes his zip and gets his cock out. Robert sighs. Just ahead, to the right, the sky is lit up by an orange glow; but surely he is not so close to the edge of the park? This path leads to a clearing, where there is a pond; beyond that several paths splay out and cross a wooded hill; there is a ditch and a stream, an impassable patch of brambles, a small fenced-off nature reserve, a football field, and only then the city begins again. The glow becomes brighter, and he approaches it cautiously. The path widens, and he leaves it, threading through undergrowth and trees. After a few minutes he reaches the pond. It is ringed by lamps. Men walk around it, through pools of light and shadow. And yet this pond was surely one of the darkest places in the park, the very heart of it.

He steps into the open, and feels the glow on his skin, an unreal, plastic colour soaking into his hair, his cheeks, the great sleeves of his jacket, his jeans, his bright new sneakers, giving him and the others that weave around the pond vague shadows that come and go; he takes his place among them and they seem to advance together, in the same direction, as if by prearrangement, as if he were joining a dance that is always going on, whose steps are never learnt but instinctively known; when one drops out another takes his place, and now it is his turn, which comes as no surprise, for the slow revolve is so much a part of life that it could not fail to happen, somewhere. At one moment they are all moving together; then the unity is broken, one stops, turns, walks against the stream, casts a look at another, assesses in that brief deep look a whole human being; and it is easier here, in the light, and easier too to be disappointed or to disappoint. They are all vulnerable, in this unflattering light, especially the older ones who, giving themselves away, stick to the shaded circumference, and Robert too does not know whether to hide himself or brave the full glare. For they are all together, all part of the same performance, and yet separate, quite unknown to each other. He stops and leans against a lamppost. Surely they were here, these lamps, before; they are old and chipped, and yet he never noticed them. Maybe, unlit, he took them for trees, or wooden posts; his attention was so focused, so body-levelled, that he never looked up to see the round glass domes.

The pond is usually dark as a crypt; it is the womb of the park, promising a little comfort, a little relief. On quiet nights you can hear the gurgling of a tiny brook, filling the pond from one side; the water, invisible, is never still; it rustles, persistent as hope, secret as the circulation of the blood. Now, with the lamps lit, everything is irradiated; the water surface reflects, transforms the light into a haze, a foam around the edge, diluting and spreading towards the centre, which is blacker than ever, an oval of deepest black; suddenly the whole pond stirs, and myriad luminous points appear, glitter from wave to wave like metallic flames, and vanish. And in the eyes of the men that pass he sees, too, the reflection of the water.

He smokes. He feels excited. He leans against the lamp and listens to the sound of feet. Somewhere there is a pair of leather soles, undisguisable, their sharp click-clack out of place. He knows that Aids too is stalking here, that any of these men might be a potential killer. Almost everybody is interested in him; they pause, and linger by the lamppost against which he rests enigmatically. He feels attractive. He could walk away, and his absence would be heart-breaking, it would pierce the air like a cry. He could walk away, sure of being followed. It is good to be desired. He is the master of the park; his whims are law.

But none of these people are for him. Across the pond is a young man, staring into the water. He is the only one who has not come to inspect him. Robert walks casually towards him, taking the long way round. Eyes are on him; is the master about to make a choice? He reaches the pensive figure, elegantly perched above the water, and waits. The boy looks at him. He feels a little of his confidence drain away, a tiny clamouring of anxiety, but shows nothing. The boy moves off. He does not seem to be interested. And yet, after a moment's hesitation, he takes a small path that leads away from the pond, towards the hill. Robert follows, his serenity gone. The boy does not go far. He steps into a clearing, explores it, and stops at one end, where a row of saplings form a hedge. His poised, languid movements come naturally; they are what Robert tries to imitate. Both wait. Their eyes must get used to the dark again. The boy turns, and faces back towards the path. Robert tries to interrupt his line of vision, stands in front of him, but the boy moves too, presents him again and again with his profile. A long sharp nose and fine, tight lips. He refuses to see Robert; who brushes against the saplings, cracks the twigs underfoot, tries to draw his attention, as if perhaps the boy hasn't yet noticed. Every part of him cries out for attention. How can the boy remain aloof? With his left hand he touches his own crutch, outlines the growing fold, exaggerates the movements of his arm, and scrutinises the boy's face; and the other, although not deigning a direct look, is surely taking it in from the still corner of his eye. With great care, like the unwrapping of an infinitely rare and precious object, Robert lowers his zip. His eyes still glued to the corner of that other eye, the edge of that pupil just visible, the lid and lashes immobile, he slips his hand into the opening and feels his flesh unfold. The boy blinks. Thrilled, Robert's flesh hardens. The boy takes a step forward, away. But no, what are you doing, where are you going? Robert turns round. Something else is happening. In full view, barring the way back to the path, stands the small bald man, his tracksuit and pants lowered to his knees, energetically masturbating. His plump pale thighs rend the darkness. This is the sight that has transfixed the boy. It is the middle-aged homunculus that he needs. With slow, awestruck steps he approaches him.

They block the opening. Robert watches them. They are, it seems, perfectly suited. From the first moment they are so rapt that they ignore him completely. They do not care if he goes or stays. His small sturdy pursuer has already forgotten about him. He is not even invited to join in. He fingers the slim branches of the saplings and wonders what sort of trees they will become. Something about this spot tugs at his memory. He watches the lovers, only a few feet away. He watches their hands and fingers, probing, caressing, undulating. He tries to climb out through the saplings, but they are too thick. So he waits. The little man's hands are broad and soft, and operate in circular movements. He thinks of all the uses that hands are put to. His own feel cold and dry. A little while ago, on the steering wheel, they were damp and sticky. What is he doing here? The absurdity of his situation suddenly strikes home.

The night is almost gone, tomorrow he will be exhausted, unfit to work. And, surely, there is no salvation to be found in these woods! Can anything be gained from what happens here? He has an important concert approaching: his 'début' at the Wigmore Hall. The word reminds him of old-fashioned dances, 'débutante' balls at which young upper-class girls used to 'come out'. Is he 'coming out'? Yes, he is 'coming out', at this moment, here, in this clearing! And soon he will 'come out' at the Wigmore Hall too. The gentle humour of this association fills him with warmth, like a burst of timid sunshine. It hardly seems to matter, suddenly, whether he is tucked up at home in bed, or out here, in this no-man's land. The same, faintly ironic eye of heaven is on him, whatever he does, wherever he goes. He watches the fingers of the homunculus as they lovingly cover the boy's body, skin to skin, allowing no air, no space at all, to intervene, as they creep over him. And this, he thinks, is exactly like legato playing on the piano. The concentration of all one's feelings in the very tips of the fingers, the almost imperceptible passing from one smooth note to the next, and the lovely seamless flow of sound, headlong or hesitant, without any breaks at all. Sometimes, like these two, you close your eyes and feel your way by touch alone, as if by excluding sight the other senses becomes more acute. And now the lovers become more passionate, the man takes hold of the boy in great handfuls, and this is another touch, another way of taking the piano; chords, clusters of notes, that fill your arms, your shoulders, massive blocks of sound that you wring from the depths of the instrument; and you must never lose your sense of orientation as these resonant handfuls leap from one position to another, you must know the keyboard's anatomy as well as any human body. It requires more skill, he thinks, as he watches, than making love.

Flavia sits in row F, her chin resting on her hand. He is beginning to play in the way she loves most, the way that can send shivers through her. She watches his crouching, tension-filled body, and remembers the first time she saw him.

How different he seemed to her then! It was in Paris, where they were both students, at the Foyer International. When she saw him in the lobby, in the corridors of the Foyer, he seemed to pay no attention to her at all. He passed from the desk, to the letter boxes, to the notice board, to the lift, to his room, without looking to right or left, while she, looking everywhere, watched him and tried to catch his attention. And yet his large, melancholy eyes surely did not spurn human contact; perhaps they just found it difficult to begin. One day, downstairs in the lobby, she saw him talking excitedly to a tall, thin woman (almost as tall and thin as he was) with extraordinary green eyes; his excitement surprised and intrigued her. Occasionally they shared the lift; she found the enforced intimacy – he made no attempt to break the silence – rather uncomfortable. Once, she met him in the street, near the Tuileries Gardens. She greeted him; he stopped and stared in confusion. 'I've seen you in the Foyer. I live there too,' she said. 'Of course!' he replied. 'I'm sorry. I'm so absent-minded.'

His voice was slow and slightly furry. She very nearly said: 'Why don't you clear your throat!' They looked at each other. Just as she saw he was about to speak (his lips already parting) she said: 'Shall we go and have a coffee?' To her surprise he agreed. As they walked, she was aware of his enormous height, of her smallness, of his loping stride, and her little steps. Just as she was thinking about this, he said: 'You take three steps for every two of mind. Does that mean I'm one and half times as tall as you?' She found this unbelievably amusing, and the rest of the walk was spent in a hilarious attempt to co-ordinate their strides. She was amazed to find him so friendly. It seemed impossible to find a café; and yet they passed several which he didn't even notice. Locked into his stride she watched them slip by, and felt she didn't have the right to an opinion. Eventually she said: 'Robert! We've already passed several cafés, and you didn't even notice!' And then it hit her: she stopped, doubled up with laughter; aware, though, that she was losing all poise, all possibility of elegance. She knew, also, that Robert was embarrassed, that he was looking around and hoping not to attract attention. He recognised this laughter, even more alarming here, outside in the street. In the Foyer it was this laugh that people heard approaching along the corridor, and quickly slammed their doors. But she simply couldn't stop. It poured through her jaws, locked open, in long hysterical cascades, punctuated at regular intervals by desperate, gasping intakes of breath. There was something about her laughter which turned the world upside down. It was the verge of madness; it made people shudder, shake their heads, and try to concentrate on something else. People had to pretend that nothing was happening, as if any acknowledgement of the phenomenon would cause an abyss to open at their feet. But she, as she laughed, felt nothing except the impossibility of stopping; it was a fit, a possession, against which there was no fighting, and which left her temporarily exhausted. At last the worst was over; she straightened, her senses returned, and she became aware of the gurgling in her throat. She closed her mouth with a click, and saw Robert, some yards away, looking into the window of a fashion shop. She felt sick. She went up to Robert and stared at him. Her lips curled sarcastically. 'I detest people who arc cmbarrassed when I laugh,' she said, and gave him a small superior smile. After that they walked on, and found a café immediately; in silence they sat and drank two black coffees, which he paid for, while she never took her eyes off him, critical, pitying eyes. Perhaps she wanted to burst into tears and beg him to forgive her, to understand her; in any case she longed to stop him hating her. But she said icily: 'Have you lost your tongue, or what?' He shook his head, smiled politely, and looked into his coffee cup.

The next time she had a chance to talk to him she invited him into her room at the Foyer and spent a whole evening with him. She had the impression of kidnapping him; but he seemed a relatively willing victim. As a matter of fact, as he crossed the threshold, he felt that it would be difficult to leave; but he couldn't refuse. Her studio had exactly the same furniture, provided by the Foyer, as his own: bed, table, three simple chairs, and an upright piano. On the wall was a huge photograph of Maria Callas taking a curtain call at La Scala. Her bed had a beautiful dark red cover, of brocade or damask; it glowed warmly, even in the crude light of the unshaded bulb that hung from the ceiling.

'You should get a shade for that bulb,' he said, 'it makes a big difference –' Immediately they were plunged into darkness; Flavia had switched it off, and for a moment he thought she was going to jump on him straightaway. She roared with laughter, and dimly he saw her fumbling with a lamp on the piano. Her fingers were sweaty and she lacked the strength to push the switch. She saw him move towards the window, and was sure he was about to leave her, by jumping from the fifth floor if necessary. '*Merde!*' she cried. '*Ça ne marche pas! Merde, merde,* shit!' 'Do you speak English?' he asked. 'Of course! I *am* English!' 'But so am I!' '*C'est pas vrai! Toi?*' and she exploded with laughter again. 'And you?' he went on in French, 'With a name like Flavia?' 'My parents came to England during the war, from Italy, and I've been trying to get out of it ever since! And *mes cons de parents* took British nationality, or whatever you call it, useful of course – but I'll never forgive them!' she cried excitedly, and miraculously the lamp came on, although she had already given up and was about to light the bulb again. 'Thank God for that,' she said; and laughed again, for it was absurd for an atheist and intellectual like her to be thanking God, and he should realise that.

'Actually I was getting used to the dark. In fact there's plenty of light coming in from outside.'

'Coffee?' she asked, and her voice suddenly had a hard edge to it.

'What a wonderful view you have from here,' he said. It was true: the Seine swept by just below, and the lights of the noble houses on the Ile St Louis glittered through the plane trees. 'Yes please, coffee,' he added. 'Well I don't mind really . . .' 'Yes, or no?' '*Oui ou non . . . Non ou oui . . .*' Somehow he felt it was all right to dither with Flavia. He was curiously carefree; he wanted to tease her, to show off; but then, remembering after all that he hardly knew her, he said firmly: 'Yes please.' The truth was he really didn't much like instant coffee. 'Wait a moment. I've got some delicious coffee in my room. Shall I go and get it?'

'I see. Monsieur is a coffee snob.'

She came out of the kitchen bearing a packet of coffee. 'Is this good enough for Monsieur?' she asked in a theatrical monotone.

'Oh yes. Lavazza . . . of course.'

'*Ces anglais* . . .' he heard her muttering in the kitchen.

'It's true,' he said. 'I am a bit of a coffee snob. But I'm sure you're a snob too. About something or other.'

'About nothing,' she said. 'Except literature.'

There were several books on the table: Reich's *Sexual Revolution, The Man without Qualities* by Musil, and Kafka's *Metamorphosis*. He picked up the Reich, and leafed through it. Then Flavia came from the kitchen, bringing cups and coffee percolating through a paper filter into a chipped brown jug. She saw what he was reading.

'Reich', she announced, 'was the link between Marx and Freud.' She went and sat on the bed, fiddling with her legs; first she folded them up, and then unfolded them. 'It always surprised me that nobody had ever really connected up those two, and then I discovered Reich.'

'I've never read him,' said Robert. As a matter of fact he had never heard of him.

'You must,' she smiled at him. 'That's a very important book. Vital. I'll lend it to you.'

'Have you finished it?'

'Of course. Many times. I know it backwards.'

He looked inside the cover and saw that Reich was a psychoanalyst. 'I'm not interested in psychoanalysis,' he said.

Flavia smiled slightly; a very superior smile.

'I don't believe in too much analysis,' he said. 'What's the point in analysing your feelings the whole time? You've either got them or you haven't.' Flavia surveyed him from under hooded eyelids. 'What's the point?' he continued. 'What else have we got except our feelings?' This struck him as an intelligent remark.

'I can see you don't know the first thing about it,' she said coldly.

Robert was taken aback. 'Why are you so rude?' he said.

At which she burst into laughter; laughter so out of place and infuriating that he decided he'd had enough, and stood up.

'No, don't go – I'm sorry.' She looked at him seriously for a moment, almost contritely, but the laughter was so irrepressible that it kept leaking through her closed lips in little pressurised bursts.

'I really don't see what's so funny,' he said, shrugging his shoulders.

But the mention of the word 'funny' was too much for her, and she exploded into billowing waves of mirth, doubling over and gasping for breath. He looked at her in amazement. 'You're mad,' he said, making for the door.

'No, no, please don't go,' she said, straightening up and nimbly coming between him and the door. 'I'm mad, I know I'm mad – but aren't you too?' She smiled a brilliant smile, and he thought, for the first time: she is beautiful. Her teeth were magnificent, extremely white, and her eyes enormous and black. But her body was alarming: huge square shoulders, a non-existent waist and hardly any neck at all. Her sensitive face swam helplessly on that massive undifferentiated trunk, as if having trouble keeping afloat.

He sat down again and fingered his coffee cup.

'Milk?' she asked.

'No thank you.'

Flavia settled onto the bed, kicking off her shoes: high-heeled, he saw. How tiny she must be. He sipped his coffee and looked round the room suspiciously. A mauve dress was hanging on the outside of the wardrobe: heavy pleats and no sleeves. With a sarcastic smile he tried to imagine her bare arms. By the window that opened out onto the Seine lay a rug: a brash imitation of an old Kelim. On it were two more pairs of high-heeled shoes, one with leopard spots. By the piano was a neat pile of music; on top of this an open packet of Tampax; against the wall, a cello.

'I thought you were a singer,' he said.

'I am.'

'And a cellist?'

She nodded.

Then silence again. They ignored each other completely. Flavia drank her coffee in noisy aggressive gulps. He was determined to take no notice.

Eventually he asked: 'Well what are you reading at the moment?'

Lazily she stretched out and picked up a book from the floor. 'This,' she said. 'Among other things. A masterpiece.'

He read: *Les Chants de Maldoror.*

'Of course,' he said. 'A masterpiece. Would you read anything else?'

She eyed him triumphantly and opened the book, apparently at random. For a few moments she read in silence, and he thought: she is utterly repellent. I shall leave immediately.

But in a soft, theatrical voice she began to read aloud: 'One should let one's nails grow for a fortnight. Oh! how delightful it is to drag brutally from his bed a child on whose upper lip no down has yet appeared, and, with wide open eyes, pretend to pass a gentle hand across his forehead, smoothing back his beautiful hair! Then, suddenly, when he is least expecting it, to dig one's long nails into his soft breast, in such a way that he does not die; for, if he died, one would miss the sight of his suffering. Then one drinks his blood and licks his wounds; and, during this time, which should last as long as eternity, the child cries. Nothing is so sweet as his blood, extracted in this way, still so warm, except perhaps his tears, bitter as salt.'

She paused and shot him a quick glance. He said nothing.

She continued: 'Blindfold his eyes, while you tear his palpitating flesh; and after listening for long hours to his sublime cries which are like the piercing death rattles of the wounded as they sprawl in agony on the battlefield, then, having swept away like an avalanche, rush in from the next room and pretend to be his saviour. Untie his hands, with their swollen veins, and give back sight to his demented eyes; meanwhile start again to lick his tears and blood. How genuine then is repentance! How the heart overflows to be able to console the innocent being whom one has hurt: "Unhappy child, you who have just suffered such agonising pain, who could have committed against you such a crime, for which no name is adequate! How you must suffer! And if your mother knew about this she could be no closer to death, no more horrified by the acts of such a criminal, than I am now."'

'That's enough,' said Robert, and stood up.

Quickly she was off the bed, and shot to the door, like a guard dog. He went to the piano. He closed his eyes as his fingers, slightly trembling, dropped into the keys, exploring them, feeling their way into a new instrument. He began to play Schumann, Kreisleriana. And this music – the fresh, wild music of the Kapellmeister Kreisler – burst into the devastating world of Maldoror, the self-tormenting recluse, like the awakening from a nightmare. She sat down again, and was ashamed of everything; even the thick damask bedspread into which she sank. He was bringing innocence back into the room, where she had tried to dazzle him with sophistication and world weariness. She felt her eyes filling with tears. But what else could she have done? She watched his face in amazement. It was so unusually alive. The set, reserved features were melting, currents of fire or tenderness rippled through his cheeks, his forehead, his lips, and many intermediate states of feeling, hard to describe in words, were reflected there too. So fascinated was she by his face, this map on which she seemed to read every possible emotion, that she hardly heard the sounds his fingers were creating. So that when, suddenly, he stopped playing, she still stared at his face as if the unexpected relaxation, the blankness of his features were all part of the drama.

He turned to her, smiling.

'Why stop? she almost whispered.

'Because I haven't learnt the last part yet!'

The playing had changed him; his eyes laughed, he was debonair. She sat on the bed, her eyes full of tears, and he sat with her.

'What is it?' he asked.

'Your playing . . . I'm sorry.'

He put his arm round her shoulders, hardly noticing how big they were, and kissed her. 'I'm happy to have played for you,' he said. And she, in return, couldn't help covering him with kisses, his neck, his stubble, for she was too short to reach any higher, the only way was for them both to lie down, which they did; and it didn't seem to be her own fault, for he hardly resisted; now they were lying full length, his arms around her, and she kissing his cheeks, his nose, his forehead, his eyebrows which were thick as fur, and crossing and recrossing his lips without daring to stay there. He moved, extracting his arm. He lay on top of her. He kissed along the line of her lips, nibbling at them. She waited, passive suddenly. He rolled off, and they lay side by side, their noses touching. She felt his breath on her, and curled up her toes; then stretched them out, against his shin. She couldn't help it: she pushed her tongue against his half-open teeth, while outside she heard the screech of night cars. She smelled the smell of her own sweat, and pressed her arms tightly to her sides. She lay, terrified of moving, frozen to the damask bedspread; she closed her eyes and tried to force her tongue through the portcullis of his teeth. He too lay without moving, and she longed to know why, to have some idea what he was feeling or thinking. But it was impossible. His long body was utterly still, opaque as lead, his eyes closed. Only his hot breath, on her cheek, told her he was alive.

In this way, the hours passed. Once, her hand slipped down to his waist, and she felt the smooth texture of his trousers and the hardness of buttons and clasps. She imagined his pianist's fingers carefully fastening all those buttons in the morning, undoing them at night. She found the idea strange, as if dressing and undressing were womanly things. Her hand explored the band of his trousers, as it cut across his shirt and divided his body in two. That dividing line was fascinating; in the darkness of her tightly shut eyes she gripped the material, and slowly, apprehensively, without any clear purpose, began to stroke it, sliding her fingers cautiously back and forth. She marvelled at the gap between the trousers and his body; slipping her fingers in she could feel a pulse in his stomach, beating through the shirt; his thinness, his protruding hip bone was extraordinarily strange, and it seemed to her that he belonged to another species altogether. Is this a man? she thought. She opened her eyes, and saw that his too were wide open, half an inch away, the whites reflecting the yellow light from the lamp. It was terrible to see them so close: they were unrecognisable. She stared into them furiously, but they refused to blink. What did this mean? She closed her own tightly, and parted her lips. If only he would kiss her, or touch her, anything to reassure her that he too was human. Let him get up and leave her, if that was what he wanted. Like this it was unbearable. But still he didn't move.

She saw herself floating in the air, looking down on two mummified bodies from the ceiling, one long and thin, the other round and fat. Both were still and silent as serpents. What form would she take as she hovered around the ceiling like a balloon? Strangely enough, although so heavy, she did not feel earth-bound. She had a very clear picture of the two of them lying there, but from far away, from a great distance, like an aerial photograph; and it might be a police photograph, of a death, a mutual suicide, on a bloodstained bedcover. In the picture they both have their clothes on, but this would be an illusion, for their souls are naked and their bodies so well known to each other that they would have dressed simply for the sake of dignity, so that no one, seeing the picture after their death, would be able to share, like a voyeur, in their intimacy. She wanted to pinch herself, to make sure she was awake; although, in a way, the situation did not surprise her, it was just the incarnation of the confused feelings that were always with her, and Robert (especially in this prone state) was almost like a figment of her imagination, her own inevitable creation. She could not pinch herself, for she didn't dare move; instead she screwed up her toes and held them tight, like a clenched fist. Then she realised she was about to get cramp in her left foot. She tried desperately to release the toes, and prayed: please God, not cramp. The indignity would be terrible. Their closeness was vitally important, it must not be broken off. The cramp passed, and she gave a great silent sigh of relief. But immediately another danger threatened: in the depths of her, she felt the birth of laughter. The wild beast was rising, and it was completely inexplicable; she could not understand what plunged her into this helpless, primitive condition, from which all civilised people recoiled. For a long while she waged a silent war with the wild beast. She tried to think of Schumann; then of her cello, leaning serenely against the wall; of Maldoror, of earthquakes and disasters at sea. She concentrated on floating bodies, crashing waves, on the captain sinking with his ship; suddenly she saw the ancient city of Pompeii drowning in a flood of lava, its fleeing inhabitants naked and screeching; she remembered Robert's face as he played Kreisleriana, his quivering eyelids, his body as it jerked from side to side, and a blob of saliva that flew onto the piano keys. She saw Maldoror at a dinner party, smiling politely, and inadvertently exposing his vampire teeth; she imagined herself singing a doleful, passionate song, and then, as in a bad dream, no sound at all coming out of her gaping jaws . . . the laughter was rising, the beast was grinning hilariously, the muscles of her stomach were contracting. The battle was lost: there was a vibration, like a death rattle, in her throat. And at that very moment she felt him moving, on the bed, and his hand, like a rasp, was on her cheek. The wild beast froze. She heard: 'Are you all right?' His hand, cool and dry, lay on her cheek, and her breathing stopped. She realised that she loved him. She said: 'I think I . . .' but then, screwing up her eyes, and clasping his hand to her face, she broke into a loud tearful whisper: 'Robert, you scare me!'

He slid his arm under her neck, and she buried her head in his shoulder, trying to stifle sobs. It was impossible: the sobs forced their way through her clenched lips, and she felt his shirt, under her face, grow damp. She was deeply ashamed. So ashamed that she, who masqueraded as an intellectual, should prove to be such a child. And yet, in the end, her sobs turned to laughter; and this time, wonderfully, he began to laugh too. They lay on their backs and laughed. Their combined laughter was like the relief of two people who, against all the odds, have come through a great ordeal together. Afterwards that night remained in her mind like a touchstone. It was, really, her first experience of love, her first night of love; against which, for a long time, she weighed all future nights.

He stands in the clearing, and touches the bursting buds of the saplings. He smiles; wistfully, for he has just remembered something. It was this very sapling, or the one next to it, on which, eighteen months ago, Johnny laid his shirt. They had grown since then, the trees; in those days their little limbs hardly reached one another, and it was possible to climb through, especially in winter. He strokes the slender trunks, and wants to retrace the path he took that night with Johnny, to feel the same earth under his feet, to search for the imprint of their steps. He squeezes past the lovers and turns back towards the pond. It is not easy to recapture the rawness of that night, the damp earthy smell, and the breeze which made his eyes water.

That night he stood beside the black pond and watched his breath creeping away through the air like smoke. Two young men were approaching. One was short, the other tall. The shorter kept running ahead, dashing into the bushes and jumping back onto the path; he would turn, look behind his companion, check on both sides to make sure he hadn't missed anything, then catch up, laugh, and walk with him for a moment; soon he would start the performance all over again. They passed close by Robert and stopped. They were talking, but he could only hear the voice of the taller one. He took a step towards them; the little one shot him a quick look and turned back to his companion. Robert realised, and this gave him sudden confidence, that they were talking in French. He wanted to join them, to eavesdrop; he moved closer. The little one was whispering excitedly, and could not keep still. 'What?' he was saying, 'You sent him out? Just like that? Because he had a National Front badge?' 'Yes, and I was sacked for it.' 'I must kiss you for that! Pierre, where are you?' Inadvertently perhaps, standing on tiptoe to kiss his friend, he moved very near Robert, who saw that the kiss he implanted, tender and quick, was not the kiss of a lover. 'You are my hero,' he said. '*Mon bel héros!* I wouldn't have dared, you know. Who is this *enmerdeur?*' he said, referring to Robert, and glanced at him. 'Oh I shouldn't have been so rude,' he went on, still in French, 'but I'm sure he doesn't understand;' and he looked at Robert again, a quick look out of the corner of his eye, and gave a very brief smile, parting his lips nervously and closing them immediately; at the same time he moved rapidly from one foot to the other, as if trying to keep warm. 'What does he want? I mean – really!' and he laughed, turning his head and smiling quite openly at Robert, but only for a moment; then Robert, reaching forward with his long right arm, touched the back of his trousers. 'People really take enormous liberties here, don't you agree, Pierre? *C'est trop, c'est beaucoup trop!*' he went on, and Robert, overjoyed that he had not moved out of the way, kept his hand on the hip, which was quite full under a pair of worn jeans; the boy's feet, so restless before, were now completely still, and his body seemed to have sent down roots, to have detached itself from the animated voice which continued as if nothing was happening, and to be embarking on a life of its own. 'Well, so what else do you come here for, one might say, if it's not for taking liberties? And I reply: for the beauty of the night, to appreciate Nature in the heart of London and to caress the trees whose shapes are far more interesting and varied than human limbs, which, after all, we know well, don't we, Pierre? We have our own.' He laughed.

'But the trees are colder,' said Robert.

And now the hip, whose warmth had just begun to seep through the trousers into Robert's hand, moved. The boy half turned, and in a completely different voice, controlled, without a hint of excitement, said in English: 'So you speak French.' The hip had moved out of reach, and Robert regretted having spoken. The warmth that had flowed between them was enough, it was the perfect expression of a deeper current, which now, perhaps, was irretrievable. But despite the cool, reserved voice he was aware of being scrutinised by a pair of very intense eyes; and yet this impression, he thought immediately, came probably from the effort of trying to see in the dark. He tried to make out the face staring up at him, but all he could be sure of was a thick crop of hair, wide open eyes, and a vague pair of lips which were not smiling. He felt that he must say something, because he had started he must continue, and so he said: 'It's cold, isn't it? I can hardly see you, you know.' But this remark sounded so lame, so obvious, that he immediately gave an apologetic laugh; which, he realised, was far more banal even than the remark itself. At the same time he knew that he was behaving true to form, he was irreversibly embarking on a downward spiral, little by little he was destroying all possibility of magic; and it was unbearable, he could not bear the fact – and suddenly he found a word for it – that he had no *charm*; the other, with his controlled voice, his searching eyes, had the gift of charm; he had a way of projecting his personality with grace, of declaring 'I am here, I am like this, I am feeling this or that' but without hesitating, without apologising; take me or leave me, he seemed to be saying – and the very fact of being so definite was captivating; his immediacy was magical, and Robert was beaten by it; he felt himself shrinking, creeping back into his shell, and all the excitement of a moment ago was gone. He had given himself away; he was an open book now; even the darkness could not save him. Unable to stand the power of those eyes, which seemed to be trying to hypnotise him, he stepped back. Nothing could come of it now. And so, feeling dull and rejected, he took a step away from that stare and vaguely looked at other shapes wandering around the pond, when the boy said, in French: 'You have very charming eyes.' Robert frowned, unsure if he had heard correctly, as if perhaps the darkness could distort hearing as well as sight. He mouthed the words to himself '*des yeux très charmants*'; and suddenly realised that he had been completely wrong, he was not rejected at all, his misgivings were a piece of purely internal chemistry, this boy actually liked him; with a single step he was at his side, impulsively put his arm around him, and answered, using the familiar '*tu*' form: 'But so do you!' They both laughed, and this laughter was perfectly conspiratorial. 'Shall we go for a walk?' he said; and the other took the initiative, slipping his own arm around Robert, and immediately leading him away; called over his shoulder in a voice that was no more than a cheeky whisper (and destined, in its cheekiness, for Robert): '*Pierre, salut! On va se promener.*'

They did not go far, they could not go far, for there was no time to lose; they had to take advantage of the miraculous situation. Their intimacy was enough to create privacy. They made love, standing up at first, in a little clearing close to the path. Once, Robert opened his eyes and gasped to see silent shapes all round, feeding off them, nourishing themselves, masturbating; like the unblinking eyes of wild animals, attracted from their lairs by a fire in the middle of the forest. But the boy smiled and whispered: 'Let them watch!' He took off his shirt, despite the cold, draped it over a sapling, and they lay on the ground, muscle to muscle, where Nature, the accomplice, provided them with a mattress of fallen leaves. The watching men drew closer, peered over them, and their breathing was audible. But the lovers were protected; no one dared touch them.

Such matings often have no follow-up. They are hermetic experiences, complete in themselves. They have the integrity of our deepest illusions; they are the luminous answer to the disquiet which gnaws, like a rat, at the core of our well-being. Their condition is anonymity, for only then the other becomes what we wish him to be. But perfect anonymity is impossible. Like it or not, we have already begun to get to know our lover. He has already given himself away: by a mole on his neck, by the particular curve of his buttocks, by the fact that he whispers rather than talks aloud, by the quality of his touch, by his hesitation, by his eagerness. And so when Robert came across a large sticking plaster on the slightly spotty back that he was caressing, and noted an impulse of embarrassment, an attempt to move out of the way, he felt a flicker of disappointment; as if he had suddenly learnt that a picture, which he had taken for an Old Master, was no more than a clever reproduction. As soon as they had pulled on their clothes, in the quiet that comes after sex, he felt his hand being taken, his fingers entwined, by other tender, communicative fingers, even before he had time to button his trousers. And this action did not quite belong to the shadowy passion of a moment before, in which each was hardly more or less than the troubled projection of the other's dream. As they walked back along the path, hand in hand, he was aware of a head with a tight crop bobbing along beside him, just above shoulder level, a real head, belonging to another, and yet seeming, now, to belong also to him – and he thought: I have never been happier than this, than this moment now. I will remember this feeling for ever. For a while they walked in silence, not the tense, fragile silence of before, but a silence which could, if they wished, be broken, and the outside world of names and facts, of pasts and futures, could, without danger, be broached.

And so he said: 'By the way, my name's Robert.'

'*Et moi je suis Johnny*,' replied Johnny without hesitation, in a voice no longer a whisper, which had about it a sort of husky vitality.

They reached the pond. Pierre was nowhere in sight. Robert turned to face Johnny and took both his hands. 'That's a funny name for a Frenchman,' he said.

'But I'm not French! Did I fool you? Oh good!'

And he realised that Johnny's French was indeed not perfect. His own critical faculties had been bewitched, like the rest of him; in fact Johnny had had a little English accent all along.

'You almost fooled me,' he said.

A man sidled up to them and stopped a few paces away. '*Bonsoir*,' said Johnny. 'Who are *you*?' The man hesitated, but

Johnny continued immediately: 'I mean, how are you?' 'Oh fine, fine,' said the man in a gravelly voice. 'Beautiful night.' 'Beautiful?' said Johnny, and shivered. 'This isn't what I call a beautiful night at all!' 'Oh no?' said the man, coming closer. 'Look,' said Johnny. 'This is all I'm wearing. My jacket isn't thick enough. I'm not used to this horrible damp place. I come from a hot climate, you see. Hot!' 'Are you really cold?' asked Robert, in French. 'Oh,' said the man. 'So you're *français*. Did I catch that right?' '*Oui*,' said Johnny. The man came closer. 'If you're cold,' he said, 'why don't you warm each other up? Go on – warm each other up.' 'Us?' Johnny laughed. 'But we're old friends . . . old friends don't do that sort of thing.' 'Yes,' said Robert, 'we're old school friends. Aren't we, Johnny?' And the pleasure from saying the name for the first time was so great that he repeated: 'Old school friends, *n'est-ce pas*, Johnny?' 'Oh yes. We've known each other for years, many many years.' 'We were at school together in – where was it, Johnny?' 'Marseille.' 'Yes, Marseille. Or rather just outside Marseille. Boarding school, you know.' 'No, it was a day-school.' 'He's kidding you,' said Robert to the man. 'He doesn't want you to know . . . what we got up to.' '*Sie sprechen Deutsch?*' asked the man. Johnny pealed with laughter. '*Ja, mein Kapitän*,' he said. 'Have you lived in Marseille?' Robert asked, surprised, for Johnny had no trace of a Mediterranean accent. 'No, of course not.' 'Where then?' 'It doesn't matter.' 'Go on, tell me.' 'In England,' said Johnny. 'But I'm Italian really. On my grandmother's side.' This conversation was all in French – which was too much for the man, who broke in: '*Ich kann Deutsch sprechen*.' Robert, still holding Johnny's hands, said: 'You see, we were lovers – at school. Ever since the age of eleven.' 'Together we discovered about sex,' explained Johnny. The man was right beside them; now Robert saw him put his arm round Johnny's waist. 'And *l'amour*,' Johnny continued. 'Eleven,' said the man. 'That's young.' 'No, he was very advanced, you see.' Johnny indicated Robert with a nod, and made no attempt to free himself from the man's grasp. 'One night I caught him doing something under the bedclothes. How old are you?' he asked the man. 'Well now, have a guess.' 'You've got lines on your forehead,' said Johnny. 'I don't like that.' The man slipped his hand below Johnny's waist; Robert could see it, a pale blob on his jeans. Johnny stood absolutely still. 'About forty,' he said. The hand began to move. 'Forty? That's generous of you.' Robert squeezed the fingers he still held, those active fingers. He could scarcely believe it; this dull, overweight man was feeling him up, and Johnny was letting him, frozen to the spot. Robert stared furiously into his eyes, shaking his head. But the eyes were remote; they hardly took him in. He wanted to shout at him: this warmth, which still flows from your fingers to mine, is it meaningless?

The man pushed his way in between them, disengaging their hands, and tried to kiss Johnny. Only now Johnny moved, a little out of the way, but not far. 'What are you doing?' he asked in mock surprise, raising his eyebrows. 'I like you,' said the man in a lecherous whisper. 'And you?' Robert broke in, in French: 'you like him?' Johnny did not answer. Robert turned, and walked away; out of the moonlight, into the shadow of the trees which lined the pond; anywhere, out of sight, out of earshot. He noticed the merry twinkling of the stars, and they seemed very far away. What was he doing here, in this fickle, devastating place? This was not the real world. There was no heart here. He heard a voice behind him, the same animated whisper, almost a shout, as before: 'Don't go!' and with a few bounds Johnny was there. 'Come on,' he said, taking Robert's hand again. 'Don't be stupid.' 'What?' said Robert. 'Come on, Robert.' He was sparkling all over. 'Where to?' 'How should I know?' Johnny was whispering again, and Robert thought: how stupid this is. He said: 'I'd better go home. I can give you a lift if you want. But I expect you'd rather stay here.' And Johnny, teasingly, provocatively: 'Come on, baby, cheer up. Are you tired of me already?' He took Robert's hand, with its long fingers, its little tufts of hair, and lifted it to his lips. 'I was only playing,' he said, and kissed it. He nibbled one of the fingers, quite painfully. 'That's for being jealous.' Robert looked around. The man was wandering away. He had a rounded, hunched back and walked ponderously.

Now, more than a year later, he retraces the path from the clearing to the pond, and when he gets there he realises that the lamps have gone out. The pond has been returned to darkness, by an invisible hand. He himself is powerless; he stumbles in a world not of his making. He cannot even choose, now, at three o'clock in the morning, to go home. He cannot leave this place. Filled with the memory of Johnny, and the bliss that he once knew, here, he believes that nothing can ever replace it. And so he circles the pond; he cannot leave, because the air here is the same air that he and Johnny breathed, when they first met, the trees are the same trees, and the hungry winter smell will soon be here again. He could spend the daytime here too, prowling amid the nature lovers, the courting couples, who know nothing of the darker life that comes into being when they are gone; for him, this pond, these paths and clearings, even in the midday sun, will be for ever nocturnal. He stands still and realises he is quite alone, as if the other prowlers have made way for him, have left him there on purpose. And this solitude, which seems the essence of his life, hangs about him like a dense, insoluble problem. He thinks of Peter, of the meal he prepared for him and ate alone. He looks into the still water and its blackness is frightening. It was Peter's rejection which made him come here, to the Observatory Gardens.

There is no one, really no one, in sight. He leaves the pond and tramps along another path which rises steeply under high branches. He stops and listens for the sound of other steps. Somewhere far away he hears a car driving recklessly, and the squeal of its tyres which echo for a moment against the tree trunks. Further still London purrs like a relentless engine. But close by, cocooning him, is silence. Even the breeze has dropped. The only sign of life is the haze of breath around his face. He sees the bursting leaf buds, the contorted branches, and they are senseless. It was only his hope that gave them meaning. He can no longer animate them. They are obstacles, alien, and impenetrable. And the absence of any other human being is pure rejection; they have all fled from him. He lights a cigarette. The feel of it between his lips is just enough to keep despair at bay.

And then he hears an unmistakable sound. Over to the left, someone is walking. He freezes, trying to gauge the distance, the exact direction. From head to toe he is immediately alert, with all his strength he concentrates on those elusive sound waves. They grow fainter. He strides out in pursuit, leaving the path, stumbling through the undergrowth. He almost falls over the roots of a tree and twists his ankle. He rushes on, oblivious of pain, fighting his way through thickets, thundering down a steep slope. He stops and listens. The sound of the steps has vanished. But, surely, that other being cannot be far away; he must have heard him coming, he must be listening too. The silence now is different; it is alive. He waits. Suddenly, very close, he hears a sigh. A shiver runs through him, and delicately, soundlessly, he steps towards it. Another sigh. He peers through holly leaves and sees two men.

Can he intrude? This is his last hope; he must have a meeting, a human meeting; he must put a barrier, a dyke between himself and Peter; and Johnny. He finds the opening to the little holly room, and the men see him and pause. They both have moustaches and short hair. They are clones. He does not like clones. But how can he leave? He stands and waits. The men seem uncertain. One looks at him, and the other turns away. He draws up to his full height and tries to broaden his shoulders. He surveys them coolly. They return to their lovemaking. They do not want him. But he steps closer. Slowly he undoes his zip. The sound of it is magic, how can they refuse? He needs so little, a spark of interest, just a moment's appreciation. Will they refuse him that? One of them is wavering. He detaches a hand, a delicate hand, and it hovers in the air, an inch or two away. Robert lowers his trousers, and puts his penis into the hand.

A little later he shoots out his seed on to the ground, and with it the sharp edge of despair. The men look on admiringly. He dresses, and says – the usual formula: 'Take care!' He steps out of the little room and away, into the park. He feels numb and tired. The clones did not excite him. He allowed himself to be fondled and gave very little in return. His madness has passed, and he can hardly understand it. He smiles grimly, and hurries on. With luck he will be in bed and asleep in one hour's time.

Gradually he becomes aware that somebody is following him. Now that he no longer needs them there are steps behind him. He does not look back. He pauses, to get his bearings. For the first time he is not quite sure of his direction. Behind him the steps have stopped too. This surprises him. He turns his head but sees no one. He sets off again. Even if this is not the right way he will surely soon come to a place he recognises. The pursuing steps are there again. He increases the length of his stride. He does not want to give the impression of hurrying. The steps keep up with him. He thinks of running, but decides against it. Where is he? This is not a path he knows. He pinches his cheek, just in case the whole thing is a dream. The path narrows, and he stops again. This is not the right way. He steps quickly behind a tree, his heart beating hard. He tries to hide, but it is too late. A figure approaches, sees him and comes straight for him.

It is the middle-aged psychoanalyst.

'It's you,' says the man. 'I thought so.'

Robert thinks: shall I pretend not to know him? Shall I be a completely different person, a hooligan, and threaten him? Shall I frighten him, reject him brutally, and have no shame about it? I do not feel like the polite, gentle person I am supposed to be.

He says: 'Yes, it's me. But I thought you had gone home long ago.'

The man laughs uncomfortably. 'Sometimes it's hard to go home.'

'Well, I'm off now. I'm tired. Aren't you?'

'Oh yes, me too.'

'There's no one here.'

The man hesitates. 'Just you,' he says.

'Actually,' says Robert, and this seems a possible way

of getting rid of him, 'there are still a few more people over there . . .' he waves vaguely.

The man smiles; then stops smiling suddenly and stares hypnotically into Robert's eyes. 'As a matter of fact I was looking for you.'

'Really.'

'It was a great pleasure, you know, in a place like this, to meet someone to talk to.'

'Oh yes. We had a nice conversation. About telescopes.'

'There's something very special about you,' he goes on, fixing Robert again with an unearthly stare. 'And . . . your eyes are beautiful.'

'Oh no,' says Robert. 'That's just the light. Or lack of it.'

'No – I don't think so.' And the man tries to grab them again. 'Of course I don't want to keep you now . . . but could I perhaps have your phone number? I would love to take you out to a meal.'

Robert looks at him again. 'But I have a lover,' he lies brutally. 'I live with someone.'

'I see.'

'And really – what time is it now?'

They look at their watches, and all of a sudden it is no longer necessary to light a match, or to have a luminous dial. They are both taken aback, as if they should run for cover. But there is no way of stopping the revolving planet. There is no escape. They have to stand their ground bravely and watch, as colour seeps back into the world. Laurel and holly glimmer with reluctant green, and the blackest refuges are exposed, as spaces between leaves become transparent and shadows begin to glow. The rule of stars and moon, though they still shine, is being overtaken. It is almost unbearably sad, so sad that they have to say: 'Look! How beautiful it is!'

But they do not look at each other. Dawn should not have caught them here. They feel naked and guilty, as if the coming of the light were the arm of the law. And yet the man knows how childish this is. There is nothing to be ashamed of, no sense in this scramble for respectability. He feels Robert's shame, and wants to reassure him. But he hardly dares look at him, as if by looking he will himself be seen. He says: 'Of course it's time to sleep now. I have a long day ahead! I just hope I'll be able to keep awake for my patients!' He hears the change in his voice: it is the cheery, daylight voice. 'I'll tell you what,' he continues. 'I understand the difficulty of your position. But let me give you my phone number – I won't take yours – and you can ring me, if you ever feel like it.'

'All right,' says Robert, and he looks at the shrink. There he is, in three bright dimensions: a large rubbery nose, a flabby mouth and many small moles.

He is moved by that face, which no longer tries to probe enigmatically into his own. It is a very vulnerable face. He feels sudden warmth, almost love, for this man, who is a human being like him. 'Do you know the way out of here?' he asks.

'Yes, I think so,' and the shrink smiles, a little wearily.

'Let's go then.'

He puts a friendly, fatherly arm round the man's shoulders, and they set off together. The shrink knows the way very well. It is not far. They soon reach the Observatory building, and the road beyond, where their cars are parked. Robert takes down the man's number. He smiles at him; knowing, for sure, that he will not see him again.

STARS

HIS father watches him fighting with the piano, the muscles in his face straining, and thinks: this is obviously a difficult bit. He realises there are some wrong notes, and feels a tiny glow of satisfaction: he's not tone-deaf after all. He makes a pained expression and turns to Yvonne. But she doesn't seem to have noticed anything. Perhaps she's not that musical after all? Then he sees her plump little hand, tense as it screws up a handkerchief. So she *is* worried. He lays his own, comfortingly, on top of hers. He smiles: a few wrong notes are not the end of the world. How often he's heard Rob say that it's the spirit that matters! An occasional lack of precision is not what it's all about. How different to his own work. There, precision can mean life or death. Surgeons must not make mistakes. Does he ever make mistakes? With his smile and the pressure of his hand he tries to reassure Yvonne. Without even glancing at him she frowns and pulls away her hand. So she's misunderstood him. He is reminded of other occasions. Allowing his smile to fade naturally he grits his teeth. From now on he will keep his hands to himself. He can see the sweat literally dripping off Rob's brow. What an effort; and what for? And why did she withdraw her hand? On the stage his son's attempt at athletics is reaching a pitch of absurdity. This music, he decides, is not grand or exciting: it is neurotic. For a moment he feels better. The discovery that Schumann's music is neurotic has done him good. He sighs, and looks round at the small audience with a vaguely proprietorial air. Hypocrites, he thinks. Fucking hypocrites. Yes, this is a word he uses, in private. For he is a man of flesh and blood, and he is not afraid of 'dirty' words. Under his breath he says: 'Fuck, shit, piss, arse, cunt, prick,' and tries to think of more. These words protect him like a rampart. He thinks of the human face, and its ability to conceal. No one could ever know what he was thinking now, nor the words he has just whispered. He looks at Yvonne: staring, brows slightly contracted, at her son, that performing ape. There *was* something a little apish about him, with his long dark limbs covered in hair. Where on earth did all that hair come from? Surreptitiously he pulls up the sleeve of his jacket and looks at his own strong, almost hairless wrist. An amusing little idea comes into his head. Supposing Robert were not his son?

The ape's wild antics come to a halt, much to the relief of the public. He turns to Yvonne and nods encouragingly. 'That was pretty exciting,' he says. 'Oh yes! He put everything he's got into it!' she whispers. 'And that's what makes his playing so exciting!' She's giving me a lesson, he thinks. 'Of course, Yvonne. That's exactly what it is. You think I don't know?' he snaps. But she puts her fingers to her lips, silencing him like a child. The ape had begun again, although so much softer that it was like a different piece altogether. But Henry knows very well what it is! He's heard it before! He looks at his wife with nothing less than hatred. How dare she treat him like a child? Does she think he's a child because he's not 'musical'? He wants to start chanting 'piss, fuck, cunt' again, but aware that this is a child's reaction, he manages to stop himself. As he watches his son experiencing emotions which music somehow, inexplicably, aroused in some people, he thinks: really, this ape can have nothing to do with me! And he tries to imagine Yvonne in a compromising situation. A classic picture comes to his mind: an operation cancelled, an unexpected return home, and there she is, copulating on the carpet with one of her musical friends. Oh, his fury – and her fear – would know no bounds! The trouble was, her 'artistic' friends were either queer, or too weak, too unimaginative (he chuckles) for such a thing. What about the so-called 'wild' artists – the Beethovens, the Van Goghs, the Dostoevskys? He realises, with considerable pleasure, that Yvonne's artist friends were not of that type: they were the bourgeois sort. And so he must think of something else. What about those evenings – quite frequent – when he was obliged to stay late at the hospital, to attend an important meeting? Evenings on which Yvonne would sometimes go out by herself, to a concert, for instance. Could it be that, instead, she went out into the street, into pubs, in search of a man? Yvonne, the serious, music-loving virgin he had once known, whose protests thinly disguised a rather extraordinary passion? A passion which was not without its perverse elements?

All day long he wielded the knife: did she not love him for it? Did she not love the implacable rhythm of his knife? Imperceptibly his left hand slides off his lap, across his leg, to the division between his seat and hers, onto the green silk of her dress which covers it. His fingertips press into the material. He observes her out of the corner of his eye. Does she know how close his hand is?

He will have her strapped onto the operating table; the powerful lights transform her into human meat, illuminating every pore, every imperfection, and make her sweat; he stands beside her, watching her writhe as she tries to escape the shameless light; from the trolley he chooses the sharpest instruments, knives and scalpels, and with these he caresses her from top to toe; then, as she moans with delight, struggling at the straps which bind her to the table, slowly, slowly he removes all his clothes (except perhaps the surgeon's mask?) and penetrates her. He tries to see her eyes, through his mask, as he caresses her, strapped to the table, with sharp knives. Are they closed, her eyes, screwed up in frantic protest? Or does she admit – staring at him, splayed open – that she is wildly excited? Does she dare look deep, chillingly, into his eyes, with love?

She notices the critic, or whoever it is, just in front; squints and tries to read. But she can't. It doesn't matter; she has confidence. Strange that she should be so sure. She is no musician; but she knows. She knows that something important is happening; or, if not now, that it will happen. On the other hand, perhaps it has already happened. In her mind past, present and future have little meaning. She is capable, like everyone, of differentiating. But in this case all edges are blurred. Her anxiety has gone; the difficult, almost unplayable second movement is over. The struggle is over. She prepares herself for the reunion. Like a baby child whose mother has come home and takes the tearful little thing in her arms. There are times when it is wonderful to be a baby again. The last movement is beginning, the movement of love. Oh, how silly she is being! She does not know, exactly, when it was that she looked at him and he looked at her. Perhaps, long ago, the very moment he was born, it happened; once and for ever. Perhaps they didn't even have to look at each other. Certainly there was nothing to say, words themselves never came into it. Neither were events important. Even his playing was not important. And yet it is the music now, the purity of his music, which makes her think of him like this, which moulds and frees her. Without the music, which is so much more than a background, she would never allow her mind to drift in this vague, senseless way . . . She wonders, for a moment, if his looks are important. He's tall, dark and handsome, she thinks, smiling at the cliché. He has beautiful hands, with long slender fingers which are strong, not effeminate. She likes the way he combs his black hair straight back, and the way a few strands rebel and flop over his ears and across his forehead. His hair is thick and straight; he gets that from Henry; but his hair is *better* than Henry's – far better than Henry's ever was! But really more than his looks it is his expression that matters. She wants to laugh. She is so happy to see him play. She closes her ears to the music and sits watching his expression, watching it change, like an old silent movie one has seen many times. Every now and again she lets the music in too, then excludes it. She is surprised and amused by the way she can switch the music on and off.

His heart pounds; for a nasty moment he wonders if he is going to have a heart attack. Then the fear passes. His hand is so close that by stretching out his little finger he could touch her leg. He can feel its warmth. He smiles: perhaps the music is having an effect on him after all. His fantasy is so powerful, so pure. Was the ability to fantasise so accurately, so exquisitely, the hallmark of maturity? And was it not remarkable, after all these years, to be able still to fantasise about your wife? Did that mean he loved her? Does he love this plumpish body, squirming under the arc lights? Who would ever guess that this was the basis of their love, that he was the dark brute in her life, that for this above all she abandoned her cosy Normandy fireside? Does she know?

He tries to think about her objectively. He thinks about her legs, which she has waxed regularly. About her cooking, which is excellent. About her face, which to him is exactly the same as when he first met her, one distant summer in France. Did he, even then, want to strap her down and rape her? She was like a butterfly, like the flames flickering above the logs in the little country fireplace. He watches her from the corner of his eye, as she watches their son. He knows that she is in love with Rob. He knows that every note their boy plays, every movement of his face, goes straight to her heart. It is more than love. He knows that their boy, the ape, is still a part of her: the flesh of her flesh. To whom else could she relate in this way? She never knew her parents, she was adopted, an adopted child . . . In Normandy she had a brother, but he was no relation; he was younger, a late, unexpected arrival. He was a real child, he had a real father and mother. Did she fully appreciate the difference? She was alone: a meteor from an unknown constellation. And he had loved her for it, for that very fact, for her loneliness, her lostness; her secret, unacknowledged lostness. She was a clever child, good at school, and especially good at drawing. She was praised by everyone. She was pretty. But underneath, lost. And this is what he, with the instinct of a master, had recognised and loved. And why, too, she had loved him. A beautiful tune reaches him from the distant piano. Even he could, for a moment, appreciate that. He sighs, and remembers what is happening. He sees Rob, and thinks: she cannot possess him, he has my hair, my eyes, he is half me. He has her heart, her sensitivity, but he has a prick like me. He is homosexual, because of her; but also, perhaps, because of me.

His eyes wander round the hall. He sees many people he knows, mostly women; friends of theirs, supporters of the arts, good people. After the concert there will be a party, and the Schwarzenbergs will be there. And he will be the charming host, the proud father. He watches Rob; he is not effeminate, his homosexuality is concealed. What does it matter to him that his son is homosexual?

The question floats above his head and hardly seems to touch him at all. Rob is a good boy, intelligent, a little ridiculous, he makes his mother happy, he will spend his life in a sort of no-man's land of the emotions, probably childless (and that, of course, is a pity), he will not be particularly successful as a pianist, for, thinks Henry, quite sure of his judgment, he does not have 'star quality' . . . I have not, he thinks, been cruel, or intolerant; I have been interested in his development, I have respected his choices, paid for his studies, and he has not been difficult. I have given him a flat, so he can be independent. He tries to put himself in the place of another type of father, a father who would be intensely worried about his son's homosexuality. He thinks: what good would that do? By the time you know about it, it's too late. The die is cast. The bed is made. The worried type of father feels responsible, he is tormented by guilt. If his son is deviant, he himself is called into question. What have I done? Or what have I not done? Absurd, unhelpful questions. He, Henry, may or may not have something to do with it, but he is far too sensible to feel guilty. Live and let live. And how terrible for a son to bear the burden of a father's guilt. Such a situation could never end happily. Is Rob at least grateful for such a tolerant father?

He glances at Yvonne as if she could provide the answer.

They have never discussed Rob's sexuality. And yet she must know. She wants to keep it a secret: between the two of them. But does Rob want that? Does he *want* that sort of secret with his mother? He shakes his head. He looks at her little well-manicured hands and the tense knuckles as they clutch a pair of white gloves. He thinks: I will punish her for you, my boy. I will strap her to the table and caress her till she explodes . . . he almost bursts into laughter. But then the same beautiful melody creeps over him again, and he can't deny it: he is moved. Amazing! Rob must be playing well. He looks at him, and is struck by his expression, full of pain; the melody, certainly, is beautiful, but what connection could it possibly have with the pain he sees on his son's face?

Two or three rows ahead, a little to the left, sits Flavia. Henry recognises her. She is Jewish, a singer. Her profile is striking: a perfectly straight nose, a dark deep-set eye with thick lashes, black curls, a dusky cheek round as an apple, and heavy mauve lips. She's obviously listening hard. Henry tries to listen too. But there is something about this music that is unbearable. Something profoundly irritating. Something against which he has always defended himself like a tiger. He feels a perverse desire to lower his defences. What is it, this invading monster? He realises: it is gentleness. What is gentleness? He draws himself back from the brink, and stares at Flavia; he has always noticed her enormous breasts. Gentleness makes him uncomfortable. Rob, his son, despite his body, hairy as an ape, is gentle. This music would make a stone weep; but when did he last weep? Has he wept, even once, in Rob's lifetime? Sometimes music can have a strange effect, even on the unmusical. He thinks: no, I have not once cried, all these years. And he feels a little sorrowful about it; at the same time he smiles, for it is ridiculous to want to cry just for the sake of it. But it seems so sad, suddenly, to have been dry-eyed for so long that he actually feels a tiny wave rising in his chest, part sob, part laugh, as he watches Rob leaning at an odd angle, away from the piano. And he is acutely aware that much, too much is happening inside his son's heart; and it is all unknowable, for Rob is another human being, another planet altogether.

What is gentleness? In his mind's eye he sees the insides of bodies: kidneys, lungs, hearts, livers; and especially the pancreas. The pancreas, with its soft porous surface, tender as a snail which has lost its shell, seems to him one of nature's most wonderful creations. He is as familiar with the body's inner world as with the outer; perhaps more so. When we grow old the skin sags and discolours, the flesh crumples, but the inner organs often remain surprisingly youthful in appearance, almost pristine; sometimes, at the end of an operation, he regrets having to sew back together old withered shreds of skin and seal off, return to darkness, the glistening Aladdin's cave where his fingers, deft and sure, have been working.

Henry is very much liked by his patients. And he too very much likes his patients. He never forgets a patient. They remain as individuals in his memory; he does not think of them as machines, all more or less alike, whose ailing parts have to be repaired. He is not a car mechanic. It is in the astringent atmosphere of the operating theatre that he feels most fully alive. A bond exists between him and his patients, a bond that is both physical and metaphysical. He takes a global view of the human body. To a man in love, the mouth or the vagina are exciting because they offer the possibility of penetrating the beloved body, of experiencing it from the inside; but how limited are these intimate explorations compared to those carried out daily by surgeons. He knows this is an unorthodox point of view. For most doctors, probably, intimacy is inhibited, not encouraged, by contact with the insides of bodies. Their emotional life is clearly separated from their work. In his case the opposite is true. Not that he is ever unprofessional. He does not, on the whole, fall in love with his patients. Nor does he, for example, get an erection from examining the pancreas of a beautiful woman. But something happens; something which, even now, he can almost always, if he wishes, experience again. In fact the older he gets, the clearer it becomes. A sensation of great complexity, born partly from power. It contains, he believes, much of what is evil in him; but also what is good. Inextricably mixed with his enjoyment of power is the feeling, despite masks, gloves and bright lights, that an operation is an act of communication. This communication, of which the operation is the apotheosis, starts with the very first consultation; the various examinations, the steps which little by little lead to the decision, the patient's trust, her courage, her recognition that something of great importance is about to happen, and the final submission of her body, about which she knows so much less than the surgeon. And afterwards, when all is over, the skin sealed again, he often lays his hands for a moment, in silence, on the sleeping body. Something passes then, through the latex gloves, from his fingers, into that profoundly unconscious being. The nurses and doctors present watch this with interest; they do not find it absurd. All in all, he is a very good surgeon.

He smiles as these feelings, perhaps under the influence of the music, pass through his mind. Something inside him has risen to meet the challenge of these notes, of his son's commitment: his own form of commitment, his own enigmatic relationship with human bodies. He remembers that once Rob had an appendicectomy; he referred the case to a colleague. While examining his son he experienced something close to fear. Rob's submission, as he lay in pain on the bed, the enlarged appendix pressing insistently against his probing fingers, the thin wall of muscle so easily breached with a knife, the pale skin already covered with hair, provoked a strong reaction. Henry felt sweat on his forehead and took away his hand. It was impossible to say which frightened him more: an overwhelming sense of potential power, or the curious intimacy, like an imprinting, a branding, which he could feel on opening up, touching and cutting the inside of his own son's body. 'Poor Rob,' he said. 'You must have it out.' And the boy, opening his eyes, asked: 'Will you do it, father?' 'No, I'll try and get Mr Schwartz.' 'Why don't you do it, father?' Henry hesitated and wiped his hand across his brow. He felt like a man to whom an interesting crime has just been proposed. 'Well Rob, it's urgent,' he said. 'Though nothing to worry about. And I'm completely booked up at the moment. But you'll like Mr Schwartz. He's much nicer than me, old boy,' he winked at him. 'And better,' he laughed. And so it was settled.

Henry remembers this episode now, but brushes aside the emotions which went with it. He sees Flavia, two rows ahead, and wonders if she'll be coming to the party afterwards. Even from this angle he cannot help noticing her breasts; closing his eyes he concentrates on them. For he likes the outside of bodies too, although he is hardly ever unfaithful. He likes the colour of Flavia's skin, Mediterranean, so different from Yvonne's; he sees her breasts, dark sails billowing at sunset . . . and suddenly (oh the music is definitely affecting him!) his fingers, all ten of them, come sharply together on the lapels of his grey, double-breasted suit, as he grasps the wonderful, turreted nipples. How enormously nipples vary! They are all different in size, colour and texture. And what were Flavia's like? He relaxes his grip and feels them nestling in his palms. He tests them for shape and firmness. How could a man not love this? he thinks. How could a man possibly be a homosexual? At last, reluctantly, he lets go; massaging the full, warm surface just below, vibrating with inner life, one hand slides down, inch by inch, down across the stomach, while the other still cups the breast and expertly stimulates the nipple and all around it. The music, in the background, is very inspiring.

Untouched, she watches and listens. The opening phrases of the Fantasy's last movement, like the opening of a heart, fill her, and she is aware more than ever that she loves him. She observes his face, and sees the expressions she knows so well. But she sees them differently. She sees him, at last, as a very separate being. She knows that his feelings are his own, not hers also, that his way through life is his own, which may cross hers, but not run with it; that the particular expression she now sees on his face as his fingers, faithful to Schumann, resolve a dissonance, is his alone, his unique experience of a dissonance resolved. And she is sad. She leans her face against her hand, the old velvet arm-rest supports her elbow. She is beautifully dressed (as Henry, three rows back, has noticed). Two emeralds sway on short silver pendants from her ears. She wears a blue silk scarf, and a black dress, which she fell in love with in Venice, a copy of Fortuny, sparkling with sequins and strange beading; which she bought one morning after singing at La Fenice. For she is becoming famous. Her voice has blossomed; suddenly she is in demand. She has sung Dorabella at Glyndebourne, Amneris in Naples, Princess Eboli in Venice. In the last two years her dream, for which she has worked so hard, is coming true.

And yet it is not easy for her to believe that dreams can come true. Ten years ago, at the age of twenty-two, she hardly knew that there was anything special about her voice. She was studying music in Paris. She worked at the cello, led an unstable life, and occasionally, for pleasure, sang Schubert and Brahms with Robert at the piano. One evening, in December, some months after the night they became friends, one evening, when snow lay in the streets, and the lights of the Ile St Louis had an unusually bright glitter, and the heating in the Foyer International broke down completely, she wrapped herself in a blanket, draped the damask bedspread around Robert's shoulders, and, shaking with laughter – for it was a beautiful clear night and despite her fear of the cold his presence comforted her and turned it all into an adventure – she began to sing. In Schubert's 'Erlkönig' they laughed at Robert's attempt to play the difficult piano part, and turned the father's horror-struck realisation that his son is dead into a melodrama; they turned the page, and began 'Gretchen am Spinnrade'. And then, somewhere in the far constellations that affect human destiny, a star changed course, a flower bloomed in the desert; her voice, which until then had never been taken seriously, began to acquire a curious life of its own, like a newly hatched creature stretching its limbs, whose existence, maturing inside an egg, had never really been envisaged, even by its mother; the walls of the little room began to reverberate joyfully and their ears were drenched by a full, powerful sound, whose mysterious origin could only be the depths of her own body. At the end of the song they looked at each other in amazement. He stood up and kissed her. Once again, as on the night when they lay on the bed together, he felt that her cheeks were wet. 'Flavia,' he said slowly, 'I think perhaps you have a voice.' And then, suddenly becoming very English, he thought: does she always have to be so dramatic? 'Why cry?' he said, almost irritated. 'You sang beautifully. Well done,' and patted her back. Only years later he accepted, and grew to appreciate her temperament, in which there seemed to be so much black and white, so few intermediate shades. (But there too he was wrong.) She nodded, her head stuck to his shirt and wetting it; gave a great heave and started sobbing.

How could he possibly understand the reason for her tears? Even she didn't know. From that night her life began to take a different direction. At first she believed it was somehow Robert's doing; that their closeness, wrapped in blankets on that frozen night, and the understanding that they shared, had inspired her, sent her into a state of trance; and from this an aural illusion was created, which deceived them both. For it was some time before it happened again. That evening, when she tried again, she had no voice at all, less than before; the newly born creature had vanished completely. But a little later she found it; and she was all alone, in her studio. Then she realised, to her joy, and a feeling of vertigo, that the voice was in her, and had nothing to do with Robert. She wasn't even thinking of him when, at six o'clock one evening, the thin, sensitive sound began almost of its own accord to fill, to multiply, like a trickle of water which suddenly finds it has become a river. From then on, supported by her teachers and friends, the cello began to take second place. The discovery of her voice was like the sculptor's gradual uncovering of life in a block of marble.

Her search for the right teachers, which took her all over Europe, her effort to maintain continuity, despite two long difficult love affairs, and her need for regular financial support, was a struggle of great dimensions. Sometimes she was so exhausted, her confidence so worn away, that she could do nothing but lie on her bed for days on end. At these times she was obsessed by her failures and a conviction that nothing would ever turn out right for her. It was often the thought of Robert that rescued her. She tried to recover that first evening when she had sung 'Gretchen', and many subsequent evenings, with him at the piano, when her voice bloomed, when she was sure that she was made to be a great singer. It was a feeling that, at last, she was swimming with the tide. But it was not easy for someone who had always felt an outsider, who had the impression of living on the fringes of society, to accept that she was to become a full member. And now, as she sits in the hall, watching him, so near and so far, in her elegant clothes, with real success already behind her and signed contracts to sing in the world's opera houses, she feels half a fraud, at least half. Is it possible, is it right, that her career has outstripped his? She hears how he plays the piece that Schumann wrote when he thought that he had lost his love, Clara, for ever; she breathes with him, she imagines that she herself is the instrument on which he lavishes caresses (and smiles at the thought that she is perhaps as big and ugly as the black piano), she knows in advance from his face how he is about to play each note; she is at one with the tender quality of his touch; she can hardly believe, and yet she has always known, that his spirit and hers have such uncanny empathy. And if the last movement of the Fantasy is a lament for an impossible love, she allows herself to imagine that he is lamenting for her, and she, as the music fills her, is lamenting for him. In this way they are joined.

But sometimes he plays in a way that she is not expecting. Just as she feels most united, so sure of the direction in which he is leading that she could herself take the lead, that it is enough for her to want, to hope for a pause, an accelerando, for it actually to happen – just then he confuses her. He brings her up with a start; he hurries forward when she wanted to linger, he interrupts her peace with a sharp accent; or perhaps he holds back, insisting on a shadowy, more internal passion when she can see no sense in restraint. And then, abruptly, she thinks of all the things they do not share. For example, she remembers Johnny. She looks at him and remembers that he has always rejected her. But Johnny he loved. Was that love?

She changes position, uncrosses her legs. Her neck is a little stiff; she lets it flop forward, then rotates her head. The emerald earrings graze her shoulder. From the corner of her eye she sees Robert's father, three rows back, looking at her. She performs another rotation, lazily, self-consciously, and closes her eyes. Yvonne, almost exactly behind, frowns. Something starts to rise up and choke her. She sees that this girl, this woman, this singer with an inflated ego, her son's 'old friend', is trying to draw attention to herself even here. She dislikes her. She remembers her hysterical laugh. There is something perverse about her. She watches as the woman begins a third rotation. She shakes her head and clicks her tongue. She hates her. She knows that she is trying to divert the audience's attention; away from Rob. Can the bitch not bear to be out of the limelight for the space of a single concert? She clears her throat. Henry turns to her, holds a finger against pursed lips; irate, furious with him too, she points at the gyrating Flavia. Henry nods, shrugs his shoulders, and – horror of horrors – a little smile plays around his lips. She stares forward, rigid as a statue. She sees nothing, hears nothing. Worst of all, Flavia has stopped rotating; and yet the horrible feeling, like a snake, continues to strangle her. She blinks, holds her eyes tightly closed, then opens them. Flavia is listening attentively. But even the way in which her hand supports her head is intensely irritating. She wants to murder her. The hall has suddenly become a most threatening place, all shadow and glare, and she can hardly bear not to throw a tantrum and lie screaming with her feet kicking the air. She knows this feeling very well, oh so well! She must sit it out, frozen to the velvet seat. Old Mrs Schwarzenberg catches her eye, makes the face of one about to swoon. Bitch! Has she noticed something? Just in time she remembers: Rob is playing, he must have done something good . . . she smiles back at Mrs Schwarzenberg, that ghoul.

Flavia has registered Henry's hungry look. She doesn't like him, but it does her good to feel his lust. What would Robert think if she had an affair with his father? She imagines his elderly body and wonders if she has ever felt sexual desire without love. If she had an affair with Henry, what would fuel her desire? Only one thing perhaps: to be the recipient of the seed from which Robert was born . . . at the same time she shudders at the idea. It would be incest. For Robert is her brother, she thinks, more than her brother, as he holds the music on the crest of a wave, which now roams above the troubled surface and will not break; she never expected such a great crescendo as this, and she is thrilled by the sheer power of it, by the passion she knows is in him, but which she has only experienced through his playing. For she has never seen his heat, his hunger, he has never thrown at her one single look of the type that Henry, she knows, is now directing at the back of her head; of the type that Johnny received, time and again, although he didn't seem to want it and tried (she often noticed) to avoid; rude, flippant Johnny who ignored this priceless gift as if it were beneath him.

She can see Johnny, in her mind's eye, as he burst into the room where Robert was playing and she was listening; he came in, smiling, and immediately poured himself some vodka, put in some ice, and then, pointedly, was looking for something else; she felt Robert's playing lose its concentration, then come to a halt, and heard him say, although Johnny had asked nothing: 'There's some more tonic in the hall. In the shopping bag.' She waited for Robert to continue, but he didn't; he sat at the piano and listened to Johnny rummaging in the shopping bag. 'You were playing wonderfully,' she said, frowning. 'Why stop?' 'You must meet Johnny,' he said, getting up and going into the hall. For a few moments she heard nothing; then the fizz of the tonic bottle, and he came back with Johnny who gave a huge grin and, to her surprise, kissed her.

Johnny paid her a lot of attention. He said: 'Robert's always talking about you. I'm Italian too, you know.' And that evening she was, for a time, captivated by him. Robert hovered around them, talking little and yet encouraging their friendship, preparing food and filling their wine glasses. Johnny said:

'I love opera. I'd like to be director of an opera house and invite singers from all over the world. I'd have fantastic productions and put on a lot of new stuff. I'd have completely bare stages and singers sitting on trapezes. Or stages so cluttered that the singers couldn't move at all. They'd be stuck in little squares with furniture and mountains squashing them in. They'd be behind rocks, so all you could see would be their heads.' He imitated the singers stuck in these tight spots. 'They'd be singing heads. Trapped. Trying to get at each other.' He clawed at her. 'And not succeeding. Wouldn't that be great? They'd be singing all this romantic passionate stuff and not be able to move, not even an inch towards each other. The only thing that would change would be the scenery. You'd have stage hands coming on and moving the rocks and furniture about. And so for a moment the singers would be free. But they still wouldn't move. And before they knew it they'd be surrounded again, by tables or beds or trees or walls, and all you'd see would be their heads, singing away like caged birds! How do you like that, Flavia? Would you be in one of my productions?' She laughed, a bit uncertainly, looking at his big white unevenly spaced teeth and his gleeful eyes, and wondered if he was really mad. 'You're mad,' she said, in French. This was obviously what he had been expecting, hoping for, and he exclaimed, in Italian for her benefit, with the greatest delight: 'Yes – mad!'

He got up – they were having supper – went behind Robert's chair, took his shoulders in both hands and shook him wildly, chanting: '*Si! Sono pazzo, pazzo, pazzo!*' Robert lowered his glass, from which he was about to drink, and she saw his body stiffen as he tried to avoid being jerked against the table; he put his slow bony hands up, over Johnny's brown fingers, and tried to hold him still. Johnny lowered his head and started to nuzzle the back of Robert's neck with his bristling hair. 'Don't you like it, baby?' he said. 'Being shaken up?' Robert didn't answer. She saw him bend his head back so that Johnny's nestled tightly against his neck, enclosed like a nut in a furry shell. They seemed to remain like this for a long time. She took a sip from her glass, replaced it on the table with a clink that rang out in the sudden quiet. Distant pop music and a boy's high voice from the street calling 'Sarah, Sarah!' floated in and out of the room. She was aware of a vast distance between her and everything, between objects and beings, between friends, between her and lovers everywhere.

Johnny said: 'Well, would you?' and looked at her, putting his arms round Robert's neck. 'Would I what?' 'Be in one of my productions, of course!' Irritated by this 'of course' and feeling, all of a sudden, that he was no more than a spoilt child, she replied: 'I really don't think the question will arise.' Johnny let go of Robert's neck, and sat down on the floor beside her. He imitated her, sticking his nose in the air: 'I don't think the question will arise . . . don't *really* think the question will arise . . .' and pushed out his chest. 'Shut up, Johnny,' said Robert and cuffed him gently on the back of his neck. 'I really don't think, do you, that the question will arise,' he went on, on purpose to annoy her, 'arise, arise . . . ,' and then, bold as a winning child, looked up, flashed a bright smile and put his head on her lap. Now she saw the side of his face, eyes closed as if asleep, and his curls, clinging to his forehead like lichen to a rock, resting on her. With a small sad movement of tenderness she stroked his hair. His legs, splayed out on the floor in turned-up jeans, looked thin and crooked, like a frog's. She tried to meet Robert's eyes, but he wouldn't play; he filled her glass, slow and distant.

'Sometimes,' she said, hardly knowing whether to laugh or cry, 'you remind me of a dinosaur.' 'Why?' he asked, after a few moments, and the slowness of his reaction seemed to confirm the comparison. 'Because . . .' she began, but couldn't continue; it was a complex matter, and the thought of his playing confused her, the speed and sensitivity of his response to music was very unlike a dinosaur. But the head on her lap was coming to life, emitting little internal sounds, and she realised Johnny was laughing. She looked down at him, struck by the odd convulsive nature of his laugh, and wondered if her own was equally peculiar. 'You're right,' said Johnny, raising his head, grinning almost to his ears, 'You're right – he's a dinosaur! I've always wondered what he was – now I know! But he's not really carnivorous, is he? I think he's a brontosaurus! And he never told me. Why didn't you tell me, bronty? It's nothing to be ashamed of! You can't imagine,' he continued in a serious voice, 'you can't imagine, Flavia, how much has suddenly become clear to me. I've been racking my brains to try and understand him, and it's all been a wasted effort. How can a human being understand a brontosaurus? Now I'll just have to accept it, and everything'll be much easier.' She glanced at Robert, to see how he was taking this; he was looking very tenderly at Johnny. It's because of his brow, she thought; and the deep eyesockets. It's just a physical thing, the shape of his skull, that always makes him look so gentle. 'If I'm a brontosaurus,' he said to Johnny, 'what are you?' 'A human, of course; just a simple human being.' 'You're a mosquito,' said Flavia. 'A very silly mosquito.'

Johnny's face fell, and she couldn't tell if she'd really offended him. 'Am I?' he asked. 'Is that all – just a silly mosquito? She doesn't like me.' He got up and went to the window. He stood there, very straight, looking out; he pushed his hands into his pockets, tightening the jeans around his bottom. She felt a little thrill of power. 'You're not a mosquito,' said Robert. Johnny didn't respond. 'Come and finish your meal. Come on.' Johnny still didn't move. Robert frowned, shook his head at her. She shrugged, and made an uncomprehending gesture. She mouthed: I didn't mean it badly! He left the table, went to Johnny and put his arms round him. She wondered if she should try to repair the damage. She saw Robert standing behind him, concealing him. She watched intently. She saw Robert move closer; his crutch must be against Johnny's buttocks. She felt a wave of anxiety, but some triumph too. She saw Robert bend and whisper in his ear. Johnny moved away, detaching Robert's arms. He turned, glared at her and said: 'Remember – mosquitoes *bite*!'

She was a little scared. She thought that perhaps he could really be dangerous; she was afraid for Robert. She looked at him and said: 'You frighten me, Johnny. I was only teasing you.' 'Oh, I know,' he answered. 'I'm sorry,' she said. 'Really.' He waited a moment, then cried: 'Good!' And from his sulky, childish pose he changed into a playful demon. He began to dance around her, rapidly opening and closing his hands, poking, jibing at her, and chanting: 'Good, good, good, she's a wicked woman and she knows it, she's confessed her crime –' then, just as suddenly, he stopped, flashed his smile at her and sat down at table. 'Where were we?' he asked.

Eventually they left her. She stayed that night, on the sofa in the living-room, and they went off together into the bedroom. She sent them to bed like a grown-up who has had enough of two over-excited boys, and wants to be alone. She breathed a sigh of relief. First, she opened wide the French window that gave onto the balcony; Johnny was an incessant smoker, and she was already beginning to develop the allergy to cigarettes that now almost makes it impossible for her to be in the room with a smoker: a reaction that is respected by others only as her success as a singer increases. She went out onto the balcony. It was June; the air was warm. She looked at the window boxes by her feet; they were a mass of overgrown weeds, and the soil (she touched it) was very dry. She toyed with a long strand of bindweed, wrapping it round her fingers. She had always found her hands peculiar. They were small and rubbery, and the fingers turned up at the ends. Playing the cello had stretched them, but this stretching seemed to run contrary to their nature. They always wanted to curl up into little balls. She pulled sharply at the bindweed, and it broke. She dropped it over the railing, and studied its capricious flight down onto the courtyard. She thought she recognised Robert's Volkswagen, but couldn't be sure; cars were of no interest to her. And yet the sight of the little car down there, locked up and self-contained, was troubling. Cars were watchdogs, spies for their sleeping masters. She had a feeling of being excluded. She was worried by things that she didn't understand. For example: why did she always end up with homosexuals? She smiled sarcastically. Her male friends were almost all homosexual, and two of the three men she had most strongly desired. But she totally refused the idea that she was afraid of 'real men'. She shook her head at the folly of the world. She knew – she had always known – that she was made for love, for passion: wasn't it obvious?

She began to touch her own body, and the first thing she noticed was her heartbeat; how often had that little heart, so warm, so giving, been forced to stand on the sidelines beating hard, and wait while the men she loved pursued others, rejected or were rejected in their turn, struggled and wept, and then came to her for consolation. She had learnt the bitter patience of a saint. Her breasts were large, and the skin very smooth; she undid her blouse and freed them. They were coffee brown against the white cotton; she bent over until they touched the top of the balcony railing; felt the nipples stiffen on the cool metal. What was happening in the bedroom? she wondered with a slight shudder. Were they performing that act which she couldn't help finding disgusting? She slid her hand down the cleavage and swayed, rubbing the nipples back and forth along the railing. The sensation was so exciting that she had to continue. She slipped her fingers under the belt of her skirt, down through the thick wiry hairs, into the secret opening. Then two things happened. She became aware of her large belly, flopping in soft rolls over the top of her skirt; immediately, with a sense of revulsion, she withdrew her fingers and the strong sour smell on them reached her nostrils; and simultaneously she had the certainty that she was being watched.

Had she forgotten where she was? Perched on a second-floor balcony overlooking a courtyard? But she did not fasten her blouse. Her heartbeat quickened. She understood: the sudden horror of her body and the fantasies of a voyeur were made for each other; their meeting was inevitable. This man, crouching in the parking lot, was her natural partner. Down there he was lusting, watching, drinking in her grossness. She stood, blouse gaping, still and silent, staring towards him, searching the shadowy space, and willed him to appear. How would she meet his terrible eyes? Would they be dim, or blaze? Or mock her? Or glint, aware of their power? She knew he was there; she waited. The summer air stroked her, the reflected lamps of the city lit her. She looked down at her breasts and saw that they were noble. Behind Robert's car something moved; she waited, trembling. She was not ashamed. She was a tragic queen; she would be dressed in rustling silks and embroidered brocades, in brilliant jewels and the fantastic head-dresses of the opera. Her voice, riding a column of air, would fill the far spaces of a theatre and thrill the hearts arranged in countless murky rows beyond the footlights. And she saw them rise, ghostly hearts, and stamp, clap, shout, call and recall her; she inclined her head, almost to the railing, squinted into the glaring lights, acknowledged flowers thrown to her feet and the bouquets brought by svelte footmen. She sighed, sweeping the parking lot with her gaze, the potholes, the cars and a few ragged bushes.

But her lover remained invisible. Even he, she reflected bitterly, belonged to the category of 'Distant Beloved'. She whispered: 'This is your last chance. It's not fair. I want to see you.' She took her breasts in both hands and smiled at him. He did not appear. She fastened her blouse and turned back towards the room. A grey streak shot out from under Robert's car and zigzagged away.

She came quickly into the hostile flat, closed the balcony door and covered her eyes. She summoned all her strength. Gritting her teeth she set out for the bathroom. She passed Robert's room and stopped. Did it matter to her what was going on in there? She considered. Serious student of human nature that she was, she stepped to the door and listened.

There were voices, but very low. It was not easy to attune her ear. Then she realised, with excitement, that they were talking about her.

'I don't really care. It's not my business, is it?'

'No, all right. But she'd like you – if you gave her the chance.'

Johnny laughed. 'I resent being called a mosquito.'

'Come to bed. Forget about it.'

'I don't want to. I'm sorry. I want some fresh air. I need to go out.'

She heard steps, and withdrew quickly. She went into the bathroom, locked the door, and studied her face in the mirror. She found herself rather beautiful.

'Please Johnny, couldn't we have a quiet night?'

'*You* can. But I couldn't sleep now.'

'Why not?'

Johnny shrugged. He himself hardly knew what was bothering him. 'I need sleeping pills,' he said.

'Aren't you tired?'

'Of course. But I can't sleep.'

'I must sleep, Johnny. You know what a lot of work I've got to do tomorrow.'

'Me too.'

'Exactly. So please come to bed.'

'Go to sleep. I'll think about it.'

He had just had a good idea. But Robert would know. He'd hear him getting out his bicycle. He looked at the bed and wondered if he was almost asleep. 'Rob?' he whispered.

There was no answer – but could anyone fall asleep so quickly? He heard the bathroom door close: was Flavia still up?

He went into the hall. 'Flavia! You're not in bed yet!' he reproached her, with his wide smile.

'Speak for yourself,' she said, and stood facing him.

'Don't tell me you're a night owl, like me.'

'Perhaps I am.'

'Mosquitoes work at night,' he said, boring into her. He could see that he'd unsettled her; she lowered her eyes, and clasped a little red sponge bag.

'You upset me,' he continued with reckless candour, 'because it's true. I am a mosquito.'

'I was standing on the balcony,' she said.

'You don't have to explain yourself.' He felt as if he was crushing her, grinding her into the dust. 'Even I stand on the balcony.' He paused, aware of his power – was he not Robert's lover? But she looked so pathetic; he was afraid she might actually cry. He had a soft heart; so he added: 'I sometimes think that ugly old yard is quite beautiful at night. You know what I mean?'

'Yes I do,' she said. 'In fact just now,' she went on eagerly, 'I had a strange feeling out there. A very strange feeling . . .'

'What was it?'

'Nothing,' she said, as if she'd changed her mind. 'It just seemed so lonely, the most desolate place on earth. And yet there were people, sleeping, all round. It was a powerful feeling.'

He smiled. 'Sometimes we get prowlers,' he said.

'Really?'

'Oh yes. Once, in the middle of the night, I went out onto the balcony for a moment, without my clothes on, and an old man saw me. He was prowling around, I don't know why. And now the silly wanker keeps coming back.'

'How extraordinary. I think I saw him tonight. What was he like?'

Johnny shrugged. 'Just a typical old wanker.'

'Did you actually *see* him?'

'Of course.'

'What did he look like?'

He was surprised that the story had such an effect: as a matter of fact he'd made it up. 'Aren't you going to bed?' he enquired.

'Yes.' But she hesitated.

'Do prowlers excite you?' he asked. This was interesting; women were not usually turned on by that sort of thing.

'Not really,' she laughed, and he had a view of her splendid teeth. 'How about you?'

'Me? Yes.'

She clicked her tongue. 'May I ask you something?'

'Naturally.'

'Do you live here?'

Johnny thought about this. 'No,' he said.

'Robert said you did.'

'Wishful thinking, I suppose!'

'But why would he lie? He said you lived here.'

This obviously mattered a lot to her.

'Well I do, sometimes,' said Johnny. He had a great sense of freedom; she seemed so gullible – he could say exactly what he wanted. And why, he asked himself, why should he tell the truth? What was the truth? Where did he live, really? 'And now,' he went on, touching his bicycle which leant against the bathroom wall, 'now I'm going home.'

'Where's that?'

'Why are you so curious?' he asked, coming up close to her and looking down; she was rather small.

'Because I love Robert. He's a very old friend. I want him to be happy.'

'Oh I make him happy,' said Johnny.

'Do you?' He felt her eyes on him, the eyes of a suspicious schoolmistress. 'Do you really?'

'Mind your own business,' he said. 'It's not easy to be happy. I'm sure you know all about that,' he added maliciously. 'But he's happy with me. Why – don't you think he could be?' He paused. 'Do you want to ask him?' He went to the bedroom door. 'Yes, good idea. Let's ask him.'

'No – he's asleep, Johnny! Leave him alone!'

He could see she was completely rattled.

'Then leave *me* alone. And how do you know he's asleep?' He looked at her. 'Even I don't know that – so how could you?' No answer. 'I'd better go now,' he smiled at her. 'I was very happy to meet you, and I won't bite you any more for tonight.' He held out his hand. 'O.K.?'

She nodded, and turned towards her room.

'Well? Aren't you going to shake my hand?'

She looked at him slowly. 'Stop playing the fool,' she said, and fixed him with one of the most reproachful expressions he had ever seen. He felt very angry.

'Fuck off! What are *you* playing at?'

He shouldn't have allowed himself to get upset. He saw – there was no doubt about it – that she was pleased. Her eyelids drooped sarcastically and a small superior smile crept across her face. Slowly she shook her head, as if to say: now I've seen you in your true colours; and I'm not in the least surprised.

He wheeled his bicycle to the door. 'Good-night, madam,' he said and winked at her. He opened the door and went out.

Oh, what a relief! The night air folded him in its arms, fondled him, and he wanted to sing out for joy.

What a wonderful invention is the bicycle. How fast and light, slicing through dark deserted streets, delighting in the slightest slope, oblivious to traffic jams, anarchic, all but invisible! His legs were so strong that the bicycle seemed to go by itself. The speed was so exciting that it almost gave him an erection. As he pedalled he sang to himself:

Late at night
I feel so lonely
Here's a body next to mine
But I'm feeling cold

He let go of the handlebars; his balance was reason enough for happiness. Only one tricky bit: the stretch ahead, though hardly noticeable to the naked eye, had a slight upward gradient. But there was comfort in the thought of straining muscles; it was good for the shape of the legs.

In the twinkling of an eye he was there. It always surprised him that this large square should be open at night. He paused at the railing, mopped his face, and took a blue peaked cap from the pocket of his jacket. He tried it on at various angles, then changed his mind. There was nothing wrong with his hair, it was thick and clean; he would go bare-headed. He switched off his lamps and rode into the square, along the gravel paths, under the great plane trees, in a high gear so that his feet rotated very slowly, as if the bicycle was moving by itself. He circled the perimeter of the square, and passed a man sitting on a bench. He drifted on, but there was no one else. No one else at all? he wondered, peering into the dark spots. Surprising – it wasn't as late as all that. He wheeled round, parked near the occupied bench. He walked casually past the bench, had a good look at the man. Really nothing special. He lit a cigarette and walked back. The man, fair-haired, fortyish, was unpleasantly plump round the jaw. He was interested, of course. Ah well, Johnny sighed, beggars can't be choosers. He paused, right beside the bench, and wondered what to do. Something to make it more interesting . . . he went over to his bicycle and remounted. He could feel the man's disappointment; but he wasn't going to disappoint him. He rode up to the bench and, still seated, put one foot over the armrest, while the other rested on the pedal. The man moved closer and looked up at him hopefully. Really the catch was too easy; without the involvement of the bike this encounter would have no interest whatever. Johnny smoked, feeling the tautness of his jeans over his right leg. He ignored the man completely; stared out at the square, apparently deep in his own thoughts. He was profoundly aware of the man's anticipation; he could almost touch it. This was a wonderful moment – perhaps it was all he needed? A moment to be captured, frozen, kept for ever. He toyed with the idea of riding off. The cigarette came to an end. He flicked away the stub, and undid his trousers. Still on the bike, he lowered the jeans to his knees: a complicated balancing act! How nice his thighs looked, against the metal of the crossbar. He paused, gripping the seat with his buttocks. Then he slid his pants down, inch by inch; they were tight. The sensation of the leather seat against his bare skin was even better than he'd expected. The man could control himself no longer. He opened his trousers and exposed himself. Johnny looked at his erect cock. This was the biggest secret he had to offer. Undressing could go no further. The man gripped his swollen prick with his right hand, and touched the side of Johnny's thigh with his left. Johnny let him stroke it, deliciously aware of his bicycling muscles, the way in which his soft flesh, in repose, spread out over the old wooden armrest.

Five minutes later he was riding home, hell for leather.

Robert was only half asleep when he came in. He was vaguely aware of the outside door opening and closing, and of the heat of Johnny's body as he climbed into bed beside him. He put out his arm and touched him. The skin was wet, he was sweating. 'Had a nice ride?' he asked, and opened his eyes.

'Oh yes,' said Johnny, moving out of reach. 'I needed a spin. Now I feel more like sleeping.'

'I heard you talking to Flavia.'

'Did you? I tried to keep my voice down.'

'You must understand if she's a tiny bit jealous.'

'What?' said Johnny, sitting up. 'I thought all that was years ago.'

'Haven't you ever been in love?'

'But you never *did* anything with her.'

'That's true.'

'Exactly. Good-night, bronty.'

Robert lay on his back, quite awake, wondering what to do. In the dim light he saw that the room was filled with Johnny's possessions: trousers, shirt and socks carelessly discarded, a small open suitcase, half unpacked, fashion magazines, a large book with photographs of Japan in the last century. Johnny had moved in, he realised. And wasn't this sensible? Wasn't it what he, Robert, wanted? But it was difficult to understand how Johnny had moved in so quickly. It was not long since he had met him in the Observatory Gardens.

Even more unexpected had been their second meeting, completely accidental, in a café in Hampstead; Johnny was sitting at a table with two girls and a man, all speaking French. Robert did not notice him immediately; their first encounter, in the moonlight, belonged to another domain, as removed from the waking world as a dream, the gap as unbridgeable. Drinking an espresso coffee by himself, at four in the afternoon, reading *The Times*, he suddenly recognised Johnny by his voice; he felt excited and guilty, as if he had violated a commandment. He blushed, and sank into his paper; in a moment he would get up, pay his bill and leave. He signalled to the waitress, but she was gossiping. A group of noisy Americans were crowding through the door; he was trapped. Quickly, bravely, he looked; and saw Johnny by daylight. His skin was lighter, he had freckles on his nose, his teeth glinted brightly and there was a little mole on his temple.

It was still possible to ignore him; that, perhaps, would be the expected procedure? But Johnny, daylight Johnny, paused in the middle of a sandwich, and saw him. And immediately, in a perfectly normal voice, called: 'Hi, Robert! Come and meet my students.' Aware of his ungainly movements (one leg was going to sleep) he made his way over, between crowded tables, only to hear the waitress reprimanding him; he searched clumsily for change, and a pound coin flew out of his pocket and disappeared into a corner. All of which was much to Johnny's liking; he started laughing, and soon the students were giggling too. *Students?* Robert asked, trying to regain control. Of course, didn't he know? An old friend, and he didn't know? That he taught English in a language school – and was an excellent teacher, wasn't he? To which the students laughingly agreed.

From then on Johnny's belongings arrived regularly in his flat. They were a more tangible presence than Johnny himself. For he, at first, was absent for days and nights on end; but his toothbrush remained, his towel, his battered suitcase spilling contents in midstream onto the floor; and these were signs that Johnny existed. Once, in the solitude of the night, he took socks, shirts, pants and sweaters one by one into his hands. They were almost alive, they glided through his fingers, sent delicate smells to his nostrils; each one spoke intoxicatingly of Johnny, of intimacy and warmth. He grasped them with both hands, and held them against his face. He dropped them, and they littered the floor like stars.

Johnny too was there, from time to time. The possessions did not arrive by themselves. But they remained the more solid part of him. Information seeped through: an old boyfriend who was still chasing him, his miserable pay (three pounds twenty-five an hour), his own language studies, the antics of his students, a film he liked (*Ossessione* by Visconti), a room in Bayswater. A momentum came into being, very much of Johnny's making; although, Robert knew, it was his own passivity which made it possible.

Now Johnny sighed and turned over, pulling the bedclothes with him. Half of Robert was uncovered completely.

He lay without protesting. He began to practise trills on his thigh, with his right hand. Fingers two and three, and three and five, were quite well controlled; but one and two were stiff and useless. The end of Beethoven's Sonata, opus 109, haunted him; he had billed it for a programme, but the end of the last movement was impossible. He tried to concentrate, to become aware of each separate finger as it tapped against his leg. It was no good; fingers one and two were stuck together. Instead he played with his genitals, but they were soft and lifeless, not part of him at all. He thought of a grand piano, and it came to life, kicking with all three legs, the keyboard an open mouth, the lid an upper lip; he was trying to play opus 109, but the mouth was determined to talk, and the keys rattled like false teeth; from time to time the lid came down with a sharp crack and he had to snatch his fingers away; then, unexpectedly, it shot open again; opus 109 was quite unrecognisable . . . he opened his eyes with a start. He was cold. He pulled at the bedcovers, but they were locked round Johnny. He felt angry. He disentangled the sheet, freeing it abruptly, but the sight of Johnny's face on the pillow, deeply and undeservedly asleep, was unbearable. Even in his sleep he was fighting for the bedclothes. They were a symbol: if he allowed Johnny in, he would take everything. But he was already in, he had moved in, he was in his own bed. Robert turned onto his side, and drew up his legs; he moved to the very edge of the bed. The body beside him was alien. It was alien and he hated it.

He was alarmed by the strength of his feeling. The nearness of this body, its regular breathing, its heat and selfishness, repelled him. He lay, throbbing, on the extreme edge of the bed. For minutes on end he heard the alarm clock ticking in the dark. He was counting the ticks. He was ashamed. This body is Johnny. Remember Johnny. Remember Johnny's laughter, his grace, his beauty. You find Johnny adorable. You would do anything to have Johnny near you. Now he is near you and you hate him.

The ticking clock became an enemy too. He felt the ticking of his heartbeat, and the two rhythms were fighting each other. His chest pulsated with a terrible need to overcome the clock. He lay there, sweating, locked in mortal contest. Far away Johnny's tight little body was serenely recharging itself. Remember me, he implored the sleeping boy. For I too exist.

Very slowly he uncoiled his aching limbs. It is not your fault, you are asleep, you cannot know what I am feeling. But if you stretched out and touched me, you would save me. A single touch, if it came from you, now, would transform me. I would be human again. I would forget the murderous ticking of this clock. And then he thought: are you afraid, Johnny? Is that why I always have to reach out for you first?

Gradually this thought took possession of him. He stretched his arm across the crumpled sheet, into the hollow where Johnny's body lay. Even asleep it was desperately alive. Johnny is afraid, he repeated. He touched his back. The heat amazed him. His fingers, dry as dust, explored the moist surface, the crevice of the spine, the quietly inflating ribs which almost pierced the skin. He slipped down, so slowly that the back became a world, with valleys, hills and plains; until he reached the coccyx, which was always mysteriously covered with two sticking plasters. He was expecting these; but one was missing. In its place he discovered a little mound beneath unbroken skin. Was this something that Johnny was trying to hide? He examined it with hesitant fingers, aware that he was trespassing. Johnny had an extra hillock in the small of his back! The other plaster was still in place; did it conceal another little bump? His first reaction was anxiety: perhaps they were cancerous. Johnny shifted in his sleep, and turned onto his back. Robert looked at the closed eyelids, which flickered for a moment, and even in the dark noticed his long lashes. He touched them; and with the other hand touched his own. Eyelashes suddenly struck him as strange. He shuddered. But was there any part of the body not capable of making you shudder?

'Johnny,' he said.

The eyes opened sleepily, and looked at him.

'One of your plasters has come off,' he began.

'Really.'

'You've got a little bump.'

'Oh yes,' he said lightly, wide awake. And then, as if reading his mind: 'Don't worry about it.'

'What is it?'

'Called a lipoma, I believe. Harmless.'

'Why do you cover it up?'

Johnny closed his eyes. 'Fancy waking me up for a thing like that. You know I have trouble sleeping.'

'I was worried, I thought perhaps it was something bad, and you were keeping it from me.'

'Something bad? Oh no,' he laughed. 'Actually I've got several of them. If you really want to know.' He took Robert's hand and guided it to his thigh. 'Try there,' he said.

Probing with his fingers he discovered another, much smaller, bump.

'See?' said Johnny. 'I get them from my grandmother. They're a sign of good health. Nothing to worry about.' He paused. 'Don't you like them?'

'Why should I like them?'

'Lipoma,' said Johnny. 'Sounds like a little rabbit. Rather sweet, don't you think?'

'Why don't you take the other plaster off?'

'I might,' he said. 'Sometimes I have them cut out. And sewn up. Then they leave scars. Haven't you noticed my scars?'

Robert reflected. 'Perhaps I have,' he said.

'I have to decide which is nicer. Bumps or scars.'

'Why bother to have them taken out? If they're harmless?'

'Scars look manly. Don't you think so?' He paused. 'It's strange, bronty, you know, when they cut one out and then afterwards they show it to you, a funny thing like a little red and yellow slug, and then you think: that was part of me.' After a moment he added: 'Not that there's any point in having them cut out. They're harmless. I'm quite fond of them.'

Robert put his hand onto Johnny's chest, and felt the heart beating with great vigour. 'I'm sorry to wake you up,' he said. 'I wasn't feeling very good.'

'Why not?'

'I felt distant.'

'From me?'

'From everybody.'

'I'm here,' said Johnny. 'Very close.'

'Are you?'

Johnny turned towards him, and saw those large quiet eyes, filled with shadow, and all that lank hair, flopping over the pillow.

'You're a little boy,' he said, and reached out for him.

Robert closed his eyes, and allowed himself to be drawn against the small tough body.

'It's all right about the lipomas,' said Johnny, but Robert had almost forgotten about them completely. 'I'm glad I told you. Not that it matters much.' He held Robert tighter, and the hair on his chest was so thick that it felt to Johnny like a carpet, or a dog's tummy; so much hair was quite inhuman. 'I'm glad you don't have hair on your back,' he said. And he started to move, with a light heart, against Robert's bony body, from which he sometimes felt youth had already flown, aware that he was making him happy.

It was almost the first time that he had confessed to anybody about the lipomas. He was a consummate actor. Feigning sleep was easy; anyone could do that. But to tell Robert about the lipomas, and to let him feel them, demanded fearful skill and courage. The relief was marvellous. Lovemaking was an act of gratitude. Robert would never know, and must never know, what was at stake. For the lipomas invaded his body like an army; they grew unceasingly and were gradually turning him into a monster. 'Funny, aren't they,' he muttered between kisses, 'my little rabbits.' They were his darkest secret, one so terrible that he did everything to hide it, even from himself.

He never looked at his naked body, least of all in a mirror. In the bath he lay with closed eyes, in order, he told himself, to appreciate the sensation fully. He avoided swimming for, as a child, he seemed to remember nearly drowning. He never sunbathed: wasn't it the height of narcissism to care so much about a tan? These were his rationalisations. His life was a race against time; against the relentless advance of the lipomas. Could nothing be done? What about vitamin pills, special diets, homeopathy, or acupuncture? No one knew what caused them. He had had them since childhood. You must accept them, said doctors. They're perfectly harmless. Nothing to worry about. Although they do grow. You don't really mind them, do you? No, said Johnny. Why did he mind so much? Because he knew the laws of the jungle. Life was a jungle, and he knew its laws.

Daniel watches Robert splayed over the piano like an anatomy lesson. With his analytical mind he tries to draw all the conclusions he can, to piece together the naked young man like a jigsaw puzzle. He wonders if he himself would have the courage to expose himself so brazenly. But what frightens him is the possibility that he would have nothing to expose. Others see him as a clever, fascinating personality. But what Robert is displaying for all the world to see is not cleverness: it is the actual core of his being. How on earth can Robert be so clear about this dark, elusive thing? His eyes almost fill with tears: tears of envy.

To be a brilliant stockbroker is really no problem. Apparently he has a gift for it. It is true that he studied economics at university; but without much interest. Instead he was looking for a vocation. Much later he drifted into stockbroking, thinking it would be a job like the many others he had tried, a small part-time job of no interest. But it had taken him over, and was making him rich. Money suddenly began to fall into his lap.

It is hard for him to take anything seriously. The fact is, he thinks as he watches Robert achieving something, imposing himself, the fact is that he is a plaything of the gods, to an unusual degree. He is the archetypal plaything. He no longer feels a clear distinction between success and failure. All the time there is an itch inside him, like an itch on an unreachable inner organ, a thirst which he couldn't quench, a need to run away, to stick out his tongue, and this itch was him, the only part of himself that he could really acknowledge. It was a sort of heroism; he was a glorious martyr for no cause. The unscratchable itch drives him gleefully on. The itch expresses itself in ideas. He is full of them; they have a life of their own, they interest and amuse other people. But he himself is rarely amused, even when he laughs. He lags behind, a reluctant dog on a lead, dragged forward by his bursts of inspiration. He builds a glittering palace with his ideas, his thoughts, his sense of humour, but the palace is empty, he does not live there. In the stockmarket his ideas have been beautifully successful. This is one of the bitterest jokes he knows. Of all things it appears that he is cut out to be a bourgeois Jewish banker. The coming of Peter is equally unexpected. All of a sudden he has a wonderful boy who loves him. Even his fits of jealousy do not drive Peter away. He invents jealousy when nothing else is happening. He cannot believe that Peter loves him.

At the age of forty he is still a rebel. His younger brother has been settled for years, with an honest career as a lawyer. His parents are German Jewish refugees, and they live in peaceful retirement in a village near Oxford. Despite the upheaval of Nazism, and their uprooting, they have succeeded in creating well-ordered lives. He himself has never had to undergo such an ordeal. Sometimes he spends the weekend with his parents, and there, in their sunny home, he is surrounded by warmth and affection. His father is a keen gardener, and Daniel helps him. He spends hours mowing the lawn, weeding and digging, under his father's kindly supervision. His father is particularly proud of his fruit trees. 'We have had so many apples this year', he would say with delight, 'that the only thing to do was to make pints of apple juice. And we have given it to all the neighbours, who think it is the best they have ever tasted.' Or: 'The new cherry tree has had fruit for the first time. After four years. Only four or five cherries, but we have kept one for you. Next year, with the right weather, we'll have dozens.' And he calls to his wife: 'Marie, where is the cherry we kept for Danny?' His mother comes out in her rust-coloured skirt, cupping the cherry in both hands. He makes gestures of wild exaggerated admiration, and eats it with an expression of rapture. His parents laugh. His mother settles down to a book in a comfortable garden chair.

'We had a phone call from Judith,' says his father. 'She is coming down to stay next weekend.'

Judith is the woman to whom he was briefly married, ten years ago.

Daniel nods. 'I'm glad you're still in touch with her,' he says.

'Oh yes. You know we're both very fond of her.' His father looks at him with his deep brown eyes, timidly probing. 'She sounded quite cheerful,' he says.

'She's fine,' says Daniel. 'Living with her boyfriend.'

'Look at this clematis, Danny. Elsie Spath, I think it's called. Last year she got the wilt, but she's recovered marvellously. You've missed most of the blooms. But there's a late bud here, just about to open.' And he touches it with his thick weatherbeaten fingers.

He looks at his father's gentle joy, from his own emptiness. How can he be homosexual in the face of such fulfilment? His parents' love has spread to the garden, to the blooming of every flower, every fruit. He touches the clematis bud, rubs the neck of the stalk, like a murderer.

'How is Simon?' he asks. Simon is his brother, the lawyer.

'He's well. He would love you to be in touch more often.'

'Well really, he has a telephone too, Daddy.'

His father ignores this remark. 'Little David is having trouble at school.'

'Oh? What sort of trouble?'

'He can't get on with maths. Simon wonders if you'd ever like to give him a helping hand.'

'Well why doesn't he ask me?'

The shadows are lengthening, and the grass is still to be mown. Daniel plugs in the machine and sets to work. His father prunes an old sprawling rose. Up and down he mows, his eyes on the ground, until the lawn glimmers new and fresh in the evening light, swathes of soft green lines.

Every visit to his parents' home emphasises his own

sterility. Occasionally he wishes they were dead. But would that change anything? Perhaps his attempts at painting are only a way of trying to have children. He knows now that he is not really a painter. If he were an artist his rebellious, challenging existence might have some justification. If he were acknowledged by the world he would have no need to hide anything. His parents would admire and respect him. But he is not an artist, and so, plagued by guilt, he has to hide everything. It is possible, he sometimes thinks, that with the years his strong attraction to boys will die down a little. Then perhaps he will be able to live with a woman again, and his profound desire for children (which he admits to no one) will be fulfilled. He loves children and can very well imagine being a father.

Why, he wonders, does he always think of his lovers as 'boys'? Peter is a 'man', but it is vital to think of him as a 'boy'. Even at the age of fifty he will still call Peter a boy. The idea of 'men' does not interest him. He finds it hard enough to think of himself as a 'man'. He is already old, but his life has passed in a way so unexpected, so malicious, that it seems never to have started. He is still waiting to be created.

His parents know something about his homosexuality, but they do not believe in it. They do not want to know too much, and he does not want to tell them. Although he is forty years old, they too still think of him as a boy; a late developer, though intellectually brilliant. They are pleased he is making money, but money in itself does not impress them. They are convinced, in their gentle way, that one day he will reach maturity and get things straight. And so they are patient. For a man who does not have a wife, a family of his own, is hardly a man at all. This is what he reads in the happy lives of his parents, and the loving looks which they still shower on each other. For them the family, and the continuity that comes with it, is the most important thing in the world. But could it be true? Could they really be as contented as they seemed? He does not know. He does not understand them. Their perfection gnaws inside him like a worm.

He looks at Robert and wishes he would play a wrong note. The logical and harmonious progression from one note to the next is unbearable. He feels trapped by it. He cannot accept such predictability. Perhaps it is only against this that he has always fought. Night after night Peter comes home to him, as promised, never more than a few minutes late. His punctuality is so terrible that it must conceal some secret perfidy. Punctuality alone is enough to make him insanely jealous. Now, willing Robert to play a wrong note, a handful of wrong notes, to slam down the lid of the piano, to get up and shout at the audience, to take his prick out, anything to shock, to break the monotony, now he laughs to himself, for he knows Peter is not really unfaithful at all, that his jealousy is as much a sham as everything else. Oh God, he thinks, what is wrong with me? But God is the last person to appeal to. Peter, that stupid, starry-eyed boy is becoming a priest! Oh that irritating, endless, absurd faith! Against which he, Daniel, can do nothing! Peter will leave him for Jesus Christ. And he understands, exultantly, bitterly: he is jealous of God. He is a megalomaniac. He watches Robert and is jealous of him too. He runs his hand over his forehead and feels the lines there, already deep; they, at least, are evidence that he has lived, that forty years of life have taken place. He tries to tap a rhythm with his feet, a completely different rhythm to the one Robert is creating. It is amusing, ridiculous and heartwarming. A big stupid smile cracks open his face, exposing the pirate's gap in his teeth. There, he thinks, concentrating intently, for it is not easy (especially for a music lover like him!) to beat out a defiantly contrary rhythm; there, I am an artist after all, I am the poet of clowns and buffoons . . .

Johnny had an urgent need for smooth, unblemished bodies. Oh, the miracle of a back which could play, unashamed, in broad daylight! Like ugly old men, who have everything to hide, he was driven to dark places. A lipoma was growing on his chest, slowly but surely; already it interrupted the harmonious channel which should, which must, run from the breast bone to the navel, dividing the flesh. He scrupulously tried to avoid touching it; but when his attention wandered he found his fingers drawn to it, kneading, squeezing and trying to flatten it out of existence. Sometimes he even seemed to have succeeded; to his joy, by pressing hard, he had squashed it, forced it into the surrounding tissue. But a few moments later, desperately hopeful, his fingers would fly to the spot; and there again was the mysterious nodule, protruding with its own boisterous life, real as ever.

He went with Robert to Rome. Italy was, for him, a promised land. He was proud of his Italian blood, and especially of his grandmother, whom he had never met, but whose picture he always carried in his wallet. During the war she had hidden partisans in her house in Verona. He loved to think of these bristling, idealistic young men, protected by the serene lady, her grey hair drawn into a bun, who was his grandmother. In Paris they bought couchettes and boarded the train called 'Palatino'. This name enchanted Johnny. As they travelled south the mood in the train changed, northern concerns were left behind, people stood in the corridors smoking, compartment doors were left open and children ran from carriage to carriage. The Italian passengers, who had seemed, in Paris, less numerous than the French, began to spread and multiply, stretching their feet up onto the seats, calling their children, playing cards noisily and passing around food, while the French shrank into corners and nervously read their books. He loved the way the Italians used the train, and turned it into a home. To them everything was natural; they had an inalienable sense of their right to existence. Such confidence gave even the fattest, ugliest old man a beauty and grace of his own.

'My grandmother fell in love with one of the *partigiani*,' said Johnny. 'He was younger than her, about thirty, I think.'

Robert was helping a Japanese woman wedge an enormous suitcase on to the top rack. 'You so tall! Velly velly taw!' she tittered.

'He was thirty and she was about forty,' Johnny went on. 'He was called Andrea, and she was called Giulia.' He took her photograph from his wallet, and showed it to the Japanese woman. 'This is my wife,' he said.

'Ah, very nice,' she said, although the picture was of a woman at least twenty years older than Johnny. 'You have children?'

Johnny smiled. 'Four,' he said; then frowned, and counted on his fingers: 'No, five. I'm not sure. There's Robert, Johnny and Martha. How many's that? Three.'

'Shut up,' said Robert. 'She'll think you're mad.'

But she was already politely engrossed in a magazine.

'And so,' Johnny went on, 'Giulia and Andrea fell in love. And Giulia became pregnant.' The guard came in and handed out customs forms. 'And gave birth, in secret, to a beautiful boy called Francesco. Her husband, by the way, was already dead.'

'Really? And what happened to Francesco?'

'I've no idea,' said Johnny. 'One night, at the end of the war, when he was three years old, Giulia had a terrible dream. She dreamed that the house was in flames and Francesco was crying, leaning out of the window. So she spread out a mattress on the ground and told him to jump. Can you imagine how brave the little boy had to be? But he was, and he jumped. And when she tried to pick him up, there was no Francesco, only a little pile of bones. She woke up in a terrible sweat. Everything was quiet in the house. Andrea and Francesco were sleeping peacefully. So she knelt down and said a prayer of gratitude. But the next day Andrea took his gun and went out with the *partigiani*; and never came back.' Johnny rubbed his eyes.

'What a sad story.'

'Yes,' he said. 'The sort of thing that happened in those days.'

'So Andrea disappeared, and she never saw him again.'

'Never,' said Johnny, and gave him a playful poke in the ribs. 'Cheer up.'

'How can I cheer up when you tell me a story like that?'

Even the Japanese lady, turning the pages of her magazine, was affected; she looked up with kind, enquiring eyes, full of concern.

'Because I invented it,' Johnny said. 'I just made up the whole thing.'

Robert shook his head. He was always taken in by Johnny's stories.

'Giulia existed, of course. But I made up Andrea. Although he might have existed. Like me.'

'You do exist, Johnny. And . . . I love you,' he whispered.

'Are you sure?' asked Johnny loudly.

'What, that you exist? Or . . . ?'

'That I exist. You can't be sure, can you? You might easily be the only person in the world, and I'm your fantasy. So if I disappear like Andrea, don't be surprised.'

'How did your grandmother die?' Robert asked.

'In a car accident.'

He went into the corridor, and put his forehead against the window. He felt sorry for Robert and regretted all his stories and deceptions. But they were necessary. He turned round, and saw Robert sitting uncomfortably, his legs cramped, hands twisted about each other in his lap, staring at nothing in particular. He wanted to laugh. He felt so excited.

'Robert,' he called, aware of his grin, which had so often proved irresistible. 'You look very funny.'

'Funny – why?'

'You look sweet,' he said; shrugged, and blew him a kiss. Perhaps I love him too, he thought. Love was a way of playing: it was a look, a smile, a sudden inspiration. The word should not be uttered aloud; at least not in the hearing of the other.

Dijon passed, and Mâcon, and Chalon, and they were rushing through the mountains, not far perhaps from the Italian frontier. The corridor was almost empty; most people had gone to bed. He looked into the compartment. Robert was lying down, and the Japanese lady was nowhere to be seen. 'I'm going to wash,' he said. 'See you later.'

He idled along the corridor, running his hand over the doors of closed compartments. He had heard of thieves boarding the train at the frontier and robbing sleeping passengers. Locked doors were interesting. Thieves must have duplicate keys, he thought. Unless they were in league with the guard. He tried to open a window, but it was locked too. He came to the toilet, at the end of the carriage. It was occupied. He waited by the main door and looked through the glass, into the pitch black. Supposing he got off at Modane, the border town, and started a new life. He checked his pocket; his wallet was there with quite a lot of money. Was it possible to start a new life? He thought it was.

The door of the toilet opened, and the Japanese lady came out. They exchanged smiles and little bows. There was something warm and motherly about her. She disappeared through the swing door, along the corridor and into the compartment. For her he was a man with a wife and children. And this was something which, surely, he could easily be, if he wanted. Women were often attracted to him. From Modane he could cross the frontier, find an Italian girl and marry her. There were various possibilities. He could present himself as an adventurer, whom a strange destiny had brought to Italy, who was looking for a wife on condition that he could come and go as he pleased. He would tell her as little as possible about himself, his past, and the reasons for the many journeys he would make. And what he told her would, mainly, be invented. He would come back to her regularly with extraordinary tales of his travels. His children would look up to him as a wild man, but full of kindness, whose lust for the unknown would fire them too to be explorers. Or he could be the perfect family man, teaching English and French at the local school, and bringing up his children strictly but fairly on a solid moral foundation. He would enjoy cosy evenings by the fireside, excellent food, and take his family for hikes in the mountains. He wondered if he could really do this. He felt that women were more understanding than men. They were warm and accepting. Perhaps he could even tell a woman about his lipomas. He could be completely honest with a woman. Women presented no problems.

He went into the toilet, urinated, and examined his face in the mirror. He was, on the whole, satisfied with his face. He sucked in his lower lip slightly and studied the effect. A completely new face was created by this small, subtle action. It turned him into an unattractive, gullible individual without much intelligence or charm. This person would have large soft limbs and be easily teased by other boys. He would fall into all the traps that were laid for him. When he released his lower lip the fine harmonious shape of his mouth, whose corners were on the brink of smiling, delighted him. He took a comb from his wallet and tried various hairstyles. The differences were small, for his hair grew in tight elastic curls which resisted interference, but they were worthwhile, for the practised eye. In this light there was no hint of a thin patch anywhere. He was so pleased that he took off his shirt and ran his eye very quickly over his body. This was a miscalculation. He blurred his focus, but it was too late. He had a glimpse of skin which was too white, and his torso, which once he had been proud of, was utterly deformed, there could be no doubt, made monstrous, actually inhuman, by the little subcutaneous lumps which had no right to be there; and which, all the time, were growing. He struck his chest forcibly with his fist, and bent over the sink. He lacked what every other young man in the world had: a normal body. The lipomas were taking him over; they were eating him up. Little by little *he was becoming them*. He then remembered something else: in a few days time he would be thirty years old. The truth was, he was nearly two years older than Robert. To be thirty was inconceivable. The horror of it made him wince. He screwed up his eyes in agony. I am lost, he thought. My time has run out.

He came out of the toilet, a shapeless, disjointed mess of skin, bone and lumps. It was a miracle that he held together. Impossible to go back to the compartment. He wandered into the next carriage. A fat old woman stood smoking in the corridor. '*Excusez-moi*,' he muttered as he squeezed past, adding under his breath: '*vieille vache*.' There was no one else. He pushed on to the next carriage, couchettes again, all doors closed. He looked at his watch: five to twelve. In a compartment at the end sat the guard, with a pile of passports and a glass of beer. 'Are you looking for something?' he asked rudely, in French. 'No.' And then, narrowing his eyes: 'Aren't we all looking for something?' The guard was in no mood for philosophy. 'Is this your carriage?' he asked, bored. 'No. When do we reach the border?' 'One-thirty.' 'Good-night,' said Johnny. Two more carriages of couchettes. He went into another toilet, washed his face and dried it roughly with paper towels, which he shredded and scattered over the floor. He came out, leaving the door to swing and slam. In the next carriage, also couchettes, three people were talking in the corridor. 'Excuse me,' he said, 'do you know what time we reach Modane?' 'Sorry, no idea.' He went on. 'This is a dead train,' he said aloud, and banged his fist on the door of a compartment. The click-clack of the wheels as they sped over sleepers was the thud of a clock. He counted these irreversible intervals: thirteen from one end of a carriage to the other.

Then wagon-lits. A different atmosphere: carpeted, dim lights, and the corridor walls, orange, looked soft. He gripped the bar of a window and pressed his legs against the wall. It was warm. He felt his prick stir. He waited for the space of nine sleepers. Next carriage: more wagon-lits. A guard approaching from the other direction, eyed him suspiciously. 'Good evening,' said Johnny. 'Could you please tell me what time we reach Modane?' 'One-thirty. Why? Are you getting out there?' The man spoke French with a thick Italian accent. 'Don't I have a right to know?' asked Johnny with a sweet smile. The man shrugged. 'Is this your carriage?' 'I was told one-fifteen. I thought the Palatino was always on time.' He noticed the fly on the guard's grey uniform was undone. He studied this for a moment. The man moved, and he had a glimpse of his shirt tail. 'I'm afraid you'll have to go back,' said the guard, and blocked the way. 'But I love trains,' said Johnny. 'I'm an explorer. I've been all over the world on trains.' 'I can't let you pass. It's against the regulations. Unless your seat is through there.' 'It is,' said Johnny, grinning from ear to ear. Inside he was afraid. 'Why don't you go and have a pee? I'll slip past while you're in the toilet.' He faced him provocatively, hands on hips.

The man was about thirty-five. He thought he saw the flicker of a smile. 'Go on,' he said. 'You can see I'm not a thief. Just a curious boy. You can search me. Look, I've got no guns, iron bars or keys.' He turned out his pockets. 'Go on, frisk me.' He lifted up his arms and inflated his chest. He stared at the guard's open fly. 'I'm a train fanatic. Just a train fanatic. And my seat *is* through there.' The guard yawned. 'If you'd seen as many trains as I have . . .' He was unshaven, unwashed, and his light blue shirt was creased and half unbuttoned. A few hairs stuck out from under his collar. He had broad shoulders and a fat belly. Johnny felt a bit sorry for him. 'You're a friend,' he said. 'Thank you. *Ciao, buona notte.*' He winked and walked past.

The next carriage had no beds. It was locked at the far end. But the train continued; he stared through the glass of the locked door at the swaying corridor beyond. Utterly predictable, more lifeless carriages, but the cul-de-sac enraged him. He was brimming over with violence and kicked at the door. He wanted to commit a crime. He lowered the zip of his jeans and thrust his hand in. Then he walked back and peered into the compartments. They were dark; bodies were stretched out on the seats. How tragic life was! All people could do was sleep. Wandering up and down the empty corridor he too felt like a sleep walker. Perhaps there is a God, he thought suddenly. *Dio mio, mon Dieu,* my God – *my* God? The possessive pronoun made him smile. Little God, he whispered, a little break please . . .

If he had a whistle he would blow it with all his might. He wanted to wake up the world, to marshal these duds and lead them into adventure. But such things never happened. Real life was a round of pointless details, failed love stories, deception and slavery. And yet trains ran, children were born, houses were built, cows were milked, men and women fucked: the world behaved as if it knew what it was doing. A fly buzzed uselessly round his head, crashing from time to time against the black windows. Like him it had strayed into the wrong place. Everything around him was alien: the narrow corridor, the plastic walls, the little metal ashtrays brimming with butts. And yet this was the Palatino; every irrevocable second was carrying him towards the country of his dreams. He gripped the window rail and watched his knuckles turn white. He wanted to put his head out into the night and let the wind blast against his face. He knew the window was sealed. Why, he asked himself, why did Italy mean so much to him? Perhaps this too was just one of his inventions.

He clung to Italy as if it was the only reality in his life. But, now that Italy was close, he began to wonder about his grandmother. He was afraid that she too might be a fabrication. He had lost touch with his family. He had no idea where his father was, and hardly ever saw his mother. The name of the village in England where she lived slipped his mind. He tried to remember; but that neat, summery little place belonged to another age. It lived somewhere inside him, vaguely, much as, he imagined, people who believe in reincarnation are said to have intimations of a previous life; like a dream image which surfaces for a moment during the day, and sinks rapidly. And yet for seventeen years he had lived with his mother. He did not understand how he could have cut her out so effectively, relegated her to such a distant, shadowy zone. It was almost murder: matricide. He tried to imagine her death, but felt nothing. He trembled at this callousness. His mother was alive, she was a fact; she had the dull, leaden density of facts; her weight was a threat, an obstacle to his freedom. And so he had disposed of her. Deep inside him she tugged against the current of his life. Oh mother, forgive me! It was not she, but his grandmother, whom he had never seen, whose picture he carried with him, who was far more vivid. The thought of her death, of her sheltering the partisans, could bring tears to his eyes. If we have guardian angels, she was his. 'Giulia,' he said out loud, 'help me.' He tried to remember all he could about her, but felt afraid, as if approaching forbidden territory. Italy was no longer a dream; its physical reality, bounding towards him, might shatter him. The truth was, he knew very little about Giulia. He knew her face from the photograph. Had he invented the story about the partisans, or had someone, long ago, told him? Did she live in Verona? When or how did she die? He was not even sure her name was Giulia. 'Giulia,' he said out loud. Then: 'Giovanna.' What if her name was Giovanna? No! His own name was Johnny, Giovanni; that was why he had called her Giovanna. The name Giulia stuck in his mind, though less and less clearly; as he repeated the word it began to lose its meaning, it seemed no longer a name at all. And yet someone must have told him this was her name; why should he have made it up? He clung to the name Giulia like a drowning man. In a flash he resolved to invent no more stories; they would destroy him. He felt that this was the bravest, most important resolution of his life. With trembling fingers he searched his pockets for a cigarette, but found none. He was denied even the reward of a cigarette.

Can't you just see me
Can't you just see me now with my head in the air
Can't you just see me
I'm going to look in your eyes
And see a whole lot of tears
Can't you just see me

He lurched to the end of the carriage and peered through the darkened glass at the occupants of the first compartment. Stretched out on the seats were two lifeless female bodies. In the second compartment a large man sprawled across the corner, his head flopping against the window. In the next, the third, the blinds were down. Johnny opened the door and went in.

Immediately he felt a sense of relief. Someone was lying full length along one seat. It was a young soldier. Johnny paused, praying that the sliding door and the sudden shaft of light had not woken him. The soldier did not move. With infinite care Johnny closed the door and locked it. In the pitch dark he heard the ticking of a watch. Silently and slowly, like a thief, he sat down. He waited for his eyes to adapt. Gradually the body opposite took on perspective, like a landscape at first light. The soldier's head was resting on his forearm; his hand dangled over the seat. His knees, fitting snugly one on top of the other, were drawn up. He had taken his shoes off; the heels protruded neatly from under the seat. His breathing was smooth and regular. Johnny sat quite still. Nobody in the world knew where he was.

I don't want to wake you, he said very softly. He was afraid that even this was too loud; but the other didn't stir. Soldiers sleep deeply; they are always tired. The train was clattering like thunder. I am unhappy, he went on. I wonder if you are unhappy. The long curve of the soldier's body scarcely dented the seat beneath him. I don't think, said Johnny, that someone so beautiful could be unhappy. For example, at this moment, I am sure you are not having a nightmare. He thought about this: could a body so perfectly in repose be having a nightmare? It is possible, he said, that you are listening to me. My voice is not loud enough to wake you; but perhaps I am influencing your dreams. I find this possibility very exciting. In your dream you will not find my presence surprising, you will accept me. He paused. Let me confess. If I were sure you wouldn't wake up I would certainly undress you. I would examine you bit by bit and tenderly explore you. And what I would discover would amaze me, as if I had never touched a young man before. I would climb into all the moist corners of your body. He leant forward and whispered joyfully: I would climb into all the moist corners of your body! I would excite you, and from the depths of your sleep you would respond. You would feel no inhibitions. I too would pretend to be asleep. You would enter my dream, and I yours. And so we would have no reason for shame. It would remain a dream. In the dark I would be beautiful.

On the rack, high above the seat, was the soldier's luggage. Just one suitcase. Standing on tiptoe he reached up and took it down. It was quite heavy: a small compact bag, a little battered, with large handles. He took it to the window and tried to read the label, but it was too dark. He pulled at it; then bit through the string with his teeth. The label came away and he put it in his pocket. He replaced the bag on the rack.

Poor boy, he said, you don't even have a couchette. I would give you mine, if you wanted it. I am used to going without sleep. I get very tired, but I never show it. Nor do I show fear. I do not think I am a coward. But if I slept I would lose time, and I have so little. In a few days I shall be thirty years old. But perhaps I still look as young as you. In any case I am never a good sleeper.

But all this, he felt, might be boring to the soldier.

You sleep so well, he said, that you don't understand what I'm talking about. You don't know what it means to be always on guard. You have a Mummy and Daddy who love you, two brothers and one sister, a nice little home in a village, not far from the mountains. At school I would have helped you if there were things you didn't understand. I am clever, and perhaps you are a little stupid. But you're a big boy now, you can travel on your own, you can even do your military service. You think it's normal for your body to grow and strengthen, so that your mother has to stand on tiptoe when she kisses you, you drink and smoke and dream of girls and masturbate. All this, you do not realise, is a miracle. You do not understand my happiness, which is to appreciate all these marvels (such as the smoothness of your chest, the hair that curls between your buttocks) in your place. My happiness is to be thrilled by all these things, which you take for granted.

His eyes were now so used to the dark that he could almost make out the soldier's features. He knelt down and examined them closely. The eyebrows were black and thick and joined in the centre. Johnny thought this was funny. He wanted to laugh. He put his hand close to the soldier's nostrils and felt the warm breath on his fingers. He watched the rise and fall of his chest and began to breathe in unison. He had the ecstatic sensation of being inside the soldier's body.

'I love you,' he whispered. He tried it in all the languages he knew: I love you, *je t'aime, ti amo, ich liebe dich, ya lublyu tibya*. His ear for languages was amazing. Each had its own resonance, its own unmistakable implication. '*Ti amo*' was a vibrant night, electric as the song of cicadas; '*je t'aime*' was a sweet and gentle game, 'I love you' clear and faithful as a woodland flute, '*ya lublyu tibya*' was an epic poem, '*ich liebe dich*' a slow flood, a dark submarine world from which there was no escape. He loved them all, all were miracles, but most of all perhaps '*ich liebe dich*', which he repeated again and again, filled him with awe, and almost frightened him.

He sat back on his seat and smiled at his lover. He let go of the soldier's breath and found his own again. A deep sense of peace came over him. He felt his limbs jerk, a sharp delightful spasm, and relax. He yawned and stood up. On the floor, close to the young man's drooping fingers, was his soldier's cap. It was an intrinsic part of him, necessary to his perfection; to touch it would be disruptive and he might even wake up. But Johnny was a realist. He picked up the cap and put it on. 'Thank you,' he murmured. He went to the door, blew him a couple of kisses, and said in a breezy, non-committal voice: '*Gute Nacht*'. The soldier still didn't budge. Johnny unlocked the door and went out.

Blinking in the bright light of the corridor, he studied the cap. It was a navy blue beret, with a little tassel, like a tail, at the back; on the left side was a badge, made of light metal. It fitted Johnny perfectly. He set off at a brisk pace along the corridor. But then he had another thought; paused, and broke into a grin. He marched back to the compartment, slid open the door roughly, and switched on the light. The soldier lay still for a few seconds, like a stunned animal; before sitting up violently, his feet thudding to the floor. '*Cosa? Chi é?*' he called out in a loud hoarse voice, shading his eyes. 'Oh,' said Johnny in English, 'I'm sorry. Wrong compartment.' He smiled at him. The soldier was really very young. He had small deep-set eyes, and acne on his chin, where the stubble grew only in patches. 'I'm really sorry to wake you,' said Johnny. He was still wearing the beret. The boy squinted at him. He had a snub nose which twitched; and his dense eyebrows made him look like a monkey. With an adolescent sigh he lay down, covering his head with an arm. This new position looked much less comfortable. Johnny smiled, his tongue peeping through his lips. He waited for the soldier to react; to ask him to switch off the light. But the boy was too shy, or perhaps he was already asleep. And so, as if putting a child to bed, Johnny made sure all the blinds were drawn;

turned off the light, and left, gently closing the door behind him.

In the claustrophobic compartment, stuffed full of beds, where Robert lay, time passed unevenly. He dozed and woke, at the mercy of the train's boisterous rhythms and his cramped bunk. He heard a buzzing, which could be a mosquito, and tried to make sure his feet were covered. But this meant that his knees were even more uncomfortably bent. He would be tired the next day, and have to deal with a city he hardly knew, and Johnny's excitement. And where was that stupid boy? He felt like a keeper in charge of a wild animal. It was this wild animal that he was trying to love. He lay on his back and thought of freedom. The beat of the train's wheels was inescapable, rattling through his body like a drill; within it one could try to establish syncopations of one's own. It was possible to carve out one's own rhythm, even a melody, in opposition to the metronomical train; according to the laws of music, tension would grow from these opposing forces, and the refusal to capitulate, the dogged pursuit of syncopation, was a powerful form of expression. He fought the tyranny of the train, and the effort of it caused his heart to pound, creating a pulse of its own; and now, like a juggler he kept all these rhythms in his head, and tried to insert another, a slow melody which exploded with the colour of instruments, of an orchestra, defying the mechanical clatter of the wheels and his heartbeat . . . he opened his eyes and sat up. He was alone in the compartment. He lay down again and smiled bitterly. He lifted his right hand, heavy as lead, and began practising trills in the air. It was his thumb that was the problem. He stared at it: a blunt appendage, a remnant from an earlier stage of evolution. He made a great effort of concentration, and worked it slowly up and down so that it moved, in one uninterrupted shaft, from the tip to the edge of the wrist. He was trying to teach it to be free, free from the other fingers, which, like nosy neighbours, were always interfering. This thumb moved like a rusty piece of machinery; ancient and yet irreplaceable.

The door opened, and Johnny appeared.

'Hello,' said Robert. 'Just doing some exercises. Each finger has to be free, you see. Otherwise you simply can't do what you want on the piano.' He smiled; he was happy to have Johnny back. 'Close the door, Johnny. We've got the compartment to ourselves. I don't know where she's gone. Her bags are still here.'

Johnny remained in the doorway, lit from behind. He was wearing a cap, a soldier's beret. 'Where did you get that?' Robert asked, touching him on the head and trying out his fourth finger. Johnny moved out of the way and leant against the open door, one foot in the corridor. The cap shaded his eyes. Robert saw the beautiful line of his lips, and wanted to make them laugh. 'Come on, soldier boy,' he said. 'I never knew you were in the army. You've kept that dark.' Perhaps, very briefly, the lips flickered. Still in the doorway, Johnny started to unbutton his shirt. 'Come on, baby, close the door. Or is this a strip-tease?' Johnny was not even looking at him; and yet his stance and attitude were provocative. Robert wondered if there was someone watching in the corridor. He stretched his head through the door. The train lurched, and he almost fell out of bed. Even this did not produce a smile. He was annoyed. Johnny stood posing in the doorway, his eyes slanting into the corridor, toying with his buttons.

And this, really, was not at all what Robert wanted. The compartment was snug and cosy; it was a little home. 'Come in,' he said weakly. Johnny undid his belt. 'Somebody'll see you!' He sounded like a mother hen; not even a father. Johnny's pants came into view, and a thin line of pale skin. He couldn't decide whether the sight fascinated or repelled him. 'By the way,' he said, 'there's a mosquito in here. Where have you been?' Johnny lowered his trousers; Robert looked away. He was helpless: the wild beast was galloping, tearing across a distant plain, foaming at the mouth. He closed his eyes tightly, and with a deep sigh threw his head onto the pillow. This journey would be a torment. Johnny came into the compartment, his trousers down to his knees, his hand on his genitals. Robert glimpsed his strong thighs. How he hated them. In his head he sang the last movement of Beethoven's opus 109. Johnny was smiling horribly. He reached out to close the door, but Johnny caught his hand and stopped him. He understood: Johnny wanted the possibility of an audience. 'So you want a public, do you?' His voice was angry and coarse; he wanted to kill him. Johnny gripped his hand. 'Let me close the door!' But Johnny was hideously strong; he freed his hand violently and saw the boy, with an angelic smile, lower his pants. Somewhere in his head opus 109 continued, obsessively, uselessly. 'I've got a headache,' he said. Never, perhaps, had he seen Johnny so sexually excited. He reached out from his bunk and touched the lithe body. Johnny withdrew to the window. He held out his arms, murmuring 'All right; come to me then!' Johnny remained aloof, his body gyrating. Robert realised the divergence of their desires. Johnny, with the soldier's cap, was a stranger, but it was not a stranger that he, Robert, desired.

'I want you, Johnny,' he said; but knew, as he said it, that the name was out of place; was afraid, even, that by naming him he would kill Johnny's excitement. And he seemed to notice that Johnny shook his head, very slightly; he pulled the beret further down over his eyes. There was nothing for it: he would have to play the game. But how? Opus 109 still ploughed through him. He moved under the sheet and touched his own body. Johnny watched him. Why should I give in to you? he asked silently, as he feigned the motions of love. The door was still open, but he was past caring. From the shadow of his bed he fixed his eyes on Johnny's graceful, selfish body. He felt like crying.

After a while he heard a distant door opening and shutting. Footsteps approached. They were small, rapid and polite. With great agility Johnny hoisted himself onto the top bunk. It was the Japanese lady. Johnny sat on the bunk, his legs dangling, and put the beret over his crutch. He was grinning. The woman entered on tiptoe. 'Solly, oh so solly!' she whispered, and closed the door.

Johnny sat for at least ten minutes without moving. He wanted to giggle. One of his students was Japanese; her confusion of l's and r's was an old joke, but always refreshing. She spoke of flying pans and brankets. In the darkness he took the cap away. The movement of the train was stimulating. He still had his shoes on, and his pants and trousers were round his ankles. What had the lady been doing? Perhaps she too had had an adventure. He pulled up his pants, removed his shoes and trousers and stored them neatly on the rack. But not before retrieving a small, crumpled luggage label from one pocket. He could, if he wished, switch on the tiny light above his bed and read it. But, instead, he put it under his pillow. He would wait for the morning. He would keep this delight for tomorrow. Besides, he did not want to shatter the darkness. He was a child of darkness; a master of the night.

He was still awake a little later when the train stopped at Modane.

Modane: a pale, odourless name. Modane was an empty space, waiting to be filled. You could enter, fill it, and make it your own.

He heard French and Italian voices on the platform, doors being opened and heavy footsteps in the corridor. He felt safe in his bunk and hoped the others were asleep. He himself was used to being awake and could cope with tiredness. And Rome, where he had never been before, would be exciting enough to banish thoughts of sleep. Exhaustion could be exciting in itself; it cast its own feverish colour across your life. He would never tell anyone about his adventure with the soldier. He realised there were many such episodes in his life, secret episodes, and each was unique. Perhaps one day he would write them all down. It was possible that one day he would write a book. In this way he would share his secret life with the world. Perhaps the world would envy him. He thought he would take a pen name, and wondered what it might be.

After a long time, so long that he had almost forgotten that the train would ever move again, doors slammed and a whistle blew. Someone walked down the platform with a transistor playing full blast. Very Italian, he thought, and winked in the dark, as if he were winking at a charming naughty boy. But he hoped that his companions had not been woken. He listened to their breathing. How strangely close they were. Imperceptibly, stealthily, the train had set off again. But it would soon gather speed, and he would be swept along with it, into Italy.

I am a pilgrim, he thought.

She is amazed by her son. Not only by his physique, so different from hers and even from Henry's, but by the force of his personality. He is so thin; how could one so thin play with such determination? As a child of four he had refused to eat. His willpower was extraordinary! She screws up her eyes.

She sees him sitting on a little chair in the kitchen, fixing her with eyes which, on so small a face, seemed even more enormous and dark than nowadays; and she is offering him a tiny sliver of roast chicken. He says nothing; merely turns his head slightly to one side. In the end she eats the roast chicken herself. She is haunted by the thought, ridiculed by Henry, that he might starve himself to death. But she knows it is possible. And she imagines the feelings with which, if necessary, she would drag him to the hospital to be force fed. He would bite and kick and scratch her, and she would ask what has she done to deserve this. As she eats the chicken she feels she is stocking up for the conflict; and he, by his own rules, is depriving himself of the strength he will need. He watches her eat, and she lowers her eyes. 'Won't you join Mummy?' she says, feeling the tears come. But it is not right, she feels, for him to see her crying. 'Aren't you my little Robbie? *Mon petit chéri?*' She wants to pick up the tiny bundle and cover it with kisses, but is afraid to do so. His eyes seem to be pleading with her, asking her for something, but she has no idea what it is. She feels very alone. Should she perhaps be angry, and slap him? How can one possibly know what is going on in a child's mind? Does he himself know? His eyes are definitely accusing her. She is afraid of him. So she potters round the kitchen, pretending to be busy, humming French songs to herself. It is the maid's day off, and she is not really at home in the kitchen. She decides to squeeze some oranges, but has no idea where to find the orange squeezer. 'Oh dear,' she mutters, 'stupid Helen. Where *has* she put it? Mummy wants to make some orange juice.' Everything in the kitchen is clean and tidy and she is afraid to disturb the beautiful order. Even the floor is polished, and it is possible she might slip and fall. She opens cupboards, searching for the squeezer, and the bristling army of cups, plates, cutlery and cooking utensils dismays her. She feels a little more comfortable with the glasses; at least they are transparent. Meanwhile Robert is obstinately silent. No doubt he has noticed her agitation. He is staring at her scornfully. She clenches her fists. What on earth is going on? she asks herself. She turns and looks at him.

She remembers that before his birth she had two miscarriages. She thinks that, perhaps, he has the same soul as those two others. The fact is, she cannot imagine having any other child. The same soul, the one destined for her, was struggling to be born. A valiant struggle. Eventually he came into the world, and her life was lit up by a ray of blinding sunshine; now, for obscure reasons, she is in danger of losing him.

She looks, and sees that it really is her own son. He sits there, in his shorts, legs dangling, quite motionless. He has eaten so little, for three whole days; she can see the bones of his tiny knees almost piercing the skin. She feels quite overwhelmed. 'Darling,' she says, 'aren't you hungry?' The child shakes his head. 'Or thirsty?' She has a good idea; she will make a yoghurt drink, with fruit and nuts. She smiles at him, noticing, once again, his straight dark hair. 'You look so sweet,' she says. She often wonders where his hair came from; Henry's was fair, and her own, though dark, has always been curly. He must have inherited it from one of her parents, whoever they were. She herself was adopted; she had never seen her real parents. She was brought up in a cultured, comfortable family; she loved her parents, and came to share their taste for the arts, especially music. Rob is her only blood relation. With his birth, a hidden part of her came to life; through him she has discovered her own past. Sometimes she found herself staring into his eyes, as if trying to extract from them her own secret, the secret of her own birth. It was a game between them, these searching looks, in which their eyes were locked together like magnets; eventually one of them would break the spell, they would giggle and kiss each other, and life would start again. Through him, in dazzling glimpses, she found her own roots. But now, as he starved himself, she was losing them.

Once, when she cut his hair, she kept back a small piece and put it into an enamel box; it was, after all, a normal thing to do, but she never told anyone about it. At night, unable to sleep and filled with agitation, she would rise and fetch the box with its cutting of hair. She took it back to bed with her; holding it, under the bedclothes, with Henry fast asleep at her side, she felt better. Once she put his nail-clippings into the box as well (they were so tiny); but thought better of it and threw them out. She did not want to be too sentimental.

She makes the yoghurt drink and takes it to him. Her hands are unsteady, and he would notice this. He refuses the drink and closes his eyes. Then she hits him. Tears roll down his cheeks from under the long lashes, but he makes no sound. 'Mummy made it for you specially!' she cries, and lifts him off the chair. He resists savagely, and bites her hand. She lets go, and he falls back onto the chair. He starts howling and covers his head with his arms. She realises that he is terrified of her. 'Why did you bite Mummy?' she says, tears flowing down her own cheeks. 'Look, Mummy's bleeding!' She thrusts her hand into his face. He might bite her again, and she would be totally destroyed; she would fall to the floor and curl up, clenching her fists, waiting for death. Nevertheless she holds her hand there, despite his violent attempts to push it away. Then the little boy cries out: 'Daddy! Daddy!' This terrible cry sobers her. She backs away. 'I'm sorry, darling,' she says in a calm voice. 'Mummy lost her temper and she's sorry.' But Rob goes on calling for Daddy. 'Daddy's not here,' she says firmly. 'He's at work.' 'I want Daddy!' 'But Mummy's here.' 'You're not Mummy! You're not Mummy!' For a long time afterwards these ghastly words haunted her. They even entered her dreams. She had no idea what to do.

Now, as he plays the last movement of Schumann's Fantasy, she has the feeling that it all happened only yesterday; and that it could happen again, that or something similar, even now, at this very moment. Many such possibilities exist within the dark corners of her mind, like subterranean rivers, never still, flowing secretly through her. As she listens to his expert playing she is full of admiration. She is convinced that he is a true artist, and a master of his instrument. And their life together, their conflicts and their love, have helped him towards this goal. He has withstood the tests of time. Now he is a man; his playing is undoubtedly that of a grown-up, independent spirit. And she accepts this happily.

His adolescence, however, was troubling. When his voice broke, very suddenly, she was deeply shocked (she smiles to think of it now) by its raucousness. Luckily this was a passing phase; later, when it settled down, his voice became gentle and melodious. But puberty turned him, nevertheless, into a stranger, and she would frown at his odd face, sprouting soft, disturbing hair. She was trying to find the old Rob again; to hear that special little voice, so spring-like, hidden somewhere within his cavernous body, and drag it back to the surface. Sometimes (and she remembers, with a pang, what a doctor once said to her) she felt he was doing it all to spite her. He was growing at an alarming rate; she almost wished he would eat less. At fourteen he was already taller than Henry, and she saw no reason for him to stop. These developments filled her with confusion. But one thought comforted and excited her; he must be taking after her own, unknown, father. She said to him: 'You look so like my father, *chéri.*' 'But you never saw your father.' 'Oh I did: once I was shown a photograph.' 'And he was like me?' 'Oh yes, very much. He was tall, with straight dark hair.' She is a great fantasist. It is not hard for her to invent stories and tell them convincingly. She never thinks of it as lying. Facts are not important in her life, nor is the passing of time.

Rob's coming gave her an allotted place in the bright swirling world where she found herself. She began to be aware, at last, that her feet touched the ground, that kitchens and bedrooms served a sensible purpose, that it took five minutes to walk to the corner shop, that Henry worked hard and expected, naturally, to be fed. But at night her dislocation sometimes returned. Henry's sound sleep and the ticking of the alarm clock were solid facts which frightened her. She lay awake and tried to shut everything out. She was like a citadel, at whose gates a strange, all-powerful enemy was beating. It was impossible to describe her anguish; whom could she tell? In the morning Henry asked if she had slept well. 'Oh yes, darling,' she always said. 'I'm so lucky; I have nothing to worry about.' It was true: there was no excuse. But she would get up, in the darkness, and wander through the flat, a small figure in a white nightie, her face coated in thick cream. She would stand in the middle of her sitting-room, near the piano, surrounded, unbearably, by chairs, carpets and wallpapers that she herself had chosen. For a long time she would watch the curtains as they whispered in the breeze, full of vague threats. She had no thoughts: only a pounding heart. She was light and empty as a skull. The sight of tiny sleeping Robbie did nothing to help. She was afraid to touch him; for the touch of her skeletal fingers would be terrible. She might even damage him. And if he woke, how ashamed she would be! Nobody must know. At last she remembers the little enamel box, decorated with a flight of ducks; she holds it tight, under her nightie.

She is deeply grateful. His existence is more real than hers; for one thing, he has a mother and a father. People sometimes said she had a strong personality. This pleased her, but it was Rob who had a strong personality; because of him, she too had a personality. And yet this was not true either. Others see in her things that she herself is not aware of. And perhaps they were right. Even without Rob, would she not still have existed? Did she not exist for nearly thirty years before he was born? But how on earth did she feel then? As she listens to his playing it is hard to believe that she existed, then. It is now, filled with feelings and memories, that she exists. As he plays she is convinced that feelings, and above all shared feelings, are the only things that matter. And it seems that, in music, feelings exist in a domain of their own and are clearer, and far more beautiful, than those we experience in the rest of our lives. Yes, but are these, in the true sense, shared feelings? Up there, on the stage, Rob is giving her so much; but what is she giving him?

She knew, twenty-five years ago, that he might starve himself to death. He screamed at her that she was not his Mummy. She left the kitchen, washed her hand and put a plaster on it. She telephoned the doctor, and told him calmly what was happening. The thread that bound her and Rob, like a tight-rope brightly anchored in the sky, along which they stepped out together, had snapped. She remembered that she was a grown-up woman, and he was a little boy. She fetched his toys, his cars, his bricks and his animals, and laid them beside him. She switched on the radio and found music: a piano trio by Schubert. She sat quietly, not too far away, leafing through *House and Garden*. She thought perhaps he was listening to the music. She asked if he liked it, but he said nothing. She wondered if he'd ever speak to her again. The doctor came and announced that he was suffering from dehydration. Dehydration: was it serious? He should go to hospital. She agreed; now she would agree to anything. The doctor took his little hand and he went with him easily, without a struggle. She followed. Immediately after she left him in hospital he started eating. A nurse offered him a glass of milk and a boiled egg. He ate with relish. He was so hungry. There was nothing whatever wrong with him. The doctor rang up and said: 'He's a little weak, but quite well. Nothing to worry about. I have a feeling he was doing it all to spite you, to prove something. Perhaps he's angry with you. Can you think why?'

For a long time she pondered the doctor's question. The words 'to spite you' rang in her mind like a monstrous, clanging bell. Were they at odds, then, he and she? Somewhere far away, she had a glimmer of understanding, but she could never quite put it into words. And perhaps it was just a general sense of inadequacy.

I tried so hard to understand. You were telling me something: did I understand? You stayed in hospital that night. In the morning I came to see you. I made up as best I could, but I must have looked terrible. If you wanted to spite me, you succeeded. I was not angry though. That night, as I lay in bed, I saw your face and I knew how much I loved you. I would do anything to make you happy. You're such a serious person, you don't laugh much, although you make jokes, very good ones sometimes. In those days you laughed more; but there was always something deeply serious about you. When I watched you, asleep, or playing with your fire engine, or just walking along the street, I felt you knew something terribly important, something I'll never know. I don't think you know what I mean, because you're so used to knowing it. But I can tell, even now, when I look at you. You have a great secret inside you, but you're not aware of it. I know, because I haven't got it. Sometimes, when I look at you, you suddenly laugh. And that's the you I saw in my mind when I lay in bed that night. Your face was creased up with laughter, and I saw all your little white teeth. I was desperately afraid of losing you.

Your father was awake; he was worried about you too. He was so pleased to hear you'd eaten an egg and drunk a glass of milk. And I was pleased too, even though you wouldn't eat when I gave it to you. He said: 'I'm sure he's all right, Yvonne. Children do funny things. They go through so many different stages.' He put his arm round me. We had a very big bed. We had to: his body was always so much hotter than mine. In the summer I can't sleep if he's too close; it's like having a red-hot log beside you. I almost jumped when he touched me. But he's my husband: I had to let him. I didn't want to, though; I wanted to think about you, and try to understand what I'd done wrong. But your father's such a determined man; perhaps you get that from him? Anyway, at first I tried to get away from him. I think I kicked him. But he trapped me, even though I said: 'Don't, Henry. I've got to think about Robbie.' He didn't say anything, but he must have felt how I was resisting. I even thought of biting him. After all, you bit me. Oh I know it all sounds childish. But sex is like that; however grown-up we may be, sex turns us back into children. Your father wanted me: do you understand how important that is? Do you too need to be wanted sometimes – at any cost? When I gave in, finally, and allowed him to take me, I think it was the most exciting time I've ever known. I'm glad you can't really hear me now, because we've never talked about sex, and that's how it should be, of course. As for your father, I don't know if I loved or hated him. I still don't know. But that night, I sobbed. I wanted to force my way into his body, just like he was doing to me. I sobbed with all my heart and soul, but you weren't there, so I wasn't afraid of you hearing.

Your father went to sleep, and I was alone again. I spent the whole night awake. That's why I looked so terrible when I came to see you in the morning. I spent a lot of time in your room, by your bed. I wasn't being self-pitying. I was questioning myself. Your father thinks my worries and questions are ridiculous. He could never understand that I felt something between us – you and me – had been broken for ever. For me connections – real connections – between people have always been so tenuous. I feel that the least conflict can snap them. But your father thinks conflict is normal, and necessary between human beings. He is full of confidence. He is a man of power. I don't understand him. Do you? Sometimes, though, a bit of feeling creeps in, something like affection. When that happens I don't altogether like it. He is a little like a crocodile; his affection gives one the creeps. You know what I mean; I am laughing now. If you knew what I'm thinking, we would laugh together. *N'est-ce pas?*

I think you'd understand, now, why I loved him so passionately that night. I hear your playing, and I know you understand about passion, even though you never tell me anything about your life.

I had to think a lot about what happened because I didn't want our relationship – yours and mine – to become a power game. At least I was clear about that. Perhaps I have suceeded. You aren't a sadist or a masochist. Are you? I know I am a sado-masochist, a bit of me sometimes, but only – please only! – with your father.

The little box with your lock of hair didn't help me, that night. It didn't seem to belong to me any more. When I came to the hospital in the morning you were up and walking around. You were very curious about everything. I was afraid of you. But when you saw me you smiled and kissed me. You said: 'Hello Mummy.' You were pleased to see me, weren't you?

I wonder if we ever played that game again: looking into each other's eyes and holding out till one of us laughed. You usually lasted longer than me. I honestly don't think that was a bad game, but I believe you felt there was something incestuous about the way we did it. There. I've said that word now. It's silly to be frightened by words. Words are only words, often misleading. They can put ideas into our heads, and we believe them too easily. Sometimes words create categories that don't really exist. They define everything too sharply. They even create guilt, all by themselves. Surely love is the most important thing?

I thought of you as mine, full of diamonds. But even if I managed to extract a few, I believe you had an endless supply. Listen to your playing. Even if I had the training I could never play like you. Your feelings are much deeper than mine. They have roots. You have more to give, much more.

I think, after that night in hospital, you forgave me. If not, *chéri*, my darling, please forgive me now. All parents make mistakes. We're grown-up now. I so want you to be happy. I've only ever wanted the best for you. I daresay all parents say that. But in my case, at any rate, it's true.

The sound of the soles of your shoes behind me, your immaculate steps, resounds through me like a drumbeat. I am your echoing chamber, emptied, and then filled, by your presence. Unlike me you are not wearing sneakers; *à l'Italienne* you are more elegant. Your feet, which follow mine, have already prepared me, opened me; but I pretend I have not yet noticed you. You'd never guess, would you, that I'm going to be thirty tonight? Nobody knows, except me. I would prefer not to know the date of my birth, like those people in Russia, Georgia, who claim to be the oldest in the world. But I have never been able to forget when I was born. Later, I might tell you it was my birthday. I could admit to twenty-five. But in fact I am very old, I am far older than thirty. Where shall I take you? There's no hurry, is there? Shall we play a little longer? You see I hardly know my way around yet. I can't help smiling. I can't help being pleased with myself for finding this place so soon. It's not easy in a new city. We saw these steps leading up from the main road this afternoon, and the name: Via del Ovino. There was no one here then, but it was a lovely walk. We couldn't get over this little winding path through the trees right in the centre of Rome. Robert was in ecstasies over the beauty of it. So was I. It was such an ideal place. I didn't say a word to him, but I had a strong feeling – and I was right, of course. At night it's amazingly beautiful. It's so perfect I may even have to tell him about it. I'm not sure I could keep it to myself. I'm walking on air. *Je marche sur l'air.* Come on, let's cross this bit quickly. Don't dawdle, the lights are too bright here. But wait a moment: I might go over that wall and have a look. There are trees down there; oh it's steep. I see, there's another path; I might go round to the side and investigate it. There are several people down there. But I can get to it from the other side too. Or I could climb over the wall. Shall I have a cigarette? Not yet. Now, who's this? No thank you. Not really. All right. I'll have another quick look. No. You see, you're a bit old for me. But you have a nice face. Ten years ago I might have said yes. I'll give you another look just to show I'd have said yes ten years ago. There. Did you get the message? It's not your fault you were born at the wrong time. You don't realise, but we're too alike. There's too much of you already in me. What a smile. No, really. I'm sorry. There I've shrugged, but nicely. I don't want to put you off completely. I do want you to think well of me. I won't try to look ugly. I want you to remember me. Don't misunderstand. I like you, it's just time that's against us. You'll find someone that likes men of your age. There are plenty of them. *Capito?* I'll give you a wink. OK? I've got to be going, you know.

There's work to be done. You're lovely. *Ciao*. Don't forget. Come on, don't follow. I've already given you a bit of me. Keep it. I'll give you a last smile, and *basta*. You can think of me tomorrow. OK? Don't take it to heart. Now look what's happened. Where's the boy that was after me before? That's your fault. Quick now, I must find him. Back. Back to where I was. Not so fast, don't make it obvious.

Can't make love to no diamond rings
Give them all to someone else
And what good is one hundred rooms

Eh, *ragazzo*! Look at me, *ragazzo*! You can't resist, you know you can't resist, look at me, for fuck's sake. Can't you see, I'm standing here like this, just for you . . . OK, fuck you, I don't care. You see me shrug? How warm it is, what a wonderful night!

On such a night as this
When the sweet wind did gently kiss the trees
Stood Dido, upon the wild sea banks

Now that just came to me, I wasn't even thinking! I do a bit of Shakespeare with the students sometimes . . . My mind's so clear now, I'm capable of anything! I'm wide open, like a creature with a thousand arms that wants to embrace everything! You, and you, and you, and this perfumed, balm-filled air that's all around me, and those dense, dark trees (what are they, ilexes?) and this high wall with those old lanterns (how many centuries have they been there?) and that flight of steps up which somebody's always climbing, this tortuous little path, and even you, old man, with your bald head, your umbrella (who could bring an umbrella on a night like this?) and the creases on your old Roman face, you're beautiful too (no – don't take my smile too seriously!) and these old cobbled stones, and this little wall along which I scrape my hand for the sheer delight of touching Roman brick and dust, and you, lovely boy, whose hair is rather like mine, just as thick and wiry, and whose ankles I can see now under your flapping trousers as you walk along (no socks, eh?) with those sharp strong tendons cleaving the air like rudders, and the great winding street far below with late cars zipping past, and the plaque up there which says, on white marble, Via del Ovino, this sloping tunnel through the trees, these two little niches in the wall which might have had statues once and which you and I can climb into now, alone or together, and the stars so close! I'm an arrow, shooting up into the sky, and breathing you deep into my lungs, Rome! I'm a calm clear lake for you to bathe in, and I'll never let you go! Now, what's this . . . so, you like me, do you, skinny, funny little fellow, you're sweet, your eyes are a bit like Robert's, all right, I don't mind, I'll follow you behind your tree, you're so serious and worried but I just can't stop smiling, what neat little buttocks, big rough hands too big for you, yes, touch me (you *are* in a hurry), undo my zip, I'll kiss you – no? No kiss? All right *ragazzino*, look I can pick you up, just like that! That's right, I wanted you to smile, oh sweet you've got a tooth missing right in front, come on now, don't be afraid of a kiss, I can't resist teeth like that. Your body's so hard it's like a splinter of rock! What's this, you're talking to me just as I'm trying to kiss you? Your tongue is twitching, vibrating against mine . . . You're Claudio? All right Claudio, talk, go on, I won't stop you. The more I fondle you the more you whisper . . . come on, don't be afraid, no one'll see us, what, you're buttoning up already? Relax, you're a little fox cub, your eyes darting all over the place, look baby, touch me, please Claudio. I'm sure this can't be your first time . . . there now, doesn't that feel good? I'm going to stop you talking, I really am, you make me want to laugh, I feel as if you were tickling me, but I'm going to kiss you so you'll have to shut up, there, you've closed your eyes – heaven, isn't it? – but now they've popped open and you're looking around everywhere like a fox cub again, I'm tame compared to you! I like the way you squirm, but now I'm going to hold you fast, I'm going to pin you down, it's no good struggling! Yes, I know you're Claudio! Don't be afraid, I'm going to make you happy. My name? All right: Giovanni, Jean, I'm French, but my grandmother was Italian, I speak a bit of Italian. Oh, French! That made you smile, yes, it's my first time here, oh I see, if we talk you don't mind me undressing you, eh?

It's all right, we'll talk, we'll pretend nothing's happening, Rome is so beautiful, no, you don't like it? You're from Crotone, where's that? Yes, I'm from Paris, but the most beautiful boys are here, here in Rome, in the Via del Ovino! What lovely proportions you have! I'd never have guessed. You hate Italians? You prefer the French? And the *English*, you like the *English*? There now, you see, nothing in the world to be afraid of . . . London's where you want to go? Yes, I have been there, I know it well, in fact I'm . . . My address? You want my address? Be brave, Claudio . . . not too bad, eh? You're what? Working on *what*? I'm sorry, my Italian's not that good . . . oh I see, for the trains. Electricity cables or something? Up on ladders all day? And you get vertigo? What's the hurry, Claudio, not too fast! I see, your father pushed you . . . of course it's not easy to get a job! No, not in London either! My father? He's dead. Slowly, Claudio, wait, not so fast! What a lovely chest, Claudio. Your mother wants you to come back? To Crotone? Wait, I'm going to come, Claudio, *momento, vengo* . . . what do I do? I'm a teacher. And a writer. Not yet, Claudio! I'm writing a book. Let's come together, OK? Ready, Claudio, are you ready? What about? You want to be a writer too? There – watch me!

You have to catch a bus? Shall I come with you to the bus stop?

And now you have nothing more to say. We walk in silence, under the pines. I ask if the women we pass are prostitutes. You shrug. And here, on our right, is this the Roman Forum? You mutter something and look away. Yes, I say, this is the Roman Forum. You smile, and in the brighter light I see that almost all your teeth are chipped or missing. I am older than you, much older. You are my little friend from Crotone. I leave you at the bus stop. There are other people waiting, you are embarrassed. You pretend you do not know me. Goodbye, Claudio. I turn back once, and see you rubbing your head violently with your big hands.

Now it's time for my cigarette. It's funny, I quite forgot to offer one to Claudio. As I light mine, I can't stop laughing.

Something inside me has been set free. I'm ready for any experience. I laugh loudly and my rough voice ripples through the ocean of air. I laugh again, just to check up on my voice. If I heard a voice like that, I'd like it. Via del Ovino, I say aloud, as I reach the steps and start climbing them again. There is a ruined arch here, a Roman pillar. Someone in a suit is leaning against it and smoking; someone else, younger, trying to attract his attention, weaves through the arch. I watch them; and it's as if I was watching a scene from another age. Those curls could just as well have belonged to an ancient Roman boy. He'd have been wearing a toga, but it could have been just as scruffy as that bomber jacket. And his heart would have been pounding with just the same sort of excitement. He'd have stretched out his arm too and wrapped it round the very same column and stood there, so that the folds of his toga would open slightly. Now it is the tightness of his jeans that sends the same message.

What colour were togas? They were purple, or perhaps white. But Johnny sees the boy in an apricot toga, almost the same colour as the skin of his outstretched arm. Others, older men, would wear purple. He himself, perhaps, would wear white. As he joins again the elegant game of life and death, he belongs to the ancient world. He is filled with love for humanity. These stones have witnessed the passing of civilisations, of religions, of customs, but people have remained the same. Rich or poor, educated or illiterate, masters or slaves, all have been prone to the same feelings. What are these feelings? Johnny knows: they are hope and fear. These are the feelings, he is sure, which govern human life. Are there, really, any others? He himself is a battlefield where fear and hope are continually stalking each other, and his body is the substance on which they feed. Sometimes they devour him utterly, so that his body is gone. And this, in turn, gives rise to a new fear; for he needs bodily love, and without a body himself he is a haunted spirit, departed too soon, eternally in love with what it can never be: mortal flesh, which is the charm of the world. To others, and to himself, he presents a bright, elusive exterior, polished as a diamond, but this image too owes its being to the hope and fear that consume him, sometimes warring, so that one is annihilated, sometimes conniving. But now, standing amid bushes and fractured columns, watching the confused antics of others whose hope is as strong as his own, in this meeting place of past and present, the navel of the earth, he realises that he is not, has never been, alone. He too is part of humanity. He is so happy: Rome has given him the key to understand himself, and so he can understand all others too.

He sees the hesitation of a man who stops and stares, willing someone to join him, but the other walks past, pretending, of course, not to have noticed him. The man scrapes his shoe on the cobbled stones, humiliating himself, imploring: you *can't* go past; but the beloved object is deaf, nothing would induce him to incline his head in that direction; he ambles on, more and more fascinating. Johnny watches: how well he understands both of them, how like himself they both are! The cord which binds them is the cord which binds him too, elastic or brittle, to the objects and people of his world. He thinks, excited: perhaps, one day, I will admit to being thirty! To himself he laughs and says: but not before I'm thirty-five. And for a moment, here in Rome where time matters so little, this deception seems more an enjoyable flirtation, a playful challenge, than a question of mortal significance.

So great is his love for his fellow creatures that he remembers the existence of women. He has no idea what women were like in Roman times, but he tends to see them as washerwomen. There may have been streams pouring down from this steep hill, across the Via del Ovino, and he imagines a procession of women in flowing white gowns and sandals, whose strong calves are just visible, with braided headdresses on which wicker baskets balance, piled high with cottons and silks of all colours. They are like a battalion as they file along the Via del Ovino, in the morning sun, and he, stepping aside to let them pass, eyes them intensely; each graces him with a twinkling glance and a parting of sculptural lips, while heads face forward to hold the baskets in place. And when they reach the water, lower down, where to this day there is a fountain set in a stone pool, they heave down their burdens with a long low cry, part word, part music, and join other women whose washing is almost done, who repeatedly slap the materials onto a flat stone. The sound of this slapping, and the birdsong that accompanies it, would be the same today. Perhaps his mother is one of them. He remembers the name of his mother's village in England. She might pause and turn, sensing for a second his almost invisible presence. The sounds and movements of these women are full of poise, though it is hard to imagine them speaking Latin, that stilted language, as they work in the sunny waters of the fountain. They are happy. Like his grandmother, charming in her photograph, they are in fixed form, a living frieze, and from their separate abode they sigh and glance in his direction. When the washing is over, with the same cry, half music, half language, they toss the baskets once more onto their heads and turn back, single file, along the Via del Ovino. Now their white gowns have water splashes on them, but these are already drying in the sunlight; and the women disappear one by one round the corner of the hill, with soft stately steps, sometimes a hand to steady the basket, never tripping, never straying; the pleated gowns are so still, except when the breeze ruffles them, lifting the edges, as they turn out of sight, so still that one could hardly guess at the movement of the full graceful bodies inside.

For a moment the slope still gleams with their luminous presence, and then they are gone, swallowed by the dark green of the night. Johnny is left with the men and boys, ancient and modern, whose presence is the cause of so much joy and distress. He saw a young man with black curls down to his shoulders and a swarthy, unshaven face, and said to himself: now why should I find a sight like that interesting? He did his very best to detach himself, to watch this person dispassionately. He noticed that, despite his aggressive face, the young man's walk was slightly feminine. There was a subtle undulation in his hips. He looked at the tartan tweed trousers (rather vulgar!), full at the top and narrow round the shoes, and said to himself: there is no reason why these trousers should have any particular meaning for me. What's more, it is stupid to wear tweeds in this hot weather. They give away as little about the legs as the long gowns of the washerwomen. What surprises, what discovery, could these legs possibly hold in store for me?

As the boy dawdled, looking for all the world as if he had landed up on the Via del Ovino completely by accident and had no idea what went on here, there was, certainly, an appealing ripple in the depths of his tweeds. But what was that to him? Johnny thought, delighting in a sort of objectivity he had never quite known before. Did he too not have muscle and flesh? To prove it, he circled his own thigh, at the fullest point, with both hands and tried to make the fingers meet. Impossible, he noticed happily. Despite its thirty years his leg was still strong and healthy. He muttered: I'm as strong as you, and my hair, though not as long (through my own choice), is just as thick. Laughter bubbled to his lips, and he wanted to stick out his tongue and snub him, fingers dancing from his nose. The young man made a languid semi-circular movement with his head, took a comb from his back pocket and set to work on his curls. Johnny could hardly stop himself bursting into laughter. Did he really expect to dazzle the world so easily? This gesture was absurdly Italian, childish as only the Italians know how. He remembered seeing ancient combs in museums, great unwieldy things made of clay, and it would certainly have a bad effect on the silhouette if one had to carry one of these in one's back pocket. But then togas probably didn't have back pockets. Johnny followed the young man's meandering progress, his pointed refusal to acknowledge the looks of passers-by, as if he was an ancient philosopher studying the habits of the twentieth century. Modern clothes, he noted, were more varied than togas, and yet, in a sense, diminishing: trousers highlighted the forked nature of the human body, perhaps its most ridiculous aspect. He thought an ancient philosopher might be highly amused by the sight of trousers. And yet, for Johnny, trousers were essential. The great variety of shapes, zips, buttons, textures, stitching, was a source of continual amazement. Without trousers, the pulling on and off of trousers, trousers right down to the ankles, or arrested, gaping open, just above the knees, legs would lose much of their charm. And belts were highly suggestive. He thought it funny to like trousers so much. Here in Rome clothes, like everything else, became more meaningful. They had a sort of purity, they were archetypal; and dirt and grime added to their significance. In London dirt was just an inconvenience, something to be got rid of, but here it was a sign of life, of action, of human endeavour, like the ancient columns eroded by the grazing of countless hands. In such a place, he thought, it might even be possible to accept old age.

The boy with the long curls was having no luck. There was no one, apparently, to his taste. But he was clearly in a state of need. Johnny, in his post-coital state, could only smile at the urgency of that need. And yet how well he knew it! He realised that cruising was the only thing in his whole life that he had ever done seriously. He had climbed under cubicles in public lavatories, stalked in the Observatory Gardens till dawn, and tried out innumerable methods of seduction. Compared to all that, his language teaching, which he'd been doing regularly for several years, was a bubble of little importance. In fact his language classes too he had mainly thought of as a cruising zone. Perhaps it was this that gave them a certain charm. But now, following the boy's baggy tweeds in the Via del Ovino, he was a philosopher, and he shook his head in wonder at the importance of sex in people's lives. If he had a notebook he would take it out there and then, sit down on a stone, and begin to write; how young he was, compared to Rome, and how much he already had to write about!

He felt so completely sexless that he grew worried. It would be awful if this new philosophical detachment was capable of taking away sexual excitement. The boy's buttocks – Italian buttocks – moving suggestively in front of him, so beautifully contained, should provoke an awakening of life between his own legs; but nothing was happening. Half amused, half panic-struck, he withdrew behind a tree and lowered his trousers, just to make sure that the bulge, on which so much depended, was still there. Reassured, he pulled his pants down too, and stood daringly beside the tree, naked for all the world to see. This was so enjoyable that his member came quickly to life and he stroked it affectionately. With the other hand he explored the contours of his bottom, delightfully full; and immediately came across a bump. This must be a new lipoma, already of some size, which he didn't remember ever having felt before! The graceful, perfectly curving surface was already hideously distorted! Horrified, he pressed with all his might, but the little fatty lump popped back resiliently; its existence could not be denied, it was an incontrovertible piece of evidence against him. He pulled up his trousers and leant against the tree, disconsolate. Philosophy was no defence against the shame of the lipomas. He had been found out: he was a sham. Sweat broke out on his face, and he had no doubt that he was the most horrible, the most monstrous of mortals. He belonged to all the squalid, refuse-filled corners of the world, where like a leper he would cover himself with old bits of newspaper and hide his head. He had no right to be enjoying Rome, the supernatural city; he could never be one of its beautiful, self-assured inhabitants, parading, justly, as peacocks; he could be nothing but a parasite, clinging disgracefully to a glittering tail feather. How could such a thing happen to him? He who was clearly made for beauty and happiness?

The lucky ones filed past, and he saw them through a mist. He felt so helpless. A middle-aged man stopped and stared at him. This man, he realised, desired him. A small part of his enlightenment returned: in the eyes of this man he was still young and handsome. Was it worth prolonging the comedy? Hardly. He looked straight into the man's eyes, and disarmed him. This man was putty. He shook his head sadly. And yet perhaps, in the circumstances . . . Thank you God, he whispered. He stretched up beside the tree, with languid movements; he blinked, like a creature just emerging into a strange new world. On his face, tilted slightly to one side, he bore the expression of one who suspects that this world is full of dangers, but trusts that his innocence will protect him. The transformation was automatic; not a moment's thought intervened. He was as much this new, fresh creature, eyes wide open to the magic of life, as, before, reduced to the state of a worm, all hope abandoned. He thought: I'm cut out to be an actor. Yes, that's what I'll do. I'll make enquiries, as soon as I get back to London. The man approached. He had a kind, greying face: the face of a professor, Johnny thought. He felt no desire for him. The man stretched out his hand, and touched the nape of his neck. He stroked his neck gently, and smiled. This is no time for tenderness, Johnny thought; and he regretted the smile: he could hardly start the intimate business of smiling with this man. He looked away. He saw the boy with the long curls and baggy tweeds walk past. 'Excuse me,' he said to the man, and left him. It was hard to do this, for he understood the man so well. He really didn't want to upset him. He gave him a smile and a little pat on the cheek.

The boy walked so slowly that it was not easy to remain behind. Everything about him that Johnny had found ridiculous now carried extraordinary promise; his lazy movements and self-conscious curls were not, after all, empty narcissism, but indications of awesome superiority. Johnny followed full of trepidation. But the discovery that he was made to be an actor gave him some hope. He started to recite, under his breath: Shall I compare thee to a summer's day? Thou art more lovely and more temperate. Rough winds do shake the darling buds of May but thy eternal summer shall not fade . . . He had no clear idea what this was from. He kept on repeating the words, and they became a marching song, a rising tide, a way of keeping up morale.

He banished the newly discovered lipoma. Once again the Via del Ovino held promise of redemption. Come on *ragazzo*, turn round. Have you seen me? I'm different now. You haven't seen me properly! The young man led him up a steep path, which Johnny had noticed but not yet explored. At the top was a low wooden fence, and beyond a flight of wide steps. The boy hesitated and looked around. His gaze swept past Johnny without pausing. He stepped over the fence and started to climb the stairs, and for a while Johnny watched him, a diminishing figure on the immense staircase, uncertain what to do. Perhaps I should go back to the hotel, he thought. It's late. Robert's waiting. After all, I've had little Claudio. But no; his feet were already on the steps, which he took two or three at a time, thinking: at least this is good exercise, and I'm exploring Rome! And then: there are so many attractive people in the world, and I am stuck with Robert . . .

He flew to the top, just in time to see his prey passing through a loggia, lit by a dim lantern. Johnny followed a little nervously. He reached the door of the loggia (how surprising to find this open at night); and saw the young man descending another staircase on the far side; then crossing a square with a curious white pattern painted on paving stones, and in the middle the statue of a horseman; Rome, I love you, he muttered, as he pursued; the boy was walking much faster now, without a trace of effeminacy. At the edge of the square Johnny caught up with him. A huge space opened up; a small staircase led down into darkness. Far below lay the Roman Forum, a shadowy rectangle in the moonlight, silent, full of wisdom. The boy stopped by an iron railing at the head of the stairs, and looked into the distance.

Johnny stood beside him. They were alone. The boy ignored him. Eventually Johnny said, in French, with his magic grin: 'Rome is so beautiful.' The boy turned, and Johnny saw his eyes. They were heavy, brutal eyes; they frightened him. He snarled: '*Che cazzo vuoi? Mi fai schifo! Sparisci!*' Johnny saw him reach in his pocket, perhaps for a knife; but he was already gone, running across the square with its mounted rider, and up the steps: Fool, bastard, criminal! through the loggia and down the steps on the far side, over the wooden fence, and onto the steep path leading back to the Via del Ovino. He stopped, out of breath and trembling. How he loathed that dull violent face. Immediately, like one trying to forget a nightmare, he started roaming again. The Via del Ovino was almost deserted; he cursed its steep slopes, hurrying from one end to the other and back again. He broke off a branch of oleander and whipped it savagely through the air. Rome had lost its charm: it was peopled by aggressive idiots, like any other city. He stood by the steps that led back to civilisation and sucked a cigarette angrily; he stared down at the road and beyond, at sleeping houses and darkened cafés. But it was impossible to leave. At any moment a perfect young man might still come up these steps.

He waited. Life was, after all, mainly a matter of waiting. He smoked several cigarettes in succession. Were there not hundreds, probably thousands, of people in this city who would jump at the opportunity he was offering? So where were they? At last someone did come; climbed the steps slowly, smoothed and patted his hair into place as if going to a dinner party. It was the kindly grey professor returning. Johnny gave a deep, desperate sigh. He led him to the same tree, demolished him with a look, turned again into a young innocent animal and stretched his limbs. This time he let him have his way. Inside he was laughing, but not a smile crossed his lips.

Afterwards he hurried down the steps, crossed the road, and took a wrong turning. He found himself in a maze of cobbled streets. The cigarettes had made him thirsty. Now he needed one of those little metal drinking fountains that were all over Rome. In his guide book he had read of the purity of the water, fresh springs everywhere. And in fact, there, against a peeling wall, was exactly what he was looking for. Water was continually escaping, but by pressing a bright, brass-coloured button you got a strong jet that flew straight into your mouth. It was infinitely refreshing. He caressed the cool iron of the fountain; how thoughtful to have one here, so near the Via del Ovino. A passing kitten mewed and stared at him in surprise, as if it had never seen a human being before. He remembered the film *La Dolce Vita*, and laughed out loud. 'Baby!' he said, and tried to catch it.

They were the only creatures about. The kitten was not sure if it could trust him; it allowed a little stroking, and even closed its eyes; but suddenly opened them with a squeak and scratched him. He wandered through the streets, holding it tight. Footsteps were approaching from somewhere, echoing sharply in the narrow streets. The kitten was alarmed, pricked up its ears and made a wild jump from his arms. It galloped for shelter into a doorway. The footsteps grew louder and louder, and Johnny prepared himself; but they veered off unexpectedly. Johnny's rubber-soled sneakers made hardly any noise. He stopped, aware of the silence. He didn't feel alone. Tall brick buildings crowded him, their noble windows protected by iron lattices. The streets were alive with people from the past, just like the ruined arches and pillars on the Via del Ovino. He was proud to be a member of the human race, which had created such a city. The whole history of man was imprinted here, recorded in stone, and he was in the thick of it. He walked, shoulder to shoulder, with men and women of the ages, ran his hand over the bricks which they had touched, bricks which had absorbed them and grown great with the infinity of their lives. Countless generations thronged these streets, and they were purified souls, stripped of flesh and blood, wise and solemn as the trees of a primeval forest. In a place like this, he thought, especially at night when the living, with their trivial concerns, make way for the mighty dead, how could one fail to be happy?

The street opened out into a small sunken square. Piazza Mattei, Johnny read. In the centre was a fountain – the very fountain, he realised, which they had seen in the guide book and failed to find! Four naked boys, perching precariously on dolphins, tipped tortoises on upstretched arms into a circular basin above their heads, so they could drink. And the tortoises were scrambling gratefully into the pool, some already safe and sound, others with their little armoured feet dangling desperately over the edge. Water spouted irregularly from the mouths of the dolphins into huge shells, which overflowed into the lower basin and onto the surrounding stone. Empty cigarette packets and coke tins floated around the feet of the boys. Johnny sat on the iron rail which encircled it and watched the fantastic, heaven-sent game. It was heartbreaking that some of the tortoises should have been fixed for ever in mid-air, their tiny heads straining hopelessly for the water, which lay, murmuring, only a few inches away. Johnny walked round the fountain and examined each of the boys in turn. They were all different. One was looking up, almost wearily; he had plump cheeks and was prematurely old. One had a little too much stomach. One smiled too much. The other was perfect. Johnny studied him. He named him: Fabio. He remembered another scene from *La Dolce Vita* and considered climbing into the water. He would caress Fabio's smooth metallic body, from his curls to his nipples, from his soft little member to his toes. He would even stroke his eyeballs. He compared Fabio's proportions to his own. He stepped back to enjoy a cigarette and thought of all the lovely boys he had known, so briefly, so intimately; there was no doubt he had been fortified by them. Certain faces, certain limbs, certain places and sensations were blinding as oases in the scorched desert night; and he could call on them at will. He looked at Fabio and saw that his tortoise was the only one whose mouth actually reached the water: and yet Fabio, unlike the others, still held its tail, affectionately, encouragingly, between the fingers of his upturned hand. Also, there was no doubt that Fabio had the most beautiful nipples. Looking at the immortal fountain boys, fixed in bronze, he thought: I'll never get to the end of it.

The fountain, for all its rustling water, was so still. He saw behind the masterly deceit of the sculptor. He saw the disintegration of the sinuous bodies and their return to liquid metal, and then to rock. The boys despite their youth and grace were dead. Night and day they stared out, unblinking, for centuries; their incipient smiles would never bloom. They could be hacked to pieces and their perfect muscles would not budge in self-defence. No amount of caresses would awaken their virility. They were as tantalising as the flesh and blood bodies that obsessed Johnny's brain. The beauty of the ringleted boy, growing small as he climbed the great steps by the light of a lantern, would remain with him. The crude rejecting language, the brutalised eyes, were almost forgotten already; or rather they seemed to belong to a different person altogether, a real person, perhaps – and they had as little meaning, for Johnny, as other aspects of the real world. His reality lay elsewhere. He looked at the heavenly, lifeless boys and thought: yes, I belong to your world. You are my judges.

He remembered Robert, and was filled with anxiety. He had a kind, sweet lover waiting for him in a cosy room, and the thought terrified him. What was Robert's love compared to the great starlit territory where he roamed? I am not of your world, he murmured, and tears came to his eyes.

He stood up; anxiety gnawed at him. He must go, he must not stay here any longer. He set off at a run and blew a kiss over his shoulder. He crossed the Via Arenula and hurried towards the Campo dei Fiori. He ran as though pursued by devils. The streets were empty; even the souls of previous generations seemed to have fled. The shuttered houses were full of new, sleeping bodies, unconcerned with the past, though steeped in it; refreshing themselves, of this life still, like him. An old man, elegantly dressed, was approaching from the opposite direction. As he passed Johnny he paused, and lit a small cigar. Johnny slowed his pace and examined him. He was bald, fat and ugly; and yet he walked with confidence, he did not hide his head in shame. Johnny thought: some men are considered worthwhile, noble, even great; and yet they can be extremely unattractive, physically, more unattractive than he would ever be, perhaps, despite the ravages of the lipomas . . . In his domain, in the Via del Ovino, for instance, such a man would be scorned and rejected; but by the world at large he might be considered a hero, even a saint. The world did not set too much store by youth and beauty; why was he obsessed by it? But what of Jesus Christ? he thought suddenly. In all pictures Jesus Christ was portrayed as a beautiful young man. Would he have the same appeal if he were a cripple, a leper, or just plain ugly? Western civilisation was in love with Jesus Christ; was it conceivable to think of him as ugly? '*Buona notte*,' he said to the old man, and the noble pendulous lips muttered something in reply.

It was hard to penetrate the human mind.

The night-watchman had obviously been woken by the bell, but Johnny did not feel guilty: it was his job. He smiled at him, aware of the sudden snap of his lips, as if they had been stuck together. The lighting on the stairs was dim: a single decrepit bulb hung from a cobwebbed ceiling. He hummed as he climbed, pleased with the raucous vitality of his voice. 'Shh! *Zitto!*' he heard the night-watchman call. He shook his head, and shouted back cheerfully: 'OK! *Buona notte!*' It was much too loud, and the man grumbled again. He walked along the landing with resilient strides, careful to prevent his rubber soles from squeaking on the lino. His encounter with the elegant old man was the final touch to the night's adventure; like the last lines in a play of genius which unexpectedly shifts the perception of the whole.

Naturally, the door to their room groaned as he opened it. He paused on the threshold until he could hear Robert's regular breathing; then closed the door with great care and went into the bathroom, where he undressed completely and washed from top to toe, avoiding the mirror. It felt good to be clean. He slid into bed and lay still, waiting for sleep. There was a little terrace garden, in the middle of the hotel, outside the window; a lamp was burning there, and sent oblique shafts through the shutters. Johnny's eyes refused to close. He looked at Robert. He felt no trace of superiority, as he sometimes did, the superiority of the wakeful. He was struck by the enormous difference between the waking and sleeping states, between his and Robert's, and the mysterious ease with which one could pass from one to the other. He found it curious, too, that people wake in the morning and are exactly the same as they were the night before; one would expect great transformations, even mutations, to take place during those strange hours. Sometimes he was so wide awake that he seemed to have forgotten how to sleep; he can hardly believe he has ever been asleep, the state seems so alien; at such times he is all jagged consciousness; faces, events and words clatter through his head like a crowd of restless ghosts. It would be so good to sleep now. Has he not deserved it?

He gets up, and sits on the side of Robert's bed. He puts out a hand, a little clumsily, and lays it on his cheek. He feels the stubble; it seems to cover the entire face. Robert stirs, and opens his eyes. Johnny looks into them, then closes his own. It seems so long, so very long, that so much has intervened, since he last saw him. Robert dislodges a sleepy arm, and puts it round his shoulder. Johnny notices how slow he is, and the arm is like an old stick without any sap. The fingers, which rub his neck a little, remind him of the bark of the trees on the Via del Ovino. Were these the same fingers which could fly across the piano keys?

'Are you all right?' said Robert.

'Of course. Are you?' He paused. 'I'm sorry to wake you. I didn't intend to wake you.' His voice sounded strange to himself. 'I had a wonderful time. I was walking about, and I came across the fountain.'

'Which fountain?'

'The tortoise fountain. The one we were looking for. It's lovely. I'll show you tomorrow. You'll like it.'

Johnny wished he could stop talking like this. His heart was bursting. He had experienced so much; he wanted to share some of it, at least, with Robert. But how? He said: 'I just couldn't stop wandering around. You know me, how I love the night. But Rome is something else. It's like nowhere I've ever been before.'

'Yes.'

'I feel I belong here. I feel I should have been born here, and grown up here.'

'Well you are partly Italian.'

Was that what it was? Did he really belong here? He no longer knew. The thought of belonging anywhere alarmed him. Then he realised that it was long past midnight, and so his birthday. He was thirty years old.

'It's my birthday,' he said.

He saw Robert smile, allowed himself to be drawn closer, and received a kiss on the lips. 'Happy birthday, Johnny!'

'Doesn't time fly, these days? At this rate I'll soon be thirty!' he laughed.

'I don't mind how old you are.'

Perhaps it was true.

'Anyway, I expect I'll die young.' He thought: yes, it's better if I die young. Before the lipomas take over completely. This actually seemed like a solution, the best solution.

'I don't want you to die young.'

'Well, one doesn't have much to say in the matter, does one?' He lay down on the bed and yawned. 'You know,' he said, 'while I was sitting looking at the fountain, I found another lipoma.'

'Another what?'

'You know – my little bumps. I came across a new one – just like that. A birthday present.'

'What do you mean – you came across one?'

'On my arm.'

'What little bumps?'

'Don't be silly. You know what I mean.'

'Oh yes,' said Robert slowly.

Johnny scrutinised him in the dark.

'I don't want you to be sorry for me,' he said in a hostile voice. He stood up and went to the window. 'I like these pots, these old earthenware pots.'

'I'm sorry, Johnny, I don't know what you're talking about. I don't know about these bumps.'

Johnny turned and shook his head. 'You're my lover,' he said icily. 'You've been my lover,' he corrected. 'Don't pretend.'

Robert sat up. 'I'm not pretending!'

'Have you forgotten the plasters? On my back?' he shouted at him.

'Oh, the plasters. The little bumps. I remember.'

'Well, that's what I'm talking about!' he shouted.

'What of them? They're small, and you say they're harmless.'

'Of course they're harmless!'

'So what's the fuss about?'

'I'm not making a fuss.'

There was silence. Then Robert said: 'I see. You think they're ugly.'

'Well, not really ugly, but . . .'

'But what?'

He was torn between two opposing forces. Flippant, joking words came bubbling to his lips. He would start to tease Robert now. He smiled and winked at him. But he bit back the words. After all, he no longer thought of him as his lover. Could he perhaps risk giving in to that other powerful temptation, the temptation to confess? What did he have to lose? Was he afraid of Robert? Of his scorn? That he would never again want to make love to him? But the excitement that he, Johnny, had once felt, in the Observatory Gardens, had long passed. It no longer mattered whether he had sex with Robert. But what did Robert feel? Did Robert still find him attractive? And if so, could he afford to confess? He might still lose him, lose his desire, even if he didn't want it, by showing how he was gradually, irrevocably, turning into a leper, an outcast . . . On the other hand, was it possible, just possible, that he was exaggerating?

Robert was waiting.

Johnny looked at him and opened his mouth. He opened it wide and held it; until his saliva ran dry and the intake of breath tickled his gums. Then he winked and began to make clucking noises like a chicken. He flapped his elbows like wings and said: '*Sono un pollo arrosto.*'

Robert took hold of his wings and led him, crowing like a cock, back to the bed. 'Giovannino,' he said. 'Just in case you're worried, even a little bit, I want to tell you. Your little bumps don't bother me at all. I'd completely forgotten about them.'

Johnny went on clucking and crowing as Robert removed the towel he was wearing and laid him under the sheet.

'Shut up, Johnny.'

It was terrible. He was afraid of what might happen if he stopped being a chicken. He would be far more naked than a chicken, even than a plucked chicken, ready for the pot. He changed his clucks into cooings, like a pigeon, and nuzzled Robert's collarbone. 'What's a pigeon in Italian?' he asked.

He felt Robert's hand on his stomach, and lay absolutely still, like an animal in danger pretending to be dead. Robert was much too close. He said to himself: Be brave. You must go through with this. To his surprise, he felt a slight sexual stirring in his own body. But it was intolerable.

'Robert,' he said, sitting up. 'I don't feel well. I've had indigestion all this time.' He climbed out of bed. 'It's suddenly got worse.' He limped to the bathroom. 'It could be that pork we had. Sorry, baby. I won't be long.'

When he came out of the bathroom, almost half an hour later, Robert seemed to have fallen asleep again. In any case he was lying very still, on his side. Johnny went quietly to his own bed. It would soon be morning now, and there could be no escape: his thirtieth birthday. He sighed; perhaps he could confess even this to Robert. He looked at the big soft boy asleep across the room, and felt enormous affection for him. 'You're a sweet baby,' he whispered. 'And it's so nice you like my little rabbits.' He almost believed it.

His mind was racing. A few weeks ago he had met a boy in the Observatory Gardens who had fascinated him. This boy was all boots, braces and torn jeans: an archetype. He had refused Johnny at first; but then, with a clever shift of personality, a new, calculated expression, Johnny had won him. Afterwards, the boy pulled on his clothes roughly and said: 'I could murder a cigarette.' Into these words, and the way they were spoken, everything that Johnny found most desirable was violently compressed. As he offered the boy his packet of Rothmans he got an erection again. They lit their cigarettes and parted with a handshake. Naturally, he never saw him again. Instead he was with Robert, and this in itself was a mystery. Robert, to whom, perhaps tomorrow, he would confess that he was already thirty years old. The big soft boy would know all about him. And he, Johnny, uncovered, out in the bright light, would never desire him again.

Was it possible that he could only make love to strangers?

He was aware, then, of the extraordinary gulf that separated him from the rest of the world. Only to strangers? he whispered in astonishment. Is that a tragedy?

Yes, it's a bit of a tragedy . . . He seemed to be looking into this great gulf, this abyss, and it was peopled far below with many little creatures, goblins, imps and sprites, who leapt nimbly about, cavorting, somersaulting and leapfrogging, covered in scales some of them, like lizards, with forked tongues which gleamed, electric, iridescent, in the dark . . . almost immediately he was deeply asleep; with a suddenness that was most unusual, it would have surprised him.

But he was so very tired.

The stage is framed with slabs of rose-coloured marble; above it, in a domed vault, a youth (with genitals delicately obscured) pays rapturous homage to the sun while a naked nymph looks on wistfully and a druid scribbles. Below, the pianist plays. Vases of tall solemn flowers mark the corners of the sacred platform. The concert is nearly over. Hats and coats will soon be on, bodies will uncurl, lips will part, words will tumble forth, hands will be shaken and cheeks kissed. But now, still, they are quiet. There is a great silence in the hall: the silence of the audience. Daniel looks at the rows of bobbing heads in front of him, each a solar system of its own, capped with a mop of hair, enormous in its variety: grey, blond, white, curly, straight, black, thick or thin. But why should human beings have such a tumultuous growth on the summit of an almost hairless body? Why this crowning glory? From an objective point of view a bald pate, or perhaps a sparse covering, would be more in keeping with the rest of the anatomy. And yet hair is lovable. From his distant seat he watches the pianist's hair as it flops forward, accompanying his efforts. The playing is full of effort; there is violence in the way Robert grapples with the piano, as if it were a creature difficult to tame. This might be a failing on the part of the pianist. On the other hand the fight is exciting. The Schumann Fantasy emerges from chaos like a creature struggling for life, still wet from its birth pangs.

Just as he is thinking this, the music bursts into his life. A separating curtain lifts and he is no longer an observer. Even Robert's grimaces, his awkward movements, the sweat that drips down his cheeks, is no longer an interesting phenomenon; it is part of him too. He sees it all through smiling, half-closed eyes. The music cuts through the surface of life; it breaks the monotony of days and nights, of small predictable pleasures and pains – in which music too has its usual, appointed place: a shaft of nostalgia illuminating, for the length of a record, the drab routine. Suddenly this music defies all preconceptions. Although the notes are so fleeting, the tension created between them so fragile, they interrupt the march of time, in all its pomposity, and hold it in abeyance. Time, linear time, and the despair that depends on it, retreats like an offended turkey. He realises, and remembers, that he loves Peter. The music has uncovered inside him the region where real life, the part of life that really seems to matter, takes place. It reminds him of all that he has forgotten: it reminds him of himself. He reaches over the arm-rest, into the empty seat beside him, and imagines it filled with Peter's presence. His fingers move, as he imagines touching Peter's hand; the hand that has driven tractors in the steamy vegetation of Zimbabwe, that has tenderly caressed his prick, that will one day give the body of Christ into believing mouths, that is expert in the use of a condom. Peter's hand: full of buoyant, independent life, strong and warm, which chooses to mingle with his own crooked fingers. How can this be? He knows, at this moment, that Peter is the greatest, and most unexpected, gift of his life. He cannot put off commitment any longer.

But he is so afraid. The music shows him this, too. The notes seem to tremble, to hesitate; but they have an inner strength, a force of conviction which is not ashamed. He realises that he has never, never trusted his own emotions. And yet Peter is waiting for him. He is here, beside him, in the empty seat. Does the world really have to be such a dark, cynical place? Does he really want it to be like that? Is it so very difficult to stand up, alone, face the world and say: this is me? If he does, the earth will not open and swallow him. There will be no disasters, no hurricanes, no volcanic eruptions, no murders even. The melody, in Robert's hands, leads him on, and the pianist's commitment fills him, little by little, with courage. And a wealth of memories reveal themselves. Peter is real, and the love he offers is real too, though incredible. How can he possibly refuse it?

Retrospectively he discovers his feelings: lying in bed, eyes closed, the feel of Peter's skin, so different, touching his own; sitting silently opposite him on the Tube and watching his eyes fill with their own thoughts; walking through London and hearing the tender thud of his shoes on the pavement beside his own: moments, he knows, at which Peter, though separate, is with him; it is he, Daniel, who tries to block him out. Moments of pure happiness which he has never quite allowed himself to feel, moments at which, with a little more trust, a little more confidence, the ice inside him would dissolve of its own accord.

He smiles, and thinks: yes, I am melting . . .

And it seems to him that this is not just another of his tricks, it is not clever enough to be one of his ideas; this time perhaps something is really happening. He stares at the pagan frieze in the dome above the piano, and tries to catch hold of this moment, to make it tangible. He feels quite at home now in this curious place, the Wigmore Hall, half temple, half morgue; and affectionate towards the listening heads in front of him, each of them, perhaps, as full of contradictions as his own. He hardly wants to listen any more; the music is too much, he will have to block his ears – and he fingers them, those grotesque loose ears, which stick out like mushrooms from a tree trunk; he understands now, he must be brave and accept what life so surprisingly has offered him. He says it out loud: Peter.

I sleep much better now, *chéri*, and you don't have to worry about me. Quite a few years have passed, and nothing terrible has happened! I'm fifty-seven years old and fit as a fiddle. I wonder if you've already reached the age when you realise you're not immortal. It didn't happen to me till I was about forty, but then I think I've always been a bit retarded. And when you were a child I was so happy that I never thought of death. Except when you were starving yourself that one time. I can't express how happy your playing tonight has made me. The Wigmore Hall is so intimate, it's almost as if you were playing for friends, in a drawing-room. It is strange that I should talk to you like this, silently, while you're playing. I've never done it before. It's happening in a separate part of my mind, and it doesn't stop me listening. I'm not really thinking all these words; it's more like a state of mind, which your playing puts me into. You see, as you get older, life becomes much less interesting. You simply have to accept the routine of it all, and that some things, which you always thought were the most important things of all, are not going to happen. It's hard to know exactly what those things are. Your playing reminds me of them, but it also helps me to accept their absence. That seems like a paradox. As you get older you realise just how many paradoxes there are in life, and you realise, gradually, that you've got to accept them.

I've got far more confidence now than when I was young, far more than when you were young. But I've also lost the feeling of being really alive – of being desperately alive. I'm alive now, but I don't care about it. This morning I got another prescription for sleeping pills from my doctor. I hardly ever need a pill for sleeping these days. When I get new pills I put them away in a drawer in my desk, the same drawer where I keep mementoes of you. I've still got the locket with your hair in that drawer, some photographs which I never stuck into our family album, and nearly all the letters you've ever written to me. There are a lot of different pills in there now, all different colours, in different shaped bottles and some enveloped like bubbles in stiff silvery card. Before going to see the doctor today I took a lot of trouble with my make-up. I put on quite a lot of rouge, but left my lips completely bare. I wanted good old Doctor Selson to see that I was under some stress, but took pains to cover it up. I wanted him to think I was a positive, happy person underneath. He was surprised when I told him that I'd already finished the pills he gave me last month. I told him that your father snored regularly these days. He said: 'Have you considered sleeping separately?' I replied: 'Oh Doctor, we already have twin beds, but I just couldn't move into another room. I do think, for me, it would be a sort of defeat. Henry and I have always been so very close. Sleeping together is very important for us.'

'Why don't you have the bed in the spare room made up, so you can move in there if necessary? When his snoring really keeps you awake?'

I told him: 'Of course I do sometimes. But to tell you the truth, it makes him so unhappy. I don't blame him for snoring. Sometimes I give him a little push, and he turns over and it's all right. But sooner or later he always starts up again!'

'What about ear plugs?' he asked.

'I've tried them too,' I said laughing, wondering if he was serious. 'But I don't like them. They make one feel completely cut off. And then I do love hearing the birds in the morning. I don't mind waking up early. At my age you don't need too much sleep. I just need something to help me get off.'

Then I told him about your concert tonight. He said he might try and come. (He hasn't, of course.) He told me about his children: one's a doctor, and his daughter's studying at art college. We chatted about modern painting. Dr Selson is so sweet. I asked if he had a vacancy for you, because it's so important to have a good doctor. But you're not ill much, are you? In the end he gave me some more dalmane. I've got them here in my bag. Darling, that little phrase you just played is one I love particularly. It is so exciting. Perhaps I will have to take a dalmane tonight! You might want one too. It must be hard to sleep after giving a big concert. I must remember to ask if you want one. Your father thinks a sleeping pill is all right, now and again. But he doesn't know about my arsenal!

I would like you to know, *chéri,* that I really do think of you as a grown-up person nowadays. I sometimes think you grew all that hair on your body just to let me know that you're a man.

It seems to Yvonne that the concert has been going on for a very long time. She notices that Henry's eyes often linger on the back of Flavia's head. I expect he'd like to operate on her, she thinks. But she feels quite confident. She is a married woman, and time has proved that Henry will not leave her. Marriage is a blessing. Human emotions are so volatile, and we're really at their mercy, but a marriage contract is wise and trustworthy. She believes that it is very unlikely for a relationship to last without marriage. And that, she thinks, must be a terrible problem for poor homosexuals. She and Henry are like two trees of quite different species which happen to have been planted close together. They get in each other's way, annoy each other often, but they also protect each other. Two are far better than one. Originally, as saplings, they seemed to have something in common. So they settled down together, much to everybody's approval. Their roots became entwined, and that was that. It's really a very earthy type of union! Their roots are entwined, so it doesn't much matter that they turned out to have such different foliage. But what of poor homosexuals? They should get married too, she thinks; to women who wanted 'convenience marriages', for one reason or another. Then each partner could sprout his own foliage. Society would accept them much more easily. Society is mostly concerned with appearances. And they themselves would feel so much more secure.

It is the security of her marriage which has permitted her to grow up. She recalls scenes of tenderness with Henry. Sometimes, even now, especially when he is leaving for work in the mornings, she flirts with him blatantly. At breakfast she wears, from time to time, a low-cut robe which reveals her cleavage. He is often preoccupied with the operations he will have to perform. So she teases him at breakfast. Often she uses Monsieur Pischik, her Pekinese. Last week she bought a fake dog turd. She placed it on the floor, close to his chair. Now, in the concert hall, she remembers this suddenly, just as Robert begins the final page of the Fantasy, in which the theme reappears with new, wonderful harmonies, and giggles to herself.

She placed it on the floor, just beside his chair, and he sat down without noticing. Henry was in his most efficient, no-nonsense mood. He was scanning *The Times*, and eating toast and marmalade. She brought him his coffee (she is completely at home in the kitchen nowadays) and uttered a shriek. Henry hardly stirred. 'Oh Monsieur Pischik!' she cried. 'Don't move, darling.' 'Bloody dog,' muttered Henry. She fetched some kitchen paper, scooped up the turd, and dropped it clumsily into Henry's lap. 'Yvonne!' he shouted, as she groped for it amid the folds in his trousers. No sooner recaptured the turd fell again, this time onto his plate, right into the marmalade. He stood up, so angry that he was about to knock the whole thing off the table. And her helpless laughter made him even more furious. She leaned backwards, shaking, the bathrobe revealing much of her breasts, which were not at all bad. She loved and feared his anger. Then he understood. He picked up the turd and approached her. He held it, covered with marmalade, over her cleavage. His face was utterly blank, and at the same time full of meaning; she saw him out of slitted, tear-filled eyes. He dropped the turd. Adroitly she moved aside, and it fell, once again, to the floor. They returned to their newspapers and finished breakfast in silence, while Monsieur Pischik barked wildly.

I am sorry, darling. Nothing could be more embarrassing than this story, and I am ashamed. It was, of course, a sexual game, and so at the time it was reassuring. Do you understand what I mean? I realise that, just now, I was thinking about homosexuals, putting them together into a category, as if you were not one. But I know that you are: and yet you belong to no category. For me you will never belong to a category. I do not even know if you are happy or sad. You are a mystery to me. Nothing about you is made clearer by knowing that you are a homosexual; it is not even something about which I think very much. Just occasionally I look at you and think: my son is homosexual, he carries a dark secret. I am not sure if this fact brings us closer together, or drives us apart. Perhaps it does both.

She knows the Fantasy is coming to an end, and she feels she must assemble all the most important aspects of her life before it is over. She must collect the straying pieces and put them together. The combination of Schumann and her son (both of them Robert) has cast a spell over her. They have loosened her mind, and memories of her life surge to the surface, in a similar way, perhaps, to the last moments of a drowning man. Although she is not drowning. And she remembers The Witness.

Listen, darling: this is my confession. Many years ago, when you were at school, The Witness called at our flat. He was wearing a dark suit, a white shirt, and a very ordinary tie. He introduced himself as a Jehovah's Witness. I said: 'I thought you always went about in couples,' and laughed. He answered, without smiling: 'Yes. But my colleague is sick today'. He had sullen, expressionless eyes. His face was very unemotional, his flesh seemed fixed; when he talked it hardly moved at all. He asked me a few questions about the Bible, and so on, in a slow monotonous voice, and I was aware that my coffee, in the kitchen, was boiling. It was one of those Italian coffee machines, and I could hear it hissing and gurgling. I interrupted him and said I had to go and switch it off. He stopped in mid-sentence, and smiled. It was a very small smile, only a slight lifting of the lips on one side – the left side, I think. He stood there, filling the doorway. And I invited him in, for a cup of coffee.

Perhaps he was only masquerading as a Jehovah's Witness. I have often thought about this, and I am not sure. It is not true to say that his face was immobile, unchanging. In fact he responded very subtly to the situation. He registered everything that was happening, everything that I said. There were tiny changes in the way he looked at me. These tiny changes fascinated me. He was like a well of secrecy, a deep well, into which you drop things that vanish for ever with the softest of plopping sounds; and the surface is completely smooth again. He was the most secret and sensual man I have ever known. We never even knew each other's names. For me the anonymity of it was quite breathtaking. I would never have guessed that his sober, ill-cut suit concealed such a magnificent body. I think it was the only time I have ever really appreciated the beauty of a man's body. I remember thinking, as we made love, that I'd never been so violently happy in my life. (Of course, when you were born, I was just as happy, but in a different way.) It was a frightening happiness, because it revealed to me an abyss, a chasm. Suddenly I felt that nothing, nothing at all (except perhaps you) prevented me from being an alcoholic, a drug addict, a nymphomaniac, even a criminal. He was The Witness.

When Henry came home that night I was full of affection for him, I listened to the account of his day's work with passionate concern. I realised how much I valued him and was quite prepared to forgive his lack of interest in the television programme I was watching: a concert by Giulini, I remember.

The Witness came back, in the same suit, the same tie; I was so pleased to see him. The fact that he wanted to be with me again was an extraordinary, frightening gift.

He came back a third time; and I refused him. Three times was too much: I turned him away at the door.

The Witness became part of her family constellation; he, Henry and Rob had their appointed places, and all three were necessary for her well-being. If she was a planet, they were her moons. By my moons I am reflected, she thinks. For years afterwards, when she exchanged glances with a strange man, she dubbed him, in her mind, 'The Witness', and this name was enough to send a strong current through her body and transform the world into an exciting place. One of her aching regrets was that the episode never repeated itself; not with The Witness himself, for he had become a symbol, and it was better that he should stay that way, but with other strangers. Men were sometimes fascinating, until you got to know them. But perhaps she was too frightened to let it happen again.

It is the vividness of the concert, and the unforgettable sight of Rob playing his heart out, that brings back to her mind the years of secret cohabitation with The Witness. But now they are past, and so are her years of intimacy with Rob. Only Henry remains. If she could live completely in the past, in the heady concoction that the past has become, perhaps she could be happy. But like everybody else she is condemned to the present. She sleeps well now; she is less troubled by anxiety. Does she really regret the past, the long years of agitation and vague hopes?

Peace is being thrust upon her, but she cannot accept it. Listen to Schumann's Fantasy, the melody close to the end which seems both to rise and to fall, which is, in its own way, an acceptance of fate. Could she not do the same? Yes, she has her fate, but no melody to go with it. Where is her melody – did she not have one once? She clenches her fists, and prays to Rob. Perhaps if she could fix this happy evening in her mind for ever, his début at the Wigmore Hall, she will be saved. But she believes that it will evaporate, retreat into a distant corner, like all other evenings, and dinner afterwards, which she has prepared with such care, will be consumed and forgotten like all other dinners. She will fill her days with telephone calls, shopping and cooking, and people will admire her and find her entertaining. Perhaps you, darling, will become famous. And perhaps, without you knowing, your success will become my melody too. I believe you will not want to share it with me. I will follow you from afar. I am spoilt, darling, I have so much to be thankful for. But please, don't abandon me. I know we see each other often, we have meals together, we often speak on the phone. But something is missing. I want you to look at me again. Is it a lot to ask? It is such a small thing, something you used to do so often, every day, several times a day. Just look at me: without first closing yourself off. I am like an instrument, which has learnt to be perfectly in tune with you. I respond immediately to your eyes, just as a piano responds to your touch. When you play the piano you are never distant, never cold, you never shut your heart; it is ridiculous, darling, but at this moment I am desperately jealous of that piano.

Now it has passed, my hysteria. I have remembered my

place. I appreciate and respect your independence. I have, after all, my little secret adventure: collecting sleeping pills. Do not worry; I will not use them. And if I use them, you will not be to blame. I exonerate you completely. I must insist, darling: you are not to blame for anything. I do not think about using them. I do not even know, for instance, what would be the best combination. They are weapons of defence, only defence. I am worried now, that I have said too much; between us it has never been necessary to say everything. I would never tell you, for it is too shameful. And yet. I do not understand it, but the pills fill a gap in my life. Perhaps they are the dark, fearful side which I cannot do without. Perhaps they give me confidence, because they prove that I can deceive the doctor and hide something from Henry. Perhaps they are my independence, because they give me control over my fate. Perhaps they are a substitute for love. I do not know. It's as if we were a triangle: you, me and them. I do not mean that literally. It is the sort of association that sometimes happens in a dream. This evening, for me, is like a dream: a happy one.

It's over. Everybody is clapping, and you are bowing, shy and charming as always. Some people are shouting bravo, and I long to, but it wouldn't be right. Your father has just taken my hand and squeezed it. I look into his face and he is quite flushed with pleasure. We are both clapping madly, and we're so proud.

Robert surveys himself in the long mirror. A serious, sweaty face, and a body on which the tail coat hangs well. There is no obvious reason for dismay. The signed photographs on the wall, of great musicians, do not oppress him. He feels neither gloom nor euphoria. He drinks a glass of water and walks slowly up and down the room. If he were now to go back to the stage and play the Fantasy all over again, it might even be a pleasure. He would call the public back and say: 'Now I will play for you.' The concert was a first test, which he had come through alive. The music is still inside him, lurking, waiting. He hears the swing door open, voices and steps on the stone stairs.

Now, once again, real people surround him. Friends and acquaintances queue up to greet him, and the room begins to buzz like a party. There is no reason to suspect all these words of praise, these smiling faces. Nobody is obliged to come and congratulate him. Do they have an ulterior motive? He shakes hands, laughs, kisses, chats. He will try to believe them. It is true that he can play much better. Is it perhaps possible that these people think he has played well? If so, would this be good or bad? He feels a strong desire to explain that this was not, by any means, his best playing, that the piano was unresponsive, etc. To one admirer he says, quite untruthfully: 'I've been ill for three days: I wasn't even sure I'd be able to play at all . . .' This is greeted with sympathetic surprise. He is not ashamed of the lie; he is being no more deceitful than this host of smiling faces. Two opposite views of human nature were equally possible: one cynical, the other trusting. If he relaxes, these people are good friends who only want the best for him. But tiny, unidentifiable signs cause him to put up his defences: then his well-wishers become tormentors. It was extraordinary how the atmosphere could fluctuate; one moment he is being condemned, the next taken for a hero. And yet the words are the same.

He sees Flavia talking to someone he does not recognise, and then realises it is Daniel. He trembles, as if the concert were beginning all over again: perhaps Peter has come too. Is it possible, he thinks, to seduce someone by the power of your playing? Could artistic admiration become desire? Would the physical accidents of nature no longer count so much – beautiful eyes, for instance, which mislead you to think there must be a corresponding depth within; or small, bespectacled eyes, which, for all the greatness of soul, remain inexpressive . . . but his own eyes, in fact, are all right, it must be something else which Peter finds repulsive. But where is he? No, he is not here.

Henry approaches. He smiles at his son, feeling at the same time that this is a repetition of something that has already happened. Yes, it's true: this Wigmore Hall début is so much in the order of things that it belongs already to the past. So much has led up to this – and yet it is only a beginning – wheels, long ago, that were set rolling, and now nothing can stop them: that I, a sadist, should have married Yvonne; that she, a masochist, should have married me; that she with her 'artistic sensibilities' should have a son like Rob; that he should turn out to be a homosexual pianist with a strong Oedipus complex; that with a father like me he should find it difficult to express his feelings, and that, with a mother like Yvonne, he should try desperately to do so; and so on, for ever. Is there nothing in all this, nothing at all, that perhaps *is* unpredictable, some tiny element of free will, something a little bit more interesting than a mathematical equation? He takes Robert's hand in both of his, and opens his mouth to speak. 'My dear old boy,' he says, feeling the first smile still on his lips, 'the Fantasy was terrific. We were enthralled.' Robert looks at him with those eyes which, though different, are like Yvonne's, and they are both automatically locked into their roles: he knows, once again, that he is being searched for something he does not possess, that whatever words he uses they are never quite right, and so, like a mirror, brilliant and innocent, he reflects the light of those eyes back where it belongs, and says: 'You could see how hard everybody was listening. They were all moved. And I was moved too. Even me.' 'Oh good,' Rob says. 'Isn't it a wonderful piece?'

He moves away. He will dare, now, to speak to Daniel. Flavia, talking to him, is laughing, as she always does with a new acquaintance. There is no doubt that Daniel is very interesting. His ugliness is positively beautiful. His features have simply been gathered from the corners of the earth and flung haphazardly together; he is the result of a curious collision. Looking at him you could lose your bearings. The design of the human face is no longer something you can take for granted. You realise that noses could just as well be the other way up, or the position of eyes and mouth reversed . . . Robert moves towards them.

Someone pulls at his arm, and he turns to see his mother.

Strangely, he had quite forgotten about her. He takes her by the shoulders and kisses her warmly on both cheeks. Her lips part, and he sees that the creases around her mouth have deepened. She smiles, and he is drawn into that small opening, the opening of her smile. 'Darling,' she says, 'you played like a real artist. Your interpretations are always so *interesting*. And you seem so sure, so confident. One never has to worry.' He feels her brave, slender shoulders, which he grasps, far below his own. 'Yes,' he says, to his own surprise, 'the Fantasy went quite well, didn't it?' And her pleasure, her happiness, persuades him that, after all, he did not play badly, that something worthwhile has come across. 'Have you ever heard me play so well?' he asks. It is a long time since he has asked her opinion about anything. 'I don't think so,' she replies. 'And now I feel sure you will go from strength to strength.' He knows that she means it, and that she is happy; and her happiness, in fact, is so important to him. For she really loves him, and if there is anything at all he can depend on, it is her love.

Mrs Schwarzenberg, a large woman with hair like a bronze helmet, pushes to the front. 'Excellent! Excellent playing!' she cries, her mouth wide open, in the depths of which, from his great height, he sees ranges of gold fillings sparkling with foam. The huge figure of her husband, the conductor, is upon him too; he takes Robert's hand and mutters something with a bemused air. 'Ve are coming for dinner!' exclaims Mrs Schwarzenberg simultaneously, rolling against his mother. 'I won't stay, darling,' says Yvonne. 'I must go home and get everything ready. You come in your own time.' 'By the way,' he says. 'I'd like to bring Flavia.' 'Of course, *chéri*.' He kisses her again. How pleased he is to have invited Flavia. He knows his mother doesn't like her. But she points to the picture on the wall, of the woman with the peke in her arms, and bursts out laughing. Isn't she upset? She must be thinking that Flavia will spoil the evening. He looks at her for signs of distress, or annoyance, but sees none. 'I'll come with Flavia,' he says again, afraid now of upsetting her. He realises his power. It is she who depends on me, he thinks, not the other way around. 'See you later,' she mouths happily from the door, with a wave. His father takes her arm, and he hears them clattering down the stairs.

Flavia is there, smiling at him. 'I'm so pleased to see you,' he says, and then to Daniel: 'Is Peter here too?' He doesn't wait for an answer. 'The Fantasy wasn't too bad,' he says, and lifts Flavia clean off the ground, to make her laugh. 'Peter couldn't come,' says Daniel, 'but I came. Your playing reminded me of the things that really matter.' 'Oh I wish it had done the same for me,' Robert laughs, and puts Flavia down. She pretends to fight, pummelling him with her tiny fists. 'Did you like the concert?' he asks. 'I don't think I've ever heard you play so beautifully,' she says. 'Oh but I can play much better than that!' He realises how much he depends on the good opinion of others. And he must always promise more. 'There were too many wrong notes,' he says frowning. 'Oh yes, but the right ones were very good!' Daniel is retreating. 'I shall remember your playing,' he says. 'And perhaps we'll meet again. I must go now – Peter is waiting at home.'

Flavia's gaze is quite luminous, like the picture, on the wall, of Kathleen Ferrier. Her eyes are so full of love, and her face blooms, like a perfect fruit. 'Flavia,' he says, 'can you bear having dinner with my parents? It might even be amusing – if we're there together.' She laughs, in anticipation. The last of the phantom crowd has gone, and, for fun, they examine the old photographs together. There is no hurry. Eventually they set off, arm in arm; and climb into his Volkswagen, which all this time has been waiting outside, like a faithful dog.

CELEBRATIONS

MR and Mrs Schwarzenberg have never been to the apartment before. It is a fine warm evening, and from the sitting-room the doors to the balcony are open. Mrs Schwarzenberg examines everything approvingly. There is a grand piano, with an array of framed photographs on the lid: Robert, a small boy on a beach, smiles up from his bucket and spade, Yvonne with her parents in front of a creeper-covered house, Henry in a black gown receiving some kind of honour; and many others. Henry's and Yvonne's parents are all dead, and they have inherited too much furniture. Yvonne is anxious to sell an enormous armchair – known as the 'wing chair' – in whose depths Henry's father spent many happy years. She prefers open, airy spaces. But for Henry the wing chair has too many memories. He would prefer to be rid of a large Empire-style console table, from Yvonne's parents. He finds it pompous and impractical. But these small disagreements rarely cause trouble between them. They accept each other's stubbornness, which at times sparks off pleasant, playful arguments. Neither is obsessed with the appearance of the flat; they are both, in their own ways, too busy for that. In any case, the wing chair is ideal for Mr Schwarzenberg; and there he sits, a glass of sherry in one hand, and a small collection of olives hidden in the other.

'Vot a fabulous apartment,' says Mrs Schwarzenberg, scanning the room as if it was more than she could bear. 'We are in Vimbledon, which is very nice. But I would rather be more close, more close to the centre.'

'Ah yes, but in Wimbledon you have so much more space,' says Henry politely, handing her a gin and tonic.

'Oh, we have elbow room,' she concedes. 'And of course this is so important. For the children it has been vonderfoll. Anne-Marie had a donkey in the garden! And Bill can ponder to his heart's content. In Vimbledon one is not harassed.'

'We have six children,' says Mr Schwarzenberg.

'Are any of them musicians too?' asks Henry.

Mr Schwarzenberg screws up his eyes. 'Oh yes,' he says, 'we have musicians in the family.'

Henry waits attentively, but Mr Schwarzenberg has come to a halt.

His wife smiles and explains: 'Our Ben is a very good pianist.' She puts a finger to her lips. 'But this is a kind of secret. We are not yet quite sure that this is the correct profession for him. I must tell you, Dr Billington – or may I? Henry . . .' 'Please,' says Henry, wondering what her Christian name could possibly be – 'I must tell you, Henry, that the musician's life, as you know, can be so very disappointing. Bill has been lucky, this is true. But then he is . . .' she gestures vaguely, searching for the right word, 'he is, you know, in his way . . . exceptional.'

Mr Schwarzenberg lifts his hand and moves it stiffly up and down as if he were pumping a bicycle tyre. 'Come now, Lotte,' he says.

'The trouble is,' she continues, 'he cannot stop. He cannot refuse an engagement.' Mr Schwarzenberg's lips part and slowly turn down at the corners. He stares at the olives in his hand. 'I dream, you know, of travel. But I have my committees. The older I get the more I am invited onto committees. And I ask Bill – why? Why not have a break? A break would be good, so good for us both, good even for the music.'

'And where would you like to go, Mrs Schwarzenberg?' Robert asks.

Sitting next to him on the sofa, she smiles and takes his hand. Hers is yellow and wrinkled, with brown spots of different sizes, and three rings, all gold. 'My dear,' she says. 'I am interested in everything. But perhaps most of all, Asia. Everybody travels these days, everybody except us! Of course I do not refer to foreign engagements. Bill is invited to foreign orchestras. And our own orchestra travels abroad, as you know. But it is always the same places, and always so quick! Have you been, for instance, to Bangkok?'

'Yes,' admits Henry. 'A very interesting mixture of old and new. A frightening place, I'd say. An example of capitalism gone wild. And yet the people are charming. And, I must say, beautiful.' He smiles at Flavia.

'And Burma,' says Mrs Schwarzenberg. 'I am told that Burma is the loveliest of all. The people there are said to be like flowers!'

'We went to Burma too.'

'Now listen to that, Bill!' she pouts, and nods her head rapidly up and down. 'I will have to go with Henry, and you will be left all alone.'

'You must go if you want, dear,' mutters Mr Schwarzenberg, and his mouth remains ajar, the corners turning down. His eyes disappear into slits, and his whole face seems to become stuck, fat and dimpled.

Mrs Schwarzenberg looks round at the others; she hopes Henry has noticed her husband's expression. In public she treats him like a large, amiable pet. She exhibits him, like a circus elephant; over the years his expressions have become more and more amusing.

'You see how little he cares!' she exclaims with delight. 'That's why I think ve should go round the world, just us,' she takes Robert's hand again, 'just us, Robert (she rolls the 'r', long and gutterally), Flavia, Henry, Yvonne and me! And ve vill leave "Monsieur" to water the garden, and ponder old Haydn and Mozart to his heart's content!' She breaks into a slow, deep laugh, in which, gradually everyone joins, including Mr Schwarzenberg. Flavia's laugh ripples through the room like the loveliest of gurgling brooks. Mr Pischik, the Pekinese, wakes and starts to bark.

Henry laughs politely. The idea of going on holiday with Lotte is particularly horrible. Fortunately there is no danger. However the way she treats her husband is intriguing. Mr Pischik, still barking, trots into their midst, attracted by an interesting smell. This turns out to be one of Mr Schwarzenberg's large brown shoes, which he licks lovingly. When Mrs Schwarzenberg sees this her laughter becomes more and more rapid, and rises in pitch until it is inaudible. Quite unable to speak she points at her husband's attempts to stop Mr Pischik. First he bends down and offers him a swollen pink hand instead; but Mr Pischik gives this a disdainful sniff, and returns hungrily to the shoe. Now Yvonne comes in from the kitchen. Aware that he is being watched Mr Schwarzenberg sits back and laughs heartily. But at the same time he tries to shoo away Mr Pischik with his feet, which become very active. They turn in and out with extraordinary agility, and even try to hide, by turning backwards, under the wing chair; then they give Mr Pischik a series of quick jabs which excite him enormously, and he runs barking round Mr Schwarzenberg's legs before hurrying back, at the first opportunity, to the shoe. Henry tries to call him off, but Mrs Schwarzenberg shouts through her tears: 'Bill loves dogs!' and Bill himself laughs good-naturedly, while his legs and huge feet continue to thrash about, as if they had a life of their own.

Yvonne has been longing to call the conductor by his first name, and this is a good moment. 'Bill!' she titters helplessly, 'Oh Bill!' And then: 'Pischik! Pischik!' Mrs Schwarzenberg observes her husband and marvels at him. She has no idea if he is being a clown on purpose, or is merely so embarrassed that he can't help making a fool of himself. Also she has never seen his feet move so fast. 'You can imagine', she cries, 'vot a genius he is on the dance floor!' Robert bends down and picks up Mr Pischik. The peke stares at him with bulging eyes and licks his nose. Mr Schwarzenberg sees this and gives an unexpected guffaw. 'Dinner is ready, everybody!' announces Yvonne.

Lotte stops laughing and frowns at her husband: his sudden guffaw seemed uncalled for. She purses her lips and shakes her head at him. Henry stands up and leads the company into the next room, where everything sparkles: brilliant white tablecloth, Georgian silver candlesticks (from Henry's parents), glass chandelier (from Yvonne's mother) and transparent hotplate laden with shining containers. Quite at home now in the kitchen Yvonne has prepared a perfect meal without much trouble. 'How beautiful, dear!' says Lotte, creasing her eyes.

They sit down in their appointed places. Henry pours wine, and they tuck into taramosalata. 'Just the local delicatessen, Lotte,' apologises Yvonne.

'But this is St John's Wood! In Wimbledon the *vord* delicatessen is unknown!'

Mr Pischik has crept into the room, and sits silently under the table in eager anticipation. He waits for a suitable moment, and then approaches the shoe cautiously. There is something quite addictive about it; one of those tastes you can never really get enough of. Mr Schwarzenberg, preoccupied with his food, does not notice for a long time.

'We are so lucky', says Yvonne, 'that you could both come tonight. You must be so busy.' 'It is a great pleasure,' announces Mrs Schwarzenberg, 'first to hear R – Robert, and now to be in your vonderfoll home.' 'It's very pleasant', says Henry, 'to be so close to Regent's Park.' 'We have Vimbledon Common, but it's not so pretty!' 'My poor Pischik,' says Yvonne, 'has been ill for three days. He has been vomiting, and his tail has been down. Henry has examined him, but he is not a vet!' 'We have only cats in Vimbledon,' says Mrs Schwarzenberg. 'They are so clean and independent.' 'Now Pischik seems to have recovered!' Yvonne exclaims, hoping to remind everyone of the hysterical scene in the other room. 'Bill obviously has a good effect on animals!' 'Bill loves cats,' explains Mrs Schwarzenberg. 'They have a mutual understanding.' Yvonne laughs: 'I think Henry prefers cats, don't you, darling? Please have some more taramosalata, Lotte. But I love dogs. Pekes are like a cross between the two, don't you think?' 'How interesting.' 'And they are all such characters.' 'I don't like lapdogs,' says Henry. 'But they are not lapdogs, darling. They are temple guardians. In China they are temple guardian dogs.' 'You have been to China too?' enquires Mrs Schwarzenberg. 'Not yet, Lotte,' Henry answers, 'but we intend to.' 'He is teasing me,' she cries, delighted that Henry has used her first name and exposing a mouthful of spongy pink toast. 'But how do *you* find the time, Henry? Surgeons are always needed – so much more than conductors!' 'But we also need time to rest. Only yesterday I nearly opened up a lady in the wrong place. That's a sign I'm ripe for a holiday.' 'Or retirement,' puts in Rob. Henry winks at him. 'I was supposed to be examining the lady's liver, and was just about to cut in above her pancreas.' 'Oh, darling – not at dinner!' 'For me, you see,' confides Henry to Mrs Schwarzenberg, who is, naturally, seated on his right, 'for me there is nothing disgusting about the insides of people's bodies. In fact I often find them more attractive than the outside.'

'That reminds me,' says Mr Schwarzenberg, and pauses. Lotte looks at him in alarm. Mr Schwarzenberg continues: 'Of a pianist who once died in the middle of a concert.' 'What a good way to go!' cries Yvonne. 'Could you make some more toast, darling?' she asks Robert. 'In a concerto, Bill?' 'Yes, a Mozart concerto. Now let me see . . . which one was it?' 'It doesn't matter, dear,' says Mrs Schwarzenberg. 'Perhaps to die while playing would be ideal.' 'I wouldn't like to,' says Robert. 'Would you, Flavia?' 'Not yet,' she says, catching his eye. 'It could have been the one dedicated to Mlle Jeunehomme,' reflects Bill, arresting a piece of toast only millimetres from his mouth, 'or . . . the Bb, the last Bb concerto. No . . . I'm pretty sure it was the A major. Yes, that was it . . .' Instead of eating the toast he puts it dramatically back onto his plate. Mrs Schwarzenberg laughs and looks round at the company. 'He is a stickler for accuracy. This is what orchestras so appreciate. But tell us more, Henry, about the poor lady's pancreas.' 'Unfortunately I never got to see it. And that was a pity, because the pancreas is a lovely organ, unlike any other.' Flavia lets off a peal of laughter. 'I've got it,' mutters Mr

Schwarzenberg triumphantly, and in a high wavering voice sings something which Robert recognises as the slow movement of the A major concerto. 'And at exactly this point, at the very start of the movement, you see, I was just about to bring the orchestra in, and instead of the end of the phrase I hear – boom!' He lays his hands, with a thud, flat on the table. 'I think, poor Otto, what has happened? I look round and he is dead, fallen across the piano keys, with a very un-Mozartian chord.' Mr Schwarzenberg chuckles sadly and shakes his head. 'One might have expected', says Robert, 'that it would happen in another part, a more tiring part technically, for instance.' Mr Schwarzenberg fixes him with his small eye. 'Emotion, my boy. Too much emotion.' Yvonne collects the taramosalata, and, at the hotplate, dips a ladle into the casserole. 'It's too awful,' she says. 'So he was dead, just like that. Who was it, Bill? Anyone we would have heard of?' Robert helps her by serving the vegetables. He hands Mrs Schwarzenberg her plate. 'Otto,' says Bill. 'Otto something. Do you remember, dear?' 'A German pianist,' says Lotte. 'Otto Preussiger.' 'Did the concert continue?' asks Robert. 'Yes,' says Bill. 'The next item. And the orchestra played particularly well after that.' 'Everyone must have been so moved,' sighs Yvonne. 'Is it coq au vin?' asks Lotte. 'Ach, what a rare treat.'

Now Mr Schwarzenberg becomes aware that the dog is secretly at work on his shoe. He gives a little kick. 'Lotte –' he calls. She looks at him sternly, and thinks: now what is it? What does he want now, this fat baby. She remembers that she herself was once beautiful, a German beauty; and she has given her life to this fat Jew; fat even when she met him, and, in those days, not yet successful. 'Yes, dear?' she says. But Bill cannot continue. His toes are growing wet now, from the dog's saliva, but Lotte's look has frozen him. He says: 'You are so clever, dear, to remember poor Otto's name.' Meekly, he cuts into the coq au vin. Women, he thinks, frowning, have often found me attractive. And yet I was never handsome. But even Lotte was once in love with me. We have had six children. Despite that, Lotte has kept her figure. He marvels at women.

He believes them superior to men. The coq au vin is very tasty, and this is Mrs Billington's doing.

Lotte turns to Henry and says: 'Do tell us, Henry. Are the cuts in the Health Service making all your lives very difficult?' Henry smiles. 'Yes. We are having to take momentous decisions. There is a real shortage of beds and staff, as you know. In many cases it's important that operations happen at a particular time – there is an optimum time – but this is becoming more and more difficult. Patients with urgent, vital problems. . .' Lotte looks at him, nodding sympathetically. She begins to be envious of Yvonne, married to a man who deals with such problems. When she herself was young she believed that music too was urgent, vital, and Bill, who seemed so immersed in it, was like a standard-bearer. But she has lost her faith: Bill's career is routine, quite humdrum, like any other profession, and she is afraid that music cannot, after all, change people's lives. It is sad; a betrayal of all she once held so dear. And because of this gradual disappointment she has become, she knows, what is called a 'battle-axe'. She nods at Henry, and hears him say: 'It is a responsibility, an unfair responsibility: one which we should not have.' Robert looks at his father; and this look is blankly returned. 'How appalling.' Mrs Schwarzenberg shakes her head and clicks her tongue. 'We are having to make many moral decisions,' Henry continues. 'It is not only a matter of medical priority, which is hard enough anyway. We may have to lie to our patients; to make them believe that their condition is less urgent than it really is.'

'Why?' asks Robert. 'Why lie to them?' 'To save unnecessary anxiety, darling,' says his mother. Mr Schwarzenberg's plate is almost empty. Lotte glares at him. She is deeply impressed by Henry's seriousness: beside him Bill is no better than a pig. 'I suppose more and more people are taking out private insurance,' she says. 'Yes,' replies Henry, 'and I must say that I am beginning to recommend this, though in a way it's against my principles.' Again he and Robert exchange an expressionless glance. 'Darling,' says Yvonne to her son, 'don't you think you should be on Bupa?' 'I don't intend to get ill,' he jokes, touching the wooden leg of the table. 'Bill and I are on a family scheme', explains Lotte, 'which includes all the children.' 'One never knows,' Yvonne continues, 'you are young and healthy, but all the same.' He wonders if she is thinking about Aids. He does not want to talk about Aids. 'It must be dreadful', says Lotte to Henry, 'to have all these extra responsibilities.' Robert tries to imagine his father lying to his patients. Does he smile and pretend to be cheerful? Does he get pleasure out of it? He thinks he must be a good liar; but, strangely enough, he is not sure. His father does not seem afraid of telling the truth. 'Do you get fond of your patients, daddy?' he asks. 'I do,' Henry confesses. 'But it is important not to become too fond. As a doctor one has to curb one's emotions; as a musician, I imagine, one has to foster them.' Robert senses a subtle rebuke. He says: 'Really? Oh God, I get sick of too much emotion. And you know, in music it can be dangerous too. In fact, to do good work, one has to have a very scientific approach.' 'I can see that. But surely you agree that music is *based* on emotion?'

'Based on emotion? I'm not sure that emotion is the right word.'

'What does Bill say?' pipes in Yvonne. Mr Schwarzenberg frowns and looks bemused. Yvonne repeats the question: 'Is music based on emotion?' Lotte too is interested in her husband's response. His expression, that of a perplexed elephant, is one that she knows only too well; in public it is amusing, in private unbearable. But, suddenly, she is not quite sure what he is going to say. Perhaps he will give a little speech, an interesting little speech, and show these people that he is not quite as dumb as he seems. She tries to look at him encouragingly. Will he understand that, this time, she is interested by what he might say? But she is afraid that he can only interpret her stare, her presence itself, as a rebuke. And this is her own doing. Bill is chewing. Eventually he swallows the last of his coq au vin and says, with a frown that seems to contradict his words: 'Music is . . . (he lifts his shoulders) just music. But it is based on emotion. Yes.' Lotte laughs. 'Of course it is,' agrees Yvonne.

Henry looks pleased. 'It must be marvellous', he says, 'to work in a field where one can allow one's emotions to have their head.' Robert says: 'Would you like that, daddy?' 'Yes, old chap.' 'Good music is based on emotions that are utterly sincere.' 'Of course,' Henry agrees. 'And they can be painful.' 'Naturally, old boy.' He smiles at his son. 'But', puts in Yvonne, 'music transcends emotions. However painful they are, music turns them into something beautiful.' 'You are right,' says Lotte, 'music transforms emotions.' 'Do have some more, Bill,' urges Yvonne. 'Give me your plate.' Mr Schwarzenberg acquiesces. Robert helps. At the hotplate his mother says quickly: 'You're not disappointed, are you? With the concert?' 'It could have been better, much better.' 'Oh darling, it was so moving.' And in a whisper: 'Lotte adored it!'

He returns Mr Schwarzenberg's plate. The conductor smiles happily and says: 'Thank you, Robert. I think your playing's very promising.' 'Promising' is a word he has often heard before. It is a word which, applied to him, his mother undoubtedly likes to hear. She wants him to be in a perpetual state of promise. What happens when you grow out of promise, when you 'fulfil your promise'? He takes Lotte's plate to be replenished. His mother, ladle in hand, beams at him. This is because of Mr Schwarzenberg's comment. Just as he thought, she is delighted that he's still in a state of promise. He refuses to play her game; he directs his eyes sullenly into the vegetables which he heaps onto Lotte's plate. 'Don't give her too much!' she whispers impatiently. He feels her sudden fury. Is she aware of it herself? What is this promise that binds him to her? It is unbearably vague. 'So I'm still promising – after all these years!' He fetches Flavia's plate, for she too wants some more. He thinks: if I were in love with Flavia, life would be simple . . . Defiantly he brings Flavia's plate to his mother. She winks at him meaningfully. But he cannot smile or wink back. There is no secret to share. What would her reaction be if he said he was going to marry Flavia? He realises that it would be extremely hard to say this to his mother. His father calls: 'Rob, old chap, could you open another bottle?' Obediently he goes about the task.

'I am told you are having a great success these days,' says Henry to Flavia.

'Things are beginning to happen at last,' she replies with a beautiful smile.

'What a pleasure that must be. When will we be hearing you at Covent Garden?'

'Or a recital,' puts in Lotte, 'with our pianist here?'

'As soon as possible,' she beams.

'Have you ever given concerts together?'

'Not really,' she says. 'Not recently. But I would like to.'

It is true. Why does he never play now with Flavia? He sees her soft pudgy hands as they manipulate the knife and fork, and thinks of his own nervous, bony fingers. His father's hands are dry and broad, with large oval nails, perfectly trimmed. It is easy to imagine them wielding the scalpel. He watches the efficient way they dismember the chicken.

'So far,' says Flavia, 'I've sung much more abroad.'

'This is often the case,' Mrs Schwarzenberg agrees. 'It is very hard to capture the English public. But if you do, you can be blind, deaf and dumb and they still love you.'

'It would be a pity', says Henry, 'if Flavia were dumb.' He gives a cunning smile; the silver filling glitters in the corner of his mouth. 'And I'm sure those big black eyes are far from blind.'

Flavia lets loose a torrent of laughter.

'Where do you live?' Henry asks.

'I have my own flat,' she says. 'In West Hampstead.'

'You seem so European, it's hard to imagine you living here.'

'Flavia's family is Italian,' says Robert.

'Jewish?' asks Mr Schwarzenberg unexpectedly.

'Oh yes,' she laughs.

'Do you sing Mahler – Kindertotenlieder?'

'Yes, of course!' Immediately she lowers her eyelids, her brow furrows, and she starts humming.

'You have performed it?' Mr Schwarzenberg interrupts.

'No – but I know it well. I've worked on it.'

Robert knows it is her policy to say she sings everything if asked by a conductor. There is a silence as everyone waits for him to continue. But his sharp questions lead nowhere. The folds of skin on his face, behind which he retires, are impervious as rhinoceros hide. There is no suggestion of a possible engagement. It was merely, thinks Robert, a little exercise of power.

'I like Mahler,' says Henry, still smiling at her. 'But Yvonne is much more musical than me. She *lives* for music, don't you darling?'

Yvonne watches his flirtation with Flavia from far away. She is quite detached, floating in her own world. 'I suspect', she says, 'that Henry thinks my love of music is slightly ridiculous.'

Henry laughs. 'On the contrary. I love you for it.'

Mrs Schwarzenberg holds up her glass. 'This is vonderfoll. A declaration of love. I always think, my dear Yvonne, that we are the lucky ones. It is possible for us to appreciate, to *adore* music, without all the trouble. Look at poor Bill. He is so *embroiled*' – she pronounces the word slowly, with enormous emphasis, suddenly exposing her upper teeth and all her gums, which are strangely pale (Robert makes a mental note of this; under his breath he practises it; afterwards, to Flavia, he will imitate her) – 'that the joy, the pleasure of discovery is gone!'

'It must be hard for Mr Schwarzenberg', says Robert, 'to keep performances fresh, if one gives so many.'

Yvonne is delighted by this remark; she has picked up, she is sure, an undercurrent of irony. She says: 'But Bill seems to manage!'

'Oh yes,' says Lotte. 'But with so many concerts we have no social life. I never see my old friends any more. Bill wants to have me there for all his performances, if possible. Even rehearsals. He likes to have my opinion on balance.'

'Now dear, you know you don't have to . . .'

'This is vot he says to you. But I know. After so many years I know very well what he needs.'

'Think,' says Yvonne, 'if Henry needed me for his operations!'

'My dear,' says Mrs Schwarzenberg, 'we should swop places. Just for a short time.' She looks at Henry and creases her eyes. His steely hair and the elegant way his head rises from his shoulders is far preferable to Bill. There is a hint of arrogance in his face which is charming. Bill is full of arrogance, but it is of another, revolting sort. He eats, slouches and snores, and expects women to like it. Gott, is it possible that she too liked it once? She coughs, holding her napkin to her mouth, as if trying to eject him from her system. Henry's arrogance is studied. He is chic and proud of it. She says: 'Bill dear. You must be tired of me. Wouldn't you like a little change? I'm sure you wouldn't say no to Yvonne?'

Yvonne peals with laughter, and thinks: could I ever sleep with that gorilla? She remembers Rob's witty description (years ago) of Bill on the conducting podium: a gorilla brushing its teeth. She searches desperately for Rob's eyes, but the boy, damn him, will not respond, although she knows, she is convinced, he must be bursting with laughter. She cries: 'How killing! All right, Lotte, but one condition: separate beds!'

'Naturally,' comes Lotte's thick smoker's voice.

Yes, it was true: she had once liked Bill for all the qualities that now disgust her. What once seemed artistic and Bohemian has turned out to be nothing more than self-indulgence. And there is, after all, no mystery, no great thoughts, lurking behind those tiny, introverted eyes. Henry's debonair appearance, his obvious vanity was all that she once despised. How horribly mistaken one can be in one's youth. She stares at Bill, and fears that inside his vast chewing head there is nothing but emptiness. Great halls of bone, like underground caves through which not even a trickle of water flows. How tragic. 'You will find him very peaceable,' she says to Yvonne.

'*We* don't seem to have been consulted, eh Bill?' says Henry, full of injured innocence. 'But' – he leans towards him confidentially, across Flavia – 'I'm not against it, personally.'

Mr Schwarzenberg stops eating and plants his knife and

fork, vertically, on either side of his plate. His face folds into rubber pleats, and his mouth slowly opens to form a perfect O.

Lotte's frustration knows no bounds. She has made the mistake of forgetting their true roles (he the circus elephant, she the trainer) and remembering that they are husband and wife. Worst of all she knows that it is because of her that he is behaving in this way. He is obeying her, she realises bitterly. But perhaps the utter absurdity of his expression can save her. She longs to gather the others into a circle, and point her finger at him. To put him out to grass, in an enclosure, with a high fence around him. Oh, what agony it is. She gives a low, hoarse laugh, and thrusts her fist at him. She needs as much credit as possible; Yvonne, at least, gives her an appreciative nod.

Henry is trying to work out the meaning of Mr Schwarzenberg's expression. He is a very shy man, he thinks. 'Well, Bill?' he says. 'Will you take Yvonne?' There is little change, at first, except perhaps a deepening of the clefts in the rubber folds, but then, Henry's almost sure, he sees him blush. 'Why, yes,' Bill answers at last, breaking into good-natured laughter, 'yes, of course!' He is a good man, thinks Henry; a poor, tormented man. 'But I haven't agreed yet,' he teases Lotte, shaking his head at her. 'Oh you will,' she laughs. 'No operations for you!' he goes on. 'I should hope not, Henry!' 'You won't have the pleasure – of seeing me at work!' He turns into a devil, and makes horrible movements with his knife and fork. 'Unless I operate on *you*' – his eyes glint, an evil whisper – 'in your sleep!' 'On the pancreas?' cries Lotte.

Everybody bursts into laughter.

'Well, that leaves us,' says Robert to Flavia. 'We're happy as we are, aren't we?'

'Yes,' she says. 'We will be married in Heaven.'

'Or perhaps a little before,' he smiles, half an eye on his mother. 'Just in case one of us doesn't get there.' For if they were married, how happy they would be; by the age of sixty, at any rate.

'I think it's an excellent idea,' says Henry. 'As parents we give our consent, don't we darling?'

'Anything to make you happy,' says Yvonne, beaming at her son.

'Four out of our six children are already married!' exclaims Lotte.

'What about the other two?' Robert asks.

'Too young, dear,' she smiles, giving him a short painful rub on the arm. Her fingers are made of steel, he thinks. 'But . . .' she whispers conspiratorially, 'they are both in love.' And she realises that these love affairs interest her much more than the married lives of the others. 'In fact, Jo and his girlfriend are thinking of marriage, but I say: what's the hurry?'

'Exactly,' says Yvonne. 'So much more fun.'

'Bill and I', continues Lotte, 'lived in sin for a whole year. In those days that was quite daring.' She realises that it was living in sin she was in love with: which she mistook for Bill. 'Living in sin was most exciting all those years ago. But it's no thrill any more. Isn't that a shame for young people?'

'Rather a perverse argument,' puts in Henry.

'Yes, but isn't it true? Danger, and the . . .' She searches for the right word. 'Flouting?' suggests Henry. 'Yes, flouting' (what a man, he can read her thoughts) – 'the flouting of social conventions is what makes life fun and spicy. Don't you think our lives are far too safe, on the whole?'

'In that case,' says Robert boldly, 'you could say that homosexuals have the most enjoyable, spicy lives.'

Henry feels a little rush of pride for his son. He adds: 'Yes – especially promiscuous ones.'

'Oh no, darling,' reprimands Yvonne. 'What about Aids?'

Lotte remembers her year of illegal cohabitation, and wonders if Bill feels the same way. She also remembers, to her shame, that it was she who persuaded him it was time to get married. She says to him: 'Do you remember that year, Bill? We lived in England's Lane.' Bill nods. 'I do,' he says; and, she believes, tries to smile at her. But it seems to have become impossible for him to smile at her. When he tries, she immediately turns into some kind of gorgon. Her eyes become fixed, like two black holes, and he is afraid that if he continues she will take a flying leap at his throat. Smiling, simple smiling seems to have become an enormous taboo. And yet, despite all this, he still sometimes wants to smile at her. She is his wife, for all her faults she is still his faithful wife. It could be the interruption of so many smiles that has given his face its curiously perplexed expression. However he has an unusual idea, and says bravely: 'Why don't we get divorced?' Lotte is staggered. She feels herself flush. Somehow this enables him to get further towards a smile than usual. 'And move back to England's Lane!'

Lotte hoots with laughter. 'That is a brilliant idea, Bill!' she cries. And she even, for a short but extraordinary moment, thinks it might be quite fun to live with Bill again, in sin. Henry looks at her approvingly. Would living in sin (an old-fashioned expression she completely rejects) be exciting, even now? Ha ha, what a joke. According to her experience only illicit sex has been worth having. Despite her six children she has no sensation of having had a sexual relationship with married Bill.

'But if', says Henry, 'it is danger which gives life all its spice, perhaps Aids is the answer.'

'Don't be ridiculous, daddy. Why joke about it?'

'Why not? Laughing about serious things is often a good safety-valve. And that's something, by the way, I often find about your generation. You all seem to have lost your sense of humour.'

'Oh darling,' cries his mother, 'you know that Rob hasn't lost his sense of humour!'

He realises: sense of humour is part of some unwritten contract. He says, frowning: 'You think Aids is something to laugh about?'

'Of course not, old chap.' He regrets it; naturally Aids is a worrying subject for Rob. He thinks: yes, most people's lives are too safe, but mine is not. 'Being a surgeon is rather dangerous,' he says.

'Especially for the patients, daddy.'

'For me too.'

'Are you ever tempted to botch an operation?' he asks.

'Really, darling!' cries Yvonne.

Secretly, Henry is pleased. He even feels slightly excited. He says gently: 'Now what makes you ask that question?'

'Oh, you know I'm always trying to understand you, daddy!' he laughs. 'I mean, I would understand that. For instance when I play the piano, in concerts, I sometimes feel all the wrong notes are trying to pull my fingers towards them like little magnets, and it's only by the greatest will power that I manage to play the right ones.' Not that, in fact, he has ever been aware of feeling this.

'That sounds rather neurotic,' says Henry.

'Oh I'm terribly neurotic, daddy.'

'Yes, I suppose you are.'

They continue eating. Nobody, not even Yvonne, knows quite what to say.

'Why should I want to botch an operation?'

Robert shrugs.

'Why, Rob?'

'Perhaps you feel angry sometimes . . . angry or frustrated.'

'I would have no reason to take it out on my patients.' He thinks: how wrong the boy is. I am far too proud to do a bad operation. 'Some of us don't suffer from lack of self-control,' he says.

'Oh Henry,' says Yvonne at last, 'you know that Rob has self-control. And *you* know, Rob, that your father is not an angry person.'

'I'm lucky,' says Henry. 'I really don't have much reason to get angry.' He pauses. 'And I must tell you – probably you won't understand. But the fact is – I love my patients.' He smiles at his son, and believes that Rob has not the courage to take this discussion any further. His smile is gentle and encouraging. He will not let him ask the question which he believes the boy would now like to ask: 'Why do you love them? Because you feel superior?' He will not let the boy ask this question. No: and he will not even let him think it. With his smile and his quiet steadfast look he is paralysing Rob's mind. 'It's an odd thing. I've always felt close to the people I have to operate on. I think, on the whole, it makes me do my job better – more lovingly.' His repeated use of the word 'love' is giving him pleasure. Neither Rob nor Yvonne is used to hearing him talk of love. He wonders if he is making her jealous. 'But I think I'm quite unusual,' he continues. 'Most surgeons are far more scientific, and reserve their feelings – love and so on – for their families.'

'It's a great pity', jokes Yvonne to Lotte, 'that he's never performed an operation on me. He might have loved me as much as one of his patients!'

'I dream about it,' laughs Henry.

'Oh, what nonsense he talks!'

Henry feels alive now. Under his suave exterior the adrenalin is flowing. What a delightful machine the human body is. It is necessary only to touch the right button, and pleasure flows. Sometimes life, the motor which drives people in one direction or another, seems very simple to him. He sees it all clearly mapped out, as a large city appears from an aeroplane, a series of interacting mechanisms. This bird's eye view confirms his distrust of romantic love. The human brain, with its multitude of neurological connections, is, after all, a machine. Needs are formed: and it is not so very difficult, with knowledge of psychiatry, to understand the origins of specific emotional needs. Only one thing, perhaps, remains something of a mystery: the frantic attempts by living organisms to survive. But let us accept this one unknown factor. The rest follows like night and day. The child's response to his environment is based on his attempts to survive. Emotional survival is just as important as physical. In fact, it is almost the same thing. An emotional language has to be learnt, derived unconsciously from his family, from the way he is treated by those around him, and the way in which they respond to each other. And all families are, of course, individual. This precise – and ultimately unique – language is the blueprint for all future dealings with his fellow men and women. Poor old sex, he thinks, is used by us in a great variety of ways. But all these ways are, in the end, traceable to the emotional language we learnt in our cradles. Sexual desire is profoundly emotional in its origins – though this is often not apparent (especially to feminists!). Sexual desire is a development: a violent flowering of the original seed. People like Yvonne use the word 'love' when they meet someone who seems to offer hope of filling the gaps, patching up the scars, replacing the losses of their childhood. The more lost, the more adrift they are, the more passionately they 'fall in love'. We are all the victims of our past. Some are luckier than others.

Henry sighs to himself. He decides to entertain them a little. 'It is strange,' he says, 'but I believe in the laying on of hands. At the end of an operation, when the wound has been sewn up, I rest my hands quietly, for a few moments, on the patient's body. It gives me a sense of completeness.'

'Really, daddy – always?'

'No, not always. I have to be in the right mood. And I am more comfortable with women's bodies, I admit. But don't misunderstand me. There are no sexual feelings involved.'

'I should hope not,' says Lotte. 'Otherwise we would sue you!'

'Is that true?' asks Yvonne. 'You've never told me before.'

'Don't you think', says Henry, 'it's important that husbands and wives keep some secrets from each other?'

He can see her mind working, clear as clockwork. She is intrigued by this new piece of information. Later, when the guests have gone, she will ask him about it. She is surprised, because she knows he is a cool, cynical scientist. This 'laying on of hands' has confused her. It belongs more to the mystic realm she shares with Rob. He smiles at her, but she does not return his smile. Her face is slightly tilted, framed by her thick curls, dyed black. He wonders how grey she really is. He sees her hands, delicate and carefully manicured, quite different to Mrs Schwarzenberg's, which are coarser, freckled, and perhaps evil, as they lay the knife and fork to rest on her plate. Yvonne's coal black eyes interrogate him. He is touched by her seriousness. It reminds him of a time, long ago, before they had ever made love, in an orchard in Normandy. Then, as now, she was weighing him up, trying to understand what sort of man he was.

Robert collects the plates. He sees Pischik's tail, jerking out from under the tablecloth. He guesses the little dog is at work again on Mr Schwarzenberg's shoe. He glances at the conductor's unfathomable face. He sees only age there, and the mysterious barriers of his flesh.

'But this is fascinating,' Lotte is saying. 'To think that a cold calculating doctor believes in such things!'

'She thinks I'm cold and calculating,' says Henry to Flavia. 'Surely you don't?'

'Is Mr Pischik still bothering you?' says Robert to the conductor. He feels sympathetic: they are both outsiders.

Flavia laughs excitedly, which annoys him. Her response is unpleasantly flattering to his father's vanity. But perhaps he is typical of the sort of man she falls for.

'What?' says Mr Schwarzenberg.

'The dog. Is he still bothering you?'

'Oh no.' He frowns, and shakes his hands, large as plates. He is most anxious, Robert sees, not to draw attention to himself. It is, of course, his wife that he fears. 'I thought you played most lyrically,' he says quickly. 'I have performed the Fantasy myself, you know. Long ago . . . and not very well.' Robert had no idea he had once been a pianist, and the thought is vaguely troubling. He hears Pischik growling under the table; bends down and pulls at him. The little dog protests strongly, and barks. When Robert eventually extracts him his whole face is covered in saliva, and he has a piece of leather sole in his mouth.

'Naughty Pischik! Look – this is part of Mr Schwarzenberg's shoe!' He pries it from the dog's frothing teeth.

'Oh Bill,' says Lotte in a deeply reproachful voice.

Everybody laughs. So Bill is the culprit; not Pischik.

'What have you been up to?' Lotte continues theatrically. She takes the mangled piece of leather and holds it up, for all to see, between thumb and forefinger.

Robert feels ill at ease. It is he who drew attention to the shoe. But he cannot help laughing. All eyes are fixed on the conductor. At first he shows the familiar bemused expression.

Robert, next to Mrs Schwarzenberg, can feel a sort of growling, half smoker's cough, half whirring dynamo, gathering like a wave in her lungs. She roars: 'Vot a way to behave – at a dinner party! Under the table!' Bill turns his head to one side, and raises his almost hairless eyebrows; deep furrows, moist with sweat, plough in parallel lines across his forehead. The tight O of his lips widens, and for the first time everyone has a glimpse of his small separate teeth. Robert suddenly becomes extremely uncomfortable. He shakes Mrs Schwarzenberg's arm. 'I take you out,' she bellows, 'and this is how I am repaid!' She leans forward and whispers hoarsely: 'In front of Henry and Yvonne! *VOT* were you doing?' Now Mr Schwarzenberg's grimace slowly splits his jaw from cheek to cheek; he lowers his head, and, in a high tremolo, begins to whimper.

Lotte allows this for no more than a couple of seconds; leaning back and grasping the arms of Robert and Henry, on either side, she breaks into spasms of thick, voiceless laughter. This is a form of orgasm, thinks Henry. 'Bravo Bill,' roars Lotte. 'You see, he can be great!' Mr Schwarzenberg smiles round at the company, and even inclines his head two or three times. Yvonne starts clapping. 'And now,' she cries, 'let's have some dessert!'

Robert catches Flavia's eye. She can hardly control herself. 'What a performer!' Lotte sighs, wiping her eyes on her sleeve. Mr Pischik is barking. 'Take him out, darling,' says Yvonne to her son. He lifts him up, despite scuffling protests, and carries him to the next room, closing the door behind him. The dog's eyes are bulging, and he wonders if he is about to have a heart attack. For a moment he sees the two of them reflected in a long gilt mirror hanging above the Empire console. 'There, there, Pischik,' he says, stroking him. He opens the balcony door, and steps out into the warm night. Pischik follows, his tail down. 'They are drunk,' he says to him. The dog splutters round among the flower pots, then lifts his leg. A small puddle spreads across the balcony and drips over the edge. He imagines his mother's reproaches. But he will allow Pischik to do as he pleases. He sees his car, parked opposite. He has a pleasant idea, and looks at the time: eleven-fifteen. He watches a young couple walking arm in arm on the edge of Regent's Park. A fire engine rushes past, sirens wailing. He is struck by the haphazard nature of the world: Pischik's pee pouring down in a thin sparkling stream, the fire engine tearing to an unknown fire, the slow steps of the lovers in the grass – unconnected events whose paths cross for a moment.

He hears renewed guffaws from the dining-room, and returns. He notices the sweet smell of pot-pourri (from Floris) which is always present in his mother's home. This smell, which would always remind him of her.

Mrs Schwarzenberg has lit a cigarette, and Flavia is trying to explain that she has an allergy to smoke. 'It's embarrassing,' she says, 'but I'll have to move my chair away.' 'Did you know', says Lotte, inhaling deeply, 'that Monserrat Caballe and Fischer-Diskau are both chain-smokers?' Yes, Flavia had heard this before. She takes her chair and plants it in the doorway, just as Robert is coming in. 'I'll have to sit here,' she says. Yvonne shakes her head: this girl is determined to draw attention to herself. 'Really,' she says, 'aren't you exaggerating, Flavia?' 'No,' answers Robert, 'it's true.' Yvonne raises her eyebrows and blows out scornfully, as if she's just been insulted. Flavia is not enjoying this at all. All her life people have thought she was trying to play the star. She herself does not know if this is true. All she knows is that whenever she has tried, even a little, to assert herself, people have objected. Her only feeling has been of someone trying to keep her head above water. Sitting four-square on her chair she begins to laugh; for her position in the doorway, away from the rest of the company, ostracised because of a protest she could not help making, accused by implication of playing the diva – this situation is more familiar, more like home, than any other. And so she laughs, although home, for her, is not a happy place. She rolls uncomfortably from side to side.

'Don't worry, my dear,' says Yvonne to Lotte. 'Henry and I don't smoke but we don't mind at all. And I'm sure she's getting enough air from the corridor,' indicating Flavia with an aggressive nod. 'And she looks beautiful over there,' says Henry, 'perfectly framed. We should take a picture.' Robert sees Mr Schwarzenberg's small eyes focusing on the chocolate mousse. He realises that his mother, in her anger, has forgotten to serve it. He stands by Flavia and runs his hand through her hair, which is thick and a little wiry; he feels the warmth of her scalp underneath. His father is watching. He knows that his father would like to be stroking Flavia's hair. He says: 'When we get married, *cara mia*, I'll give up smoking, I promise.' She looks up at him, grateful for his support. Perhaps she has taken him seriously; perhaps she thinks they really will get married one day. And it seems to him, at that moment, that only the flimsiest of barriers prevents him from being in love with her, like a veil in the theatre which temporarily blurs the action behind. But the blur is so slight that the audience, after a while, forget about it; when the veil lifts they are surprised by the sudden clarity. When she looks up at him he is amazed by the light in her eyes, the softness of her skin, her perfect teeth, but in another part of him, the part where chemical reactions occur, the veil is drawn. The necessary catalyst, the swift wheels which could so easily lift the transparent gauze out of sight, are stubbornly dormant. He stares into her face, smiling; inside he is filled with sadness. 'You look happy,' she whispers to him. 'Oh yes,' he answers, bending down so that his cheek, with its rough shadow, is almost touching hers. 'I'm so happy you're here.' 'Lovebirds,' cries Mrs Schwarzenberg. 'Look, Flavia dear, my cigarette is over!' And she stubs it out, her red nail grating in the ashtray.

'The mousse!' exclaims his mother. 'I quite forgot!' She gives it to Robert, to hand round. Yvonne watches his agile fingers, which, a moment ago, were stroking Flavia and before that were stroking the piano. She can seen nothing in common between the shape of those hands and either hers or Henry's. She is sure they must be the hands of her father, her real father. 'Was it Rubinstein', she asks, 'who said that playing the piano was like making love?' 'Yes,' Robert answers, holding the mousse while she serves herself. 'Do you have that feeling too?'

she asks.'I think I understand what he meant.' 'Don't you think he was just making a joke?' says Lotte, her teeth coated in chocolate. 'Such a *farceur.*' Yvonne dips into the mousse, her hands so close to his. A small drop of the brown foamy cream falls onto his thumb. 'Sorry, *chéri,*' she whispers. She can hardly believe that they are two separate beings. They are a team, working closely together, he serving, she taking. A reciprocal process. There seems no good reason to believe in the skin that seals off his being, confines it to a particular space, when, after all, only thirty years ago she and he were one. The months of her pregnancy are as vivid as the concert she has just heard. She looks at his thumb stained with her chocolate mousse, which she made only this afternoon, and wonders if she could lick it off. It would be hygienic and quickly done. Is it not, after all, almost her own thumb? She takes another little spoonful, amazed by everything: the independence of her own muscles, the pliability of the mousse, his white cuffs peeping out from the sleeve of the tail coat and partly covering his palm, and the fingers themselves, strong, independent, a young man's and yet also hers.

'Come on, mother! I want some too.' 'Sorry, darling,' she laughs, and then to Lotte: 'Do your children call you Mother? I always think it sounds rather cold.' 'They call me Mama,' Lotte says, 'but then they are such babies. And Bill they call Papa. Even the grown-up ones.' 'What would you prefer, mother? Shall I call you Yvonne, from now on?' Robert asks, smiling. 'And Henry?' 'If you like, old boy,' says his father. Yvonne toys with her mousse and considers the sound of her name in his mouth. It had a gentle ring. And supposing she said 'yes, call me Yvonne' and never again heard the word Mother from his lips? It would indicate a most profound change, even a revolution. It would create a new and interesting tension between them; it would sound for ever artificial, forced – perhaps delightfully so. The ramifications of such a change would be endless. She imagines him ringing up with a cheery 'Hello, Yvonne!' She could not take it at face value; it is impossible to believe that he would ever achieve *that* degree of distance –

and yet did she not want, she thinks once again, sincerely want, his independence? Yes, but distance and independence are not the same thing. If he called her Yvonne, something in her would react, a strange, unimaginable reaction. She would be just as friendly as usual, calling him, naturally, 'darling', or '*chéri*', but in her voice, in the smallest inflexion in her voice there would be a subtle difference. She does not know what that difference would be; she could not plan for it. And he, of course, would pick up that tiny difference. Everything would be just as warm and cosy, but a tiny difference in her voice (unnoticeable to anybody else) might change everything. He would say: 'Have you got a cold, Yvonne?' or 'Yvonne, how is Pischik today?' And the tiny unidentifiable difference in her voice, as she answered him, might have enormous consequences. Perhaps he would be surprised, as if the response (although inevitable) was not what he bargained for. Something inside him might shatter and collapse. But does she want to have such a destructive effect? No, his life is rich and full of exciting experiences. And she is fooling herself. She has, surely, no such power over him. She smiles wistfully. She remembers her sleeping pills, and the way she tricked dear old Dr Selson. She sees the pills building up, an armoury, in the drawer next to his photographs and letters.

'I think', he is saying, 'all one's emotions, all possible emotions, are there to be used when one plays the piano, however subtle or obscure they may be. And so much is just in the way you touch the instrument. You have to turn it into a living creature, encourage it to respond. And there is love in that.'

'Well,' Lotte laughs, 'if you could confine your lovemaking to your instruments, musicians, at least, would not get Aids!'

'And we could be as promiscuous as we liked!'

Yvonne remembers a curious fact: her father, her real father, had committed suicide. At least this is what her adoptive parents had told her, when she was grown-up, of course. How strange that she should have forgotten. How little, she thinks in amazement, she had bothered to find out about her real parents – but this was, surely, out of loyalty to the kind, civilised, rather elderly couple who had brought her up?

'It seems', says Henry, 'that all HIV carriers are likely to get the full disease at some stage.'

'Oh daddy, you can't possibly say that. There's no proof at all.'

'I agree – there's no proof. But it looks as if it's going that way.'

And now this nice, generous couple, her parents, were both dead. It was possible that her real mother was still alive.

'This is horrible', says Lotte, 'for those who know they are carriers. And the poor haemophiliacs!'

'An excellent reason', says Robert, 'for not having the test. Why live under the shadow of death, which may or may not strike at any moment?' He feels the blood invading his neck, his ears.

'Yes – but there is a responsibility!' Lotte protests.

It might be possible to trace her mother. What sort of adventure would that be?

'There are many things to be weighed up,' says Robert calmly. 'And, in any case, there is such a thing as safe sex, remember.'

'Saf*er* sex would be more accurate,' says his father.

He remembers Johnny.

Henry looks at him kindly. 'I expect they'll find a cure soon,' he says.

'Do you really think so?' asks Lotte.

He is filled with the darkness of the Observatory Gardens, the muddy paths, the black leaves and branches, the angels of death that stalk there. Johnny once boasted that this was his own back garden. Johnny, who was able to escape any trap, to transform himself and creep through the bars of cages. But this disease would catch him. And even so he would fight to the very end; skeletal, deformed, his fearful optimism would persist.

'They will find a cure – and a vaccine,' answers Henry. 'But nobody knows when.' He has never talked to Rob about the dangers of Aids. But it was a good thing to have mentioned it.

He does not imagine that his son is very promiscuous. Henry himself has never had a homosexual experience; but he accepts homosexuality as part of the natural order, much as he accepts, for instance, that some spiders (female) try to eat their mates after copulation, or that it is natural for baby cuckoos to oust all other chicks from the nest without delay. Such activities are all based on the clumsy laws of survival. He wonders if this tall gangling youth, his son, so different to him in mind and body, has nevertheless a prick of similar shape and size. He smiles secretly: he has always been proud of his genital formation. It would be pleasant to think he had passed this on to his son. He looks at him slyly: a homosexual look, he thinks. He does not remember having met anybody who might possibly be a boy-friend. Or is his son one of those wandering souls who confine their sexual encounters to dark anonymous places? He has heard that the Observatory Gardens are one such place. An interesting atmosphere, no doubt. What if equivalent places existed for heterosexuals? A place where men and women could meet and with few words, or none, have the most exciting, fantasy-full sex based on mutual respect and attraction. Why did such places not exist? Surely this was proof of the fundamental difference between men and women. Or, at any rate, a societal pressure so ancient and inbred that it has become an instinct. For women, it seems, do not in general feel the need for these places. But how many heterosexual men would turn down such an opportunity, if it were easily to be found? He says: 'It is bad luck that homosexuals have so many opportunities to be promiscuous.'

'What do you mean, daddy?'

'I mean', says Henry, 'that men being men have many things in common. And one of those things is the ability to be sexually aroused on the spur of the moment, and to wish to consummate straight away. The elaborate and time-consuming process of courtship is done away with. And so a high number of sexual couplings is inevitable. This is what we mean by the so-called "promiscuity" of homosexuals. From the scientific point of view it is understandable and natural.'

Could any homosexual son have a more considerate father?

'Very good,' says Lotte and almost claps. 'So this is a clear explanation of the activities of the poor homosexuals. But what about women? Do we not have sexual feelings too? And surely the "elaborate time-consuming process of courtship" is one of the most beautiful of human activities?'

'But,' says Robert, 'you yourself said that living in sin with Mr Schwarzenberg was very exciting. Or do you count that as courtship?'

Lotte has an inkling that this boy might be homosexual. In which case he is, very likely, carrying the Aids virus. She has a strong impulse to move her chair. And it is possible that tiny drops of his saliva might have landed on her plate. She wipes her lips, and her cheeks too, with her napkin, and lays her arm on the table, a little clumsily, between her plate and his. If she was sitting opposite she would not mind. But here she can almost feel the warmth of his blood, circulating dangerously. She glances round the room and is struck by its smallness: apart from the table, chairs and sideboard there is room for hardly anything else – only a narrow pine dresser, its shelves crowded with too much china. And the room has red wallpaper! A strange lapse of taste which makes it quite claustrophobic.

'I try to be modern,' she says, smiling at him and shifting her chair ever so slightly, so that she seems to be facing him more squarely, but is also fractionally further away (the difference, possibly, between life and death). She thinks: Henry, you are a remarkable man. You are not an artist (thank God) but you know everything. Your view of life is Olympian and you are saying all these things to reassure your son that it's all right to be queer. (But *is* he queer?) She says to Robert: 'Love is more important than sex, which is so ephemeral. And the beauty of courtship is that it prepares the ground for love.' She looks at Bill and smiles serenely; forcing him to lower his eyes. She is surprised by her own eloquence. Of course the German accent is still there, her gutteral r's, the confusion of v's, w's and f's, the clipping and compressing which gave such an impression of efficiency – all of which was desirable, she would not part with it – but she has a command, a genuine command of the English language. Saliva, she remembers, is not supposed to transmit the Aids virus. But the small distance she has created, between her chair and his, is nevertheless a sensible precaution. It also means she is slightly closer to Henry.

'Of course,' says Henry. 'I'm sure we all agree about that. Now – I've got some excellent sweet wine here, Beaumes de Venise; shall we try it?'

'Oh yes, darling,' says Yvonne. 'I'm sure Bill and Lotte would like some.'

It is so easy, he thinks, to impress others. Occasionally he would like to come up against a real opponent, someone whose intellectual grasp is as keen as his own; but where? In his own environment, whether at the hospital, or in consultation with his patients, or with Yvonne, with her 'artistic' friends, or with poor struggling Rob, he is in a permanent state of superiority. It is gratifying, but boring. He pours the wine into the glass which Bill lifts towards him. Some people, he thinks, are driven by a passionate search; but why, what are they looking for? It is all a misunderstanding, the replay of an unhappy, insecure childhood. And yet for them life remains open, full of anxiety, but also adventure. While for me it is already a closed circle, a book which I have read too many times. I am complacent. I am caught in the circle of my own overbearing, analytical mind. Only the 'life force', the struggle to survive, is mysterious to me – and this is not enough to shatter my monotony, for the life force too is predictable; I do not understand where it comes from, but it does not vary; I know it inside out. Oh Yvonne, how full of sadness you are; now that we are getting old, now that sex is no longer important, I cannot satisfy you; my practical answers, my confidence, can reassure you, but never match your deeper needs; and you know, you must know, how much a prisoner I myself am, of my strength, of my infallible explanations, but I cannot change, I can never really share with you your thirst, your endless need . . .

Mr Schwarzenberg sips the Beaumes de Venise with evident delight. Standing beside him Henry notices a small patch of eczema on the top of his head. He will probably lose the few hairs that remain to him, he thinks with faint satisfaction. 'Excellent,' murmurs Bill, swilling the golden liquid around in his mouth. The sheer pleasure of the taste is a profound experience, which no one can take away from him. He closes his eyes while the nectar remains in his mouth, and tries to keep it there as long as possible, extracting every advantage. But then something calls to him from his throat, and he knows he must swallow. For there are taste buds too at the very back of the mouth, and only by swallowing can these be reached. But swallowing also indicates the imminent end of pleasure. How sad that pleasure, by its very nature, should be so transient. Fortunately his glass, with which his fingers are in contact, is still almost full. He swallows, opens his eyes and cannot help glancing at Lotte. Her face, pouched, is coming at him, features distorted into a hideous sneer. It is her parody of a smile, the only one he is allowed to respond to. He has played her game more than once already this evening; he is damned if he's going to do it again. He will not smile back. Nevertheless, he will be more circumspect in his enjoyment of the next mouthful. It was not, strictly speaking, necessary to close his eyes. Despite all his good resolutions he feels a tightening in the corners of his lips, as if they were being drawn apart by fearful magnets, but he resists with all his strength. He can feel them twitching. Lotte is smiling, indulgently, as one might smile at a small boy who has said something childish that he considers very funny. And yet he himself has not tried in any way to be funny. He thinks of the squid, which is able to blow out a cloud of ink and hide behind it. He breathes out slowly, invisibly, as if this hot air were a gas capable of deflecting Lotte's rays.

'You are giving Bill such pleasure,' she says to Henry.

Bill smiles affably. 'As Lotte knows, I am very fond of sweet wine,' he says.

Yvonne envies him. She herself has never had much pleasure from food and drink. The world of flesh and blood means little to her, until it is transformed by her fantasy. This is also the way she has enjoyed sex. As she and Henry have grown older their lovemaking has become almost non-existent, and this is only normal. They lie in bed, flat on their backs, without touching. Sometimes he gives her a little peck on the cheek; but, at the wrong moment, even this can be unbearable. They switch off the light, after a few minutes' reading: Henry, usually a medical journal, or a biography, his bifocals low on the bridge of his nose (on which grows a repulsive, insistent hair) and she, naturally, a novel. They turn onto their sides and soon Henry, she can tell, is fast asleep. This is a delightful moment for her (yes, she thinks, perhaps that is a real, tangible pleasure); she loves him to be defencelessly asleep (she can watch over him), and the room with its sweeping chintz curtains, squares of light from the street illuminating curious unexpected bits of the walls or ceiling, her quiet dressing-table with its old, generous mirror and pictures of Rob and Henry stuck under the glass top, all this is intensely peaceful, like a majestic ship cleaving the ocean, and so full of happy security that it can even excite her – and it was sometimes this excitement, the excitement of such security, that used, in the old days, to keep her awake; she would step lightly from the bed, in her loose nightgown, and touch these beloved, solid objects and then touch herself – to make sure that she and they belonged to the same world. Now, in middle age, she has only just begun to understand that her furniture, her flat and Henry are there to stay.

'Do you think', asks Lotte, 'that all homosexuals will eventually die from Aids?'

'Why on earth should they?' says Robert; something is strengthening inside him, for battle if necessary: it is the thought of Johnny.

'They are not all promiscuous, Lotte dear,' says Yvonne.

The word 'promiscuous' is unusual in her mouth. She tries it again, under her breath, and the repeated sibilants, separated only by a vague 'u', are like the sinewy movements of a snake, as it swerves through the grass. The word 'promiscuous' is strange and fascinating; addictive, when whispered softly, as though a communication with dark, potent forces of nature. The very sound (she tries again), with its four stealthy syllables, is like a call, a recall, to a primeval state, before dinner parties and polite conversation were invented. And this snake, she thinks, is still alive, has always been alive, inside me, thrusting its sleek head through roots and sap-filled stems, its belly scraping the earth, moulding the dust to its own shape, out of sight, mute, alert . . . and indeed there were times, rare now, as she lay next to Henry, when the orderly routine of her life was invaded by something from a different source, when the spirit of the wild managed to creep in among the laundered sheets. Sex is really a funny thing, she thinks. As you get older you begin to take it less seriously, with a sense of humour. You don't quite take it at face value. And then all of a sudden out it pops, in all its vigour, suddenly urgent again. Then she would lie, filled with apprehension, next to this hateful man who understood nothing about her finer feelings, who brutally explained everything in terms of nerves, electric charges and unhappy childhoods. She hates with all her guts the slavery to which this man subjects her, and most of all she hates his thick complacent silvery hair and his body which is gradually rotting away despite his exercises and all his vanity. And then, when her hatred has reached a peak, she feels his hand, which is not hot but cold, press gently, evilly, through her flimsy nightgown, just below her breast (she always sleeps on the left); there is still time, now, to pretend nothing has happened, she can still say 'good-night, darling' and turn onto her side. But if she does not, if she lies still, like a hare which plays dead when the panting, salivating dog has caught up with it, he will begin to murmur in her ear. 'It's all right,' he whispers, 'nothing to be afraid of, you're comfortable' and she waits, her mind blank, like a child who is about to be told a story, the same story, and she feels the excitement of the child, but it has passed through a magic grid and turns her body into something soft and clammy, unlike his unmoving hand which is always dry. 'Now the lights are on, they're coming down slowly,' he continues, his mouth only a centimetre from her ear; and she should, indeed, be frightened of his voice, for it is so calm and purposeful; she is face to face with his pure, unadulterated soul, the soul that lives by her side, with her, in her bed, but which she manages, most of the time (with the help of food, gossip, television) to keep at bay. 'I'm putting on my mask,' the relentless whisper continues, and the hand moves a little, up or down. What on earth is he talking about? This is quite absurd, and so degrading! 'Other people are with us, also with masks, they're here to help, they won't say a word . . . the table of implements is ready.' The phrases are beautifully spaced, like an actor building a climax; she knows only too well that it is a trick, a performance (this is what makes it so real); she wants to scream and kick and run away from this squalid rigmarole! She begins to squirm like a fish under his hand, her eyes tightly closed. She wants to block all her senses against the lights, the masks, the despicable onlookers, but she cannot escape the brutality of his soft voice, the warm air against her ear which comes from the depths of his body. 'Which implements shall we use today?'

'Thank God', says Lotte, 'we are not living in the last century. Can you imagine what would happen to the homosexuals? It would be seen as the hand of God, and no one would be able to think differently.'

How Robert hates this line of thinking, the most banal and the most insidious. 'Don't forget', he smiles, 'it is not a homosexual disease. World figures show that heterosexuals are the most affected.'

'You are thinking of Africa,' says Henry. 'There are no reliable figures for Africa.'

'All the same,' he continues, 'it seems likely that, the world over, the greatest number of sufferers are heterosexual. Then homosexual men. Only lesbians are completely spared. So if the hand of God is at work, it is clear that He favours lesbians most, then homosexual men, and is most displeased with heterosexuals, of both sexes.'

'Very well put,' says Lotte. Yes, it is clear the boy is queer, '*schwul*' in her own language. 'You hear that, Bill?'

Yvonne laughs. She squints at Flavia, and tries to catch Rob's eye. She would rather like Flavia to be a lesbian. She herself is not concerned by Aids; it is the least of her worries. It is not transmitted by breath, or words, or implements. Of all the images of those dark rare nights, the implements are the most powerful. On the shining table lie the grey, blind tools, heavy and indistinct. 'I am choosing an implement,' he murmurs, 'I am testing it.' And the fingers of the hand which rests on her come, dreamily, to life, they mould and caress a rod, a point, they invent curves, ridges, blades, and she can hardly bear it, she has to touch herself and moans in rhythm to the motion of his fingers.

But no, no, no! she thinks. No, none of this has ever happened, these are crazy thoughts, thoughts all her own! Never, never has Henry made love to her like this! And she looks at the elderly man opposite her at the table, and indeed there is nothing godlike, nothing devilish, about the wrinkles around his eyes, his double chin, the brown spots which materialise, year by year, on his face, his hands, how very mortal he is! Poor Henry, you are not at all a monster, you are kind and brave, like everyone you have your anxieties (I can see it now, in your eyes) which you try, proudly, to hide: poor darling, you need me, and I will do my best to give you my support, my companionship! And I am grateful, so grateful! Suddenly she feels herself blushing; and Lotte's implacable eye on her.

'Could you give Bill a refill, darling?' he calls to her, passing the bottle.

How strange is the use of the word 'darling'! Never, on those demonic occasions, never with The Witness, did she say 'darling'! 'Darling' belongs to her everyday life. She takes the bottle of Beaumes de Venise, her fingers grazing his. She does not know where his fingers have been, what they have touched today, whose hands they have shaken, what operations they have performed, and yet on them, surely, is microscopic evidence of all this, so that his actions, even in sequence, could be read by one who had the key. And so, perhaps, could all the movements of Rob's heart be traced from his playing; the particular emphasis he might give to a special note, his use of piano and forte, the significance of a pause, an accent, the way he grades ritardandos – all this must have a correspondence with his deepest self, his soul. And so she understands why playing the piano, according to Rubinstein, is like making love; although did that include the sort of lovemaking she sometimes fantasised about?

'Do give some to Bill,' says Henry, slightly irritated.

She laughs, realising that she is holding the Beaumes de Venise in mid-air. She catches Bill's small eye, flickering anxiously on and off the bottle. She fills his glass lavishly. 'No, no, not too much!' he protests, covering the glass with his hand.

But then she calls Rob 'darling' too. And even Lotte, in a fit of enthusiasm, she might call darling. Does Rob, in his mysterious life about which she knows nothing, call some people 'darling'? She remembers, hazily, that there has been talk of Aids. And she experiences a mighty rush of anxiety, on two counts: first, that she has not been concentrating, she has not been leading and shaping the conversation as a hostess should: and, second, that Rob might be in danger. She remembers, some time ago, meeting a young man, Johnny, who she knew immediately was his lover. Is he still around? Does he share Rob's bed? He was a curious '*petit bonhomme*', constantly flashing a toothy smile and unable to sit still. She seems to remember that he spoke French, although not perfectly. Rob brought him around, for some reason . . . perhaps to borrow a cookery book? Yes, Rob wanted to borrow a cookery book, and brought Johnny. Actually she remembers having rather a lively conversation, about Normandy, and the boy got his geography muddled up, confusing Granville and Honfleur. And insisted on talking French. But most of all she remembers the curious way he sat on his chair, somehow only on one buttock, and fidgeting . . . not very '*sortable*'.

'Of course,' she says, 'we all have to be very careful about Aids now.'

'Why?' asks Robert, with a twinkle. 'Do you think you're in danger?'

'You never know,' she shrugs, returning his sweet smile. 'Of course I'm old, but it's such a bore for young people.' He's sensible, she thinks, I can see he's sensible. 'They're trying out several different vaccines, I believe.'

He can see her mind working; she's longing to know if he's had the test.

'I think everyone should have the test,' she says. 'I mean, if one thinks there's a possibility.' She sips her Beaumes de Venise.

'No, I don't agree,' he says. 'It's fine if you find out you're negative, but if not . . .'

'But one mustn't infect others!' she cries, bitterly regretting the hysteria in her voice. 'I mean', she controls herself, 'knowing, if you have it, that you have to be careful – not to give it to other people.'

'Safe sex is the rule these days,' he says.

'Saf*er* sex,' put in Henry.

'We've already had this conversation,' Robert frowns. 'Obviously you weren't listening.'

'I was, darling!' she protests. 'But it's, well, it's almost criminal to . . .'

'Of course,' agrees Lotte. 'The responsible thing is to have the test, if you think there's any danger.'

'That's all I meant,' she says desperately. 'Only if one thinks there's a good chance. And most people don't seriously have to worry about that. I mean, like us, probably, around this table . . .'

'I know someone who's got Aids,' says Flavia.

Everybody looks at her.

'The full disease?' Robert asks.

She nods.

Henry smiles at her kindly. 'Someone close?' he asks.

'Quite a close friend.'

'A homosexual?' enquires Lotte, trying to look concerned.

Flavia nods again, pursing her lips. Robert is furious with

her. She is betraying him. In fact, she is boasting. She forgets all about his feelings for the sake of creating a stir. He can feel the curiosity of the others bursting out from their civilised, tolerant faces: who is this creature? Was he promiscuous (did he deserve it)? Did *you* ever have sex with him? Did Robert have sex with him? How ill is he? How long has he had it? What are his symptoms? How much longer has he got? Is there a chance you might have caught it from him? Even Mr Schwarzenberg's little eyes light up. They all stare at her. But nobody asks these questions.

'Life is so unpredictable,' says his mother. 'We could all be run over by a bus tomorrow!'

'Exactly. Mr Schwarzenberg,' he says, taking the bottle, 'a drop more?'

He fills the conductor's glass quickly.

'I must make the coffee,' she exclaims, standing up.

'What a gloomy subject,' he says cheerfully. 'But it's good to talk about it, don't you agree?'

Would his mother survive, if he died of Aids?

'Of course, darling! One must always talk about these things,' she says, putting on the kettle and handing round tiny coffee cups with great efficiency.

He remembers introducing Johnny to his mother. They had chatted about France, and he had been irritated by Johnny's efforts to charm her. Afterwards Johnny had said she was a most attractive lady, and he had felt flattered. He had been horribly pleased that Johnny liked her, that he admired her flat, her status, her maid, her money: all the things Johnny did not have, and which Robert cared nothing for – and yet Johnny's admiration gave him a good feeling.

'Delicious coffee,' says Lotte.

'Oh darling, it's only Marks and Spencer.'

Did he and Johnny play a power game, like his parents?

'Bill and I don't take sugar,' Lotte says.

'I'm afraid I do,' smiles Henry, exposing his silver filling. 'It's one of my little vices. I've got an impossibly sweet tooth.'

'He simply can't resist a cake – or a patisserie,' his mother laughs. 'So I don't buy them.'

'I get plenty at the hospital!' He screws up his face at her, and she puckers her nose and almost, Robert thinks, sticks her tongue out at him.

Flavia coos with laughter, like a satisfied dove, and this reminds him of Johnny. For Johnny often gave the impression of being satisfied, of being self-contained; and his body was full and firm, not unlike the feathered breast of a happy dove. But soon that warm vital body became untouchable, and Robert could only appreciate him from afar, aesthetically; like a sculpture protected by a glass screen. In Rome, he remembers, the night before his birthday, Johnny said: 'I'm going for a walk. I want to experience Rome at night. You know, see the street prowlers, the tramps and so on.' Robert too would have liked to experience Rome by night. Johnny added: 'I know you're tired. You go to bed. I won't be long.' He smiled, but without opening his lips. The light from the passageway shone diagonally across his face, hollowing his cheeks. He stood there, blocking the narrow corridor, calmly ordering Robert to bed. And so Robert yawned obediently and said: 'Yes, all right. I am rather tired. Be careful.' Johnny's smile expanded. 'I'll tell you all about it,' he said, blowing him a kiss and disappearing with carefully controlled strides.

When he came back, and woke him, Robert knew it was very late. Johnny's hand on his cheek was hot and full of vigour. 'Aren't you tired?' he asked stupidly. Johnny ignored this remark and closed his eyes. Robert thought: what does he want from me? He felt angry. Johnny had woken him up, pointlessly. And yet he nearly said: 'I'm glad you're back. I still love you.' Instead, with the sort of paternal concern that must have been so un-aphrodisiac, he asked: 'Are you sure you're all right?' And Johnny snapped instantly into flippant, elusive life. He chattered about his lipomas, about this and that, clucked like a chicken, cooed like a pigeon. Robert longed for a moment of silence, the silence that existed when Johnny's hand was on his cheek and he first opened his eyes. But he himself broke that silence, and nothing could bring it back. When Johnny got into his bed and lay quietly (although still clucking and cooing) he touched him, but without love or desire. It was painful, a painful duty, to touch him. So when Johnny sat up and said he felt sick – which Robert didn't believe – it was a profound relief. As he left for the bathroom Robert saw his face as he had never seen it before. 'I've got indigestion,' Johnny said, 'perhaps it was that pork chop.' His face was changed, as if an obscure pain had burst to the surface, right into the pores of his skin, his forehead, into the muscles of his lips and cheeks, over which he usually had such masterly control; all the flexibility, which was so intriguing, was gone, and the flesh seemed to have stiffened, drawn tight against the bone. Robert looked in surprise, as Johnny's eyelids drooped and a cleft appeared between his brows. It was almost the face of an old man. Johnny said, raising his eyelids a little: 'Sorry, baby. I won't be long.' From the back, as he went to the bathroom, it was the Johnny he knew: movements lithe as a cat, hair spurting like water jets all over his head and down to a point on the nape of his neck. Perhaps the change was wilful, an over-dramatisation of the indigestion he didn't feel; or perhaps it was just a trick of the light, sloping obliquely through the slats. He heard water running in the bathroom; imagined Johnny turning on the taps and, probably, looking at himself in the mirror. If so, he would not be pleased by what he saw. In place of the mythical creature, always graceful, was an uncomfortable human being, trapped in clumsy flesh and skin. The actor was glimpsed off stage, without his makeup. And Robert saw: Johnny was no different to him, only more selfish . . .

When he came out of the bathroom, Robert closed his eyes and listened to his all too human steps as he crossed the room, to his own bed. He heard him sigh, and whisper something. Johnny had no respect for the sleep of others. He would always wake you, though gently, if he wanted company. A few moments later he was snoring, quite loudly, and Robert was still awake.

'*Ach*, it's almost midnight!' says Mrs Schwarzenberg. 'Ve

have so far to go! And I've drunk so much. But so has Bill. We're sure to be over the limit!'

'In the case of Bill,' smiles Henry, 'he would need quite a lot, I think, to push him over the top.'

'You hear that, Bill?' Mr Schwarzenberg lowers his eyes, preparing automatically for an insult. 'It's sometimes an advantage to be fat! But then his eyes are not very good. For driving at night.'

'It's all right, dear,' he says, trying to push back his chair. Just in time he notices that the tablecloth is caught under one of the chair legs. 'I can drive perfectly well. Because I do think, perhaps, you've had a bit too much tonight!' Looking round at the company he compresses his lips so that his cheeks swell out like small balloons; he gives a quick succession of winks with his right eye.

'*Ach, ach!*' cries Lotte, 'He's giving me orders!'

And so, thinks Yvonne, the day is over. The concert, the cooking, the dinner, the day belong already to the past. If only this day could impregnate itself on her mind, so that she could possess it, like an object . . . As she helps Bill, in the cramped space, to disentangle his chair and push it back, she tries to turn her brain into a camera, a photographic plate, and concentrates on the sight of Rob, his head jutting forward, his eyes turned upwards, at a particular moment (the exact music escapes her) in the last movement of the Fantasy. Now Bill has made it to his feet, and Henry is leading Lotte by the arm into the hall. The Schwarzenbergs are going, and she desperately wants Rob to stay a few more minutes for a post-mortem, but bloody Flavia is with him, and she doesn't think she can face a threesome . . . nevertheless she smiles at them both, and whispers conspiratorially: 'Do stay a bit longer!' She would like to close the door and leave Henry to deal with the Schwarzenbergs! But Rob and Flavia are already following them out. She is left alone in the dining-room, with the crumpled napkins, the greasy leftovers on the pretty floral plates (inherited from her parents), crumbs everywhere and all the smudged glasses; and especially the vacated chairs, roughly pushed aside, with the seats still warm. 'Just coming!' she shouts, looking at the chairs, empty, abandoned like her. Memories of the evening flicker through her mind, as if it was all long ago: Flavia astride her chair in the doorway, Lotte's baiting of her husband, Henry's remark about the laying on of hands (now that was interesting; it rather scares her) and Rob, so sweet, so charming, so *fair* – yes, undoubtedly that was a most important aspect of him, he is so fair, so determined not to have any prejudices whatsoever, so much so that she almost feels ready to cry – so serious during the discussion about Aids . . . she hears Monsieur Pischik barking in the hall; perhaps he has again discovered Mr Schwarzenberg's shoe! What is she doing here, alone, preferring this roomful of ghosts? She runs her hand over the tablecloth and collects a few crumbs; piles the dessert plates, with Rob's at the top – is it hers below, or Lotte's? She stares at the remains of the chocolate mousse; how strange to think that the ingredients, which she herself mixed and stirred a few hours before, were now being absorbed into the stomachs, the alimentary canals, the blood and bodies of her guests! She hears Rob laughing and calling Pischik.

What if he caught Aids? Her heart beats ferociously; she feels as afraid of everything as when she was a little girl, and at the same time she is inexplicably playing truant, refusing to do her duty. Don't they miss her, in the hall? If he had Aids, would he allow her to nurse him? This is a question of the utmost importance. She grips the back of a chair and stares at the deep red wall. What she is thinking is worse than terrible. For she would like to nurse him. She already pictures the situation: her continual, slavish presence at his bedside (if he wanted it – and wouldn't he?) and the mighty, spiritual, transcendental effort to transfer every ounce of her strength, physical and mental, to him. Her life, at this tragic time, would acquire unprecedented meaning.

Robert appears in the doorway. He sees her standing bolt upright, gazing into space. 'Mother! What on earth are you doing?' She is so relieved to see him strong and healthy that she runs up and kisses him: a nice, demure little kiss from pouted lips which hardly touch his skin. 'I'm sorry,' she says. 'I felt slightly faint . . . I'm better now. Will you stay?'

'I'd better take Flavia.'

'Yes, yes, all right, darling. We'll have a post-mortem tomorrow,' she whispers, screwing up her face, for the evening has been so funny.

'They're going,' he says. And then, because she hesitates: 'Are you sure you're feeling better?'

She doesn't answer immediately; the interrogative, in his mouth, is like music; a gentle phrase, unfinished: and hers to complete. 'Of course, *chéri*.' She puts her hand on his arm. 'You really did play beautifully.'

And he smiles at her, from his height.

'Poor mother wasn't feeling well,' he tells the others.

'Just a little turn,' she explains. 'I sometimes have them. It's been such a wonderful evening! And so very nice', she says warmly to Bill and Lotte, 'to have you! You really must come again.' Surrounded as she is by the aura of love, she means what she says, and the whole evening, it seems, has been unforgettable, a blaze of light. Lotte, on the doorstep, gives her hard, passionate German kisses, crying: 'And you must all come to us! Bill is so busy, but I'm trying to get him to cut down!'

In his pocket Bill crosses his fingers. Over my dead body, he says to himself. Music is his lifeline, his little patch of freedom. The Beaumes de Venise has given him unusual courage. He says: 'Now, now, Lotte. You know how much I enjoy giving concerts. I'm not cutting down – not yet! But of course we'll find an evening – when we're all free.' All his toes are soggy, and from one shoe part of the leather sole is missing; he can feel the grain of the haircord carpet with the ball of his foot. He looks down at Mr Pischik, into that wide wet face, and slowly shakes his head. Mr Pischik can't tear his eyes away; he has never seen such a man. Flavia laughs; Robert takes her hand. 'Congratulations,' says Lotte, and kisses him. 'Yes,' says Bill. 'Keep working, young man!' Flavia is like a shield; with her beside him he is almost invincible. He would like the Schwarzenbergs to think they are lovers.

They stand on the landing, waiting for the lift. Yvonne does not want Robert to leave with the Schwarzenbergs. But she cannot bundle in Flavia, and keep him back. 'The lift is not really supposed to take four,' she mutters. 'Especially if Bill is one of them,' adds Lotte. The lift arrives, and the doors slide softly open. 'We'll stay, mother, and give you a hand with the clearing up.' The Schwarzenbergs get in, filling most of the space. The automatic doors close with a gentle click, and Bill and Lotte are framed for a last moment, waving cheerfully, against the little rectangular window. Robert has his arm around Flavia.

'What a pair of clowns!' exclaims Yvonne, and Flavia begins to laugh. 'Pischik, you were very naughty,' says Robert. 'Poor old Bill . . .' Flavia's laughter is growing, and threatens to engulf them all. 'Shh! The neighbours . . .' reproaches Yvonne. 'They're a dear old couple,' she adds sternly. 'I wouldn't be in Bill's shoes for all the tea in China,' says Henry. 'Oh no! Nor I in Lotte's!' They all giggle and Robert says: 'We'll help you clear up.' 'Oh no, darling, I'm going to leave everything tonight. Sally's coming tomorrow.' She feels awkward, standing with all her weight in her right leg; her foot, in its soft green shoe with a sensible heel, is getting cramped; but she doesn't want to move, not an inch, not even to shift her weight onto the other foot. There is something fragile about the way they hesitate, there on the landing, like a balancing act; they are together still, yet poised on the brink of separation, and the slightest move on her part could ruin everything . . . Henry bids the young couple good-night, kisses Flavia and gives Robert a number of taps on his shoulder. He goes in, and they hear the clinking of glasses and empty bottles. 'He likes to do a little basic clearing', whispers Yvonne, 'before going to bed.' 'Well, mother,' Robert says, 'you made us all a wonderful meal.'

She sees him let go of Flavia: it is natural enough, as he must be about to kiss her goodbye. She steps forward, and prepares to receive him. It is always easier, she thinks, to leave than to be left. They will go out together, into the night, and she will stay here. Oh how dirty the carpet is, she notices, clicking her tongue, out here in the corridor! The porter is not doing his job properly . . . Can he know, does he guess, how empty her life is?

'You must go, darling,' she says. 'Have a good night – you've deserved it.' She does not want him to know: she will not put this burden onto his shoulders. 'You're so tall,' she jokes, 'don't you ever feel you're going to topple over?' What, after all, could be gained by his knowing? 'I've got big feet,' he says, 'they keep me upright.' She hears a rattling behind the door opposite, of dark polished wood like hers, where another middle-aged couple lives. Flavia is laughing again; she always finds Robert so funny. 'Quick!' says Yvonne, 'Someone's coming!' She flings her arms round his neck. '*Bravo, chéri!* It was a wonderful concert!' She gives Flavia a nice little peck on both cheeks, and presses the lift button. But he says to Flavia 'Let's walk down', and leads her to the stairs. 'Yes, walk down,' she agrees in a bright voice. 'Speak to you tomorrow,' he calls.

'A *demain!*'

She listens to their steps as they go down, muffled almost immediately by the thick carpet. She decides not to go to the bannister. He will drive Flavia home, and then return to his solitary flat.

Are you unhappy, darling? Are you, like me, insecure? I am here, if you need me . . . She sends out her love after him, as if she were releasing a bird, to comfort and protect him always.

The rattling at the door opposite has stopped. A pity: she would like to have a word with old Mr and Mrs Wilkes, and tell them about the concert. She waits, but no one appears. Behind her, she hears a door close: Henry has gone into the bathroom. She takes a few steps along the corridor, and looks at the stained carpet, littered with bits of paper, fluff, and even cigarette butts. Her eyes fill with tears. She wipes them away with both hands, and waits for the emotion to pass, covering her cheeks with her palms; she feels the flickering of her eyelashes against her fingertips. 'I'm so lucky,' she whispers. She walks back and gazes at the open door of her home. She dabs at her cheeks with the sleeves of her blouse, and wonders if she is still pretty. This unexpected thought makes her smile. She has never been pretty, not really. Automatically her hands go to her hair, to make sure the lacquered curls are still in place. They are. She realises, with another little smile, that she is humming. *Au clair de la lune, mon ami Pierrot, Prête-moi ta plume Pour écrire un mot . . .* funny the way that sweet little tune is always bubbling to the surface; nothing at all, in some ways, has changed since she was a child, and yet how far away is her childhood! The little song is an anchor for her still. She will return now, to her home, lock the solid door behind her, switch out the lights, repossess her objects and her furniture; join her husband in bed. What sort of a man is Henry, she wonders, a little afraid. She hesitates, caught between worlds; her feet seem to float above the floor. She must be brave, once again.

Oh – then she remembers. Pischik has not been out for a last pee! She calls: 'Pischik! Pischik darling!' Gratefully she takes down the lead from behind the door.

Still wearing his tailcoat and white bow tie, Robert walks down a narrow street, and stops before a small door, flush with the wall and painted dark blue. A ribbon of light, from inside, frames the door; above, in thin neon tubes of different colours, unlit, is the word: TALENT. He presses the bell, runs a hand through his hair, and wonders what effect his unusual clothes will have. The door opens and a man with bleary eyes stands in the entrance. His hand, which holds the door, has thick white fingers with heavy folds of skin around the knuckles. Robert smiles brightly and says: 'Good evening!' The man nods, and asks for five pounds.

Talent is a large, low-ceilinged room with a piano at one end and a bar at the other. It is full of people, cigarette smoke, and noise. He advances slowly, pushing between bodies. There is red plush wallpaper, and worn velvet benches running the length of the walls; small wooden tables and little chairs with velvet seats and black frets, all occupied. He reaches the far end of the room, and waits by the bar, amid the crush; his head protrudes, and instinct tells him to stoop. He is aware of a familiar tension, as if he were trying to shorten and compress his joints. He notices that a young man close by is doing the exact opposite. He is trying to elongate himself; his shoulders are slightly raised and his body is straight as a rod; he stands on the very outside rim of his shoes. Even so, his curly hair hardly comes above Robert's shoulder. On the counter behind the bar is a porcelain bust of a man's torso with a hand thrust into it, fingers coming out just below the neck, white and pristine. He remembers that this image flashed through his mind during the concert. The hand is strong and fleshy, the little finger almost as long as the others. In his memory the torso was headless, but in fact there is a head; with broad classical features, a high shock of hair brushed back, and a serene, secretive smile; the lowered eyes gaze at the fingers which split open his chest.

He is surrounded by people. Only minutes ago, alone, he stood at the gate of Flavia's house, his hand resting on the wooden bar, and heard her laughing, inside, as she climbed the stairs. He looked up at the windows, and they were dark. He could stay there as long as he liked, until his fingers stiffened and merged with the wood, and night creatures relaxed their guard and crept over him. Or he could go, explore the slumbering streets, converse with cats, pursue a tortuous route back to his car, a great loop which no one would ever know about. Like this he would delay the night's last adventure. A tiny spider crosses his hand. He leaves the gate and immerses himself in the landscape, the houses which are flimsy silhouettes against the sky, or thick opaque masses, alleys that twist into the darkness of gardens, sleepy windows ajar with half-drawn curtains, lighted windows into which he peeps from hidden vantage points, windows aglow with the grey blur of television and the silent forms of viewers; everything is vivid, even the black curve of the tarmac road, sinking towards the gutters, the sharp angle it forms against the pavement, and the rough grain of the pavement itself. Alone now, he can observe everything; as scientists study the habits of animals from their tracks and their spoor, so the emptied city grants him insight into the lives of its inhabitants, their minds, their habits; like his father he is a surgeon, investigating the body of a sleeping patient. The city has a life of its own, more real than by day, as if night has released its spirit.

By the bar an old man, whose red swollen fingers hold a glass of whisky, is slowly revolving. His eyes flicker across faces: he makes two complete revolutions, then frowns and shakes his head. He stumbles towards a young lad, who leans against a corner of the bar, and puts his arm round him. The boy, wearing a kind of leather harness over a bare chest, takes no notice. The old man lurches vaguely against him. Robert orders a brandy, and sees the barman hand a pint of lager to the boy; the white-haired old man fumbles in his pocket and pays. His companion already has a soft little belly, which flops out, an inch or two, over his jeans. The old man chuckles, moves his eyebrows up and down, and taps this protruding flab. At each tap the boy's cheek gives a sharp involuntary twitch. The rest of him is completely still, heavy flesh weighing down the bar. The old man fidgets, and moves away only to return; the boy is his anchor.

Robert takes his brandy and weaves through the crowd, looking for a seat. By the piano a tall drag queen has begun to sing, her voice relayed throughout the room. 'My story is much too sad to be told,' she croons, 'but practically everything leaves me totally cold . . . The only exception I know is when I'm out on a spree I suddenly turn and see your *fabulous face*', and her own huge oblong face trembles against the microphone.

She smiles, a small vulnerable smile; and it seems to Robert that she is wearing the same lipstick as Yvonne . . . as he sits, sipping his brandy, he is drawn towards her smile, a smile very different to Flavia's open brilliant smile, a smile which suddenly stabs him in the chest; the drag queen sings on, no longer smiling now, but the whole evening, the concert, the dinner, comes back to him vividly and he sees his mother congratulating him in the artists' room; in his mind's eye he sees her smile, as she smiled then, and it makes him shudder. His true life, it seems, has taken place, and still takes place, within that small space, that tentative opening between white-powdered cheeks. Her smile is omnipotent, and yet vulnerable. What is the meaning of it? Is he responsible for her happiness? Or she for his? The parted lips, between which he flounders, half in, half out, command devotion, and yet beg him to take the lead. He stares at the mechanism of their relationship, as at a watch whose back plate has been opened; and it is a hermetic, magically adjusted system, never still, whose cogs and wheels fit together so perfectly that nothing can disturb their timeless play. And the sight of her, too, as she stood bravely in the corridor, after dinner, smiling and bidding him good-night, and yet somehow lacking a vital organ, invades his brain. Inside his black leather shoes he screws up his toes and stubs them against the floor. She is as much a part of him as a malformation: a hump he has to drag around on his back for ever. Oh come now, isn't it terrible to think of your own mother as a deformation, a parasite on your own body? He shudders, and rubs his neck against the velvet seat, trying to scratch it off, a hump stuck onto him. But he cannot. Wherever he goes, he cannot get away. She is always there, pleading, searching for him like a wanderer in the desert, lost, seeking an oasis. Her thirst knows no bounds. And he understands. He loves her, and feels infinite compassion.

People file past, greet each other with loud kisses like long-lost friends, or stand alone, like islands, with a firm grip on their glasses, searching among the crowd, staring or ignoring stares, as bar staff glide through their midst with drinks for the drag queen and her pianist. He sinks back into the soft seat, and tries to be invisible. He cannot join these people. With Flavia, driving home, he laughed at the events of the evening, at Pischik and Bill and Lotte; at the fateful net which long ago gathered his parents together, and the Schwarzenbergs, and condemned them to couple, for the hell of it; so that one day they will celebrate silver and golden weddings, nurse each other's last illnesses, surrounded by the grandchildren, and lie in the same grave: marriages which last so long must be happy marriages . . . the sheer weight of the years is Nature's secret weapon, undreamt of by the young; trim bodies and idealistic eyes are no match for wrinkled brows and sagging stomachs. He bores into the velvet seat, quite invisible; submerged by secret, bitter envy. For he *envies* his parents; their comfortable, acclaimed lives; with an envy that must never be spoken, which must be dismissed with a shrug as a passing aberration, for to admit it would strip him of all defences, and he would be no more than an infant abandoned in a den of lions.

But why, why should this be? Who is out for his blood?

Flavia laughed, and put her hand over the gear lever, telling him what a marvellous evening she's had: his playing, the hilarious party, and the wonderful warmth of his presence; she adores him, she will love him for ever. He nodded. His only freedom was in his foot on the accelerator, his hand on the wheel. At the traffic lights he took a violent left turn: a small, useless stratagem, as if he could thwart the rays that spanned out, like a cloud of irradiated dust, from the apartment by Regent's Park. Flavia was surprised, asked where he was taking her (was this really the way to West Hampstead?), laughingly thought that he had a secret plan, for she too, perhaps, like Yvonne, believes him omnipotent.

But he has nothing, nothing to do with all this. He has given a concert, been clapped and praised, he has been the guest at a dinner party, kind to his mother, communicated with his father, charmed Mrs Schwarzenberg. What a personality: how warm, how funny – and an artist into the bargain! Also he is pointlessly tall, covered in black hair, with bony limbs. He can feel his skeleton, like a brittle frame, grating inside his flesh. 'Do you ever think of yourself as a puppet?' he asked Flavia. His expression – he felt it – was both comic and tragic; she picked up the comic side, and laughed. He wanted to hit her, to knock some sense into her. But long ago he started to play a role with her, that of the gawky humourist, or passionate pianist, alternately. So he laughed too and said: 'I just feel I'm a puppet on another person's stage, in another person's hands; I never know what those horrid strings are going to make me do next.' And he made a comic movement, as if he was trying to get away, to avoid something. They zoomed on. After a long silence she said: 'Are you happy, Robert?' And in this question he recognised his mother, her insistence on whether other people were or were not happy. 'Happy? You think I'm happy? The fact is, Flavia, all this time that I've been playing the fool . . .' he broke off. She looked at him with intolerable compassion.

Apart from the spotlights on the singer and the piano the room is lit only by small coloured ceiling lights. Next to him a woman in a white blouse has her arms around a young balding man; sitting opposite another man leans forward, puts his hands on their knees, and repeats drunkenly, shaking his head: 'I love you, how I love you both, oh I love you, how I love you both . . .'

Supposing Johnny was suddenly to come in? Did Johnny come here sometimes? He glances anxiously at the door; he would not know what to do. Perhaps he would remain in this corner, unnoticed, and try to pretend he was seeing Johnny for the first time. Watch him pass through the bar, darting glances, his compact body squeezing into empty spaces; in tight trousers, as always, on his lips a small smile (not the big one in which all his teeth were dramatically exposed), happy to be in this cramped place, for bodies were his element. But Johnny would be certain to see him first; Johnny always saw everyone first. He would think Robert a bore, sitting like a wallflower in his absurd clothes, talking to no one, serious as always. And the possibility, which he feels is imminent, of the door opening and Johnny walking in, alone probably (but how terrible if he came with someone else, someone who felt at home in this sort of place, 'who went out with him', took him dancing) – this possibility affects him strongly. He lights a cigarette, with fingers which almost tremble. For Johnny, at this moment, is somewhere; he is invaded by Johnny's presence in the world, talking, laughing, sleeping, eating, thinking – alive, at this very moment. And suddenly he feels close to him, as if he were with him, observing him from shady doorways, slipping unnoticed behind him onto buses and tubes, present even at his classes (which he directs with such flair) and keeping him company, invisible, in his moments of solitude. He has no desire to intrude, to absorb or be absorbed; he is aware of Johnny as a quite separate life; and this awareness, which is the opposite of possession, is enriching, as if he had stepped into a painted screen and found it to be three-dimensional, full of depth and perspective.

And the clear recognition of Johnny's existence makes him aware, also, of his own. He realises that he too has an independent existence. He has a physical being, which now sits on a seat in a club, smokes a cigarette, and looks around him. He has a soul of his own. He is not a dog, puffing and panting, straining at a leash which will violently rein him in. Nobody is in a position to command and control him. Another, quite different view of the world is possible. A new Robert appears, one who surveys his surroundings with a clear, self-possessed gaze. As if, until now, he had looked only through odd tinted lenses, grafted so tightly onto his eyes that they were an integral part of him, a vital organ without which life was inconceivable. But now, effortlessly, they become detached, they slither down his nose and lie discarded; and . . .

From his seat in Talent he watches this interesting, unfettered person. He sees his fine dark hair which flops pleasantly on the top of his head. This person walks along the street with careful steps, but his caution is the result not of fear but of sensitivity to others. Aware of his strength he does not want to step on anybody's toes. And so he is polite and calm. He smiles at a graceful youth who passes; stops and waits for him. The youth hesitates and turns back. Their meeting is harmonious and inevitable. Meanwhile, on the opposite pavement, a tall uncomfortable young man watches and bites his nails. He moves nervously from one foot to the other and tries to hide in a doorway. He frowns and twitches. One hand flies from his mouth and practises a desperate trill in the air. He lurches forward as if fired from a rocket, his head flies back, and he rushes along the pavement with wild gestures, to the amazement of passers-by.

Robert leans forward and stubs out his cigarette, laughing. The trio at the next table join in, with hearty drunken laughter. The woman in the white blouse kisses him on the ear.

'I get a kick', sings the drag queen, 'every time I see you standing there before me . . . I get a kick though it's clear to me you obviously don't adore me!' Yet her voice is so warm that it's clear her situation is not desperate, she must still have some hope. Or perhaps the kick she gets just from *seeing* him, which makes all other kicks, such as champagne, cocaine, flying in a plane, completely worthless, perhaps this feeling, even unreciprocated, is enough to flood her veins with the beauty of life. Over to his left he glimpses again the old man at the bar, in his dowdy coat and grubby white shirt, flitting around the boy, who takes so little notice of him, except to receive drinks. And perhaps the old man, whose situation is so ridiculous and, to the eyes of the world, degrading, is far more to be envied, lit up as he is, than the other as he stares full and unblinking past the bar staff, into the rows of dripping glasses. And yet what of the rejection that the old man is constantly inviting, and receiving? Is it possible that he has grown immune to rejection?

'I get a kick', throbs the drag queen again and again, beaming at her audience, 'every time I see you standing there before me . . .'

What is the meaning of the warmth in her voice? She seems to love all the people here; protective, motherly, she wants to draw them all to the comfort of her great size, her vast wig and tremulous cheeks. But without her make-up, her wig and false bosom, she must be a different person altogether. He half closes his eyes and tries to imagine the tall, middle-aged man she must also be. But her disguise is so accomplished that it is hard to imagine her without it. In her voice, in her personality, there is no hint of a misfit. Here, in Talent, she is queen and brims with confidence. But out in the street, in the world, stripped of her face, her high heels, her motherliness, how does she feel? She has a skin to slip into, a skin which shields and protects her. He recognises the need for an extra skin. His bow tie and and tails do not serve that purpose. He too lacks a skin. Without it he shivers like a dog. The woman next to him takes his hand and gives him another kiss on the ear. Loud as a thunderclap it drowns the music. He wipes his ear with his sleeve and cleans it out with a finger straight as a ramrod; his face contorts in mock disgust. Everybody roars with laughter.

The song comes to an end. The drag queen is applauded, bares her great teeth to the public, and starts again.

> In a restless world like this one
> Love's ended before it's begun . . .

He gets up and makes his way to the bar, squeezing between all these souls, chattering their heads off. Muttering 'excuse me' he has to graze two young men whose touch is very pleasant (he doesn't linger), three women whose corseted bodies leave him cold, an Asian boy who glides out of the way as if he hardly existed, one laughing blonde woman whose curves are vaguely warm and comforting, a small fat man, perhaps an expert in stolen touches, who backs lightly against him, two men who don't budge at all so that he has to force his way between their middle-aged paunches. At the bar he squeezes in beside a transvestite, foursquare and bespangled. She turns to him and her eyes dilate in mock astonishment.

'Well, well, well,' she intones, grasping his bow tie. 'Look who's here!'

Robert tries to order another brandy and free himself from her hand at his neck, its broad fingers tufted with blond hairs, but she has a grip of steel, reminiscent of Mrs Schwarzenberg.

'Some of us *are* posh!'

'Excuse me,' he says.

'Ooh!' She releases him with a sharp twist, as if setting a ball in motion, and shows an offended profile. She observes him from one eye while he gets his brandy and then deftly blocks his way. 'Come on, darling, give us a clue,' she says, fingering his lapels. 'What's all this in aid of?'

'Oh, the clothes . . . well what about yours?' he asks recklessly.

'You're the odd one out, sweetie pie.' This is true. 'So give us a clue.'

'It's for my job,' he says.

'Pianist?' she asks, with extraordinary insight. 'In some posh do?'

'No,' he says. 'Actually I always dress in this stuff. I like it. So why not? I think it suits me.'

'You're a naughty boy. Lying to Auntie.'

'Isn't that why you dress up too? Because it suits you?'

She bursts into a cascade of laughter, and throws her head so far back that he's afraid for her wig. But in case he might take the opportunity to slip away, she seizes his arm.

'You know,' she says, bringing her head forward violently and stretching up her chin so that it's on a level with his, 'you've . . . you've . . . you've . . .' She's stammering, and he tries to help her out. But no, she was waiting for something – and there it is, she mouths along with the loudspeakers 'you've . . . you've got the cutest little face . . .'

Robert laughs and withdraws a little, but her square powdered jaw pursues him. 'What's your name, honey?' she whispers. 'I'm Lucille.'

'Robert.'

She winks at him. He tries to look beyond her mascara and curled lashes, into her eyes.

Her glance shifts. 'Do you have a fag?' she asks.

'Of course.' He lights one for her.

She looks away. She does not like his probing eyes. Her wrist tilts back as she holds the cigarette and puffs elegant rings of smoke into the air. She nods dreamily to the music, her eyes closed.

'Do you come here often?' he asks.

Her lips fly apart in a parody of a smile, then snap shut.

'I like your dress,' he says.

'Ditto,' she coos.

'So many people here,' he says.

Her eyebrows soar towards her wig, and she stares at him, her eyes huge blue discs. 'Where?' she gasps.

Despite himself he sees her spotty, pock-marked skin beneath layers of foundation cream. He cannot stop scrutinising her. He studies her like an animal.

'I'm sure those big blue eyes see everything,' he says.

'Oh yes.' Now she screws them into slits.

They are silent. She wants to get away, he thinks. I cannot play her game; when I say flippant things she does not laugh, for she does not trust me; she knows that I am from the outside world, that I see her as a case history; my eyes and my words strip away her make-up. He steps back, apologetically. But her five o'clock shadow fascinates him. He wants to know more: where does she live, how does she live, does she always dress in women's clothes, does she feel an outcast, does she hate all those who are not outcasts, is she depressed and insecure, or is this masquerade a bold solution which gives her life meaning?

'Do you have a husband?' he asks, smiling.

He is afraid of her reaction. His brutal curiosity deserves to be punished. He waits, ashamed. One blow from her thick muscular arm would send him reeling. Slowly she raises her eyes and stares him full in the face. Between her mauve lips the tip of her tongue appears. She hunches one shoulder towards her cheek; takes his hand, and holds it very gently. 'And you?' she asks softly. 'Do you have a girlfriend?' She lifts her head and strikes a statuesque pose. He feels her strong fingers, slightly sweaty, encompassing his. She runs the other hand slowly down his white shirt, grazing the buttons. Her lips suddenly twitch nervously.

'No,' he says. 'But I'm not looking for one.'

He dislodges his hand, and stares at her stockinged legs in silver high heels. She shifts her weight, from one powerful foot to the other. He can think of nothing more to say. He is afraid now, afraid of her anger. He has humiliated her. He backs away, abandoning her. She opens her mouth and emits a screech; she is going to mock him in front of her friends. But no: the screech is directed at the fat little man who rubbed against him in the crush. She seizes the little man by the shoulders and he kisses her, leering at Robert as if to say: this juicy kiss, of course, is really meant for you.

He finds another seat, and the drag queen begins a new song:

I love to go a-wandering, along a mountain track
I love to see my rucksack hanging on my back

His own words pour out, and his lips move vestigially, like a ventriloquist: I am getting drunk, Johnny, and I keep seeing you, as if you were here, next to me; perhaps in reality you are not far away . . . in one hand I hold a glass of brandy, and I lay the other here, on the seat beside me. All around, in this club, there's quite a commotion, but I am not part of it. Someone is singing, and a pianist is playing, but I am not listening. I am thinking of a concert we once went to together. Pollini was playing at the Festival Hall. Do you remember? You were wearing the same clothes as usual: jeans, white socks and Doc Marten shoes. Didn't you think it was rather a cliché, those three items? Just like so many other young men? But perhaps that was what you liked about them. I suddenly caught sight of your ankles in their white socks, crossed over each other. I watched your crossed ankles, hoping you wouldn't notice. Pollini was playing the Barcarole of Chopin – did you take in the depth, the great sense of space in his playing? They were the same as usual, your rather fine ankles with sharp Achilles tendons. But what was so unusual was their stillness. They were still as never before, and I found myself smiling. You never knew it, but that was when I first saw how vulnerable you were. I understood why you kept moving all the time: because you were afraid of anybody seeing you. By moving you thought you could confuse everybody, blur our vision. At that moment, listening to music – taken off your guard – you were still. Later, when Pollini was playing the Debussy Studies, you put your hand over the armrest, and took mine. You held it for a few seconds. It was the last thing I was expecting. Perhaps you only did it because we were in public, and of course you are an exhibitionist. But I don't think so. It's possible you loved me then, at that moment. I am sure you have forgotten. Afterwards you told me you liked that music very much, the Debussy Studies; which surprised me, too.

At the table next to him sits a man with grey receding hair, thick glasses and a high forehead. He sits alone and looks at no one, sipping occasionally from a glass of thin milky liquid. On the fourth finger of his left hand he wears a ring. He has a blue tweed jacket with frayed cuffs and a loosened tie. He looks like an intellectual, a professor lost in his own thoughts. Robert feels a wave of sympathy. He would like to make contact, to share a smile at least. He decides to ask for a light; takes out a cigarette and leans forward. But at that moment the man looks up and greets a tall youth who pushes his way through the crowd. The boy's legs, in baggy white flannels, move with curious flexibility, as if made of rubber. He sits down, and Robert sees that there was a chair and a pint of beer waiting for him. The boy immediately lights a cigarette and starts talking. His face is extremely mobile, and he laughs often, curling back his upper lip so that a whole row of pink gums is visible. And the intellectual by his side changes completely. He shifts on his chair so that he sits at a rakish angle and drops an arm loosely over the back. From time to time he brings his hand forward and makes florid movements; his thin gold ring twinkles in the reddish light. He laughs noisily at the boy's remarks. His voice is nasal and he spits a good deal; a few drops of saliva land on Robert's table, after spurting, iridescent, through the air. His right hand, with a flamboyant sweep, continually picks up and puts down his glass. His fingers have a life of their own, gyrating in unpredictable directions. They seem flabby and boneless. Occasionally the boy kisses him on the cheek. Suddenly the man holds up two rigid forefingers, and they listen to the words of the song:

> There was a young man from Nantucket
> Whose cock was so long he could suck it
> As he wanked with his chin he said with a grin
> If my ear was a cunt I could fuck it

The whole room laughs, and the drag queen stops, appalled. She wipes her brow and says: 'Ohh dear!! Now *what's* got into me? How could I EVER let that slip out?? (Pause) I'm from Nantucket, by the way.' More laughter, and she resumes in a croaking voice, with raunchy hip movements: 'I *love* to go a-wandering, along a *moun*tain track . . .'

One summer night, as we lay silently in bed, I tried to touch you. Your body was hot, as always. That heat frightened me, because it was an animal, soulless heat. You moved away, as if my touch revolted you. I said: 'Johnny, what has happened?' And you replied immediately: 'Nothing.' I touched you again, reaching out to where you were, and my touch became hostile, my fingers wanted to probe under your flesh, to split you open. You said: 'Leave me alone, I'm too hot.' I went on touching you; my hand was cold, like a knife. As I stroked you I was afraid, for it was wrong; it felt like a taboo. I wanted to say: 'Giovannino, a few weeks ago touching you was the greatest pleasure in my life. For then it was not just your skin, it was *you* that I touched. And when you touched me, my whole being responded, not just my body; your touch set my soul on fire. But now we are dead, both of us, heavy, useless bodies; the connection is gone, and no music is set in motion. What has happened? Is the connection gone for ever?' But I said nothing. I stroked you like an object, forgetting that I was stroking you. My hand ran all over your body, like a spider, I was hardly aware which part of you I was touching, it was all the same. I knew that the more I stroked you, the more you hated me, and yet I went on, incapable of stopping. For a time we hated each other, we wanted to kill each other, and then that too passed, my compulsive stroking became a nervous gesture, something I might do in my sleep, and my hand gradually came to rest. It lay on the sheet between us. 'Good-night,' you said. The wind ruffled the curtains and I lay silent.

A young man passes and winks at him. Robert knows him; his name is Billy. On previous occasions in this bar he has tried to talk to him. As usual he has been tongue-tied. He is no match for Billy's curt remarks and physical ease. But probably nothing he could have said would have made any difference. He is not Billy's type, though Billy is his. Love does not work according to the laws of supply and demand. Billy's name must be added to the great army of those who have rejected him: the great army who carry within them a mystery that is beyond his reach.

At the next table his companions seem to have run out of conversation. What has happned to all their animation? The man sits in an unnaturally erect position, supporting himself on a stiff right arm. A sophisticated smile plays across his face, and his eyelids droop, as if he is trying to impress the lad next to him, to say: naturally I've seen all this before. But the boy, who has big unhealthy bags under his eyes, takes no notice. He stares across the table and mouths blankly to the words of the song: I know a man with a great big dick It's long it's ethnic it's awfully thick

Is this a tango rhythm? Robert wonders, watching the drag queen as she gyrates her hips. He does not know, and feels ashamed. If someone asked him now he would be ashamed to admit he was a musician. Like his life his music is narrow, frightened, masturbatory.

Lucille, the transvestite, passes by and studiously avoids him.

But how can I, he thinks, how can I change?

What of the awareness, the awareness of himself, of freedom, that he felt a few minutes ago? What of the coloured lenses, whose distortions, just now, appeared so clear, as they fell away to reveal a truer world? He tries to recapture the sensation, screws up his eyes and blinks; but nothing changes. The other Robert, who strode for a moment into the light, has fallen fast asleep again.

Lucille stops behind the intellectual's chair and puts her hands over his eyes. 'Guess who?' she whispers into his ear. The man springs into elasticity and frees himself with flailing fingers. Lucille plants a wet kiss on his nose. 'Oh Norman,' she says reproachfully, 'you're not making up to that old tart, are you?' The boy laughs and gives her a resounding slap on her behind, which, in its tight glittering material, seemed to be waiting just for that.

Billy passes again, smiling coyly at a man twice his age, and Robert winces. He understands: all happiness, all excitement in his life has come from the sense that he is about to step out of his skin, into the skin of another. He sees the plaster cast behind the bar, in which a hand takes possession of another's body, driving through it, and understands. He is in a perpetual state of wanting, of wanting to be something else; whatever that may be, it is clearly something that he will never, can never become. He is looking for himself: on condition that the self he is looking for is not him. This is the power of sex. He is not in the least interested in other people; only in certain aspects, certain qualities which he himself does not possess – and they are irresistible. He is incomplete; and so he falls in love with the missing parts of himself, when he thinks he sees them in another. It was not, after all, Johnny that he loved: only his gifts, which he longed to appropriate. Sexual love is based on despair; its joy stems from a moment's suspension of reality; from the temporary illusion of possessing, and being possessed. Sexual love is materialistic and grasping; it is not interested in understanding others. On the contrary, it prefers an animal, dehumanising mystique. It makes use of others for its own ends. But what of the other? Does the other, too, believe he sees what he lacks in Robert? Is it possible that he, Robert, in a similar way, contains elements that are mysterious and desirable to others? Sex is based on mutual misunderstanding. No wonder it thrives in the dark.

The sight of Lucille pinching the intellectual's cheek with her long varnished fingernails fills him with revulsion. 'He slaps my face,' sings the drag queen, 'and I let out a grunt', at which she roars like a lion into the microphone. There is a high-pitched giggle on his left, and he sees that the Asian boy, whom he had passed in the crush of bodies, is sitting next to him. He has a view of a wide open mouth with large uneven teeth, and looks away. Strange that he had not seen him sit down. This boy has a way of moving without being noticed. But he could hardly fail to notice those powerful carnivorous teeth. He realises that human beings disgust him. He sees his own prehensile hands, one of which clutches a cigarette, and his ragged, bitten nails. His long thin legs, concealed in the black folds of his concert trousers, are tightly crossed; he can feel the thigh bones as they huddle against each other. All around him people are getting drunk and chattering aimlessly. These people are lustful and self-seeking. And he himself is no better. Survival at all costs is the first law of life. Sexual desire, or lust, is a matter of survival: survival of the race, and emotional survival of the individual. It is quintessentially selfish. It is the one great force in human affairs which cannot be won over by fine words or high intentions. Erections are never idealistic.

He sees his mother tottering helplessly on the landing as she bids goodbye to him and Flavia. Her helplessness is a plea and a threat. Even here it reaches him, spreading like a gas which has escaped a test-tube. And his father's surgical mind, dissecting life like a body, winks at him. However, he stares steadfastly at his father, and refuses to yield before those clear blue eyes. In fact his father, at this moment, is doubtless fast asleep, and probably snoring. He inhales the smoke-laden air and fills his lungs with his mother's invasive emanations. She too is probably fast asleep.

Next to him the Asian boy giggles again. He feels the seat they are sharing moving, pulling forwards. He turns to see the boy leaning down, fumbling with yellowish fingers for something on the floor. He has lost his lighter. Robert sees it, hidden behind the heel of his own shoe. He will conceal it. The boy searches amongst dust, used matches and cigarette butts. His continuous high-pitched giggle is irritating. Robert moves his foot so as to cover the lighter completely. Later he will pick it up and take it away with him. He too can play the game. But he has miscalculated; somehow the boy has got there first, and now Robert is crushing his fingers under his shoe. The boy lets out a yelp. Robert bends down, moves his foot away, and lifts up the hand, which has recaptured the lighter. 'I'm sorry,' he says. The boy shakes his head, laughing. 'Nothing . . . no, nothing!' Robert looks closely at the hand. It reminds him of a skeleton leaf. He used to enjoy tearing off the delicate green tissue and exposing the tendrils. The hand is quite unharmed. It is dry and hard with callouses under each fingertip. 'Thank you,' says the boy. 'Thank you for what?' Robert asks, but the other just goes on smiling, even wider than before, so that his eyes almost disappear. His face is already lined.

'What's your name?' asks Robert.

The boy says something, but Robert does not catch it.

The drag queen blares through the speakers: 'I like a nice cup of tea with my dinner, and a nice cup of tea with my tea . . .'

He puts his ear close to the boy's mouth, but there is too much noise. He hears something like 'Buddy'. 'I'm Robert,' he says. He realises he is still holding the boy's hand, and releases it.

'Please,' says the other, and lets his hand rest for a few moments more in Robert's, perhaps out of politeness. The drag queen pauses to catch her breath, and the boy says, pointing to himself: 'Manbadu.'

'Oh, I see. Man-ba-du,' he repeats slowly.

The boy nods.

'Where do you come from?'

'Nepal.'

Nothing could be more remarkable, amid the murky happenings of Talent, than someone from Nepal. The name itself, which Robert repeats, belongs to another planet.

'You come', says the boy, 'to Nepal?'

'No,' Robert begins, trying to clarify with expressive gestures; 'I mean – no, I have never been to Nepal. But I will. I hope I will, one day. I love mountains.'

Manbadu smiles. 'Big mountain. Annapurna. Sagarmatha.'

A man passes, his face disfigured by blotches. He is not old, but he walks with small steps, as if his joints are stiff, almost paralysed. He stops by Robert's table and leans on it. His hand is pink and swollen. Lucille appears suddenly and clasps his arm. 'Hello, *darling*,' she says warmly, but without kissing him. 'Drinkyboo?' The man nods. He looks around him, scanning the entire company. His head rotates like a film camera which, very gradually, covers a scene from one horizon to the other. When his eyes meet Robert they are innocuous, without bitterness. They have hardly any expression left; they are dark and slow; as if waiting to be devoured by the seething, angry flesh that surrounds them. Lucille leads him to the bar. When people see him, they clear a space.

The thought of Johnny stabs him again. He cannot tear his eyes away from the sick man at the bar, who is smiling a little now, at Lucille. He is afraid that Johnny too is sick. He must find him, and look after him. But Johnny would not want to see him if he is ill. His pride, which has grown like a lush, opaque flower, would not let him. He would prefer to waste away and die alone, in the gutter, unseen and unheard. Robert wonders how he could overcome this pride. He tries to plan a strategy. A strategy of love, he says to himself, his eyes still fixed on the man at the bar. First, like Lady Macbeth, but with a different aim, he must un-sex himself. For if Johnny thinks of him as an object of sex he will not allow him to see his suffering. He will go to him, he will help him. For Johnny was, yes, he must admit it now, the only person he has really tried to share his life with; the only relationship he has known which started with real attraction, and which lasted, even a few months. And so if Johnny is ill, he will go to him. But Johnny is gone. Even sick he will not want him now. His departure is irreversible. (Manbadu, beside him, is still smiling. Robert moves a little closer.) He remembers, once again, Johnny's smile, and the little furrow which appeared in his upper lip. Oh Johnny. I like to think there were some things you were not aware of. For example, there was a tiny fold of skin at the back of your ears. That, at least, I am sure you never saw. But, in secret, I drank in that little fold of skin. And then you had a way, sometimes, of laughing: a spontaneous, loud, full-throated laugh – which I never mentioned. That too I enjoyed in secret. There were certain things about you which gave me the feeling that I was coming into contact with the real you: because they were things of which you were not aware, and so you had no control over them. I believe you didn't know much about the real you.

You were frightened of knowing, weren't you? You thought you were only attractive when you were putting on an act. But, I understand now, it was the real you that I loved. Yes, I am aware of this, at last, as I sit here, half drunk. Now that I have lost you. Sometimes the real you peeped out despite all your defences. When you came back to the hotel, that night in Rome, and woke me, it was there in your eyes. For a moment you forgot yourself; you looked at me as if taking me in, as if you saw me as a real, separate person. But I was not ready; I was sleepy and annoyed with you. Later I saw something else which was real: your face was flooded with pain and you lost your immortality. I realise now that night was a turning-point. For the first time I saw you were as human, as earth-bound, as me. If you had allowed it, that discovery, that glimpse into your heart, could have led to another sort of love, more profound and no less exciting. But I fell into the trap which you set for me, and for everybody; you wanted us to appreciate only Johnny the actor. I understand now: you hated and mistrusted yourself. And in the end you persuaded me to do the same. You persuaded me that there was nothing, really, worth loving in you. As soon as you knew I had seen behind your make-up, you turned your face away. And yet you were still there, half sharing my life. We lived as savages. We made no attempt to understand each other. I lost sight completely of the real you. You forced me. You still lived in my flat, went out to your teaching classes, and sometimes we ate together and watched television. Gradually you separated your clothes from mine, and put your books, your tapes, into cardboard boxes. Of all the things you possessed it is your jeans that I remember most clearly. You had three pairs. One was threadbare, torn in various places to give tantalising glimpses of your legs, tears into which, if you allowed, fingers could probe. These you wore in the Observatory Gardens. Another pair, which had buttons instead of a zip, were new and clean. These were for your classes, and for formal occasions. The third pair was old, and onto it you had sewn patches of an exotic silky material. The blue denim had become almost white; and the little patches, of embroidered leaves and birds, were full of colour and sparkled like islands: on the knees, in the crutch, on one buttock. You were longing to get away. I too was relieved when you told me one of your students had found a room for you. I spent as many evenings as possible away from you. Neither of us showed any signs of unhappiness.

Manbadu says: 'You come to Nepal? I am Sherpa. We climb mountain. One trek.'

'You are a Sherpa?' It is, perhaps, the very first time he has ever said the word. He tries it again, repeating it softly, for it is really a delightful sensation, this new word, amid so many old words. Manbadu sees or hears this repetition and laughs. He says again: 'I am Sherpa.'

But how on earth could a Sherpa from Nepal be in Talent?

'What are you doing here?'

'My sister here . . . married.' He nods vigorously.

'You like London?'

'Yes, why not.'

'How did you learn English?'

'In Nepal many English. English, America, Australia. I am Sherpa guide. I speak English.'

'Why did you come here – to Talent?'

Manbadu laughs again. He has no shame about showing his teeth, several of which are out of line with the others, and form a double row. He has large brownish gums and a crooked white scar from his upper lip to his cheek. Nobody could say he was beautiful, but he doesn't seem to care at all. His high-pitched laughter suddenly strikes Robert as musical. It reminds him of some other sound altogether. Eventually Manbadu says: 'Sometimes in my village – I am woman.'

He looks at Robert very seriously.

'Woman? Oh, I see.'

Manbadu takes his hand and says: 'If you want, I am woman for you. Tonight.'

To his surprise, Robert feels himself blush. He squeezes Manbadu's hand and laughs. 'Do you want to?' he asks.

'Yes, why not.'

'Manbadu, you must be careful. Here in London there is a very bad illness. You must not be woman here.'

Manbadu shakes his head.

Robert points to the sick man at the bar: 'Look, that man is very sick. He has caught the sickness, from being a woman. Do you understand?'

Manbadu smiles. 'I am all right,' he says, giggling.

The drag queen announces, through the microphone: 'Oh, I had a terrible time getting here tonight. I've been in Dusseldorf. That's why I was late. I missed my plane – it wasn't my fault. You see I was RAPED! In Dusseldorf airport. By one of the pilots. Helmut, to be precise. He went at me like a bloody tiger! In the personnel toilets. He laddered my stocking. And my ticket got shredded in the process. Naturally he gave me another. A real gentleman. I've got his address and statistics, in case anybody's interested. Lovely man, with a wife and three kids. Anyway, I came here hotfoot from Heathrow. I'm still wet, you wouldn't believe it. I haven't had a moment to change my knickers. You'll have to excuse me while I go to the bathroom. I can feel it running down my leg. But first of all a big hand for our pianist, the very best in London, Johnny Carlton!' The young pianist stands up and bows. 'And this is a very special night because he's brought along his sister, and she's very proud of him, because she never knew until tonight that he's . . . (her voice drops to a whisper) *musical* . . . There she is, come on dear, don't be shy – a big hand for Mandy! Don't worry, darling, there's nothing wrong with being musical, but don't tell Mum and Dad – oh!!' she screeches, closing her thighs with a bang, 'it's trickling down . . . before I soil the stool, highest quality velveteen, let me introduce our guest for tonight – this is George! And he's going to sing for you while I go and mop up.' She staggers away from the piano like a hobbled goat, clasping her great bosom with both arms.

Everybody laughs riotously, including Manbadu. Robert sees his wide open mouth, and a vein that appears in his forehead, throbbing right down the centre. The room, the piano, and the people with their drinks, cigarettes and noise, recede. For gradually he is being gathered together, into a whole, and this whole is focusing more and more directly on the person from Nepal sitting beside him. His thoughts of Johnny, of his mother, of the concert, are all becoming irrelevant. And so he turns to Manbadu and looks into his small black eyes. He is not ashamed of his own eyes. He fixes Manbadu with that slow deep gaze, which even Johnny appreciated, and says: 'I could take you home.'

He is a little nervous, but it is not a matter of life or death. Usually the clichéd words 'Will you come back to my place?' or 'I have a car – shall we go?' are more like an end than a beginning. They are spoken almost for the form, as if a cycle of hope followed by disappointment were a path he has to tread, however painful. And so when he speaks these words, tenders an invitation, his heart already sinks. If the answer is in the affirmative he is catapulted into space, out of his orbit, and it is in a state of confusion that he leads the way to the car, drives home, unlocks the door and receives his guest, who always accepts a drink and sits in the armchair, emanating light.

But Manbadu does not provoke these feelings. He is like an unexpected bonus, a being who does not quite fit into the preordained pattern.

'It's very late,' Robert says. 'Shall we go?'

'Yes, why not?'

They pick their way through the tables, and stop by the piano. Everything is different. He no longer has to defend himself; to stoop, to lower his eyes, to sift the world through a tight mesh. Two people are dancing, and it is a funny sight: a young man and a girl who each have a drink in one hand and a cigarette in the other. Their arms protrude stiffly behind their partner's back, and they clasp each other with their elbows. The pianist sits tall and straight on the piano stool; his eyes flicker from the singer, George, to the small group around the piano, to the music on the desk in front of him, and back to George. His eyes are never still, and without expression, as if their constant movement was no more than a nervous twitch.

He is concentrating on his hands, on the placing of each finger. I wonder if he can play legato, thinks Robert. Legato is the joining of notes, the releasing of one only to pass, simultaneously, to the next: an act of physical intimacy. It is like falling asleep against the warm body of one you love and waking, hours later, to feel him still there. Legato is allowing no space at all to come between you and the piano keys; the sustained, uninterrupted contact through which your spirit passes most directly into the instrument. But here the pianist is managing very well without legato. And George, the singer, is excelling himself. Glittering silver and gold tinsel decorate the wall behind him, and this he pulls forward, over his shoulders, over his balding head, as he sings:

I've got a crush on someone
Guess who?
I've got a crush on you sweetie-pie
All day and night time hear me sigh
I never had the least notion
That I could fall with so much emotion

And now he fills his lungs to bursting and hugs the tinsel streamers against his face, covering it almost completely; rolls his eyes upwards so that the pupils disappear, lifts his shoulders and clenches his fists as if the emotion were more than he could bear:

But you had such persistence
You wore down my resistance
(softly, gently) I fell and it was swell
You're my big and brave and handsome Romeo
How I won you I shall never (exultantly) *never* know

Bright lights suddenly come on, for the club is closing. Smoke curls in sluggish eddies across the ceiling. Two couples look up sleepily from solemn, drunken embraces: a man and a woman, leaning on the bar; and two middle-aged men, sprawled on the velvet seat by the piano. The drag queen returns beaming from the bathroom. He imagines his father here, observing. Could his father ever take seriously the sight of two men embracing?

Manbadu pulls at his arm. He resists, for the pleasure of being pulled again. He feels another gentle tug, and looks down at the boy's fingers taking hold of his sleeve: slim fingers, with long tough nails. He takes Manbadu's hand, aware of its difference, and allows himself to be led away. In the street Manbadu still holds his hand, and pulls him along. Despite his excitement he feels suddenly exhausted. But, as usual, he asks his polite questions, behaving as if this were normal, as if words bore some relation to reality. And so he learns, in the car, that Manbadu is twenty-two years old. That he has a sister of over forty. His mother, according to him, is seventy-five. His father died ten years ago. 'He was sick?' asks Robert. 'I think so, yes.' One of his sisters is married to an Englishman. London, he says, is 'too much', but does not seem to surprise him unduly. In Kathmandu, he explains, 'there are some cars.'

When they arrive, Manbadu inspects the flat with great interest. He takes off the blue and white spotted scarf he was wearing round his neck and ties it round his head. 'Now I am woman,' he says, and then, stroking the bulge in his grey cotton trousers (too short for him): 'Woman with banana.'

He moves nimbly around the room and stops in front of the piano. With great care he presses one of the keys. Robert hears the sound of his fingernail as it hits the surface. 'Now you play piano?' he asks seriously. 'It's too late, Manbadu. The neighbours will wake up and get angry.' Manbadu is very interested by the piano. He puts his head inside the lid and runs his finger across the strings.

Robert undoes his white bow tie and opens his collar. He feels the hair from his chest spurting out.

'By the way, I'm a pianist,' he says. 'Tonight I gave a concert. That's why I'm wearing these funny clothes.'

Manbadu's head appears from inside the piano. He looks at Robert and then his eyes flicker away. It is not clear how much he understands. He goes to the door which leads to the balcony and says: 'Can go out?' Robert obediently opens the door and they step outside. It is still dark. They stand, side by side, at the railing and look down into the courtyard. All the cars are there as usual, his own among them. Their hands, on the railing, are close; but now to take hold of Manbadu's would be as hard as, in Talent, it was easy. He looks at Manbadu's face, his profile, and feels the intensity of his own stare. He sees the lines, quite deep already, round his mouth, and the eyebrow made up of coarse, separate hairs. All this he sees, by the dim light that creeps out from the room. His stare is driving Manbadu away; he feels him retreating, regretting his decision to come back. The young man looks out across the courtyard with still, unblinking eyes. It is so hard to speak, to find words that are natural and yet intimate. But with Manbadu, of all people, words are surely not necessary? They stand together on the balcony and the silence grows. He waits, like a dog with eyes fixed on its master at the dining table, hoping for a titbit. But Manbadu makes no move. His concentration on the little courtyard is complete. Or is he, in reality, waiting for Robert? A moth flutters past them, into the room. Manbadu runs after it, catches it, and brings it back in cupped hands. He throws it out, as far as he can, but it flutters straight back. Manbadu laughs and points into the courtyard: 'Look, your car!'

'Yes, that's right . . .'

'In my village I have one water buffalo. And some goats.'

He wanders into the room and sits on the floor. Robert follows, grateful to the little moth, which has, perhaps, saved everything.

'You are married?' Manbadu asks.

'No.'

'I have one wife,' he says. 'Next year I think I make one baby.' He wags his head, with the scarf round it, from side to side. Then he lies flat on the ground, giggling, and starts stroking his banana. 'You show your banana, I show mine,' he laughs.

Robert kneels down and slides his arms under the boy's body. He tries to lift him, but he is surprisingly heavy. Manbadu thinks this is a great joke and curls up in his arms. 'Now! Now!' he cries in his high voice, and gives Robert a sharp tug so that he overbalances, and they roll around on the floor like children. Meanwhile he thrusts his bird-like hand under the top of Robert's trousers and takes hold of his banana. 'Oh big, big!' he whispers into his ear. It is fun to roll around like this, squashing his concert clothes.

Soon Manbadu lies asleep, his head on the edge of the pillow, facing the window. His eyelids swell like petals of flower buds about to bloom.

Before long it will be morning; Manbadu's eyes will open, he will stretch and smile, and go away; the telephone will buzz and his mother will be gushing, it will be the concert (will there be a review?), the dinner, Monsieur Pischik and the Schwarzenbergs, as if nothing else has happened.

But so much more has happened; so much more happens all the time, behind the scattered events which are the framework for a story. Awake and observant, while Manbadu sleeps in his bed, he is filled with this secret existence; a dramatic existence which responds and reacts constantly to people and circumstances around him. A continuous dialogue exists, which questions and evaluates, interprets everything, and creates a link with the world outside himself: an unceasing dialogue which rarely takes the form of words. He remembers that a cough, during the concert, provoked a stream of feverish thoughts, distracting him from what he was trying to do, more vivid at that moment than the motion of his fingers as they negotiated the piano keys; and yet these fingers continued to perform, automatically, and even to express the feelings associated with the notes they played; while another part of his mind, excited and fearful, was overwhelmed by a host of useless thoughts – which, in their turn, were also part of the secret life.

Now, in the quiet room, the seconds pass to the rhythm of Manbadu's soft sibilant breathing. His foot, with wide fleshy toes, sticks out from the bedclothes. His Asian hair falls in disordered strands over his forehead, and his mouth, ajar, is a gash in scarred, weathered skin. In a moment Robert will climb into bed and curl up against that different body, rub his own pavement-weary feet against other feet unused to pavements, revel in the warmth of such a different life. He fetches a glass of water and places it on the small table by the bed. As he stands, naked, next to the sleeping Manbadu he loses the sense of strangeness which his own body usually provokes. He looks at his sinewy limbs, at his penis receding like a flower at night, and thinks that if he must have a body, it might as well be this one. It is a strange, but perhaps acceptable fact that this body belongs to him, and that one to Manbadu. The fullness, the peace, that he experiences is the consequence of making love. He remembers, with surprise, his bitter thoughts about sex as he sat in Talent. For now it is clear to him that sexual love, which had seemed then the very essence of selfishness, is, on the contrary, pure communication. And this communication has made him whole.

He kneels down beside the bed and runs his fingers through the fine black hair that spreads across the pillow. Through Manbadu he feels a connection with all the distant people of the world; with the sweat that runs down skins of all colours in sunbaked fields, with children and mothers, with joy and suffering everywhere, as if the thread of feeling between him and this sleeping Sherpa could spread and encompass the whole planet. How easy it is, sometimes, to be filled with love for the whole of humanity. And with this sense of connection to others, countless others, comes the realisation that each has his own separate life, an outer and an inner life, an individual destiny. It is a clear fact that each of these people exists, fully and independently, and that he, Robert, is only one of them; and yet the internal grasping of this fact, known to everyone, the true awareness of it, is a moment of enlightenment. It is such a mystery that it gives faith.

He is filled with happiness. This moment belongs to the rare collection when life seems, obscurely, to be right. Such moments are nourishment for the soul. The moment when he first felt Johnny's body against his in the winter night of the Observatory Gardens; a moment during the concert (it comes back to him) near the end of the Fantasy when the melody reappears – and this time, for the first time, it comes to rest, as if finding the answer it has been searching for, like a seed which flowers after long germination; but just as this seems to be the final resting point the music moves on, rises one last time, passes through a series of magical harmonies, unmistakable shafts of light, so that you could say in amazement: why yes, after all, perhaps life is worth living, it is rich, despite everything I will try again. And the perfection of that moment, during the concert, was that, despite the unpromising circumstances, he played the melody as if it was playing him, he was so free from inhibitions that the awkward wood of the piano yielded, and a dialogue came into being, as if it had always existed. Moments too when Johnny, quite unaware, gave up a little of himself, and the look in his eyes, the shape of his lips, or the tension in his hand, were like sirens, drawing him to them, as if about to confide their secret. He stands by the window, and the grainy curtain, in which strands of different colours have been woven together, flutters and fills, as though the new morning were trying to come in. He touches it. Suddenly it is possible to communicate with everything. With a pang he thinks of his mother. Perhaps the gentle breeze, trying to reach him, reminds him of her. Why must she keep coming back to him? And yet he cannot tell, now, if it is pain or pleasure that he feels. It seems to him that moments he has shared with her, many moments, were also in their way moments of perfection. He imagines her voice, in a few hours, a voice which he knows so well he cannot describe it – a pleasant, bright voice, surely, and yet somewhere in it is a small undefinable emphasis which tugs at him, like a barb. But why? What can he do? He shifts uncomfortably, unable to separate love from hate, attraction from repulsion. It might be possible to stand back a little, or to take a single step in an unexpected direction, so that the layered web of their bond would appear, shimmering in space, in its entirety: and he would see it for what it was, with a beginning and an end, and he would be outside it.

He looks at the Sherpa, and the sheet which rises and falls with his breathing; his flesh-and-blood presence almost succeeds in banishing his mother's ghost. And really there is no justification, he thinks, with a sudden shiver, no justification for being under such a spell. Perhaps, long ago, he was bewitched, forbidden to step beyond a charmed circle – but no one can in fact control, take control of another, no one can really know or possess the totality of anyone else; it is only our impression, as much our doing as theirs, for no one holds the key, the mainspring of life. What are the bargains, the compromises, he struck long ago, without knowing it, without agreeing? It's all a matter of survival, his father would say, as the silver tooth in the corner of his mouth glitters; the rest is simple!

But this secret life, this moment now, the existence of Manbadu in his bed, this happiness, is his alone. Another spell perhaps, but his own. He kneels by the bed and lays his head on the sheet close to Manbadu's body. Now he realises something else. There is an emptiness in his life, and he himself has created it; by the gradual, ineluctable separation from his mother. There was a time, a mythical time, when his relationship with her was like heaven, a time when their perfectly shared conspiracy seemed to answer all his needs. And the dissatisfaction which haunts him, as he wanders through his life, is the almost impossible task of finding anything to compare with the completeness he has experienced with her. He feels the heat of his breath as he breathes into the bedclothes, into the body of Manbadu. He is afraid to move; afraid to lose the exquisite sensation that making love to Manbadu, and being loved by him, has given him. For this sensation is as rich and complete as anything he has ever known with Yvonne. For this night, at least, the emptiness has been bridged.

Everywhere a storm of vibrations and charges jostle for space, and he is in the midst of them. It seems that so much is possible, possible simultaneously, that these possibilities have no clear borders; they run into each other and confound each other, and he must constantly make choices, although there is little room for choosing anything. But his feeling for Manbadu, for everything about him, his comprehension of him, has risen from the swirling fog like a clear pinpoint of light, a star. It is trust, the trust in his own particular perception, his own desire, which has made this possible. He, this night, has loved Manbadu, and a connection has been made, beneath the surface of things, which has nothing to do with the writhing of their two bodies as it might have appeared to an onlooker. This understanding is like a small hold on reality. He realises the profound respect which is due to feelings. Without this respect, which is also self-respect, life loses its most vital points of reference. For our feelings, however chaotic, are alone capable of bringing some order into chaos. And when the feelings are of love, even a drop of it, we are nourished, and life immediately shows its true magical face.

He wonders if he will ever see Manbadu again. What if, one day, they went together to Nepal, walked through villages, forests, valleys, among the immortal peaks, slept in tents or under the stars – and what must the stars be like there? Manbadu would show him all this, his normal world, and he would absorb it, fill himself to the brim, so that nothing would again be able to imprison him. He looks at Manbadu, fast asleep, complete, tightly sealed. What is it like to be inside that head? He remembers that Manbadu, somewhere, has a wife.

Outside, the birds are singing. He realises that their chirping has been going on for some time, but only now he notices it. He smiles, feeling the mysterious pulling of the lips and cheeks which, for no good reason, certain thoughts provoke. And this sense of the strangeness of the smile makes him smile even more. He touches his face, feels that the stubble is prickly. All this time, with complete indifference, his beard has been growing. He wanders into the other room, aware of his muscles as they connect his joints, the way in which his knees link his lower and upper legs, the bending of his ankles, his foot which hangs loosely before coming into contact with the next patch of carpet, his toes as they spread out to take his weight and balance him as he lifts the other foot . . . and this awareness of the inner life of his limbs is like the work he tries to do at the piano, the laborious teaching of each finger to be free, to become the last link in the chain from his mind to the glittering keys . . . and there it stands, a large shadow against the wall. Reproachfully it stands there, eyeing him up and down. Keep away, it seems to say. What sort of voice would it have? Shall he tease it, draw a huge penis, for instance, on its underside? Or buy a dildo and attach it there? He actually thinks this would help him play better, as if he were domesticating it, making it his. But these are flimsy ideas; they cause a chuckle and leave a void behind them. There the piano stands, quiet and patient: there is nothing wild about it.

The singing birds deafen him. They are symbols of the day, when everything will take on again its real, hard aspect, a body will be no more than tired flesh and bone, Manbadu will be an ordinary boy to whom he will serve breakfast and say goodbye, he will scan the grimy newspapers for reviews of his concert; in the bright light of the morning the world will again be a shadowy place through which he must tread cautiously . . . already his happiness, his sense of being so urgently alive, is retreating, and he hardly knows what it was that he felt so clearly. Only the events remain with him now for sure, all the rest, the vital part, is draining away, like water which runs out through fingers, leaving only a little sediment behind.

He goes back to the bedroom, where Manbadu is becoming more and more differentiated from the other objects, no longer a vague hump in the bedclothes; his foot sticks out harshly, with calloused toes and yellowish nails, and a few coarse black hairs growing unevenly round the ankle. 'Manbadu,' he whispers, determined not to be taken in by this crude reality appearing around him everywhere, 'if you could . . .' but what could Manbadu, or anybody do? And what does he, Robert, want? In what way could anything be different? 'If only,' he stumbles on, 'if only you could stay like this, breathing, away in your dreamworld, and yet here too, almost inaudible, your breath, but not quite, all yours and yet mine too, just for now, in my house, in my bed, my sweat still on you, my sheet around you, my mattress under you, how can one make a single short night last for ever?'

But his words are drowning in the noise, the light, the coming of materialistic day. Everything will soon be as before; already the world is turning into an adversary. He is so afraid of the chasm that will open up, of Manbadu who, in the morning, will be a stranger; of being alone. And yet, as he gets into bed, he knows that the next day will be no worse than any other. And now, for a little longer, he has Manbadu with him. He rubs his fingers lightly over the boy's brow; he wants to share a last moment with him, in all consciousness, before the intoxication is quite gone. And Manbadu, returning from his mountains, his water buffalo (or his *wife?*) wakes, observes Robert quietly from dark slits; opens his mouth, shows his gums and big rotten teeth, and suddenly whinnies like a horse. Yes, it was that all along, Robert thinks, the whinny of a little horse, that Manbadu's laughter reminded him of. The boy stretches out a foot, and all the toes come to life, one by one, with extraordinary independence; then, contracting, hug each other tightly. He shivers and screws up his eyes; turns over, draws the pillow roughly round his head, the sheet up to his mouth, sniffs, curls up; and sleeps on.